Nueva Vida

Nueva Vida

Mauricio F. Ochoa

iUniverse, Inc.
Bloomington

Nueva Vida

iUniverse books may be ordered through booksellers or by contacting:

iUniverse
1663 Liberty Drive
Bloomington, IN 47403
www.iuniverse.com
1-800-Authors (1-800-288-4677)

ISBN: 978-1-4620-3778-0 (sc)
ISBN: 978-1-4620-3779-7 (ebk)

Printed in the United States of America

iUniverse rev. date: 08/09/2011

A NOTE FROM THE AUTHOR

The main characters of this story, as well as the towns of Nueva Vida and Mar del Sol, are fictitious. Most of this story is loosely based on events that unfolded in Colombia from 1948 to 1996, starting with the assassination of Jorge Eliecer Gaitan in 1948 and ending with the country's turbulent political crisis of the mid 1990's. However, this is by no means an accurate historical depiction of Colombia, as the events occurring in the story are fictitious as well.

CHAPTER ONE

THE FOUNDING OF NUEVA VIDA

Looming over what was then an Indian village deep in southern Colombia was a beautiful, snow-capped volcano. This was the site where, according to legend, sometime in the early 1500's, a band of weary Conquistadors, struggling with hunger after a grueling journey through the Andes Mountains for several days, turned on some pursuing Indians and attacked out of desperation. Their mission was to take over the village lying at the foot of the spectacular volcano and they were not about to give up. With the help of a couple of horses and some muskets, the Conquistadores were able to defeat the Indians against incredible odds. Upon conquering the village, they gathered plenty of food and liquor, and had a grand feast in celebration of their victory. The lead Conquistador, viewing with awe the breathtaking landscape, named this little Indian village Nueva Vida not only for the 'new life' given to his men after their miraculous victory, but for the new sense of intimacy he felt with God after surviving so many narrow brushes with death. The volcano itself was then named after the man's long-deceased wife, Luisa, because it was strikingly beautiful like her.

He and his men decided to remain in Nueva Vida to regain their strength and prepare for new journeys. They also had to wait for the arrival of a representative of the Spanish King from the port city of Mar del Sol so that the new town could be officially registered into the empire. News of the area's vast pastures and ideal geographical location, nestled between the Pacific Ocean and the dense jungles of the Putomayo region close to the Amazon River basin, spread like wildfire among local Spanish officials attempting to stretch out the empire. They believed the area would be perfect for building a trade outpost accessible to areas where large amounts of gold were discovered.

However, something would get in the way of these Spaniards' ambitions. The volcano, Luisa, soon began rumbling as thin clouds of smoke streamed from the crater. Tremors were felt for three days before the Conquistadors grew concerned. They asked their Indian captives, through a guide, if there was anything to fear from the volcano. The captives told them the volcano was not known for major eruptions, only occasionally letting off some steam as it was then doing. With their fears momentarily tempered, the Conquistadors busily continued preparing Nueva Vida for the King's representative, who was expected any day. They cruelly forced the Indians to build abodes for this prestigious visitor and his entourage, as well as a small, crude chapel in the town's center. The men were also gathering supplies for their new mission northwards through the Andes, filling up many large bags of maize to be carried by mules. As they finished with their preparations, the Conquistadors anxiously waited for the arrival of the representative. Before they could go off on their mission, they needed to discuss urgent business matters with him. These included, among other things, payments for their services and land ownership guarantees granted by the future Viceroy, who was then on his way to Colombia from Spain.

Yet, after two whole weeks, there had been no sign of this official. The men were angry with his tardiness since the journey from Mar del Sol to Nueva Vida only took three days on horseback. As each day passed, the tremors beneath their feet grew stronger and the smoke from Luisa appeared thicker. Not knowing what to do, the lead Conquistador again consulted with his Indian captives. Again, the captives told him that such activity from Luisa was normal and no eruption was forthcoming. The Conquistadors stayed put, although very timidly.

That night, the Indians, knowing the volcano was about to blow, silently fled from their confined quarters after killing some of the sentinels on duty. They had secretly planned their escape for days upon Luisa's increasing activity. The Indians supposedly reached the safe heights of neighboring hills when torrents of mud smashed through the little town just before dawn, killing all the unsuspecting Conquistadors in their sleep. After having tricked their captors to their deaths and narrowly avoiding the mud avalanches themselves, this group of about a hundred natives rejoiced for a couple days. They viewed Luisa as a towering symbol of both their salvation and the terrifying vengeance of the gods, serving as protection against the cruel, light-skinned invaders.

* * *

When the representative of the Spanish crown did finally arrive on the scene a couple days later, he and his men were confounded and disturbed by the absence of the Conquistadors. Luisa had stopped erupting and much of the mud had dried up. The valley was barren and there was no sign of a town, people, or anything. The only visible sign of devastation left from the eruption were a few uprooted trees. The representative eventually reached the conclusion that they had followed an errant map. He was convinced the town and Conquistadores they were searching for were somewhere else. However, an Indian guide accompanying the doubting official reassured him they were at the right place. An old, grey-bearded, long-nosed ex-Conquistador known simply as Felipe de Granada, who knew the area well from previous missions and traveled with the entourage as a military advisor, seconded the guide and convinced the representative there were no mistakes. It was decided they would stay overnight and wait until the following day for the missing Conquistadors. If they did not appear by late morning, the official and his group would return to Mar del Sol. As the skies turned darker and night drew closer, the representative remarked on the eerie silence of the area, as if something bad was afoot.

His fears were justified. The surviving Indians had witnessed the entrance of these Spaniards into the valley earlier in the day from the surrounding mountains. They were now preparing for a surprise attack on these intruders, sharpening their spears and daggers. During the middle of the night, forty of the Indians quietly moved down into the valley where the Spaniards set up camp and pounced on them. There were fifteen men traveling with the representative, only about half of them armed with weapons. All of them, including the representative, were slaughtered, except Felipe de Granada. He was able to get away by swiftly mounting his horse after killing one Indian with his sword, escaping the surrounding mob of natives in the nick of time.

As these natives celebrated yet another victory over the invaders, Felipe de Granada reached a small garrison containing no fewer than a hundred Spanish troops within twenty-four hours of the attack. This garrison was located somewhere between Nueva Vida and Mar del Sol, and was steadily receiving more soldiers for the conquest of Colombia's vast, mountainous interior. When the old warrior informed the troops of the massacre, there were no immediate calls to arms. Instead, the soldiers were listless and offered the weary messenger some food. Felipe quickly understood the apathy of the troops, for they were only salaried conscripts of the Spanish Imperial Army. They neither had the burning ambition nor the enterprising minds of the Conquistadors. These men were not fanatics for God or gold. They were only content with following the orders of their corrupt commanders.

When a soldier brought Felipe de Granada a bowl of soup, he furiously threw it against the wall and grabbed him by the collar. "I tell you of a massacre," he roared at the young soldier, "a massacre of our fellow Spaniards by those bloodthirsty savages and all you do is quietly shrug your shoulders and offer me food? What the hell is wrong with you?" The wily ex-Conquistador then harangued the rest of the troops in the garrison, trying to convince them to take up their arms and avenge the deaths of their countrymen.

According to legend, the motive of this scrappy veteran of the New World battlefields was not solely vengeance for the deaths

4

of his colleagues. He was disappointed with his meager military accomplishments and longed for more glory. Why continue working as a petty bureaucrat when one can still become viceroy or, better yet, ruler of his own kingdom? In essence, Felipe de Granada viewed the massacre as an opportunity to fulfill his boyhood dream of being a great conqueror like Alexander the Great and Caesar. He was getting old and this probably would be the last chance to make his dream come true. His ambitious plan was to lead these troops to the site of the massacre, defeat all the Indians there, set up camp, and use Nueva Vida as a springboard for new missions into the Colombian interior. Maneuvering through this vast area would not be much of a problem since he knew it well, everything from which passages were to be avoided to which groups of natives were friendly. More importantly, the old warrior knew how to get to the gold deposits in valleys north and east of Nueva Vida. All he had needed was a large group of men for such expeditions and he now found them!

As he spoke to the soldiers in the garrison, Felipe de Granada noticed a change in their collective demeanor. They were now growing angry about the atrocities committed by the Indians. At first, he cleverly appealed to their sense of patriotism. He reminded them that they would all be thrown into battle against the natives eventually, so what was the use of waiting, especially right after their countrymen were slaughtered. The old warrior told the troops that the native 'savages' wanted nothing more than to kill, castrate, and butcher them all, recounting personal stories of their supposed acts of cruelty against captured Conquistadors. He then appealed to their sense of greed. "Why, the King is giving all of you pocket change to sweat, fight, and die out here so that he and his cronies can continue enjoying a life of luxury and privilege," he stated. "Why continue receiving orders from him when you can instead control your own destinies and tell them what to do?"

Felipe de Granada went on to explain that they could all go and conquer the new lands themselves and then negotiate the sale of the territory to the King on their own terms, which would make them all rich. "Each of you will be making a million times more money than what you earn now as a salaried soldier, and for basically performing the same job!" The troops were also told they would fare better under the old Conquistador's leadership because he knew the region well and how to best fight the Indians. "The King's commanders will only throw you into deadly traps because they usually don't know what they are doing and they don't give a damn about you," he told them. Most of the troops were now almost totally convinced by these arguments, if not by the logic, then from the force of the old warrior's fiery willpower.

A couple soldiers were not completely swayed. One proclaimed that it would be unpatriotic to go against the King. Felipe's quick response to this was that the King, Charles V, was not Spanish, but German. Since Charles V was in fact an emperor who did not even reside in Spain, but somewhere in central Europe, why should they then worry about being unpatriotic? "I don't believe that man has ever set foot on the soil of our motherland. Why should we consider him to be our King?" Many men enthusiastically agreed with this assertion.

Another soldier asked a more practical question regarding the possible reaction of the King, and if they might not be pursued and tried for treason. "Treason in this no man's land?" the old warrior cleverly asked. "Even the King himself would understand that only the rule of the jungle applies here, and that it's every man for himself." He also told them it would take the King months to gather a new army in that area, let alone track them down. By the time that would happen, Felipe and his men might have total control of the territory, which would mean a most favorable position in the bargaining table with the monarch. "Gentlemen, remember that the king will need us!" he went on. "His army will not dare come in here without the Conquistadors clearing the way." The old warrior explained that other groups of Conquistadors already in the area had been missing and most likely killed by Indians. "Thus, all we are doing here is taking their place, nothing more. If it is not us, there will be others happily taking their place."

When the passionate Felipe de Granada was finished with what he had to say, his audience was won over and waiting for his first order. They all were Conquistadors now. The former military advisor had finally got his wish, as he had a large group of armed men in the palm of his hand. He immediately directed them to gather their ammunition, horses, mules, and food supplies, since they would be heading out the next morning for Nueva Vida. This they did with boundless energy, as thoughts of gold and power had suddenly provided them with all the motivation in the world.

However, these Conquistadors were soon beset with one problem. The commander of the garrison was to arrive that evening from Mar del Sol. Since most commanders of the Spanish Imperial Army were loyal to the King, they feared he might seriously object with their newfound mission and cause trouble. He may run back to Mar del Sol and inform the King's minions of the situation in the garrison, thus causing troops to be sent swiftly to the garrison. After some discussion, it was decided the commander should be killed as soon as he arrived. Felipe justified this decision by proclaiming they were the true soldiers for God and Spain, not the commander, who only represented the interests of the corrupt emperor.

The persuasive, almost hypnotic powers of the old Conquistador worked well on his men that evening, as they brutally killed the commander and two of his aides when they arrived, stabbing them with their long knives. Their bodies were unceremoniously buried in a wooded area not far away. With that accomplished, the men spent their last night at the garrison and departed early the following morning for Nueva Vida, leaving nothing behind. While the men marched the entire day through some treacherous mountain passes, Felipe prepared them for their eventual clash with the Indians. He taught them some battlefield tactics using horses and guns which worked well against the natives in the past. When the men set up camp that evening, they went through some war games, rehearsing their individual parts for the upcoming battle.

*   *   *

Since they were due to arrive in Nueva Vida late the following afternoon, many of the men, anxious and excited, were unable to sleep that night. Thus, it was a shock for them all when there were no signs of Indians upon their arrival. Felipe de Granada reminded his men that he and his colleagues were attacked in the middle of the night a few days earlier, and that they should anticipate the same thing happening again. He made the bold decision of setting up camp at the same exact location that was chosen three nights before, in the middle of the valley. He judged the natives were hiding somewhere in the surrounding hills, preparing to attack deep into the night. He calmly told his men to get ready. "We will patiently wait here for their attack, and when they come, we will pounce on them." With a hundred armed men hunkered down, he was confident of his chances for a sound victory.

In the meantime, the Indians were indeed hiding atop the hills watching the Conquistadors set up camp. There was some concern about the rather large size of the group now positioned before them. They wondered whether an attack on these new intruders would be wise. This small, tough group of Indians had already survived two Spanish incursions on their land and a horrific volcanic eruption within a week's time. After much spirited debate, it was decided that an attack on the invaders would be forthcoming that evening. The tribal leader based this decision on two premises. Firstly, they would be launching a surprise attack, giving them the upper hand. He reminded his men of how well that strategy worked a couple nights before. Secondly, as a witness to miraculous events over the prior few days, he was convinced that the gods were firmly on their side. They would certainly be guided to another victory over these treacherous invaders.

He retold the myth of how the gods gave their forefathers that fertile piece of land beside the spectacular Luisa in return for their allegiance. Every subsequent generation maintained that historic bond with the gods to their benefit and, according to the myth, if that bond was ever broken, the generation responsible for its severance would never be welcomed into the kingdom of heaven. All of their ancestors would also be cast away from this celestial palace of the gods, forever disgraced and passed off into oblivion. For the sake of their ancestors and themselves, the tribal head stated they had no other choice but to fight. They had to have faith in the gods at this critical moment or else the bond would be broken. The men followed his advice.

As the night skies fell over this desolate, quiet valley, Felipe de Granada instructed his men to remain in their tents until the Indians closed in. As soon as they were within a few yards of the tents, the Conquistadors would leap out and attack. "There will be no need for the horses. We will engage them in hand-to-hand combat." The Indians were unaware they were about to fall into a big trap. Thinking the element of surprise and the gods were on their side, they became a bit overconfident. So when they launched their attack, reached the camp, and were immediately confronted by a hundred men, fully armed and awake, the thirty or so Indians were stunned. Within a minute or two, they were slaughtered. Only the lives of three Indian warriors were spared so they could be used as guides. Thanks to the thoughtful planning of their leader, the Conquistadors did not lose a single soldier in the battle.

* * *

Felipe de Granada and his men decided to stay in Nueva Vida for a couple of days, during which time the Indian captives led them to farms and food storages in the hills. The Conquistadors were amazed by the abundance of rich farmlands and pastures in the area, at least those unaffected by the eruption. Since the area was deemed so valuable, Felipe decided to leave twenty men there to protect it. The surviving women and children of the tribe were to work for those men staying behind, farming and harvesting as much land as possible.

Felipe de Granada made Nueva Vida his base for the moment, a place he could return to in case things did not go well elsewhere. "In time, it will be our grand capital," he boasted. After sufficient rest from their recent victory, the old Conquistador soon led his men to the eastern jungles of the Putumayo region. He hoped to find an abundance of emeralds and gold long rumored to be held in a remote Indian enclave. Using Luisa the volcano as a guide, the pack of men made their way through the mountains, eventually climbing down towards a river which led to the jungle. The group, some eighty men strong, began feeling the effects of the journey after only a couple days, suffering from cramping, stomach ailments, and fatigue. Things did not get any better as they marched deeper into the jungle, the stifling heat and humidity only serving to aggravate their physical ailments.

Yet, the Conquistadors persisted with their mission, determined to reach this mysterious jungle hamlet. Felipe explained to his men that a banished Indian prince founded the village with his followers a hundred years before, having brought all his prized possessions there. His descendants fiercely guarded the treasures throughout that time, warding off a host of incursions from rival Indians and Conquistadores. Felipe recounted how he and his fellow comrades had fought with this tribe of Indians twice before, their superior numbers and tenacity too much to overcome. He was sure of victory this time, however, since there were a lot more men with him. A week into the expedition, Felipe, through his trusted old map and familiarity with the area, knew they were close to their destination. They set up camp for the night deep in a jungle clearing, the old warrior telling his men they were perhaps only a couple of miles away. He also told them to get ready for battle against at least a hundred Indians. "These are tough Indians we will soon be fighting," Felipe told them. "They swarm you with arrows from all over the place."

The old conquistador closed things off with a pep talk to lift up their sagging spirits, reminding them about the incredible wealth the booty would bring to them all. He also brought a sense of urgency, telling his men if they did not retrieve the emeralds and gold, their mission would be a failure. "If we obtain these treasures, we will have unimaginable power!" he declared. "We will be able to manipulate any group of people, including the King and his cronies! However, without this loot in our hands, no one will listen to us."

Felipe de Granada, himself, was becoming madly obsessed with the mission. He felt it was a do or die situation for him. Never before did the old warrior have so many men at his service and he was clearly succumbing to the pressure. His desire for power and glory was burning out of control. The heat and humidity of the jungle was leaving him increasingly delirious. There were times when he lashed out at his men, even threatening them with execution. They were beginning to wonder if his intensity was indeed giving way to insanity.

Nevertheless, Felipe's mounting obsession and paranoia was actually necessary at this stage in the mission, just before an important battle. It left no room for incredulity among the ranks. "I may have been denied twice before, but I will not be denied a third time! We will not be denied! We will be victorious tomorrow!" Like all good leaders, deranged or not, Felipe de Granada provided his men a deeper sense of being and purpose which ascends above the selfish, superficial trappings of everyday existence. "Gentlemen, this is not just about becoming rich," he told them. "This is about who we are as true servants of God, willing to make sacrifices for the benefit of all men in the world. We are here, gentlemen, to build an advanced, Christian community, where the natives will live not like animals, but like civilized, respectable human beings. We are only humble servants of God and our motherland, and we will not be denied from performing this sacred duty of ours!" The troops stood up and cheered like no other time before, their sense of self-righteous superiority fully restored.

Throughout the following day, Felipe and his men slashed and pushed their way through the dense jungle foliage until, at long last, a village was spotted in the distance. There was a clearing and beyond it, perhaps a hundred yards away, a few homes made of animal hides, branches, and leaves. Felipe sent a couple of men to scout the area. The news they would bring back a few moments later was so startling, the old warrior almost fainted on the spot. Apparently, the entire area was abandoned. Indeed, as the men scoured through the small village, there was not one Indian to be found. Yet, much of the place was intact, leading to all sorts of speculation from Felipe and his men.

Nothing was known about the fate of the original dwellers of this jungle enclave, whether they were killed off by neighboring Indian tribes, massacred by roving Conquistadors, or forcibly abducted *en masse* by Portuguese slave traders through the Amazon River. Felipe had suspected they fled the area for some reason since many personal belongings were left behind, including, much to everyone's delight later that day, an abundance of gold and emerald studded artifacts that were discovered in vats buried underneath one of the homes. They celebrated during the evening, drinking fermented corn from large containers found in one of the village huts. They could hardly believe their fortune, not having to fight for such treasure.

While his men celebrated, new concerns swirled inside Felipe de Granada's head. The old Conquistador realized that many of his men would now want to make a deal with the King, cashing in their share of the plunder and enjoy their newfound wealth. Yet, he wanted to continue his mission, going to other parts of the region in order to accumulate more wealth and power. Somehow, he needed to persuade his followers to continue in this struggle without making them realize they were serving his interests only. He was also worried about the potential for insubordination, considering there was so much loot in their possession. Some of the men may kill him to take over the mission themselves, or simply run off with the treasures.

To reassert his authority, the old warrior gathered his dazed men and delivered a stern lecture. He told them they should not trust the King and his government. "Gentlemen, I tell you from experience that the King and his servants are now our worst enemies, worse even than the Indians." He bitterly described how so many Conquistadors were mistreated by the Spanish government, from not receiving payment for their services to being executed on false criminal charges. "They can do anything they want with you because they have all the power," he explained. "They have the world's largest navy and land army at their disposal, and what do you have? Nothing! They will laugh at you! If you think you can make a deal with the King now, you better hope you come away with just your lives!"

Felipe de Granada told his astonished men that their only recourse was to continue with the mission, plunder more towns, and raise a large army of Indians through the loot they had acquired.

"Only when we have raised a large army and allied ourselves with many of the native tribes around here," he concluded, "will the King raise his eyebrows and listen to us." The men, overcome with exhilaration a few moments before, were now pensive and somber. Their hopes of getting rich quick were painfully shot down by their leader's words of caution. Once again, the old man did a masterful job of convincing his men to follow his direction. Not only were they scared for their lives, since they realized they were truly alone, but were now dependent on their leader more than ever, since he was the only one who knew his way around this remote part of the world.

*   *   *

Felipe de Granada's fears of the Spanish government were well-founded. Columbus, Balboa, and Cortez, to name a few, were obvious examples of Conquistadors who died powerless as a consequence of the Spanish government's pettiness and treachery. He was absolutely correct to assert that the King and his court were now their worst enemies. In fact, at the very moment he finished speaking with his men after their discovery of the emeralds, the King's officials in Mar del Sol found out about the abandoned garrison.

Earlier that day, a huge galleon carrying about a hundred and fifty Spanish soldiers had docked in Mar del Sol. It was scheduled to remain there for four days, to be repaired for damage caused by storms in the Pacific. The troops were being transported to Peru from Panama. The preeminent official in Mar del Sol, a man by the name of Count Ricardo Velasquez, was desperate to impress his king. According to the official archives of Mar del Sol, he was supposed to have been of short, paunchy stature with a pug nose and large blue eyes. His black, wavy hair and handle-bar mustache were always groomed and his clothes were tailored by the very best designers in Europe. He was notorious for his excessive cruelty and vanity, which certainly did not inspire much love from his subjects. Like most Spaniards in the New World, he wanted to climb the prestige ladder and become powerful. He was in charge of settling most of the area in southern Colombia, making sure all the Indians were defeated, converted to Christianity, and abiding by the King's laws.

The Count was shrewd enough to detect something odd from news about the abandoned garrison. He suspected there might have been a mutiny, the missing conscripts preferring to conquer the area on their own rather than under the King's directives. After all, such unruly behavior was not uncommon in this desolate part of the world, since the rule of law had not been firmly established yet. The concerned Count quickly came up with a solution to the problem of the abandoned garrison. He was going to take the one hundred and fifty soldiers currently docked at the port and use them to hunt down the missing conscripts. If it was discovered there was a mutiny in the garrison, he would make an example of them all by meting out the strictest punishment. He could not afford to have chaos persist in this region, considered so valuable for its abundant natural resources.

When warned by his advisors that using the docked troops for hunting down his own missing conscripts would anger the Viceroy of Peru, who was very close to the King, the ambitious Count remained obstinate. "Since when do those troops belong to the Viceroy of Peru?" he asked his advisors. "They belong to the Empire, not to him! The King would agree with me on this." With those words, the Count left Mar del Sol for the garrison with the one hundred and fifty troops from the galleon, eager to take matters into his own hands.

*   *   *

Meanwhile, the Conquistadors in the Putumayo jungle were ready to depart after a couple days relaxing and stuffing several large bags with all the treasures. It was decided they would return to Nueva Vida to rest and recuperate from the long, successful expedition. They departed the jungle enclave in high spirits and began making their way back. Three days into the trip, however, some of the men began getting sick. A slight aching of the joints would soon turn into high fever, vomiting, and, finally, lack of consciousness. Within thirty-six hours of getting sick, the afflicted men were dead. During the span of four days, the epidemic wiped out fifty-two of the Conquistadors, leaving another six survivors terribly weakened.

This was a severe blow for Felipe de Granada, who had suddenly lost half of his men so quickly and mysteriously. The treasures were retrieved, but at a very hefty price, since the lost men were irreplaceable. They were now down to a staggering twenty-eight men, who were tired and demoralized from the recent misfortune. After having survived the epidemic, during which he anxiously hoped for nothing more than to live another day, the old warrior was now overcome with deep depression, concerned his mission was in trouble. He ultimately emerged from the depression, clutching onto the thought that things were not all lost. He still had all that loot and enough men to accomplish his goals, although a softer, friendlier approach with the Indians would be necessary from then on. He simply did not have enough men to defeat any of the local tribes in battle.

As the weary band of soldiers were slowly making their way back to Nueva Vida, Count Velasquez and his troops had entered the abandoned garrison. While they were there, one of the dogs brought by the troops barked continuously in a nearby wooded area. This drew the attention of some troops, who walked over to the distressed dog. Within minutes, the Count was summoned over to the area, where the poorly buried remains of the garrison's commander and his two aides were found. There was clear evidence of foul play, the clean, deep wounds in the bodies indicating murder rather than slashing injuries from battle. The Count took it hard, since he personally knew the commander. He vowed a bloody vengeance on the murderers, whom he now firmly believed were the missing conscripts. With nothing left to do at the vacant garrison, the troops hastily left for Nueva Vida. The Count hoped to at least find some clues there not only of the missing troops, but also the officials originally responsible for settling the town, who had not been heard from in a couple of weeks. If nothing else, he would settle the town himself, not having to worry about that dilemma anymore.

As the men approached Nueva Vida the following day, Count Velazquez grew more obsessed with finding the missing conscripts. When he heard one of the troops make a sarcastic comment regarding the search, his reaction was cruel and swift. To everyone's horror, the unfortunate, young soldier was dragged to a nearby tree and hanged, his desperate cries for mercy coldly ignored by the Count. He was not even given his last rites, despite the pleas of a friar accompanying the mission. As the soldier dangled from the rope's end, still kicking and flailing away, the Count brazenly warned the soldiers not to question his leadership.

On his orders, they then continued marching toward their destination, leaving the poor soldier's body hanging from the tree. Everyone was now deathly afraid of the Count, yet they despised him all the more. His haughtiness, wickedness, and apparent lack of scruples revealed him to be nothing but a self-serving egomaniac, craving only power, status, and the King's affections. They were resentful of being forced into this mission against their will, since they had long anticipated going to Peru, to serve under the benevolent Viceroy there. Instead, they were recklessly trekking through the harsh Andean terrain on a petty manhunt.

The group eventually reached Nueva Vida and found the twenty missing conscripts there with the small group of Indian women and children. The startled ex-conscripts were quickly apprehended and questioned by Count Velazquez. When told they were charged with treason, the men vehemently denied committing such a crime, claiming they were attacked by Indians instead, forcing them to flee the garrison. However, their ruthless interrogator would have none of it, throwing the murder of the garrison commander at their feet, and threatening them with immediate execution if they did not tell the truth. With the threat of death looming over their heads, the men succumbed and told the Count everything.

When his trembling captives finished making their confessions, the incensed Count thought of executing them right on the spot. However, he stopped to gather his thoughts for a while, not wanting to be viewed by his soldiers as an impulsive hothead. His two advisors had reproached him for callously executing the soldier the previous day. "Remember, these aren't your men!" they nervously told him. "They can turn on you too!" Knowing the other missing conscripts would soon be returning from their mission to the Putumayo jungle, the Count needed his troops to be firmly on his side. Consequently, he changed his tune entirely. He decided to act benevolently for the time being.

This startling transformation began when he simply placed the captives under arrest, to be tried in the courts of Mar del Sol at a later date. To the astonishment of everyone, there were to be no bloody mass executions. More incredibly, the once aloof Count walked over to each of his soldiers and engaged in intimate conversations with them, asking for their names and where they were from, telling them they were needed by God and the motherland to keep this region of the empire together. For the first time in days, smiles gradually began appearing on the soldiers' faces, a confirmation that the Count's clever change in social manners was working well.

∗   ∗   ∗

As Count Velazquez and his troops regrouped and prepared for a possible battle in the near future, Felipe de Granada and his band of men were slowly approaching Nueva Vida. There were now only twenty-three of them, five others dying from the combined effects of the mysterious disease they encountered in the jungle and hunger. The survivors were downright weak from a lack of food since their supplies ran out a few days before. There had been no Indian villages to pillage along the way, and the rough Andean terrain did not yield anything edible for the hungry men. They longed for Nueva Vida to such an extent, they were becoming delirious, especially Felipe. He was now only a shadow of his old self, so emaciated in appearance that his ribs were sticking out. He had regressed mentally, falling into the clutches of an implacable madness triggered by the bitter knowledge that all hopes for a successful mission were dashed, having lost most of his men not through glorious clashes with the enemy, but to an invisible force. "This cursed disease has destroyed my mission!" the old warrior would declare aloud repeatedly, oblivious to everything, not caring whether the others were beginning to question his sanity. Despite the hardships, they still had the bags of treasures, enough to perhaps purchase half of Colombia, as the leader liked to believe. The disturbing question was whether they could profit from such loot. They were considered outlaws by the Spanish authorities and mortal enemies by the Indians, to be permanently brushed aside either through imprisonment or execution. Unless they formed a large army, there was no way the sale of those treasures could be negotiated.

The old warrior put off those concerns for when they returned to Nueva Vida. They were having enough trouble trying to survive the trip back to town, for the cold Andean winds were proving to be as formidable as any large Indian army. It was through sheer determination that these Conquistadors finished the journey. When these twenty-three Conquistadors did enter Nueva Vida, they were immediately met by Count Velazquez and his forces. The Conquistadors were told to surrender at once, for they were charged with treason and the murder of the garrison commander and his two aides.

The old warrior defiantly looked at Count Velazquez and declared he would never surrender, claiming he and his men did nothing wrong. He then tried to convince the one hundred and fifty soldiers facing him to ignore their leader, declaring that he was nothing but a 'stooge of the King'. Before he could finish, the Count, understanding the danger of allowing this clever adversary of his to talk any further, ordered his troops to attack the outlaws at once.

Outnumbered seven to one, Felipe de Granada and his ragged men did not stand a chance. One by one, they were killed during the battle that ensued, as they put up a valiant effort, knowing that surrender meant a cowardly death. The Count lost about thirty of his men in the clash and was slightly wounded himself. Yet, when the dust settled over the battlegrounds, he had his prize in hand. On his strict orders, Felipe, the last man standing and entirely surrounded, was not killed. "I want him alive!" Count Velazquez commanded excitedly. The crusty veteran would have continued fighting had he not lost his sword during a melee with five soldiers.

With the main culprit of the rebellion now in his possession, the Count hastily wanted to set an example of him. The old Conquistador was to be executed, but not until the following morning. The Count wanted to savor his victory, and, out of cruel sadism, desired to see Felipe de Granada suffer some more before his execution. He was gagged immediately upon his capture and eventually tied to a tree. The Count, reverting back to his evil ways, walked arrogantly over to his ailing prisoner and announced the charges, guilty verdict, and sentence, which was 'death by hanging'. He then ordered a noose to be tied to a branch hanging directly over the old warrior, so that it can dangle in front of his eyes, to serve as a reminder of his imminent fate.

All of the victorious troops were appalled by this, as the Count quickly lost whatever respect he might have gained from them in recent days. They admired the old Conquistador's courage, believing he did not deserve such despicable treatment. Despite pleas from the friar, who claimed the torture was not reflective of Christian virtues, the Count continued with it until the old warrior was finally unbound and ready for execution the following morning. He was not allowed to have any last words or rites before his head was unceremoniously placed inside the noose, and hunched body dropped from the clutches of three tall soldiers. Just before the fateful drop, Felipe de Granada bitterly saw his bags of gold and emerald-studded artifacts being placed onto the Count's mules. "The King prospers from the broken backs of the Conquistadors," he mumbled through the gag, just before the drop. After a minute of struggling in the air, breathing his last agonizing breaths, the old warrior's body finally went limp.

Thus was the fate of the first true colonial settler of Nueva Vida, dying like a forlorn criminal rather than a conquering hero, far away from the family he left behind in Spain. Instead of finding immortal glory and infinite riches in the New World, he was killed and buried in an unmarked grave like so many other Conquistadors before him, killed not by the Indians he detested, but by his own people. "I predict a sad future for my land," one of the three captive Indians said as he witnessed the execution, astonished at the spectacle of these barbaric Europeans killing each other like pigs.

*   *   *

Count Velazquez would live on to a ripe old age. Yet, he may not have survived the day of Felipe de Granada's execution if cooler heads had not prevailed. Some of the troops were so angered with his behavior that they conspired to kill him. However, they were advised by a wise comrade overhearing them, to not go through with the assassination. "Does not the death of this Conquistador tell you all something about the power of the King?" he calmly asked them. "This mission is over. Let us all now go to Peru in peace while we still have the chance." Convinced of the King's power, and desiring to go to Peru, the plotters decided against assassinating the Count. Swallowing their anger and pride, they quietly marched back to Mar del Sol, content with the thought of leaving the 'god-forsaken' area with their hides intact, and continuing their budding careers in the Spanish Imperial Army.

The clear winner from this bloody, tragic footnote in Colombian history was indeed Count Velazquez. He came away with the treasures, giving most of it to the King, but keeping a substantial amount for himself. He was able to live lavishly from the abundant loot, building a huge palace in a remote area outside Mar del Sol, containing one of the most spectacular gardens found anywhere in the New World. He developed a reputation for corruption, enriching himself and his cronies through the lucrative gold trade, hefty taxes on the settlers, and grand slave auctions on the port. Many men hated the selfish Count, but that did not matter to him, so long as he had the King's blessings to do whatever he wished.

This abuse of power was eventually brought to the attention of the Spanish Imperial courts, however, which charged him with serious corruption offenses to the delight of all his subjects. Yet, the Count was only forced to abdicate his seat of authority over the province without having to serve any prison time. Furthermore, a replacement for the Count was not named by royal officials in Valladolid, which left the door open for him to hand-pick his own son for the job. This led to speculation that the King had a hand in the court's sentence, not wanting a serious shake-up in Mar del Sol, since the gold trade was running smoothly there. Consequently, the Count continued to run the province from behind the scenes, stuffing hoards of money into his pockets and those of his cronies through all sorts of dirty schemes until the day he died.

He was to officially receive credit for being the founder of Nueva Vida, viewed as a hero by subsequent generations of historians. Of course, neither the Count's subjects, exploited for so long under his rule, nor the troops forcibly used to hunt down the missing conscripts, were consulted by these historians. Neither, for that matter, were the judges who sentenced each of the twenty-five conscripts captured in Nueva Vida to ten years in prison. Two weeks later, all twenty-five prisoners were awoken in the middle of the night, marched to a wooded area nearby, and unceremoniously executed.

The Count publicly declared the following day that he personally ordered the executions, claiming the ten year sentences for such 'bandits and murderers' to be too lenient. Yet, when his cronies were charged with far worse crimes, such as ordering the bloody crackdown of protests in their districts, allowing young native girls to be routinely kidnapped for sex, and encouraging the illegal slave trade of Indians, he forced the humiliated judges to acquit them. If all his embittered subjects would have had input in recounting the life of Count Velazquez, there would certainly be no statues of him standing in Nueva Vida or Mar del Sol today. He would simply be brushed aside as another deplorable royal official not worthy of any mention in Colombian history.

CHAPTER TWO

ENTER GABRIEL

More than four hundred years after Nueva Vida was founded and settled by the Spaniards, little had changed politically and socially. The year was 1996 and things were still a mess. Colombia was racked with all sorts of problems, ranging from a half-century-long civil war, powerful drug cartels, corruption, and poverty. Geographically, things had not changed. Southern Colombia retained much of its natural beauty through the years, not affected by overpopulation and pollution like other parts of Latin America. It continued to be a remote neck of the woods, deep within the mighty Andes, sandwiched between the dense jungles to the east and the Pacific Ocean to the west. The only thing that changed was Nueva Vida, becoming a bustling city of three hundred thousand, no longer a small, rural town far removed from the rest of civilization. It was now a major hub of activity in southern Colombia, while Mar del Sol, the old center of business and politics in the region, had long been in decline. The old port city was now only a tourist destination for those wealthy Colombians wanting to enjoy some beach and good weather.

Nueva Vida prospered from its close proximity to the Ecuadorian border where many Colombian merchants and people would flock to do business, taking advantage of the exchange rate between the two currencies to either buy or sell goods in great quantities. However, Nueva Vida really grew during the 1990's when the drug trade first penetrated the region. The city served as an important link between Colombia and Ecuador, some of the drugs ultimately destined for the port of Guayaquil, to be shipped to the United States and the rest of the world. It also linked Colombia's mountainous interior with the Putumayo jungle, where much of the cocaine was processed. Yes, those jungles were still important, not just serving as a hideout for contraband dealers and guerrilla fighters, but for its newly discovered oil reserves.

The drug trade and oil boom brought a lot of money to Nueva Vida, as many fancy homes, buildings, and cars suddenly appeared, transforming its old-fashioned ways very quickly. The drugs, with its mythical lure of easy, fast money, also brought a lot of people from all over the country, many of the unsavory type, turning the once peaceful town into a more dangerous place. Within ten years, Nueva Vida's population almost doubled. The older natives of the city were horrified not only with the surging crime, but with the congestion and pollution. There was a time, they sadly recounted, when one could take a leisurely stroll through the streets after dinner, as the sun would set behind the snow-capped Luisa, and not have to worry about dodging cars or stepping over garbage, let alone being attacked by some thug. These were different times indeed, the old charms and coziness gone forever. Not all those characteristics were gone, as Nueva Vida remained a beautiful place with its surrounding hills and mountains, cascades, exotic birds and butterflies, lush vegetation, and agreeable climate. Luisa, in all her glory, was still there keeping vigil over the town. Yet, the changes in the city left an unsettling feeling inside the hearts of the old dwellers, undoubtedly sensing there was trouble down the road.

* * *

Soon to enter the scene was a young, impressionable man by the name of Gabriel Ferrero. He was a twenty-one year old American hailing from Troy, Michigan. The youth had just graduated from college and, like many young people his age, was a little lost. He would come to Colombia searching for an identity, trying hard to find his place in the world. He received a degree in political science with the intention of going to law school. He enjoyed political science, but grew disenchanted with law. "Law seems so boring and tedious," he would tell his friends. He could not see himself buried behind a pile of papers every night, frantically conducting petty legal cases.

Being young and romantic, Gabriel wanted to lead a purposeful existence, making a difference in the lives of many people. His dream was to become a politician, but he was not sure how to get started. Law would have been logical but that was now out of the question. A job in government would be the ticket, he thought, so measures were taken to get one. He applied for several high-profile internships in Washington D.C., but was turned down by all. After these initial setbacks, the young man then applied for an unassuming position at UNICEF, to work as a volunteer in Africa. After waiting anxiously for a few months, Gabriel received a cold letter of rejection from UNICEF, leaving him utterly surprised. "For Christ's sake, I can't even get a volunteering stint!" he ranted to his mother.

For weeks, Gabriel despaired over his bleak prospects, with no job offers or opportunities appearing on the horizon. He began wondering if a future in politics was attainable for him. For the first time in his extremely sheltered life, our friend received a painful dose of reality. He had lived atop an ivory tower for too long, living his life through books without actually encountering the complex, harsh ways of the world. University life can certainly be insulating, yet that cannot be an explanation for Gabriel's naïveté and lack of preparation. The lad simply was introverted. He never felt comfortable in the presence of other people even though they certainly did not shun him. The youth was tall, slender, and good-looking, his quiet demeanor and dark features immediately drawing the attention of people. Gabriel, however, was unwilling to open up and preferred being left alone.

Gabriel's shyness may have stemmed from his sense of alienation growing up in the United States. Despite being of Colombian-Chilean descent, he was considered too *caucasian* in appearance and manners to be Hispanic. Yet, he was too *dark* in the

Irish-Italian neighborhood he was raised in. He also could not fit in with any particular group in the schools he attended, whether it was the jocks, musicians, academic achievers, and so forth. With no group to identify with, Gabriel was left to associate only with other outcasts. This he did on occasion only out of the sheer necessity to save face. Otherwise, he was perfectly content to chart his own lonely path, marching to the beat of his own drum.

As for mentality and values, the youth also believed he did not measure up to American standards. He was never quite the ambitious one, never getting A's in school nor having clear, tangible goals to strive for. He was pretty lazy most of the time, hardly doing the things necessary to get ahead, contemptuous of the rat race so many others eagerly, slavishly devoted their lives to. Not being a shining symbol of hard work himself, Gabriel often had a difficult time connecting with others who obviously did not share the same values, further separating him from most of his peers.

Compared to the few friends he made in college, Gabriel was lagging far behind, as many of them were already starting their careers. He was satisfied with having modest, dead-end jobs and spending much of his free time in café's, reading and discussing history, literature, and philosophy with other outcasts like him. He enjoyed this lifestyle, it being free and easy. For a while, he likened himself to a beatnik living in Greenwich Village during the 1950's, often writing poems, despairing over lost opportunities of love or rejoicing the beauty of a clear, starry night. Gabriel's bohemian ways led some people to suggest he needed to move off to Paris, with all its café's and lounge philosophers. There, he could discuss Nietzsche, British Empiricism, and Marxism all he wanted with other pseudo-intellectuals like himself. Materialistic America was no place for him, they would say.

The youth always realized he was not a typical American, long suffering from feeling like a foreigner in his own country. Nonetheless, he gradually began reveling in this feeling of alienation and isolation, identifying himself as a true rebel of the modern age, proud not to have succumbed to the trappings of America's consumer-driven culture like so many others, remaining a true individual amid this growing sea of followers and pretenders. He now accepted, with open arms, the divide separating him from the rest of society, for it confirmed in his mind that he was not just an ordinary man. No longer ashamed of being radically different from others, Gabriel felt his outcast status was a blessing rather than a curse. He was in fact destined for greatness! "Were any of the great figures in history normal?" the youth would ask his fellow lounge philosophers. "They were not! They were strange characters. Who wants to be normal anyway?"

With this renewed feeling of confidence, Gabriel subsequently set his sights for politics once again. Many people would tell him his anti-social manners were ill-suited for such a career. Rather than discourage the young man, these criticisms emboldened him further. Gabriel understood he had weaknesses, his rebellious and shy nature not exactly right for a life in politics. However, the youth believed he still had qualities indispensable for such a life, like his solid, if not exemplary, educational background, profound knowledge of history and philosophy, presentable appearance, and ability to mix, albeit in a limited sense, with all kinds of people. Through such qualities, the young man could fit in with any group of people on at least a superficial level, having enough social skills to get by for a brief time, for he was by no means socially inept. He was well-mannered and had a decent sense of humor, enjoying a good laugh once in a while. Besides, many successful politicians were not necessarily dripping with gregariousness, ala his hero Sam Rayburn. That quiet Texan was the longest-serving House Speaker ever, he would tell his numerous detractors.

The one thing Gabriel perhaps did not fathom completely was the contradiction between his rebellious aloofness and the diplomatic conformity required for a job in politics. A politician could not simply get by through quick handshakes and warm smiles. He needed to endure long hours of backdoor meetings with all sorts of people, hammering out deals and appealing to everybody's wishes, often putting his convictions on the backburner. He simply chose to ignore this contradiction out of youthful optimism, naively believing he would easily make the transition when the time came.

What Gabriel feared most was to lead an irrelevant life, so he made the attempt to get things finally moving. This was hard at first, considering he had very much fancied his bohemian lifestyle, not wanting to part with it completely. Nevertheless, our friend realized he was not accomplishing anything sitting around in café's. He needed to become a man of action and get off his laurels! "Why sit around and think about politics and history when you can actually do something about it?" he asked a friend euphorically. After a couple of months thinking hard about how to get started, Gabriel finally came up with an idea. With the encouragement of his loving parents, he would go to Colombia and spend a year there. His main objective would be to find some work, even if only a volunteering stint, at the U.S. embassy in Bogotá. If that proved unsuccessful, then he could continue living in the country, find some kind of job and perfect his Spanish. By thoroughly learning another language, Gabriel thought he would make himself more marketable.

Thus, his trip to Colombia would kill many birds with one stone. The young man would not only end up fluent in Spanish, but more experienced, savvy, and knowledgeable of the world. He also would be back to a place he loved. He had been to Colombia several times before, even living there for a year when he was a little boy. Each trip was pleasant, the odd, romantic charms of that country always providing a welcome change from the austere drabness of life in the States.

As Gabriel was packing and getting ready for the trip, the atmosphere in the household was one of enthusiasm and relief. His parents, having been concerned about his aimlessness in recent months, were happy he was going to at last do something productive with his life. They were a little worried about the chaotic situation in Colombia, but were comforted by the knowledge that their son had many relatives there who would look after him. After bidding an emotional farewell to his parents, having soaked up all his tears, and as the plane departed from the gate, Gabriel, to be gone for a long time, resembled a young Conquistador leaving his family behind on the shores of southern Spain. Off to some distant place and taking charge of his life, he felt like a grown man for the first time, free from the sticky vestiges of adolescent irresponsibility.

CHAPTER THREE

ARRIVAL IN COLOMBIA

As soon as the plane touched down in Bogotá later that evening, an uneasy feeling came over Gabriel. He sensed things would not go as smoothly as planned. He stayed with two of his cousins, acclimating himself to his surroundings for about a week before his planned visit to the U.S. embassy. He would take walks outside periodically to gather himself mentally, scanning the hectic scenes of Bogotá, a city of five million inhabitants, and prepare for this new mission. It was indeed hard to ponder deeply about his situation with all the activity on the streets, particularly the motorcycles and scooters zigzagging about everywhere. "Be gone already!" the American would yell at them as though they were pestering flies. They had become a symbol of the swarming trouble already brewing in his head. Gone were the tranquil days back home where he could lounge away freely. Gabriel was now alone and had to fend for himself, anxiety now taking hold over his mind and body.

The current desperation of his situation rendered little sleep for our poor friend, as he sorely missed his family and easy lifestyle. The first couple days were torturous since his cousins were away working most of the day, leaving him alone in a cramped apartment. With nothing to do, the days dragged on endlessly and thoughts of returning home popped up increasingly. Talking to his cousins helped raise his spirits, since they were both warm-hearted young women intent on making their guest feel comfortable. But his spirits would be raised only momentarily, the dark thoughts returning quickly thereafter.

After going through the motions for a week like this, Gabriel finally decided to take care of business. He was in Bogotá specifically to explore job opportunities at the U.S. embassy. This he finally did one early afternoon, taking a fifteen minute bus ride to the embassy. "I might as well find out now," he thought, brushing aside his nervousness. Upon arrival, he was immediately displeased. The color of the embassy was stark gray and it stood well behind a tall iron gate and fence topped with barbed wire. It looked very much like a prison. With a long line of people already waiting to get in, Gabriel thought about giving up and returning to his cousins' apartment. However, he decided against leaving, realizing he had already gone through so much trouble to get there. So he went in line and waited about twenty minutes before going through a couple security checks and entering the building.

When he entered the grim complex, there were more lines. In fact, there was *one* long line that weaved its way like a coiled snake through the entire ground floor of the embassy, ending up in the reception area far on the other side. There, the long line, like a river delta, branched out into five smaller lines. At the end awaited five stone-faced clerks, not looking too pleased about handling such a large crowd of people. Another thing Gabriel noticed was that most, if not all, the people working in the embassy appeared Colombian. He could not spot an American anywhere. He wanted desperately to speak to a fellow countryman, someone who could understand his plight. Inching his way forward, he figured the wait could last as long as an hour at the very least, making his search for a fellow American all the more frantic. He just had one question to ask. During this time, Gabriel grew ill from the warm, humid, and cramped conditions inside the building, the lack of air making him feel a little dizzy. "I don't know if I can work in a place like this," he thought.

A few minutes later, however, a blond man in a white-collared shirt and beige khaki pants suddenly emerged from the reception area. He was heading in Gabriel's direction. The man most certainly looked American and as he approached Gabriel, the youth waved at him. "I'm sure he can help me out," he wearily thought. The man saw Gabriel waving at him and walked over.

"Excuse me sir, do you work here?" Gabriel asked him.

"Yes I do," the man said in a smart, southern accent.

"Well, I just have one question to ask."

"Go ahead," the man said politely, but keeping his distance, looking at the nerve-racked Gabriel impassively.

"Well sir, I just graduated from college back in the States and I would like to know if you guys are offering any jobs here?"

"I'm sorry, but we are not hiring at the moment."

"Well, would you accept volunteers?" Gabriel asked with a trace of desperation in his choked-up voice. "I mean . . . I would be willing to do anything, help in any way. I would just like some work experience."

"I'm sorry, but we are not accepting anybody."

"Not even volunteers?"

"As a security measure, we are not accepting volunteers," the man answered coldly.

"Well, I'm American," the annoyed Gabriel remarked. "I don't know why I would be considered a security risk."

The man, remaining stoic, then responded: "I understand you may have good intentions, but according to the rules and regulations of the embassy, we cannot accept volunteers for reasons of security. Believe me, we get plenty of young people who come here all the time asking to volunteer or help, and we have to turn them down. That's just the way it's been here for a long time. I'm sorry. I wish I could do something for you, but there's really nothing I could do."

Gabriel looked at the man's cold expression and knew there was no other option but to leave. The man bowed his head apologetically to Gabriel before walking down a corridor leading to the other side of the building. Our dejected friend looked at this man walking away. He watched him in a despairing, obsessed manner, as though the man held the very key to his future and that he must run after him to retrieve it from his hand. He was about to run after him, but then stopped himself. It was futile. Not only was it futile, but, in reality, Gabriel did not want a job at the embassy. The youth did not really know what he wanted. Confused and upset, he slowly walked out of the embassy with his head down and shoulders stooped. "What the hell am I going to do now?" he wondered.

He called his parents later that evening to voice his concerns. "I've come all the way here for nothing," the disappointed youth dejectedly told his mother. He expressed anger at the embassy for not allowing him to volunteer. "What kind of a threat would I pose?" he asked his mother. "I'm an American who just graduated from college, looking for a little work experience, that's all!" Now, he was not only feeling resentful towards the United Nations, but his own country's government as well. "I'm not asking for money and they still turn me down! They can all go to hell!"

In truth, even if Gabriel had been offered a job at the embassy, it probably would not have done him any good. Such a job would have made perfect sense for someone wanting to be a bureaucrat, to work for an agency like the C.I.A. or State Department; certainly not someone wanting to be a politician. His simplistic plans to launch a political career were doomed from the start and he now finally began realizing it. "Without connections in politics, you go nowhere," he told his mother. His mother, however, did everything to comfort her disheartened son and told him not to give up. Her warm, loving voice was the perfect cure for his current disillusionment. "Don't worry, honey. God has a plan for you," she told him reassuringly. "I'm sure you will find something. In the meantime, just enjoy your time over there, okay?"

Gabriel was deflated for a couple days after the embassy visit, ashamed of coming away empty-handed. "I am as lost as ever!" he would lament to himself. "All that college education has gotten me nowhere!" However, our friend would soon rise from the doldrums with renewed hopes, encouraged by what his mother had told him. For better or worse, he decided to continue with the trip. He was determined to make it a productive one, at least learning some more Spanish along the way. If he could not decide what career path to follow, he definitely was not going to sit around and do nothing. In these uncertain times, Gabriel Ferrero was going to make the best of his situation. "I'll find something," he thought optimistically.

*   *   *

Gabriel would soon make the decision to leave Bogotá for Nueva Vida, where many of his relatives lived, including his Aunt Teresa and Grandmother Celia, who had invited him to stay with them. Nueva Vida was a city Gabriel knew well, being dear to his heart. This was his mother's home town, where he lived for a brief time early in his childhood. The youth figured the city would be a good place to stay for a while and do some soul searching. "I just need to be somewhere where I can feel comfortable," he reflected.

Gabriel departed for Nueva Vida a week after his disappointing trip to the American embassy in Bogotá. Upon his arrival in Nueva Vida, he immediately sensed things would get better for him. As it turned out, the young man enjoyed the first couple of days there, as many of his relatives greeted him with enthusiasm. The red-headed Aunt Teresa was beside herself with happiness on receiving Gabriel at the door of her apartment, embracing and kissing him so much that he was overcome with embarrassment. "Thank God you are here with us," she would tell him. "We are so happy!" This incredibly warm and emotional woman considered her nephew to be almost like her son. Grandmother Celia would greet the youth from her bed shortly thereafter, as she was unable to do much walking by then. She projected the sign of the cross on him and shed a slight smile. Her body may have been failing her, but Grandmother Celia's coffee eyes still reflected some of her old fire and spunk. "Good to have you here, Gabriel," she quietly told him, grabbing him by the arm. "Come sit here and talk with me." They went on talking fondly about some old memories for a good half-hour before lunch was served. Aunt Teresa delightfully remarked how that was the first time in months she had seen Grandmother Celia so animated.

*   *   *

Gabriel's new home was a significant improvement over his cousins' cramped apartment in Bogotá. Grandmother Celia and Aunt Teresa lived in a two storey apartment close to the bustling heart of Nueva Vida. The white and green building was old and creaky. It was, nonetheless, spacious and distinctive, with a large garden in the back, glorious Spanish tile roof, high ceilings, and large windows with spectacular views of the surrounding landscape. Gabriel had loved the apartment since he was little. In every nook and cranny of the place lurked a fond memory, whether it was the bedroom, kitchen, living room, or bathroom. He particularly enjoyed the long wooden hallway in the middle of the apartment, where he used to spend hours as a child rolling marbles with his cousins. Such was his love for the place that he did not at all mind putting up with the cold drafts at night, forcing him to sleep underneath several blankets. Despite such cold, the apartment exuded an intimacy and warmth that brought comfort to our friend.

The beauty of Nueva Vida would recharge him as well, providing hope and inspiration that can only be surpassed by a serene form of religious conversion. It was as if he was instantly transformed into a new man. Many qualities of the town contributed to this dramatic change in Gabriel. Perhaps most significant was the astounding charm and quaintness of Nueva Vida. The place was always magical for the young American. First, there was Luisa, the majestic volcano looming over town, the same peak which the Indians had worshipped for so many years. Many inhabitants feared the volcano as it spewed thin clouds of ash every now and then. They did not exactly warm up to it, despite its magnificent appearance, for it was most capable of wiping out the city and the lives of its inhabitants in a flash. The volcano, however, had not had a major eruption in almost five hundred years, since the time of the first, ill-fated Spanish settlement in Nueva Vida.

Some of those fearful inhabitants of the city claimed to admire and love Luisa, though it can be assumed those feelings were traced to the volcano's awesome destructive power. Their admiration and love for Luisa was similar to a believer's sentiments toward God, uttering prayers and singing songs of faithful devotion, yet trembling at the thought of angering the deity, fully aware of his grip over life and death, fortune and misfortune. Gabriel did not have these feelings of trepidation toward Luisa. Ever since he was a little kid, he had nothing but a genuine fondness for the volcano. He had always reveled in her sheer beauty. "Why should something so beautiful be feared?" he would ask himself. Having now arrived there, Gabriel drew much inspiration from Luisa, as though it were a benevolent spirit signaling the end of his recent travails.

* * *

Another aspect of Nueva Vida that Gabriel loved was its *oldness*. Three hundred year-old churches and buildings from the Spanish colonial period were everywhere. The ancient cobblestone streets were home to legions of stray dogs, food vendors, and prostrate beggars. Horse-drawn carriages, though dwindling in number, still made appearances in these streets during the mornings to carry milk from surrounding farms. Many people, especially the older ones, were pleased to see these 'milk horses' for they represented a sort of nostalgic link to the past; change was scary for them, as they were not fond of the increasingly complex, computer-driven world of the 1990's.

Other visitors of Nueva Vida's cobblestone streets included lost cows straying far from their pastures in the outskirts of town. Still a common sight, the cows usually would lumber aimlessly through the city streets, sometimes causing traffic to clog until their owner found them and herded them away, using the time-honored method of lightly hitting them with a stick. Of course, the town also contained many features of modernity, such as cars, glitzy shopping centers, and a couple glass high-rises. However, Nueva Vida still looked old, retaining many aspects from its colonial past which distinguished it from many other cities and towns throughout Latin America. Most of the townsfolk would not have it any other way, successfully pressuring legislators to place a ban on demolishing most old buildings and churches during the drug and oil boom of the 1980's and 1990's.

Gabriel was absolutely entranced by Nueva Vida's oldness. He enjoyed nothing more than to walk through the narrow streets and sidewalks, passing through the outstretched arms of those strange-looking beggars; gazing at the colorful, little stores packed tightly together; and whiffing at scents ranging from freshly baked bread of the *panaderias* to horse dung on the streets. Nothing in the United States compared to this! It was like being brought back in time at least fifty years, which changed Gabriel in the process. He felt freer here, more in touch with his *human* side. Uptight rigidity was replaced by a calm looseness, even though danger lurked in many sectors of town, with its legions of bandits and rogues roaming about. One needed to be careful walking the streets of Nueva Vida, for any of those criminals could sneak up from behind and deftly snatch a wallet, or, working in pairs, physically strip men and women of their watches. Women were their favorite targets, grabbing purses and necklaces often in broad daylight and in front of many people. Before anyone could react, the thieves would be off and running down the next block.

Armed house burglaries and kidnappings for ransom were on the rise at this time, though still not enough to cause panic among the town's residents. Yet, all this danger did not bother Gabriel, for its very presence represented *life* for him, a degree of excitement which he had not encountered for quite some time. Anything was better than the dreary suburban existence he led in the States. Oblivious of the danger, the tall, gangly American roamed about town, observing with fascination the many colorful parts of the city.

*   *   *

Viewing his grandmother's beautiful garden from the kitchen one morning, an endearing, old memory suddenly hit Gabriel. There were all sorts of exotic flowers and plants everywhere in the lush garden, with a huge fig tree in the corner. Many years before, when Gabriel was visiting as a small child, some neighborhood cats had wreaked havoc on the garden. Each night, several cats would pay a visit to it, leaving their excrements along the many paths crisscrossing it. The youth remembered how upset both his grandmother and aunt would get with those 'night cats'. "They just poop all over the place!" Aunt Teresa would angrily remark while cleaning things up. Sometime before, they had shards of razor-sharp glass placed atop the high walls of the garden to keep them away. That never worked, as the cats kept coming in during the cold nights.

Gabriel grew obsessed with the cats like his grandmother and aunt, though in a different way. He was dying of curiosity to witness them personally, seeing them in action. He wondered how the cats entered the garden, whether they climbed over the walls, or slid beneath the doors or through large cracks. He also wondered when they would arrive there, how long they would stay, and what they would do once inside. So the boy would stay up very late just to catch some glances of them. He would climb out of bed when everyone else was sleeping, and walk over to the second-floor bathroom facing the garden.

Gabriel remembered sitting in the toilet seat of the bathroom for long periods of time, waiting for the arrival of the cats. Intently watching the garden, he noticed how eerily dark it was, some lights from an adjacent school not penetrating its depths. The garden was so vast and dark, like a calm ocean in the night with its intense blackness, that little Gabriel would get frightened. So frightened was he that there were never any thoughts of going down there alone. How different it was during the day, with all its colorful flowers and butterflies! Nevertheless, the little boy was drawn to the dark garden, captivated enough to keep returning every night to watch it.

The sense of awe he derived from the garden at night was indeed captivating, making him feel transported to another world or dimension of time, where the little things in our daily lives do not matter. It almost suggested that there was life after death, where other timeless, spiritual realms dwarfed the fleeting, tangible confines of Earth, rendering it nothing but a speck in the grander scheme of things. Of course, the little boy could not comprehend what such a grander scheme consisted of, but still sensed it was there, existing much like the dark garden, a place or dimension without any knowable qualities. This is essentially what frightened Gabriel as a little child, the unknowable, vacant aspect of the garden at night, and that it would suck him in much like a black hole. Thus, it seemed a force representing both life and death, the two intertwined in an indifferent, meaningless way within the parameters of the garden's walls, where blackness and nothingness seemed to prevail in the end.

Such ominous thoughts would paralyze the little boy perched in the bathroom, making him succumb to despair until his attention suddenly turned back to the cats. How those troublesome thoughts of life and death disappeared in an instant! He would then frantically search for the cats through the darkness of the garden, using the adjacent school lights to spot them perhaps climbing over the walls. He would sit there endlessly, waiting patiently for those creatures to appear much like a cat would for a mouse. He noted to himself how his behavior was becoming like a cat's, staying up late at night, staring out a window at apparently nothing, anticipating for something to appear or happen. The only difference was that he did not have a cat's uncanny sense of knowing if something was actually there, which made him waste a hell of a lot of time waiting.

As it turned out, he would never spot any of the cats at night. The search lasted for about two weeks, with little Gabriel staying up well past midnight the whole time. Yet, one of the cats would appear every morning on the roof of the neighboring house overlooking the garden. This splendidly orange cat would lie on the red-tile roof, basking in the warm morning sun, resting after a long, playful evening. Once in a while, he peered over at little Gabriel sitting in the kitchen eating breakfast, almost giving him a teasing look as if to say, "You couldn't spot us again, huh?"

After eating breakfast, the little boy would go shower quickly. After finishing, he peered out the window to look for the cat, only to notice it was no longer there. This happened every morning, the same exact routine. The appearance of the orange cat every morning would further embolden Gabriel to continue searching for the frolicking felines at night, leaving him very frustrated at times, as though he were being outwitted by them. Those sneaky creatures were challenging him, and he was determined, even growing desperate, to spot them during the evening once and for all.

However, the orange cat did not show up on the roof one morning. Little Gabriel was left wondering what happened to it. He did not think much of it and continued with the same routine that night, staying up late searching for the cats. The following morning, there was no sign of the orange cat again. At first, Gabriel was hurt, feeling betrayed by the cat. Then it dawned on him that the game he was playing with them was futile and silly. That was perhaps the message the morning cat was attempting to convey by not returning to the roof. The little boy never looked back, not bothering with the cats anymore. Those devious, mysterious animals were better left alone, he realized.

This memory of the cats made Gabriel a little sad. He remembered the time like it was yesterday and was astounded at how rapidly the years slipped past. Yet, he was grateful to have enjoyed such a moment, for it was truly special. It was a time of childhood innocence, when the world seemed so simple, when spotting cats at night constituted one of the few challenges to be faced in a given day. Such pleasant memories tickled his heart, reminding him that life was good to him once and it may be good to him again. The memory of the cats particularly made him believe he was in the right place. It was an example of Nueva Vida's charming allure that Gabriel loved so much. It depicted the town's mythical, supernatural aura, very much resembling New Orleans with its old-world charisma. The youth was certain he would now bounce back onto his feet in this place.

CHAPTER FOUR

LANDING A JOB

A couple weeks into his stay, a friend of Aunt Teresa informed Gabriel of a job opening at a language institute. The institute needed a person who could teach English. The young man procrastinated a bit, but ultimately decided to investigate the situation. He desperately wanted to pay his own way at his grandmother's apartment, and, for all he knew, there were probably going to be no other job opportunities available during the rest of his stay. One day, the youth walked over to the institute, a modest, two-storey glass and steel structure seemingly built in the late 1960's, which was not too far away. Shortly after his arrival, he met Dr. Ricardo Granados, the director of the school, who was a friendly, genteel man in his late fifties. His appearance was neat, as he wore an elegant olive-green suit, white shirt with gold cufflinks, and an amber colored tie. His graying hair was combed back straight, revealing his thin, tanned face. Behind the lenses of his thick, black framed glasses were his brown eyes, big and piercing like a hawk's. He looked every bit the part of a cool professor with his reserved, confident demeanor. The visual contrast between the short, up-right, dapper Dr. Granados and the tall, lanky, casually dressed Gabriel, wearing nothing but a t-shirt, blue jeans, and baseball cap, was sharp indeed. Both of them were standing outside his office, not too far away from the front entrance. Right away, the professor warmed up to Gabriel.

"So, you come from the United States," mentioned Dr. Granados, who spoke English very well. "What part of the country do you come from?"

"I come from Detroit, Michigan," Gabriel responded readily.

"Detroit, Michigan . . . hmmm," Dr. Granados replied quietly, not so much trying to locate the city in his mind, but retrieving other information connected to it.

"Well, I am not from Detroit exactly, but a suburb of it, Troy."

"Yes . . . Detroit. A good friend of mine lived there for several years, back in the 1970's. He was teaching there, I believe high school."

"Do you know which high school?" Gabriel asked.

"I do not remember exactly. Hmmm, I believe it was a St. Mary or something like that. I am not sure, but he did live there for a time. Now, he lives in Spain. He teaches linguistics in a small university in Seville."

"Have you gone to the United States, professor?"

"Oh yes. In fact, I lived there myself for a few years. I lived in Fort Lauderdale for two years, then one year in Miami. I taught Spanish at some small colleges. But I went to all parts of the country . . . Mesa, Arizona, Santa Cruz, California, Provo, Utah, Las Vegas, New York, Boston, Chicago, Atlanta, Dallas, everywhere."

"You know my country better than I do!" Gabriel responded with astonishment.

"But I was just there for a little while."

"When were you there?"

"Like my friend, I was in America during the 1970's . . . from 1971 to 1973, '74. It was an enjoyable time. I can't believe it has been such a long time ago. My God, it seems like yesterday when I was there!"

Gabriel sensed the close rapport he was developing with the affable Dr. Granados and began relaxing a bit. He enjoyed conversing with him, since he was obviously a very knowledgeable man. "Where are you from, professor?"

"Please, just call me Ricardo. I am from Bogotá."

"How long have you been here in Nueva Vida?"

"I have lived here for many, many years. Twenty-one years! I opened up this institute in 1975 and I have been here ever since."

"So, you must like it here in Nueva Vida?"

"Well, I have this business here," Dr. Granados answered as though embarrassed. "There have been times when I considered moving elsewhere, like Bogotá or Medellin, but I decided to remain here. When you get older, it is so much harder to just pack your bags and move to another place. But, I like it very much here. It is beautiful and peaceful."

"Yes it is," Gabriel replied. "I was going to say, how do you keep up with your English? You speak it very well."

Dr. Granados readjusted his thick glasses, scratched his leathery forehead, and answered, "Well, I have been back to the States several times. I have many relatives and friends that live in Miami, so I go there a lot, maybe once every two years. I have also gone to America to attend education conventions. Most recently, I have been to Dallas and Atlanta to attend these conventions. That is how I have kept up with my English. I also read a lot of books and magazines in English."

"That must be nice, being able to take such trips," Gabriel said in an effort to create more small talk.

"Oh, it certainly is. I cannot complain. But enough about me! What about you, Gabriel? What brings you here to Nueva Vida?"

"I just graduated from college, and I guess I'm here to learn some Spanish and spend time with my relatives," Gabriel responded timidly, as if he was somehow ashamed to admit there was really nothing going on in his life at the moment. He nervously took his baseball cap off his head, placing it on a nearby table in an effort to appear more presentable in the presence of the dapper Dr. Granados. With the cap off, the youth's dark wavy hair flowed in all directions, adding to the messiness of his appearance.

"You have family here?" asked the curious professor.

Gabriel was disarmed by this friendly question and felt comfortable again, realizing there was no need to be so self-conscious and worried with Dr. Granados. He was now sensing the kind man would be willing to help him out. "Yes, my mother is from here, and a lot of her family still is here."

"Wow, that is great!" the professor declared with hardly a trace of a discernible accent. "That is interesting. I have never met an American or any foreigner who has family from here." The two continued to talk at length about Gabriel's family, his Colombian and Chilean roots, and the several trips he took to Colombia. They also talked at length about life in the United States. "Things are so rigid in America," Gabriel went on to say. "You almost feel like a robot because you're always running around doing this, doing that. Everything there is work, work, work! You never seem to have time for other things, or even to think about them."

Dr. Granados eventually looked at his watch and peered outside as though he had somewhere to go. "We need to continue talking about this sometime Gabriel, but I now have to attend a meeting. Is there something I can help you with?"

"Yes, Dr. Granados . . ."

"Please call me Ricardo."

"Oh, I'm sorry . . . yes, Ricardo," Gabriel uttered softly, blushing with embarrassment and a sense of apprehension. "I was told that you were looking for someone who could teach English."

"Well, we have enough teachers now, but I suppose we can always use another teacher," the professor responded coolly, weighing his options. For about a minute, he stood there motionless, deep in thought with his hands on his hips and eyes gazing at the floor. The minute seemed like an eternity for the increasingly anxious Gabriel, as he looked searchingly into the professor's eyes for any signs of hope. There was a pained look on the professor's face for he sincerely wanted to help Gabriel, but was not sure about the feasibility of hiring another teacher. "I would be very interested in teaching here at your institute," Gabriel confirmed, attempting to trigger some positive response from Dr. Granados, who continued gazing at the floor in thought. Then, a few seconds later, the old man quickly lifted his head and looked straight at the youth. He gave a warm smile which seemed to confirm good news. "Yes, I can have you teach."

"Excellent!" responded the relieved Gabriel.

"Would you like to work at night?" Dr. Granados asked with a little hesitation.

"Oh, that would be fine by me."

"Good, because our evening classes are a bit overcrowded now, so there might be enough room for another class to open up."

"Okay."

"Now, the class would have to take place on Tuesdays and Thursdays. The sessions will each be about ninety minutes long. Would that be okay with you?"

"That would certainly be fine with me," Gabriel replied enthusiastically, as he picked up his baseball cap from the adjacent table, wanting desperately to leave with job in hand.

"Before you accept this job, you need to know one thing," Dr. Granados cautioned. "The pay will not be so great. We are on a strict budget at this time."

"How much would it be?"

"About six hundred pesos an hour, more or less."

Gabriel appeared slightly befuddled as he was trying to figure out the mathematics in his head. He was not so sure how well he could live off that salary in Nueva Vida. "Will that be enough for me to live here?" he eventually asked.

"Oh yes, that will be enough to get you by," Dr. Granados replied reassuringly. "You will not be living in luxury by any stretch of the imagination, but it will be enough to cover for basic expenses."

"Great! That will be good enough for me then," Gabriel responded, confident he would make enough money to help pay his way at his grandmother's. He was also sure there would be enough spending money on the side to lead a comfortable existence. In case there were serious problems, he knew his doting parents could always be relied upon for emergency cash anyway, so there was no need for worry.

Gabriel agreed to work Tuesdays and Thursdays between six and eight in the evening. He would begin as a tutor and then work his way up to be a teacher within a month. With that, Dr. Granados congratulated our young friend and shook his hand. "Come over anytime in the morning tomorrow to sign the papers," he said as they both exited the building. After bidding good-bye to his new boss on the sidewalk, Gabriel was overcome with relief and excitement. He found a decent job. "This will look impressive on my resume," the excited youth thought. Finally, it seemed things were going in the right direction.

CHAPTER FIVE

THE BLACK BIRDS

A couple months into his stay in Nueva Vida, Gabriel was happier than he had been in a long time. He really enjoyed working at the language institute. The light work schedule left him with plenty of free time. The classes were also small, comprised mainly of adults desperate to learn English. The atmosphere was very relaxed as Gabriel was free to engage in long discussions with his students, especially about life in the United States and Colombia. He had quickly gained a good reputation at the institute and made many new friends.

Gabriel enjoyed a pretty relaxing lifestyle in Nueva Vida. In the mornings, he would mostly read in his bedroom or accompany Aunt Teresa to shop in some nearby stores. Everyday at noon there was lunch, usually consisting of boiled chicken, rice, and beans along with a bowl of delicious vegetable soup. This was always followed by the hour-long siesta. By two o'clock, he would take an extended stroll through the city, sometimes walking all the way to the beautiful downtown plaza. Unlike in Bogotá, he could calmly proceed through the streets of Nueva Vida without any fear of getting hit by motorcycles or scooters. This was Gabriel's favorite time of day for he could freely meander about and gather his thoughts. By customarily taking such strolls, Aunt Teresa and Grandmother Celia could not help but be reminded of the young man's grandfather.

The long-deceased patriarch of the family also enjoyed taking a long walk after siesta.

Gabriel never met his grandfather for he died before he was born, but he heard much about him through his mother and aunt. His name was Hector Duarte, and he was a successful lawyer in Nueva Vida who became a federal-level Senator later in his life. He was a member of the Liberal Party of Colombia and was a staunch supporter of the poor. During the late 1940's, when the Cold War began heating up, Duarte's leftist beliefs brought accusations from his enemies in the Senate that he was a communist. Those accusations were never denied, which intensified suspicions among others in Congress about his perceived allegiance with communist subversives, and when there was a right-wing power-grab in 1948 after the assassination of popular leftist presidential candidate Jorge Eliecer Gaitan, Duarte was one of the first individuals to be apprehended. The Senator was abducted just outside his home by a couple armed men, thrown in a car at gunpoint where he was blindfolded, gagged, and bound, and quietly transported to an unknown location. The Senator was not informed of anything as he was simply locked in a room and told to keep his mouth shut. He was kept there for about three days, not knowing what was to become of his fate.

The assassination of Gaitan was indeed a very serious affair, triggering perhaps the worst upheaval in Colombia's history, a lengthy ten-year bloodbath known simply as *La Violencia*. The assassination immediately set off huge riots in Bogotá, as the mob hunted down and murdered prominent Conservative Party officials in the streets of the capital. Much of Bogotá was burned down after only a couple days. The army responded by rounding up and killing leftists throughout the country. This would also, in effect, mark the beginning of Colombia's extremely long civil war.

So when Gabriel's grandfather was kidnapped, his life was very much in danger. Hector Duarte, however, would have someone very powerful in his corner. A high ranking army general who was a close friend of the Senator ordered his immediate release upon discovering his detainment. Duarte, unlike many other leftists, was allowed to live. He eventually reentered the Senate, remaining there for another fifteen years. He never held any grudges from his 'kidnapping', which he knew was certainly supported by many of his right-wing colleagues in the Senate. This gesture of forgiveness drew much respect from many people in Bogotá, including his rivals in the Senate, and he was allowed to serve the rest of his tenure there in peace. He would be known as one of the leading leftists in the country, quietly pushing the agenda of Colombia's poor.

It was his grandfather's success that encouraged the high-minded Gabriel to envision himself becoming a lawyer or politician since childhood. His mother always seemed to put this idea in his mind. But it had now created a big problem. The shadow of his grandfather was looming large and hanging over him like never before. He would sometimes look at a large painting of him in the apartment hallway and feel humiliated at his own failures and lack of direction. Gabriel felt overwhelmed by the pressure of following in his grandfather's footsteps. His fear of failure had become insurmountable, almost paralyzing, which prevented him from understanding there were other alternatives to the lifestyle he had long envisioned for himself. It was politics or bust! Viewing the painting of his grandfather only served to remind the youth that he had fallen far short of reaching his lofty goals.

This personal dilemma Gabriel encountered was, as noted before, a result of his terribly sheltered life. He developed unrealistic expectations for himself, living far too long in a dream world of his own making. He believed he was going to be a politician one day. He was entirely convinced of this. There were no back-up plans in case things did not work, so blissful was Gabriel's outlook. He coasted through four years of college thinking everything would turn out well in the end, that he would accomplish his lifelong mission. But Gabriel never put much effort in guaranteeing this outcome for himself, never taking the steps necessary for ensuring his future in politics such as getting good grades, joining clubs, attending seminars, meeting people, applying for internships early in college, and so on. Gabriel always thought he was above the 'rat race' and that the rules of survival in it did not apply to him. Getting good grades and joining clubs? Such activities and requirements were beneath him! He refused to be a mere 'follower and pretender'. Instead, the out-of-touch Gabriel expected his goal of being a politician to materialize on its own without him having to do anything. It was just going to happen, he thought.

So when Gabriel arrived in Nueva Vida and wrestled with his grandfather's legacy, it was indeed another painful dose of reality. But it was different now. There was a sense of finality this time. He realized at long last that his mission of being like his grandfather, of becoming a politician one day, was over. Whereas there was still a glimmer of hope before his arrival to Nueva Vida, absolutely none existed now. He was paying the price for years of arrogance, ignorance, and laziness. He was paying the price for stubbornly blazing his own path for so long, one that ultimately led nowhere. And what a price it was. Gabriel was devastated. "It's too late," he thought. Gabriel for a short time would become ashamed of his own failure and shortcomings. "If only I had known how stupid this plan was from the beginning!" he thought on one occasion.

With time, however, Gabriel's harsh view of himself would diminish considerably. In an ironic sort of way, Gabriel's afternoon strolls through town would finally bring peace between himself and the burdensome legacy of his grandfather. In taking such strolls the first couple days, he would emulate his idol, placing his hands behind his back much like he did in his mother's photographs, looking and feeling like him, even hunching his back a little. His grandfather looked so dignified and peaceful in those photographs, so secure with himself and life. This image had always impressed the insecure Gabriel.

However, the young man would grow tired of trying to be like him. He finally had enough of it one afternoon. "I just don't care anymore if I turn out like him or not!" an exasperated Gabriel thought. The young American realized he had to find his own way and not live in somebody else's shoes. Through the act of emulating his grandfather during those walks through town, Gabriel was beginning to find himself. 'Do not act contrary to thy

49

nature' was the Daoist message the youth discovered for himself in the colorful streets of Nueva Vida, for everyone has a different identity and purpose in the world, much like all the things he saw in that town—the shops, birds, cats, stray dogs, beggars, thieves, cars, mountains, clouds, and pebbles in the sidewalk. These were all different and separate from each other, and with this in mind, Gabriel at long last walked away from his grandfather's shadow. He was not going to be a politician and that was okay. He would live on. Like a butterfly pupa reaching maturity, he was breaking out of the self-encasing cocoon, representing all the anxieties and ill-conceived hopes that held him back for so many years. He was not totally free yet, but he was getting there.

*   *   *

After the strolls, Gabriel would go back to his grandmother's place and prepare lessons, grade papers, or read, usually for about two hours, to be followed by a much needed coffee break at around five o'clock, very much a Colombian tradition. Usually, he and his Aunt Teresa would gather at his grandmother's bedroom for the coffee break, where she would be lying on a chaise in front of a medium-sized television, knitting away. There was a large window right beside her, from which she would periodically watch the bustling street below. She spent long periods of the day on the chaise, for she was too old to walk around much. At night, when it got cold beside the window, she would leave the chaise for her bed on the other side of the room.

The coffee break was, in Gabriel's judgment, a very important part of the day, a time to socialize with his aunt, grandmother, and other people who may have dropped in to visit. It was a time to revitalize the mind and spirit, and get prepared for the evening, which always began when the sun set at around six o'clock. After the coffee break, our friend would be off to work or visiting his cousins when there were no classes to teach.

It was precisely this light but eventful daily schedule that helped Gabriel bounce back from the recent disappointments he had encountered. His childhood dreams of becoming a politician all but crushed, the young American would soon discover something in himself through the daily routines in Nueva Vida. He discovered an energy and work ethic in himself that he thought never existed. He had grown accustomed to being alone and doing nothing throughout much of his life, getting by with as little effort and energy as possible. It was the sort of life highlighted by the usual trip to the café or bookstore, and, at times, to the bar at night.

But now in Nueva Vida, Gabriel found little time to loaf about. He was now a teacher and the job certainly changed the way he viewed things. For the first time in his life, other people were depending on Gabriel. They needed him for learning English and knowledge of this fact gave the youth a sense of power, a most gratifying kind at that. He was molding other people's minds, helping them learn a valuable skill, making a real difference in their lives. Gabriel could no longer view himself as an outcast for he truly mattered to his students, many of them needing to learn English to win new jobs or keep old ones. Gabriel had become indispensable to these people and this idea boggled his mind at times, for he long liked to believe that society shunned him. And in turn, he liked to believe he did not depend on it for much. These beliefs, however, were now being challenged and Gabriel learned that he was capable of far more than just lounging about at a café, living in seclusion. He discovered that he could make meaningful contributions to society, albeit not as a politician.

But being a language teacher made Gabriel feel important and this did wonders for his confidence. He would bounce around from place to place, meeting people, keeping appointments, attending seminars, going to parties, and learning Spanish along the way. It was hard at first for the taciturn Gabriel to get used to such a busy life, but he quickly began enjoying it. He could never have envisioned such a hectic lifestyle for himself just a few months before.

* * *

Despite all the good things that were happening to Gabriel in Nueva Vida, including a renewed sense of direction and satisfaction with his life, there still was something missing. During his afternoon strolls, he would sometimes go to a little bakery on 19th Street, only a few blocks away from his grandmother's apartment, to get some coffee and read a newspaper. He would sit down on one of the wobbly, red-colored tables close to the entrance, facing the street. The sun always beat down on his angular, chiseled face, causing him at first to squint, which then quickly gave way to a more comforted expression. The warmth of the sun was certainly pleasant, especially when one did not have to brave the brisk Andean winds just outside the entrance. Once seated, Gabriel would then have a smoke, inhaling ever so slowly in an effort to enjoy it fully, to really kick back and let the nicotine relax him mentally and physically. He would look at the spectacular Luisa in all its snow-bound glory in the afternoon sunshine, and silently speak to it as though it was a living person. "How are you, my Luisa?" he would always ask in greeting.

One afternoon while at the bakery, he looked at some large black birds hovering far ahead, way off in the distance. Gabriel could not figure out what type of birds these were, whether these were ravens or some sort of vulture, but they were rather large with big wingspans. These birds flew so effortlessly, hovering in the windy air for long stretches of time without seeming to move its wings a millimeter in any direction, almost motionless in the sky. The youth was captivated by these graceful creatures, entranced by them as though he was flying with them, his spirit freely dancing amid the thin clouds; a realm so calm and quiet, where the only sounds to be heard were gentle echoes, not at all startling but beckoning, of the birds' wings occasionally flapping against a streaming wind; a sound that for Gabriel marked the liberation of his soul from the troubles of Earth, as if he died and was entering the gates of Heaven, to be greeted by a benevolent, loving God about to cast away all his haunting doubts and fears.

Taking another puff of his cigarette, Gabriel then saw the distant birds swoop down from the heights of the sky and glide low over the

Earth. There they would glide for a while, their wings pushed tightly against their sides to achieve the lowest degree of wind resistance. Seeing this, Gabriel then sank back to Earth and began looking at his surroundings with awe and a renewed sense of appreciation. He no longer was dancing amid the clouds high above, flying away from the turmoil of Earth, but reveling in its glorious beauty. He looked at the people passing by in the busy street and was *delighted*. Watching a mother walk with her two children brought a tear of joy and love to his eye, reminding him of his warm childhood, when his mother used to take him and his siblings out for walks when he was a little boy.

He then looked at a dingy shoe store across the street, where two of the workers were taking a midday break and sitting on the entrance steps. The workers were young men with a rough appearance, their greasy hair slicked back to reveal hardened faces blackened from shoe polish. They were doing nothing more than speaking to each other and watching the street life proceed before them. Yet, these young men represented a noble picture to Gabriel, a portrait of proletarian virtues symbolizing the toughness of mankind. These boys were bent, but not beaten, from the extreme rigors of life, and they would continue confronting those difficulties and survive. Gabriel was in such high spirits that nobody could do wrong, not one member of the human race!

Our young friend also admired and appreciated his physical surroundings, even that drab shoe store across the street. Its gray walls and darkened interior were certainly not a treat to the human eye, by far the ugliest shop in a street lined with many colorful stores containing an abundance of decorations and wares on display. The shoe shop displayed no such trappings outside or inside of it; just the gray walls and unlit interior which appeared empty for the most part, aside from probably some shoes that were being fixed and readied, tools to repair them, and a stack of dominoes on a wooden table to wile away the time.

However, even this ugly shop, like those two chaps working in it, appeared noble to Gabriel. The shop did not at all detract from the overall appearance of the street, but contributed much to it, an appealingly dark, somber contrast to all the other lively stores. The shoe shop might have looked less fancy and attracted less people, but it still added a necessary dimension to the street in physical terms, a dark, lonely, isolated feature which served the purpose of making the neighborhood not look so bright and gay. In this sense, the shoe shop was necessary in Gabriel's brooding eyes, even beautiful. "Beauty encompasses all things: the old and young, rich and poor, big things and little things, pretty things and ugly things, everything," he thought while viewing the street.

As Gabriel continued taking in the environment around him, he noticed his cigarette was almost finished. As the burning end was closing in on the filter, there was a look of despair in his face. As he slowly put out the cigarette, Gabriel was suddenly snapped out of his euphoric trance. Finishing a cigarette would sometimes deflate the young man, but not like this. There was suddenly a profound feeling of emptiness inside of him and he did not know why at first. He looked up at the sky for answers, but none could be found. The sky now only seemed like some sort of transparent lid suffocating everything beneath it, shallow and obscure, not the infinitely free and joyous realm Gabriel visualized moments before. The youth then looked at the surrounding landscape to find some hope, which also proved fruitless. Everything around him, including the lively street, was devoid of any color or life, and the people walking through were nothing but a blur; their eyes, mouths, hair, skin, and most other physical features lost amid a chaotic tangle of forms and shapes. As soon as he calmed down a bit, the blurriness faded away and things perceptually returned to normal, with color reemerging everywhere. But our young friend was still feeling empty, and he knew why soon thereafter while having another smoke.

When Gabriel was finishing the previous cigarette, noticing the burning end quickly closing in on the filter, the thought of time flashed before him like a thunderbolt; time, that is, running out on him, fleeting ever so rapidly. Very soon, he would be left with no time. This then made him think about his future once again. The young man realized he could not remain in Colombia for long, and that he eventually had to return to the United States. He could have

54

stayed in Colombia if he really wanted to, but then what? He was enjoying a good time in Nueva Vida thus far, but was he to remain working indefinitely as a low-paid teacher? Furthermore, what about his destiny? Was he to languish through life like some anonymous wave rolling amidst the sea of humanity, to be forgotten once his journey unceremoniously ends on the shore? These questions continued pestering Gabriel, as he was more determined than ever to find some answers.

CHAPTER SIX

THE CANDIDATE

Gabriel would continue feeling a bit lost, but kept soldiering along. He was still enjoying his stay in Nueva Vida and as long as he did not think too much about his future, there were no problems. He took to heart the advice of his Aunt Teresa, who noticed how despondent he was one day and told him to live life one day at a time. This he tried to do although the old fears would make it difficult once in a while. Yet, one individual did arouse his attention at this uncertain time in his life. The person was Vicente Sanchez, a presidential candidate who was receiving unusual fanfare from the politically cynical people of Colombia. This was because the energetic, quirky, almost fanatical Sanchez was delivering an unusual message which was beginning to take the country by storm. "Colombia for Colombians!" was the slogan. Considering that Colombia was not under foreign occupation at the time, many outside observers were a little baffled by the slogan. "Is not Colombia a free and independent country?" they would ask. What such observers could not perhaps comprehend was that many Colombians felt they were in a sense besieged. They certainly were not besieged by some foreign army, but by indigenous forces seeking to take control of the country.

On one side were leftist guerillas, which had splintered into several different groups over the years, often warring against each other. The guerrillas were splintered because they were not all on the same page—one group advocating the poverty-stricken peasants in the countryside, another supporting exploited workers in the cities, and others representing university students throughout the country. By 1996, however, there were only two guerrilla groups left, the largest by far being the one backing the peasants in the countryside with a force of some 30,000 strong. The guerrillas wreaked havoc all over Colombia, blocking roads, destroying oil pipelines, and cutting off electricity almost on a daily basis. They were even able to pull off some victories over the Colombian Army, thanks to their newfound wealth from the drug trade, enabling them to acquire more weapons and recruits in the process. The Civil War between the government and guerrillas had indeed entered a new phase by this time, one which seemed to be favoring the rebels.

The rebel groups long considered themselves leftist revolutionaries even though their involvement in drug trafficking, ransom kidnappings, and mass executions left many wondering what their true intentions were. "Can a populist movement get involved in such criminal activities?" Dr. Granados once asked Gabriel. According to the wise professor, these groups ceased being populist revolutionaries long ago, and were now only criminal organizations bent on wreaking havoc and grabbing power, nothing more. That was the sentiment of most people throughout the country, which did not seem to bother the guerrillas the least bit. They continued with their unscrupulous ways, kidnapping priests and children for ransom money, and terrorizing the countryside in order to maintain their power.

Standing in the way of the guerrillas was the government and its faction of armed supporters. Whereas the guerrillas represented at times a sort of chaotic rabble, a camp divided into several pieces, the Colombian government was large and cumbersome, a wounded, dying elephant too slow to keep up with its smaller, quicker enemies. The Colombian Army was too weak to take on all the guerrilla groups. The government was too corrupted to rectify the situation and whip the army into shape, ultimately allowing the guerrillas to take control of more lands. Generals were accused of selling weapons to the guerrillas, while some politicians were suspected of profiting from the drug trade.

Realizing the ineptitude of the army, the government pinned its hopes on right-wing paramilitary groups. These tough mercenary bands proved very effective in curbing the guerrillas' territorial advances, fighting them wherever they could. However, the mercenaries could not wipe them out. Frustrated with their inability to defeat the guerillas, the mercenaries resorted to barbarous acts such as mass killings of peasants suspected of siding with the rebels. The government never took responsibility for such atrocities, claiming the mercenary bands acted independently. Indeed, these bands, empowered by the government during the drug wars of the early 1990's and receiving substantial aid from it, became increasingly independent as they controlled more land. As more land was seized, the mercenaries walked away from the government's shadow, no longer willing to act as mere pawns in the civil war. Losing control of the mercenaries proved to be a public relations disaster for the government, as it was quickly losing the Colombian people's confidence. In the end, the guerrillas and right-wing mercenaries were killing thousands of innocent people while the government could only watch, leaving people more furious than ever about the situation.

Lastly, there were the drug cartels. But by 1996, the cartels had ceased being a very powerful force. They could no longer pose much of a threat to the Colombian state like they had in the 1980's when Pablo Escobar laid siege on the government through carrot and stick, bribing numerous politicians while assassinating a handful of judges opposing him. By 1996, with Escobar already dead, the power had shifted from Medillin to Cali. But the Cali drug cartel was very much a quiet outfit, deliberately choosing a low profile to evade the attention of Colombian officials and U.S. prosecutors. And by then, the cartels were losing much of their business to the guerrillas and paramilitaries operating in the countryside, where much of the cocaine was processed and trafficked.

Things had very much changed for the cartels indeed, but they still wielded some influence over the affairs of Colombia. Their expertise in the manufacture and sale of drugs coupled with their links to international criminal rings still made them an indispensable force. Though they were now quiet and no longer paralyzing the country like before, the cartels retained a powerful presence through their vast wealth. And, most importantly, the guerillas and paramilitaries had now perfected many of the terrorist tactics that the cartels introduced in the 1980's to fight the Colombian government, resorting to mass murder and assassination to achieve their aims.

So when Vicente Sanchez was declaring "Colombia for Colombians" during his spirited campaign, the Colombian people perfectly understood what he meant: no more massacres, kidnappings, warfare, car bombs, electrical 'blackouts', and ineffective government. Above all, they wanted peace. They wanted their country back. And Vicente Sanchez was there, like some prophet sent by God, to give it back to them. Unlike so many other politicians offering the usual suggestions of 'peace through war' and 'not giving in to the rebels', Sanchez bluntly spoke for the people. "The people of Colombia need to take a stand against their oppressors," he would proclaim passionately to the thunderous applause of audiences throughout the country. "We are sick of the guerrillas, the mercenaries, the corruption, the war, the drugs, and all the madness! We will take our country back, with or without the government's help!" This was not just empty, political rhetoric either. The presidential candidate truly meant what he was saying, as he showed all the heartfelt emotions of a frustrated citizen while up on the pulpit. His face would be flushed red with anger when he talked about the civil war, often pounding the top of the pulpit with his fists during his speeches.

Vicente Sanchez was not your typical hothead either. He was a young, thin man in his forties who was very well educated and mannered, always dressed in a suit and tie. He personified class and culture, for he taught economics at an esteemed college in Bogotá and was an accomplished pianist. He loved literature and history, reading a lot in his spare time, a quality very rare among politicians at that time. So his hot-temperedness did not come across as petty ranting or bombastic ignorance, but the justified emotion of a dignified, purposeful man. He was a person with a specific mission, one that was heroic and noble in the eyes of his fellow countrymen. If anything, his emotional nature made him all the more attractive to voters bored with stiff, timid politicians. Colombians had a gut feeling that he was going to be the man to finally set things straight. His popularity rose with every stump speech he delivered during the campaign, which took him and his staff everywhere in the crumbling country, from the Amazon jungles in the south to the Caribbean coast in the north.

Every campaign stop was greeted enthusiastically by the people, as they clamored to see this new person on the political scene, a man they considered their savior. Not since the doomed Luis Carlos Galan had a presidential candidate generated this much buzz in Colombia. People would cry in his presence, especially the older women, who had long lost hope for their country until this charismatic man suddenly emerged out of nowhere. And when it was announced that Vicente Sanchez had showed up in town and was soon to deliver a speech at a certain location, people would immediately stop what they were doing, even if they were working, and run over to the place. The fanfare had become incredible considering the Colombian people were notoriously cynical and indifferent when it came to politics. Yet, they were swept up by this man. When he started his campaign, Sanchez would speak to small audiences in street corners, hardly noticed by the press. Now, he was speaking to thousands in stadiums, and even the foreign press was beginning to pay attention.

*   *   *

The government, guerrillas, and mercenaries were also paying close attention to Vicente Sanchez. This firebrand was becoming a real thorn in their sides and they nervously watched his every move. The young presidential hopeful posed a real threat to the guerrillas and mercenaries, for much of his campaign was directed against them and their massacres and ransom kidnappings. The government also was a big target of the campaign, as its corruption, negligence, and incompetence were blamed for the ruinous shape of the country.

A complete overhaul of the government was suggested as the only feasible way to revamp the rule of law in Colombia, and that idea became extremely popular with the people. "If we had an effective government, there would not be all these problems hanging over our heads," Vicente Sanchez would say on many occasions, to the overwhelming delight of audiences, many of whom felt betrayed by the government. "The government has the duty and obligation to defend you from these butchers stalking the countryside," he would say. "The very least thing they can do is make an effort! But they don't and that makes them as callous as the guerrillas and mercenaries." While such bold comments gave the people a much needed lift, they felt like terrible hammer blows to the ringleaders of destruction in Colombia. For once, someone was taking a stand against them. And for once, they were feeling united about something, for they all wanted nothing more than for this troublemaker to disappear.

At first, they attempted persuading him into being less belligerent and hostile. When that failed, numerous death threats were issued, forcing leading members of the press to warn that Colombia's hero was in peril. All the death threats were from anonymous sources, but it was universally understood that the guerillas, mercenaries, and cartels were behind them with the acquiescence of the government. However, this did not faze the bold presidential candidate as he continued traveling around the country, making speeches to larger audiences. The death threats only made the people rally around Vicente Sanchez more, which certainly buoyed his spirits.

There was no way he could abandon them now, but that did not even cross his mind. He had long realized the danger he was getting himself into by running for president, and was prepared for it. He publicly addressed this issue by stating that the threat of death would not deter him. "I know what the stakes are, which includes the possible taking of my life by some assassin's bullet," he told a reporter. "I know that full well. But my life is not at issue, for it really is insignificant when one considers the big picture. What is at issue is the life of our country, and I am willing to die for it." It was these types of quotes that really enhanced Sanchez's heroic image throughout the nation and fueled an astounding surge in his popularity. His show of courage at this moment, with death staring him straight in the face, is what completely won the hearts of the Colombian people.

Yet, they were worried. Many other courageous political leaders in Colombian history had been assassinated, usually for standing up against the powers that be, whether they were colonial viceroys, right-wing governments, or drug cartels. As soon as they had become popular, the established rulers gunned them down mercilessly, leaving the peoples' hopes utterly crushed. Having very long memories, the Colombian people did not want history to repeat itself as they anxiously waited for the outcome of the elections. They prayed that things would run smoothly, that there would be no assassination this time around.

To save face, the government announced it would do everything possible to ensure the safety of all the presidential candidates, offering each of them police escorts and armed bodyguards. With much pomp, the exiting president issued a statement saying that "the government will not allow terrorists to threaten the sovereignty of our nation." He further was to state proudly that Colombia was one of the oldest democratic nations on Earth, and that "the election process will proceed, and nothing would stop that." This declaration was a source of amusement for much of the public, since the government had long lost effective control of the country, but was now intending to 'defend and protect' the election process. Even some conservative journalists were making light of the situation. "The government's assurances of safeguarding the election process is an indication of how low it has fallen," wrote one. "Does the government really believe that offering some bodyguards to the presidential candidates is a show of strength?" wrote another.

The situation became even more humorous when Vicente Sanchez turned down the government's offer of armed protection. He kindly saved it from further humiliation by giving the reason that he did not want to use the public's money for such a purpose. In reality, the presidential hopeful did not trust the government and considered their armed protection a threat to his own personal safety. "Those bodyguards will only be used to keep tabs on me," he suspiciously told one of his aids. Ironically, the moderate candidates, whose lives were not in jeopardy, gladly accepted the government's offer of protection. Not accepting the protection proved to be another huge coup for Sanchez, as it further demonstrated his courage to the public.

The gap between him and his opponents was widening to such an extent that many insiders were already predicting he was going to win in a landslide. Yet, the new popular hero did not let the success get to his head as he continued traveling around the country, delivering stump speeches that were more inflammatory than ever. Against the advice of his aides, who were cautioning him to ease up on the fiery rhetoric at that late stage in the campaign, Sanchez continued with his crusade against the 'destroyers' of Colombia. He responded to the advice of his aides by saying it was not solely a matter of winning an election. "So, I should let up on the tough talk now that I am winning easily?" he asked one of them. "So, when I win the election and become President, I should just sit on my ass and stop what I am doing? You see, it's not about winning the election, but about changing Colombia. To that end, I cannot just stop now."

As the campaign continued, more death threats were received. The tension was starting to mount in the Sanchez camp, with most advisers concerned about the direction of the campaign. They believed their boss was acting carelessly, unnecessarily inviting danger onto them with victory at hand. There was even talk that he was on some sort of death wish, wanting nothing more than to be a martyr for his country. Eventually, three of the five advisers left camp, offering the usual reasons of having philosophical differences with their boss, when they actually departed out of fear. The press attempted to generate much commotion from this setback for Sanchez, as some newspaper headlines, to list a few, read as follows: "A CHINK IN SANCHEZ'S ARMOR!", "MAJOR ROW IN SANCHEZ'S CAMP!", and "TROUBLE FOR SANCHEZ!" The press desperately wanted to give a bloody nose to the heavy favorite in the presidential race, but their sensationalist attacks fell well short of the mark, for the public was not at all interested. The papers underestimated his incredible popularity in the country and, by attacking him, were making themselves out to be sympathizers for the despised warmongers. They quickly learned from that mistake, and subsequently withdrew back to a more neutral position to restore any lost credibility.

The government, with hardly any credibility to lose, desperately sought a way to sabotage Vicente Sanchez's run for the presidency. They dug for any dirt from his past that could harm his campaign, but none could be found. There were no torrid affairs, mistresses, illegitimate children, crimes, abuses, character flaws, or other serious defects to be discovered. Sanchez had been married for eighteen years, having one daughter during that time. By all accounts, he was a loving, committed family man. His academic career was also free of any troubles, with no trace of corruption, cheating, or incompetence on his record. From his students and colleagues at the various academic institutions that employed him, he enjoyed an enduring popularity and respect. To them, he was a responsible man committed to his profession, an accessible and helpful educator.

With nothing unearthed that could derail his campaign, the government had begun considering other ways of handling the Sanchez problem, including assassination. Numerous congressmen and senators did not want their lucrative associations with the drug cartels to be exposed. Military generals were worried about their treasonous arms deals with the guerillas being uncovered. And certain eminent police officials? One hardly had to ask. Their double-dealings were so notorious during the civil war, helping both the guerillas and mercenaries conduct their wars and massacres, while profiting from the drug trade, that they would have certainly traded their uniforms for prison jump-suits at the snap of Sanchez's finger.

Most members in the government were fearful of this maverick being elected and were willing to do anything at this point to undermine him, so they started throwing death threats his way to see if that would soften him up. It seemed like a good idea since the use of death threats had worked several times before as a means of intimidation, 'softening' up many other would-be mavericks in the past that initially challenged the status quo. Many of these 'rebels', whether they were crusading judges, disgruntled senators, or big-headed activists, would crumble in the face of such death threats, so frightened were they that a single peep of resistance was never heard from them again. Their rabble-rousing attacks on the status-quo would stop suddenly, to be quickly replaced mysteriously by more moderate and, in some cases, even hard-line conservative positions.

This is what the government hoped would happen to Sanchez, that the pressure of any harm being done to him or his family would force him to change his ways. This was not working, as noted before. The maverick candidate continued campaigning hard, promising the people of Colombia that many high-ranking officials would be going to jail, as well as the leaders of the guerrillas, mercenaries, and drug cartels. Now, assassination seemed to be the only option left, as plans were being drawn up to carry it through. For the time being, the government waited to see if Sanchez would cave in. It wanted to avoid the trouble of having to assassinate the candidate and deal with the unforeseen consequences.

* * *

The whirlwind campaign of Vicente Sanchez swept up the young Gabriel Ferrero. His spirits and hopes, much like that of the Colombian people, were raised up to lofty heights. The Colombians visualized hope for their own country, while Gabriel visualized it for the world and humanity. The youth was astounded by this man. He had never seen anything like it before: a country mesmerized by a presidential candidate and his message. The atmosphere throughout was electric and everyone in Nueva Vida was certainly feeling the pulse. Posters of the intense Sanchez were all over the place. Most of these posters contained the slogans "COLOMBIA FOR COLOMBIANS!" or "WE'VE HAD ENOUGH!" Every image of this maverick was one of seriousness, as he was never shown with a smile on his face. This was in sharp contrast to the other candidates, who always were portrayed with complacent smiles.

"These candidates come across with the message that everything is fine, that our country only warrants minor tweaking here and there," Dr. Granados told Gabriel once. "The Colombian people are sick and tired of that nonsense."

Gabriel considered himself lucky to be experiencing this phenomenon firsthand. His life was no longer boring! He relished this frenzied time in Colombian history, talking with people on the street about the upcoming elections, listening to fiery speeches by supporters of Sanchez, and reading newspaper and magazine articles about the new 'revolution' about to take to place. Indeed, Gabriel felt like he was living through the French Revolution or in 1960's America, a time when people clamored for reform, when materialism took a backseat to idealism.

For our young friend, this current phenomenon taking root in a troubled South American country had wider implications. To him, Vicente Sanchez was the type of figure the world so desperately needed. For so long, Gabriel hoped that individuals like him would jar the rest of humanity loose from the tight, suffocating grip of computers and corporations. Leaders like Sanchez would chart new paths for the human race, saving it from irrelevance and making it dynamic again. A new world would be forged, where the creative abilities of the human mind would retake its place as the engine for global change and evolution, replacing efficient but 'inhuman' machines. Now, something truly exciting was happening in Colombia, where people were fighting for their own existence, not waiting around for 'tweaks' to be applied by the powers that be, but taking action themselves.

This was the human dynamism that Gabriel had longed for, and he hoped that what was then happening in Colombia would begin spreading rapidly everywhere else, in the form of revolts and popular revolutions. "Change, as an end, is not so important," Gabriel once told a friend. "What is of importance is the act of changing, the act of struggling." Before his very eyes, such an active push for change was occurring, as a monumental struggle was forming. He was extremely delighted that the visions he had for the world were finally taking shape. This more or less accurate prediction made him think all the more highly of his own intellectual prowess. "My predictions are coming true!" he enthusiastically told his Aunt Teresa one day. "I must say that I'm impressed with myself."

Gabriel spent a lot of time discussing this situation with Dr. Granados. Like our young friend, the professor was also excited, though he was more even-tempered, and feared a possible assassination on Vicente Sanchez's life. Gabriel did not know nearly as much about Colombian history as Dr. Granados, which explained his boundless enthusiasm and lack of concern. The young man was completely assured of his vision for the world and that nothing would disrupt it. The two had a long, animated conversation one day about this and the elections.

"I tell you, Dr. Granados, the situation here in Colombia is a precursor of things to come throughout the world!" Gabriel said with his usual naïve charm.

"Ah my boy, Colombia is such a small country. How can you possibly believe that the rest of the world will be affected by what goes on here?"

"I just have a feeling, a sensation that this will happen."

"Do you have any valid reasons for believing that?" asked the wise professor.

"I don't really have any valid reasons for believing this. But, the world cannot continue the same way for long."

"Why not?"

"Because there will always be change," Gabriel answered confidently.

"You may be right," Dr. Granados replied.

"People everywhere will eventually react against whatever is oppressing them. Here in Colombia, the people are reacting against the oppression of war. In other parts of the Third World, the people may eventually react against the forces causing their own misery and squalor. And in industrialized countries, they may stand up to the oppression of the computer age, where they feel like a number or a statistic rather than a human being."

"I admire your views, though they seem a tad over-simplistic," the professor said in a respectful way. "Who knows, your predictions may prove to be correct one day. However, I don't believe that Colombia will serve as some sort of beacon for global change. What you also need to consider is that change ultimately may not occur here in Colombia after all, since Sanchez might get assassinated, which would ruin your vision."

"Well, even if Sanchez does get assassinated," Gabriel replied eagerly, "the wheels have already been set in motion, and the people here in Colombia will continue to struggle for change, leading to similar struggles in other parts of the world."

"My boy, the wheels have not been set in motion just yet."

"What do you mean?"

Dr. Granados looked at the youth more seriously, as though he were about to reprimand him at first. What Gabriel soon realized was that the argument struck a very sensitive chord with the professor, since it was *his* country being discussed, *his* country being watched under a microscope, *his* country being smashed into pieces with its future hanging in the balance. This was a delicate matter for him. "What do I mean? What do you think I mean?"

"You think the wheels are not set in motion, that nothing has been established yet, right?" Gabriel asked in a slightly startled way, believing he had angered the good professor.

"That is precisely what I am saying," Dr. Granados responded in a more relaxed tone, the furrows in his forehead not as deep now.

"Why do you think that?"

"Because I believe that if Vicente Sanchez dies, so will the entire movement."

"You don't think there will be others to carry the torch and succeed Sanchez?" Gabriel asked somewhat innocently.

"No, I do not," Dr. Granados answered with the confidence of knowing Colombian history all too well. "Great leaders cannot be so easily replaced. That is what you fail to understand. You underestimate the importance of a leader, especially if that person is charismatic."

"So, you are saying that the fate of the reform movement, if it ever does arise, is strictly tied to that of Sanchez."

"Yes. If Sanchez dies, so will the movement. It will be nipped in the bud. If he lives, it has a chance of surviving, but only during his lifetime. Once he dies, the changes that were implemented, all the reforms, will either no longer be enforced or be removed altogether by the people that succeed him. That is what always happens, especially here in Latin America."

"Well professor," Gabriel said, attempting to salvage his argument a bit, "perhaps I have underestimated the importance of leaders such as Sanchez. But there is something special going on down here in Colombia, and it is still my belief and hope that what is happening here will spawn similar movements in other places of the world. Even if the movement does not end up taking shape here, it would have raised a lot of eyebrows everywhere. It would have given hope to other people and encourage them to take action."

At this point, Dr. Granados flashed a grin and looked at Gabriel almost amusingly. "You are ready to go fight, aren't you?"

"No I am not," replied a smiling Gabriel. "But, I am very interested in what is going on. I prefer actually to witness things from afar, not from the front lines."

"Well, you certainly are talking like someone who should be in the thick of the action."

"No, I am just really excited about what is going on here, that's all."

"Because I am sure Vicente Sanchez would welcome your support, even if you are a foreigner. You could volunteer your services toward his campaign. That would be a lot of fun!"

"I'm doing just fine here, peacefully watching from a distance," Gabriel said, trying to convince the good professor he was a pacifist.

"Well, you may not have that luxury in the near future," the professor warned. "The action of the campaign, and of the war, may come to you before you know it."

"I hope not, Dr. Granados. Anyway, what is your take on Vicente Sanchez? Do you like him?"

"I really do like him. I agree with everything he says. He has the right ideas, and more importantly, he comes across as an honest man, which is why he has gotten popular with the people. He is also very brave. It takes a lot of cojones for someone to stand up to the guerrillas, the mercenaries, the drug lords, and the government all at once. The Colombian people have definitely responded positively to his stand, for they have suffered a long time."

"What is it that the Colombian people want exactly? I mean, in the end, do they want democracy or socialism?"

"You are getting ahead of yourself," quickly responded the professor. "All what the Colombian people want now is peace. They want an end to this war. What happens after that is almost secondary."

"So that is why they want Sanchez to win. They think he will deliver peace."

"Somewhat," Dr. Granados replied. "They certainly believe that he has a better chance of delivering peace than the other candidates. But, it is not just a matter of whether he can deliver peace or not. The people simply like him. He speaks for them. He expresses their sense of frustration very well. He really is a fantastic speaker, as I am sure you know. He is similar to Castro in the sense that he is a convincing speaker and has a magnetic personality, which people are naturally drawn to. But what makes someone's personality magnetic? The person has to be honest, brave, intelligent, and charismatic. Sanchez has all these qualities."

"Do you think he is honest?" Gabriel asked.

"I think he is honest. Most people do. He is risking his life right now. A dishonest politician would certainly not be risking his life for anything. So far, Sanchez has not been caught lying on any single occasion, and he probably will continue being honest, even after he becomes president. He comes across to me as incorruptible."

"Some people say he is crazy."

"I do not think he is crazy. He is just an honest, dignified person who believes that what he is doing is right. These people probably think he is crazy because they think he has some sort of death wish, that he is in fact suicidal. I have heard these arguments before. But I do not think that way. I believe that individuals like Vicente Sanchez are noble and principled. Thus far, Sanchez has acted courageously and admirably, and I believe he will continue to do so."

"No, I agree with your assessment," Gabriel said defensively, not wanting to give the impression that he was a basher of Sanchez. "I also believe that he is honest and principled, and that he won't change for the worse as some others are saying."

"Who knows how Sanchez might turn out if he were to become the president," the professor remarked, scratching his head. "He may change for the worse for all we know. Power has corrupted many people who seemed idealistic and good at first. So, it is very hard to determine how a person will act under certain circumstances. It is very hard to predict the future. But, judging from how he is behaving now, I do not think Sanchez will change for the worse. He wrapped up this election a long time ago, and yet he continues to berate the government and the guerrillas. He is still on the offensive, even against the advice of his aids. What does that tell you?"

"That he is sticking to his guns," Gabriel answered boldly.

"Well, yes, that he is sticking to his guns," the professor replied as though he was answering one of his student's questions in class. "More specifically, what it tells you is that he will not change, he will not be corrupted. At this point, if he was your typical cut-throat politician, he would have eased up on the hard talk and began preparing for the presidency, making deals with at least the government and mercenaries. There would have been a marked change in his behavior by now. But, that has not happened yet, and I do not think that it will. He is too firmly committed to his cause to change his ways and make deals with the government."

The rest of the conversation was devoted to Vicente Sanchez's plans upon becoming president. Dr. Granados, like the rest of his countrymen, was unsure of those plans. The professor figured Sanchez would probably have some government officials indicted on various criminal offenses and that this would become a 'messy' affair. "Sanchez will also try to help the poor, I'm sure," the professor added. Aside from this, there was little else he knew about Sanchez's plans for the future, predicting all the while that the reformer was going to encounter many obstacles along the way as president. "Let's hope he does not get killed," Gabriel told the professor.

"We will keep our fingers crossed," the professor replied.

CHAPTER SEVEN

SANDRA

During his stay in Nueva Vida, Gabriel met many people. A good number of them were from his work at the language institute, but many of them were from the street. He would meet a lot of them during his long walks through town, or in cafes, usually through discussions about the upcoming elections. Many people were milling about town during this time, contributing to the campaigns of their favorite candidates either for the presidency or the local legislatures. Many billboards, posters, and leaflets were appearing throughout the city, as this mad sea of paper was signaling the height of election campaigns. Despite the competitive jockeying going on in the streets, these 'campaigning days' were usually festive, generating a carnival-like atmosphere. A constant stream of cars and trucks blaring advertisements for candidates through loudspeakers would slowly pass through. Stands emerged in certain busy street corners, serving their respective candidates where leaflets and posters would be distributed. These stands would also frequently play loud music, sometimes attracting large groups of people who would form a circle and begin dancing nearby. During the weekend, colorful, intoxicating street parties would usually take place and last well into the wee hours of the night. One would often encounter the sight of individuals toasting to their 'man' for president or 'old friend' for Congress. It was all a very personalized experience, as if their candidates were extensions of themselves. Sometimes, fights would break out between members of opposing camps because of insults directed at their candidates. However, such fights never got out of hand and put a damper on the festivities, for most individuals were really in the mood to celebrate. They would not let a small number of drunken troublemakers ruin things.

Gabriel immersed himself into this setting, observing the spectacles around him like a dazzled child. He enjoyed it, especially the street parties. At that time, several people would become familiar to him. There was Puma, an older man who always appeared in a red jumpsuit. The two would bump into each other so many times in the streets, that Puma, out of agitation and curiosity, finally introduced himself one day.

"Are you some C.I.A. agent following me?" he asked in a friendly tone, correctly guessing that Gabriel was an American.

"No," responded the startled youth.

"Good, because I thought you were going to kill me," Puma remarked with a big laugh. Puma was a semi-retired civil servant who was busy campaigning for an alderman associated with his old boss. He would do small favors for the man he worked for part time, such as putting up posters, delivering food to rallies, or running a stand. This man, with his short-cropped gray hair, deeply-lined face, little eyes that shifted rapidly to and fro, and toothpick in mouth, was the image of a tough survivor. Gabriel marveled at him. This was a man the youth aimed to be in certain respects, someone who had experienced the hard blows of life from the pits of humanity; someone who had not lived in an ivory tower far above the fray. He supposedly received his nickname after surviving an attack from a puma during a hiking trip in the mountains of Peru when he was a teenager. According to him, he wrestled free from the large cat after it had jumped on his back, using nothing but his bare hands. He still had scars on his forearms from the attack, which he would often display proudly.

Puma and Gabriel fast became friends as the youth would sometimes help him put up posters or deliver leaflets. The relationship, though, was not based on shared political views, for Puma was apolitical. "Nothing will change in this country," he once told Gabriel. "The people are getting excited about this man Sanchez. They should know better than to get too excited around here." He had learned over the course of his long life that to get too hopeful in Colombia would only lead to bitter disappointment. "As soon as a man that the people think might be their savior comes along, he either sells out or is killed," he explained. "Therefore, I don't think much about politics. I just focus on making it through each day with some food in my stomach."

He attributed his current involvement in politics to helping out an old friend, nothing more. What Gabriel valued much from his friendship with Puma was his crude yet penetrating wisdom of the street, of everyday life in Colombia. Their conversations were not as high-minded as those Gabriel had with Dr. Granados, but they were equally significant in describing the present state of the country and how the average Colombian lived. Puma was an average Colombian who vividly communicated to Gabriel the challenges his countrymen faced in towns everywhere, whether it was hunger, unemployment, crime, inflation, or other deprivations caused by the civil war.

*   *   *

Another person familiar to Gabriel was a blind homeless man that sat on a little stool in the same street corner every morning. His long silver hair, slanted eyes, and yellow complexion made him look Chinese. The lifeless, light-blue eyes seemed to have a supernatural quality about them, which led Gabriel to think he was not quite human. His incoherent mutterings, sounding as though he was speaking in other-worldly tongues, further convinced the youth that this tiny, shriveled, old man was some sort of mystical figure. He sat there, with his back to the concrete wall, beside his wooden cane, which stood up against an adjacent doorway entrance. He held out a small tin cup to collect money, shaking it once in a while to attract attention to himself. Gabriel observed that he was not completely blind, noticing he would look directly up into the faces of people who dropped a coin or two into his cup, his nearly vacant eyes following them as they walked away. He would softly say to them, "Thank you. Lord be with you." He would repeat saying that a few times before reverting to incoherence, quietly mumbling to himself as he looked straight ahead onto the street.

Curiously, this homeless man, who Gabriel eventually referred to as "Chinito", only appeared on his corner during mornings, never in the afternoons. The youth began to wonder where the blind man would spend the rest of his time, and if someone was taking care of him. So curious was Gabriel of his whereabouts that he went looking for him a couple afternoons, walking around the vicinity of Chinito's neighborhood a few times to no avail. The man simply could not be found. "Where could he be now?" our friend wondered. "Where does he go in the afternoons? Where does he sleep at night?" So, seeing him in his usual corner one morning, the youth ventured over to him. Gabriel was so determined to find out some information about the old man that he temporarily lost all reason and sense.

"Hello," the youth awkwardly said in greeting, crouching down so the little man could hear him. The man slowly turned his wizened face toward Gabriel, like some sleepy lizard, locking his vacant eyes onto the youth's. Gazing at the large, slanted pale blue eyes of the old man, slightly aware of the youth's physical presence but not completely, which had a disturbing quality of lifelessness as though the man were indeed inhuman, Gabriel had briefly become startled. He was all the more puzzled when the man continued mumbling incoherently, seemingly oblivious of him. Gabriel finally regained his composure after this uncomfortable pause and proceeded to continue the conversation.

"Uh, hello," Gabriel said again, a little more forcefully this time. The old man continued giving the youth the same blank stare, but stopped mumbling as if aware someone was there trying to talk to him. Again, there was a long pause. The old man said nothing. "I do not mean to disturb you, but I wanted to know where you go in the afternoons," asked our young friend very hesitantly. This inquiry made Gabriel feel extremely uncomfortable and embarrassed. He could not believe he went so far as to ask a decrepit stranger what he did on his spare time! This uneasy feeling was compounded by the old man's immediate reaction, which was one of unpleasant surprise. An alarmed, almost angry expression overcame his gaunt face, as if he found the youth's inquiry a little distasteful. He withdrew further back against the wall, away from Gabriel, and subsequently began waving his arms around defensively. However, he quickly stopped doing this as an expressionless look reappeared on his face. He was calm once again.

Yet, the youth was still feeling uncomfortable and was having a difficult time trying to figure out a way to continue the conversation. He felt he needed to make up some sort of lie to justify such inquiries into the man's personal life. After pondering for a few moments, our friend came up with the perfect lie. "Well, sir, I am asking about your whereabouts because I am volunteering on behalf of the church, and I wanted to know if there is someone taking care of you." The homeless man did not reply. Gabriel pressed further in a more relaxed manner. "The church is initiating a drive to provide shelter for the homeless citizens of Nueva Vida. But, before it can proceed, the church needs to find out some information, like how many homeless people are living here and if they are receiving any support from relatives and friends in the area. Would you like to give the church any information regarding your situation?" Certainly not a smooth liar, Gabriel was now more embarrassed than before, correctly sensing his interrogation was going nowhere. He became ashamed of his own ridiculous irrationality, stooping so low as to harass and lie to this poor man. The man, himself, then began jiggling his tin cup at the embarrassed youth, finally saying, "Money, please! Money, please!" Giving up, Gabriel finally stood up, dug for a couple pesos in his pocket, and dropped them into the cup. "Take care of yourself, now," he told him on his way out, wanting to forget this strange episode as quickly as possible.

Gabriel would continue to see Chinito often during the mornings. He was still curious about the whereabouts of this man, but never again considered bothering him about it. The youth realized the man was better left alone. As the elections were coming up, Chinito began donning a blue shirt and baseball cap advertising the candidacy of a local alderman. He wore it everyday, leading

Gabriel to wonder if he was being paid to wear the apparel. "Even little Chinito is wrapped up in these elections," the surprised youth thought.

*   *   *

Finally, there was Sandra. She was a beautiful young woman appearing to be in her early twenties, with long, wavy dark hair, ivory-colored skin, and exotic green eyes. "My God, she looks like a young Elizabeth Taylor!" Gabriel observed excitedly. He would frequently encounter her at a stand near the downtown plaza, on the corner of 18th Street and Avenida de la Independencia, where she was campaigning for a man running for the national congress. He saw her for the first time while she was delivering a stump speech in front of a small group of people, imploring them and all others in the vicinity to vote for Lucindo Gomez. "I want you all to cast your vote for Lucindo Gomez on Election Day because he will speak for all of you in congress! He will address your concerns there and he will bring the necessary changes that will improve your lives here in Nueva Vida. Please vote for Lucindo Gomez! He is the best man for the job and he will finally set things right!"

She normally would appear in the afternoon, delivering about two fifteen minute speeches a day. Her intelligent manners, sweet voice, and pretty smile immediately enchanted Gabriel, as he fell in love with her instantly. But he never made an attempt to meet her despite a couple of good opportunities, one in which she even smiled warmly at him while she stood alone next to the campaign booth. He felt terrible for not taking advantage of that opportunity, but he hoped there would be others in the future. Our young friend believed he was simply not ready to take such a girl on at that moment, preferring to bide his time instead.

Gabriel found out her name when overhearing one of her friends call out to her after she delivered a campaign speech. He would recite that name to himself constantly, in a state of bliss or torment depending on what kind of mood he was in. He ultimately could not keep this secret to himself, as he began talking to others about this divine girl. The unanimous advice to Gabriel was for him to go and meet Sandra. "If you are that interested in her, do something about it," Aunt Teresa told him. "Don't be afraid!" Puma said. "Just go ahead and meet the damned girl!" Their advice was good and Gabriel realized they were right. However, he could not follow their advice. He was petrified of making a fool of himself in front of her or, worse yet, finding out that she was with someone else. "Anyhow, a girl like that has to certainly be taken," he would coolly tell Aunt Teresa and Puma in an attempt to justify his reluctance to follow their advice, and to hide his true feelings. So the youth would continue avoiding the chance of meeting Sandra for fear of eternally losing the hope of being with her. Better to have some hope than none at all.

Nonetheless, this strategy eventually brought more agony rather than comfort to Gabriel. Each time he saw her, a feeling of despair overcame him. As each day passed without her in his arms, this despair got worse. It got so bad that the youth, finally running out of patience, boldly decided to end his misery by meeting her. "Puma is right!" he said to himself. "I have nothing to lose." During one sunny afternoon, he gathered all his courage and set off for Sandra. Gabriel felt total exhilaration as he walked out the door, as though he were set free from some terrible burden. He was doing the right thing, after all. He was elated about not having to wait anymore, no longer having to be a passive spectator on the sidelines. "I am just going to go up and talk to her like many other people do," he said to himself.

Gabriel hatched a clever plan in which he would simply ask her for a leaflet, and perhaps have her answer some questions about the candidate she was campaigning for. This would at least provide a smooth prelude to a conversation with the girl, without betraying any trace of aggression which might make her feel uncomfortable. The plan also allowed for a dignified escape in case things did not work out, for she could only guess that Gabriel was there to inquire about Lucindo Gomez, not her. He could then approach her again another day, for he would not have made an idiot of himself, and not have to feel bashful upon seeing her again. "No, this is a good plan," he thought, emboldening himself while he started walking toward Sandra's campaign stand a few blocks away. Like many other young people, appearances were everything for Gabriel, as he was conscious of his image, desperately not wanting to suffer embarrassment over it getting tarnished somehow.

As our friend was getting closer to his destination, the exhilaration was replaced by a more subdued calmness. With a couple blocks to go, Gabriel could not so much as think. He could only faintly sense the environment around him: the sound of running car engines nearby, the sight of stray dogs roaming past through the sidewalk, and the feel of Andean winds gently blowing against the back of his head. It was as if he was aimlessly floating about like a balloon. If a huge truck was barreling down on him, he perhaps would have noticed at the last second, so unaware he had become of his surroundings.

When he was only a block away from Sandra's stand, things began really changing. The strange calmness now turned into an overwhelming numbness. He could not see, hear, or feel anything. He stopped immediately to gather himself. The youth noticed he was short of breath and perhaps on the brink of a panic attack. He took a couple of deep breaths to keep himself from fainting, for he felt very dizzy and weak. The street, buzzing with all sorts of activity, did not make things any easier for him, adding to his feeling of an impending panic attack. As he stood against a wall alongside the street, recovering from his dizzy spells, Gabriel realized he was feeling sudden anxiety over the meeting with his beloved Sandra. Our friend, looking harried and flushed, did not escape the notice of others, including one old woman wearing an elegant flower hat. She went over to him and asked if he was okay. Gabriel said he was all right, that he was winded after a long walk.

"But you look terrible!" the old woman responded, grabbing him by the elbow. "You look like you are about to collapse! Let us go to this shop down the block and get you something to drink."

"No, no, it's okay," Gabriel answered back emphatically. "Thank you. You are so kind, but I really am okay."

79

Regaining his composure, Gabriel soon made his way towards Sandra. He was still feeling a little weak but persisted onwards. The young American proceeded down the street and approached a corner, knowing full well what would soon be upon him: the sight of Sandra. He braced himself for it, taking a couple more deep breaths before turning the corner, making a sharp right. As he made the turn, he did not immediately see Sandra around the stand across the street. At that moment, there were only a few individuals milling around, some readjusting the podium while others were working on the speakers. The small campaign booth, or stand, which usually had someone working inside, was empty. Only a few leaflets stacked up on the front counter and a small portable television in the back were to be seen. Sandra would normally spend a lot of time in there, either reading a book or watching television.

Her strange absence made Gabriel pause. "So, she's nowhere to be found," he thought, somewhat frustrated. The youth lingered across the street from the stand, trying to figure out what to do next. He stood there on the sidewalk for a while, undistracted by the pedestrians walking past him. Then, he decided to cross the street and investigate further. He snaked his way through the slow-moving cars, and reached the other side with his wavy hair a little ruffled from the wind. As Gabriel got closer, the lovely Sandra suddenly emerged from behind the booth. Our stunned friend stopped in his tracks. Sandra, only a few feet away, did not see Gabriel, as her back was turned to him. The girl, holding an ice cream cone in one hand and a magazine in the other, was looking at some of the men working on the speakers.

"Are they getting any better?" she nervously asked them.

"Not yet," answered one of them in an agitated tone. "We will find out soon. Give us a couple of minutes."

"Have you heard from Gonzalo, by any chance?" she asked.

"No, we have not," the same man responded.

"If the loudspeakers do not work shortly, we will just go without them because Gonzalo will want us to start soon," she told them.

Gabriel was close enough to hear the whole conversation. Too startled to proceed toward her, he quietly took a few steps back while

Sandra was talking to the men. He then casually walked to a bench behind some trees inside the square, well hidden from her view. From this safe distance, the rattled American would gather himself and decide the next course of action. He sat on the bench and hastily took out a cigarette. While he was having his smoke, some resigned, sobering thoughts crossed his mind. Sandra's interaction with the men by the stand bothered him a little, in the sense that it revealed a human side to her not witnessed before. Gabriel had always seen her from afar, whether she was speaking from behind the podium or nestled inside the booth. She was the very picture of beauty and serenity from such distances, her apparent perfection mustering an extreme, but ill-conceived passion from Gabriel. He placed her on a very high pedestal, fueling his passion even more.

However, Sandra's human side showed something different. Her nagging questions to the men working on the loudspeakers and rush to get things back in order at the stand made her seem petty and superficial. She momentarily fell from Gabriel's high pedestal, leaving him puzzled. He wondered how this could have happened. It felt like his whole world was coming apart. The cigarette dropped from Gabriel's limp fingers, for he had not the power even to hold it any longer. The energy to continue living had been sapped from him at that moment, but his mind was too numb to fully comprehend this stark reality. Faintly sensing this dangerous bleakness rapidly overcoming his soul, our friend made an instinctive effort to save himself. He chose the easiest path, one that had the least amount of risks: *not* meeting with her at all . . . that day or any other time in the future. He would deny himself the chance to meet her in return for preserving his wits. By not meeting Sandra personally, Gabriel would save his previous image of the girl, unrealistic as it was. By saving this impression of her, he would also save a part of himself.

For Sandra was not just a pretty girl to Gabriel. There was something else here. The young American had dated and known other women before. It was not like he was utterly lacking in experience. The only thing that could explain Gabriel's paralyzing trepidation before Sandra at that time was his state of mind. There was something supernatural and surreal about her, much like many things in Nueva Vida. She in fact had become a sort of deity for Gabriel, a symbol of human perfection. And in being perfect, she ceased being human in his eyes. She symbolized everything that was right with the universe, providing the terribly idealistic Gabriel with some remnant of hope for himself and humanity. Having seen some of his dreams crushed in recent weeks, the youth was desperate to keep whatever hopes were left.

So, Gabriel decided to get up from the bench and leave the scene immediately. From then on, he would continue worshipping Sandra from afar. Whenever he passed by the stand and saw her either speaking aloud on the pulpit or sitting inside the booth, the same blissful thoughts would continue to overwhelm him. Sandra might have briefly fallen from the tall pedestal Gabriel erected for her, but he wasted no time in placing her back up there again. In fact, she stood higher on that pedestal than ever before. He would forever bury the memory of her petty exchange with the workers at the stand lest he be reminded that she was only human! And he certainly would not meet her ever lest he discover other imperfections about her, which might be the death of him. Gabriel even reckoned it would be best for him to see Sandra less often so that the idealized image of her would remain in his mind, however delusional it was. Better to endure unrequited love at this point than another disappointment.

One day, Aunt Teresa asked him if he had ever gone and met Sandra like she had advised him to. "No, I have not," Gabriel responded tranquilly. "That would be too much trouble for me now."

This response left his aunt a little perplexed. "What do you mean by that?" she asked. "What is the trouble of going up and talking to her?"

This line of questioning was irritating our young friend, who clearly realized that his aunt would not understand him or his predicament. "No, no, no" he said. "It's not that. I just do not believe I am ready to get in a relationship with a woman like that."

"Gabriel, how will you know if you do not try?" she asked.

"Because I know, that's all," he said as he walked away, not daring to even bear his soul to his own aunt. Life was already complicated enough as it was, he thought. Why would he want to complicate it further?

CHAPTER EIGHT

NUEVA VIDA, HERE I COME!

Meanwhile, the elections were only a month away and it was widely expected that Vicente Sanchez was going to win in a landslide and become the next president of Colombia. Sanchez, though, did not ease up on the campaigning. He continued traveling throughout the country extensively, making as many speeches as he could to further spread his message of a unified Colombia. The inhabitants of Nueva Vida were extremely shocked and delighted when they discovered early in the morning of Tuesday, October 22nd that Vicente Sanchez was going to make a stop in their town. "Nueva Vida, here I come!" he announced on national television. He was scheduled to visit on Saturday, October 26th and depart the following day. The atmosphere in Nueva Vida, already abuzz with heightened activity and excitement over the upcoming elections, became all the more electrifying. The citizens of Nueva Vida simply could not believe Sanchez was coming to their long forgotten and forlorn town. The city, itself, was an important economic and political hub in southern Colombia. Its importance had always been acknowledged by business leaders and politicians, but it never received a whole lot of nationwide recognition. Nueva Vida was nowhere near in the same glitzy league as other larger cities like Bogotá, Cali, Medillin, Cartagena, or Baranquilla.

Instead, it was often referred to as a lonely, distant outpost, 'that town way up there in the mountains'. It still suffered the same reputation it did during colonial times, as a town too remote for important people to visit. Not only was the city high up in the Andes Mountains, but it was also surrounded by dense jungles. But even when air travel was born and an airport was constructed for Nueva Vida, the town still continued to be avoided by high-profile leaders of the country. So when Vicente Sanchez declared that he would be visiting Nueva Vida, the people were genuinely surprised. Indeed, his visit was going to be historic since it was the first time a presidential candidate had gone there.

While the rest of the city was jubilant over the news of Sanchez's visit, the alcalde, or mayor, of Nueva Vida, Juan Carlos Rivera, was fuming mad. He despised Sanchez and even went so far as to call him a 'big mouth' and 'a threat to Colombia' in public. The portly, silver-haired, sixty-seven year old Rivera was an arch-conservative politician from the old school. Sanchez's wild outbursts and accusations did not sit well at all with the traditionalist Rivera, who was accustomed to playing within the rules of the old democratic order in Colombia, not breaking them. Rivera, himself, was a popular, long-serving mayor. He had been the leader of Nueva Vida for fourteen years, ruling over city hall like a powerful autocrat. It was generally perceived that his term would end whenever he died in office or felt like leaving it; that is how entrenched he was as mayor. But he had been in office that long for a reason, and it was because he had done many good things for Nueva Vida. He had brought a sense of stability and prosperity like no other mayor before him. He vastly improved the town's commercial appeal by making it an attractive hub on the Pan American Highway between the big city of Cali to the north and the Ecuadorian border to the south, between the jungle interior to the southeast and the rest of the country.

Under his initiative, a big highway connecting Nueva Vida with the jungle interior was constructed, instantly bringing a lot business from all over the country. The heads of the lucrative mining and ecotourism industries of that region subsequently moved their headquarters there. Some left Bogotá, the capital, because it was too far away, and others departed Leticia, a town located on the

Amazon River, because it was too remote and underdeveloped. Any business flowing in and out of the jungle interior now went through Nueva Vida, further bolstering its position as a vital financial hub in southern Colombia. The economic boom resulting from these developments did raise the town's population and crime rate significantly. However, the crime in Nueva Vida was no worse than in most other cities in Colombia, and it did not leave much of a dent on Mayor Rivera's impeccable reputation. He was viewed as the town's savior, the man most responsible for its impressive turn around.

Yet, there were indications that chinks were developing on the once-formidable armor of Mayor Rivera. Charges of corruption within his administration were beginning to circulate throughout Nueva Vida. Some of his closest advisers were suspected of accepting and offering bribes, money laundering, and drug trafficking. None of the accusations were directly linked to the Mayor, but they revealed his weakening grip on power. There were rumors that the aging patriarch, long suspected of having serious health problems, was losing his touch. Some insiders were saying that he was staying away from the office for longer stretches of time, leaving others to run the affairs of the city. His absence from city hall is what many believed to be the cause for the recent scandals, and they were concerned that things would spiral out of control. These concerns eventually forced the Mayor to vehemently deny in a press conference all accusations of corruption directed at his administration. Reports of his poor health and absenteeism were also denied. "Look at me," he jokingly asked one of the reporters at his press conference. "Do I look sick?" He explained away the charges of his 'extended absences' as nothing more than attacks by his political foes. "I am always at the office!" he declared. "Everyone knows they have to drag me out of there!"

No official criminal charges were handed down, but the Mayor felt someone was poisoning the well, leaving him increasingly paranoid and embittered. "This dirty business has been going on for years," he confided to his brother about the alleged corruption. "But it is suddenly brought up now." He was astonished by the ingratitude of those whom he had long considered friends, including the local media. "How can they so enthusiastically ride this story after what I have done for this city?" he cried. "They are all too eager to see me thrown in the mud. How despicable they are!" In some ways, Mayor Rivera was right to be upset. Corruption was rampant throughout the country and usually went unreported by the media. In the Mayor's eyes, the charges against his administration were minor, considering the instances of wrongdoing were isolated and sparse, not widespread. Yet, the media was strangely making a very big deal about it, "making a mountain out of an ant mound", as the Mayor put it. He believed they were going overboard with the story in an attempt to tarnish his image.

Regardless, the Mayor's scornful attitude at the time was also a reflection of his losing touch with reality. Having been in power for fourteen years and enjoying an enormous amount of success during that time had left him with the perception that he was invincible. He truly believed he was a divine personage, a legend already in the making entitled to nothing less than deferential treatment from everyone in Nueva Vida. He fully expected for there to be smooth sailing until the end of his historic term. What Mayor Rivera could not understand was that this arrogant complacence made him a huge target. He failed to comprehend, or did not want to accept, that some people were growing tired and jealous of his rule. Many younger politicians, hungry for power, were angry with the outright cronyism that developed under his watch, which kept them from climbing up the ladder further in city hall. For so many years, only his small inner circle of friends enjoyed the spoils of power to the exclusion of everyone else. This increasingly led to resentment among those who were excluded, to the point where some of them quietly began conspiring against him.

These conspirators, which included local representatives, officials, and businessmen, did not exactly expect the Mayor to be removed from power, but they wanted to do away with his brand of cronyism. They began mobilizing against Mayor Rivera just before the corruption charges had surfaced, by blocking the passage of a couple legislative initiatives important to his administration, including a proposed airport expansion bill. This particular bill was deemed crucial because the airport was then too small to accommodate the growing number of flights that were coming in. "Nueva Vida is growing," the Mayor announced during his introduction of the proposal. "The airport now needs to grow as well." This plan was his baby and he took pleasure in overseeing its initial development. He campaigned hard for it, believing a lot was at stake since the project might be his last great contribution to the city.

So when significant opposition to the proposed bill unexpectedly popped up, he blew a gasket. "Who are those punks?" he barked at the objecting representatives during the vote. "Who do they think they are? Do they know what they are doing?" He was so shocked because he had not been seriously challenged on an important issue for several years in city hall. Private civilians had challenged him throughout that time, but not politicians. He thought they were all in his pocket. Rather than rolling with the punches and letting diplomacy take over in this high stakes political game, something which he would have instinctively done many years before, the Mayor let things get personal. "Don't worry, I'll get the ringleaders," he told one of his aids. "When I do, their careers will be finished."

Another way in which Mayor Rivera was losing touch with reality was his confusion regarding the media. He seemed to have forgotten that he was living in a democracy, where there was freedom of the press. Ten to fourteen years before, the Mayor would have understood perfectly that members of the press were out to make a quick buck and owed no allegiances to anyone. If they eagerly threw mud in his direction, he would have ducked out of the way. He certainly would not have slung the mud back by publicly calling them 'stupid ingrates' and 'worthless parasites'. Like a dictator, he felt that the media was his property, a mere extension of himself and his regime. It was his tool to serve only him and his interests.

The problem was that he was only a democratically elected city official with no actual ownership of anything in Nueva Vida. The Mayor was deluded into believing he was in full control of everything, including the press, because there had been no resistance to his rule. He had been successful and popular, so the reporters chose to be on his side, writing good things about him and his policies through the years. Many of them did favors for him by writing favorable articles he wanted them to write, whether it was to push his legislative agendas forward or to hail a political friend. They were literally at his beck and call. This went on for so long that the Mayor could not fathom the local press as a body free and independent of him. So when it went against him during the recent corruption scandal, he was stunned. Above all, he was embarrassed to have taken the media's servility for granted. "How silly of me to have believed in them!" he told an aid.

Feeling betrayed and fooled, Mayor Rivera immediately lashed back at the media. He accused the papers of lying to the people of Nueva Vida and jumping to false conclusions. He also called for the dismissal of the papers' editors, claiming they were more suited for work in the department of sanitation as garbage collectors. By attacking the media in such a way, the Mayor thought he would receive the support of the people. Instead, his actions elicited the opposite response, as people were more convinced of his complicity with corruption. They also did not approve his handling of the media, which left many of them wondering about his sanity and decency. "He has never behaved like this before," Puma told Gabriel, who spoke for many concerned citizens of Nueva Vida. "Something must be really wrong with him. It's as if he has gone cuckoo."

At this time, Mayor Rivera was more isolated than he had been in a long time. Politicians and members of the media were giving him a hard time, but he was not in immediate trouble. To begin with, there was no real proof that acts of corruption had taken place. Yet, the goal of triumphantly ending his run as mayor with an impeccable record was now in jeopardy, thanks to "those ingrates" in city hall and the media. He viewed the younger crop of politicians and reporters with disdainful suspicion. "These younger people are only interested in easy money," he complained to a friend. "They have no values, no etiquette, no principles, nothing. They will do anything to get what they want, even if that means selling out their own mothers." The Mayor thought his younger opponents were going against the old Colombian traditions of respecting their elders and everything they built. Thus, by going against him, they were not only wrong politically, but morally. "They are attacking our generation," he angrily told an elderly colleague. "They are saying 'no' to us and everything we have accomplished, all the good things we have done. What does that say about our society, if the youth no longer respect their elders? If this does not change, our society, as we have known it, will go kaput!"

Like many proud older men, Mayor Rivera was not willing to change with the times. He could have easily diffused the shaky situation in city hall by striking some compromise with his opponents. He could have at least partially put an end to the spoils system of his administration by allowing more outsiders to climb the political ladder. With the wave of his hand, he could have offered prestigious jobs to some of them, which would have certainly helped matters for him. But he refused to do those things. The Mayor would never consider bowing down to such troublemakers, catering to them as if they were worthy of his full attention and respect. He was unwilling to admit there were any problems with himself or his administration. "I will fight these bastards!" he proudly declared. "They will never get anything from me or this office!" Even if he had done wrong, the Mayor, out of principle, would still not acquiesce to his foes. "If they ever did catch me doing something wrong, for Christ's sake they should still shut their mouths and wait their turns like everybody else! That is what I had to do for so many years, and I did it out of respect for those above me and for the system." Such were the views of an old-fashioned politician, a traditionalist who favored a system based on seniority rather than fairness.

* * *

In Vicente Sanchez, Mayor Rivera saw everything that was going wrong with Colombia. Like most of his foes in city hall, Sanchez was from a younger generation which had supposedly turned its back on the old traditional values of Colombia. Like them, Sanchez was an ingrate bent on destroying the moral fabric of his country. In the Mayor's increasingly paranoid mind, Sanchez became the very symbol of his enemies, the embodiment of his opposition. He actually believed that the popular presidential candidate might have had a hand in the conspiracy against him, who had personally plotted the corruption charges and the resistance to his airport expansion proposal. "What a coincidence!" the Mayor told an astonished friend. "This guy becomes popular and things suddenly start falling apart for me." He reacted to Sanchez much like he did to the media, with hostile anger. It spewed out of him uncontrollably as he publicly attacked the man several times, often referring to him as a menace to society. Once again, the Mayor miscalculated the mood of the people, as his criticisms of Sanchez only alienated him further from them. The jubilant reaction of the people to his surprising visit to Nueva Vida infuriated him.

"Why do they like this man so much?" he asked his staff members during a closed door meeting addressing Sanchez's approaching visit on the morning of his historic announcement. "Don't they see this man for who he is? Don't they realize that he is a threat to our government, our democracy, our way of life?"

One bright, realistic member of his staff, Cesar Rubio, who was anxious to shake some sense into his boss, was bold enough to tell him the truth to the amazement of his timid colleagues. "Mayor Rivera, the reason why the people like this man is because he speaks for them."

"What?" the Mayor barked. "How does he speak for them?"

"He communicates their sense of frustration," Cesar Rubio said with composure.

"Frustration? Why should the people of Nueva Vida feel frustrated?"

"They feel frustrated with the civil war."

"Well, if they feel frustrated with the war, shouldn't they be on the side of the government?"

"Not if it is weak and corrupted and losing the war," Rubio said while the others nervously motioned for him to stop.

To everyone's surprise, the Mayor did not look upset as he calmly looked out the window. "Maybe you are right," he told Rubio with a soft, resigned voice. "Maybe this man, Sanchez, is right to attack the government. Maybe the reporters are correct when they say I am losing touch with the people. Maybe I don't have what it takes anymore to be an effective leader, and I should just step down and let some new people take over."

This immediately drew protests from everyone, including Rubio. The Mayor's tall and dapper right hand man, Victor Ascencio, stood up from his chair and began pleading with him. His dark, receding hair revealed an aristocratic, lean face with icy-blue, persuasive eyes. "Juan Carlos, how can you think that way?" he asked theatrically, raising his arms in disbelief. "Of course you are still an effective leader! C'mon, you have been the finest mayor in this town's history! You have been mayor for fourteen years! Just because you have recently encountered some minor troubles doesn't mean you should suddenly quit. That would be ridiculous. Despite what some stupid people might say in the papers, this town needs you now more than ever!"

"Well, maybe not," the Mayor answered unemotionally. "Maybe the times have passed me by and Nueva Vida doesn't need me and my services anymore. As they say, nothing lasts forever. The people are totally in love with this Sanchez character. He is young, good-looking, full of wonderful ideas, while I am old and decrepit."

"Stop talking this way Juan Carlos," Victor Ascencio angrily protested. This clever, corrupt man certainly wanted to retain his glamorous position in the city government, which would potentially be lost if his boss decided to quit. "The times have not passed you by! That is nonsense! You are overreacting to what Rubio said, which is really nothing. He may be right about Sanchez and his popularity, but it doesn't mean the end of the line for you. All you have to do is greet him here, give him the keys to the city, and walk away. You don't have to shower him with much fanfare. He will get enough of that from the people. All you need to do is be courteous, that's all, which is something you have always been good at."

"How can I do that when everyone already knows that I despise him?" the Mayor naively asked in an attempt to make the others feel sorry for him.

"Juan Carlos, you have been in politics for almost forty years," Ascencio sarcastically told him. "I don't think I have to answer that for you as I know you are just putting us on. But in case you are not, I will gladly tell you what you need to do. You will go on and greet the man anyway. Hating Sanchez or not should be of no consequence when you are engaged in the simple act of welcoming the man to the city. Its only politics and the people will not care much about it."

"Ah Victor, you have really done a good job of setting me straight through the years," the disturbed Mayor remarked quite absent-mindedly, as though he had something else on his mind.

"Well, that is my job, boss."

"Mr. Ascencio has, I think, made a good point," the Mayor said after a long pause, now addressing everyone. "Do you all go along with what he said?" They unanimously agreed with Ascencio. "Then I will welcome that son of a bitch into the city. That's it gentlemen, this meeting is over. Enjoy the rest of the day."

After all the members of his staff left the room, Mayor Rivera walked back to a lounge chair in the corner and sat down on it. He took a bottle of scotch on the adjacent stand and poured himself a glass. He looked at it for a while, entranced by the scotch and its rich golden color. He slowly swirled it around within the glass, watching various brilliant sparkles of gold light shine through with each slight rotation. "How pretty these sparkles of light are," he thought. He then finally began sipping the scotch, hoping it would bring him some peace of mind. At first, he felt wonderful. He was happy and relaxed, thinking about seeing his family over the weekend in his lake house not too far from Nueva Vida. His grandchildren were reaching adolescence and he was looking forward to spending some quality time with them. He wanted to go fishing with them in the lake and take them off for a brief hike in the surrounding woods.

All these pleasant reflections came to an abrupt end however when the Mayor came across the thought of Vicente Sanchez entering his city. As he began consuming his second glass of Scotch, the old politician thought about how the meeting with his staff members went. He was troubled by their unanimous support of

Victor Ascencio's suggestion to welcome Sanchez into the city. None of them supported the Mayor when he railed against Sanchez. They all seemed as excited as everyone else in town about the presidential candidate's impending visit. "They really love this man too," he thought in reference to his staff. This made the Mayor feel all the more alienated, especially since he expected his own aids to be loyal to him. Instead, they appeared not to take much notice of him during the meeting; they were certainly not their usual selves, fawning over him as though he were a king. "They talked down to me as though I was some idiot who could not tie his own shoes," he reflected painfully.

This feeling of isolation made him very desperate for a way out of his bitter predicament. He became more obsessed with Sanchez and his rising popularity. In his darkening mind, the young presidential candidate now stood directly in his path toward a glorious, successful end to his long tenure as mayor. But he felt powerless to do anything about it, which left him only more confused and frustrated. Slumped in his chair, the tired, old politician felt like he was going to die right there. Despite it still being rather early in the morning after a good night's sleep, he suddenly was overcome with weakness, experiencing dizziness and shortness of breath. He began perspiring around his neck and chest.

CHAPTER NINE

A HAPPY DAY
FOR GRANDMOTHER CELIA

The early morning announcement of Vicente's Sanchez's visit to Nueva Vida sent shockwaves throughout the city. Upon hearing the news, many people immediately went out to the streets and began celebrating. The town soon became a merry spectacle of confetti, dancing, singing, balloons, and honking cars. They could not believe the next President of Colombia was coming to see them. Neither could Gabriel's grandmother. When Aunt Teresa informed them of the news, Grandmother Celia asked her if she had gone mad. After she exuberantly repeated the news to her three times, the old woman still refused to believe it.

To make sure her daughter was telling the truth, she turned on the radio. When several stations on the radio were issuing the news of Sanchez's visit, she still was not convinced. "It's true, mother!" Aunt Teresa proclaimed, as she then ran over to Gabriel and gave him a big hug. "How wonderful!" she shouted wildly. "He is coming! He is coming!" Gabriel was excited, but not nearly as much as his aunt. His grandmother, still not sold on the news, went out to the balcony as quickly as she could. Never did she step out to the balcony alone, for she was eighty-five years old and ailing. Amazingly, she mustered all the strength she could, and walked over there without assistance.

95

The very idea of Vicente Sanchez coming to her hometown seemed to have extraordinary healing powers!

Alarmed to see her mother already on the balcony, Aunt Teresa ran over there. "Oh, she cannot break her hip again!" she cried. Gabriel followed her onto the balcony and saw his grandmother there, leaning against the old railing and waving to someone below. His concerned aunt tried to pull her away from the railing, imploring her to go inside. But she refused to go inside. She then hollered at a man walking underneath the balcony. "Hey! Do you know, kind sir, if it is true that Vicente Sanchez is coming here to Nueva Vida?" The man looked up and told her that it was indeed true. She thanked him and motioned for her daughter and grandson to walk her back inside.

Without commenting on the news, she then asked Aunt Teresa if they still had their large flag of Colombia. "Yes, we still have the flag," she responded. "It is in the garage downstairs." The old woman requested them to bring the flag upstairs. When her daughter asked why, she responded that she wanted it hoisted up on the balcony. "Today, I feel proud to be Colombian," she declared. Within a couple hours after the large flag was positioned securely on the balcony by Gabriel, other flags were seen hanging from the windows and balconies of apartments throughout the sprawling neighborhood. "Wow, look what you have done mother," Aunt Teresa remarked as they viewed with some amazement the transformed neighborhood from the large living room window. "All of our neighbors are now hanging out their flags too!" As Grandmother Celia stood there watching, a rare smile slowly appeared on her face.

*   *   *

Up until that moment, Gabriel's grandmother had been in a steady decline physically and mentally. About two years before, she had badly broken her hip from a fall down the stairs in the apartment. The injury left her hardly able to walk, as she needed assistance every time she wanted to move about. This was a terrible blow to the fiercely independent woman, who was now unable to live like she once did. The simple pleasures of strolling to church every morning, walking down the stairs to retrieve the milk in the morning, or going to the kitchen to do some cooking were denied to her. She was confined to the second floor of her home, as she rarely ventured down to the ground floor, let alone outside her bedroom. Grandmother Celia gradually was losing her appetite for life. She spent most of the day either praying or looking out the window. Aunt Teresa and Gabriel could only look on with distress.

Once in a while, she showed some signs of life, whether by engaging in humorous conversations with visiting friends and family, playing some checkers with Gabriel, or delighting over a fresh piece of sugar bread with coffee. The presence of Gabriel did recharge her a bit, as he brought some much-needed energy and 'noise' to the apartment. She no longer worried about herself so much, for there was someone else to look after. Her maternal instincts were not quite dead yet. Whenever Gabriel was out of the apartment, she would always ask Aunt Teresa about his whereabouts. "Where's my Gabriel?" she would inquire with genuine interest. "When did he leave?" When these questions were answered, she predictably asked when he would return. The youth would spend a lot of time chatting with her or watching television in her bedroom. Gabriel's presence in the apartment helped distract her enough to push most serious thoughts of death in the backburner.

Nevertheless, there were times, even with Gabriel there, when Grandmother Celia would sink back into the depths of hopelessness. She would silently lie in her bed for long stretches of time without doing anything in particular. She did not even have the will to talk to anyone. "You should not try to speak with her now," Aunt Teresa would tell Gabriel during those occasions. "She is feeling a little sad." Her eyes would stare vacantly at the wall in front of her or out the window, as her hands would gently feel and pull at the blanket's ends. She would respond to questions with a simple nod of her head or shrug of her shoulders. Once in a while, she would break the monotonous silence with some brief chants of prayer, which did lift her spirits a bit.

Gabriel liked to compare his grandmother's plight with that of Colombia. "Both are prostrate and dying," he often thought. His grandmother's sadness could not only be traced to her immobility, but to losing the country she once knew, or more specifically, the city of Nueva Vida; for she only really knew Nueva Vida, having ventured out of it only a few times to the outlying areas and to the town of Ipiales on the border with Ecuador. This despite her husband having been a Senator of Colombia for several years, living in Bogotá! She never went to the capital, not even once, while her husband was Senator. Feeling very comfortable in Nueva Vida, she dared not leave it for fear of being separated from her precious children and home. She was deathly afraid of traveling through plane or the treacherous Pan American highway. To her, Nueva Vida was *the world* and it did not make much sense to leave it.

Yet, her world had seen much better times. Grandmother Celia had longed for the 'good old days' like most other people her age. She fondly remembered Nueva Vida when it was smaller, quieter, and safer. Back when she was growing up as a child, the city had a much more pastoral quality about it. It was not even a city, but a hamlet in the countryside. Only a few thousand people lived there, their residences closely huddled around the plaza at the heart of town. The farms were much larger at that time, dominating the landscape as well as the lives of the people. Most of the male residents worked in the farms, while the women stayed home. Things were simple and secure, with people living according to strict routines. The work week revolved around the cherished lunch and siesta, when families could get together and relax at home during the middle of the day. On Sundays, everybody went to Church in the morning, and then went off on picnics during the afternoon. It really was a pleasant life, a time when people were friendly and respectful to each other.

As the years passed, Grandmother Celia painfully witnessed her hometown transform rapidly, as it grew larger. In the course of her lifetime, Nueva Vida went from a small hamlet in the countryside to a bustling, large city. It became less pleasant and secure with the passage of time, especially during the tenure of Mayor Rivera, when the population grew at an alarming rate. With the surge in population and crime, the town's old pastoral charm died forever, leaving Grandmother Celia and most others of her generation embittered. She deeply resented Mayor Rivera for this.

In fact, she had once feuded with Mayor Rivera thirteen years before over the destruction of some old four-storey apartments in her neighborhood. The apartments had been around for as long as she could remember, and were probably first constructed shortly before she was born in the 1910's. Apparently, the apartments were bought one day by a mysterious group of people. Their identity and whereabouts were unknown. The city would eventually reveal that the apartments' new owners did not reside in Nueva Vida, fuelling plenty of speculation from those living in the area. Many people, including Grandmother Celia, believed that these mysterious owners were probably members of the drug cartels.

When it was discovered that these historic treasures of the city, with their arched windows and distinctive pilasters, were going to be demolished to make way for a string of new condominiums, residents of the neighborhood rose in protest. They demanded, through a petition, that the old apartments not be demolished since they were landmarks. The Mayor's office disagreed, explaining that 'architectural' landmarks had to be at least 150 years old. Since the apartments were only about 70 years old, they could not be qualified as landmarks and could be demolished. At that moment, the protesters, which steadily grew in number as residents from other parts of the city were joining in, leaned on the one woman who they thought could win the sympathy of the Mayor. That person was Grandmother Celia. She was the widow of a well-respected Senator, and having been a long-time resident in the neighborhood, could lend a dignified voice for the cause. She gladly accepted that role since she believed in keeping the neighborhood the way it was. "I will not allow this tragedy to occur!" she told her neighbors. "Those buildings have been there throughout my whole life. If they fall, the city will be stabbed in the heart."

She arranged a meeting with Mayor Rivera through his office. When the meeting took place in one of the backrooms of City Hall, the Mayor was absent. One of his representatives was there instead to the utter displeasure of Grandmother Celia. She immediately objected. "Where's the Mayor?" she demanded.

"Unfortunately, the Mayor could not make it to this meeting for he is away on personal business," the man answered.

"Tell me, what kind of personal business can be more important than the demolition of those beautiful apartments?" she asked passionately.

"Well, that is not for me to judge," the representative replied.

"I am not asking for your judgment," she snapped back. "I am just making an observation. This whole thing is so terrible. Anyway, how can we have this meeting without the Mayor?"

"I was instructed by the Mayor to conduct this meeting. The Mayor finds this matter to be important, and intended to go to this meeting personally. But, like I said, he was unable to attend because some urgent things popped up."

"If he cannot attend now, then we should reschedule this meeting. I want to meet with him personally."

"That may not be a good idea," the man cautioned.

"Why is it not a good idea?" she asked.

"Because by the time you get a chance to meet with the Mayor personally, the apartments might have already been demolished."

"Tell the Mayor that there will be no destruction going on until he meets with me personally!" Grandmother Celia demanded, as she got up from her seat, ready to depart. The representative, who was not mean-spirited and wanted to accommodate the old widow, tried convincing her not to leave. "Ms. Duarte, please stay. We can resolve this now."

"As I told you, this meeting will not . . ."

"There will be no meeting between you and the Mayor," the man firmly stated, cutting off Grandmother Celia in mid-sentence. "There will be no meeting between the two of you today, tomorrow, next week, or the week after that! He is going to be very busy over the next couple months. He will not be able to meet with you, period. So, you have no choice but to work with me today for there may not be another opportunity in the future." This momentarily stunned Grandmother Celia, as she stood there with a puzzled expression on her face. "Please sit down Ms. Duarte, so we can begin this meeting," urged the representative. Still stunned, the old widow did what the man asked, and slowly sat down. She sat there quietly, waiting for her host to begin talking again.

"Now, what I wanted to tell you is that the Mayor's office cannot do anything to stop the demolition of those buildings," the official began after regaining his composure. "They cannot prevent those buildings from being demolished based on the fact that they are landmarks, because the law stipulates that architectural landmarks here in Nueva Vida have to be at least 150 years old. As you know, those buildings are nowhere close to being 150 years old. Also, it is very hard for the city to prevent such a demolition from occurring because of the various laws protecting the rights of the owner. This is private property we are talking about here, and the owners of those buildings have every right to do whatever they want."

"Yes, they do," Grandmother Celia half-heartedly agreed.

"Look, Ms. Duarte, the Mayor wanted me to tell you that he did everything possible to prevent the demolition. He also admires those buildings and he feels badly about what is going to happen. Believe me when I say the Mayor has been doing everything he could! He looked into the matter closely. He and his staff spent several hours trying to solve this problem, figuring a way out of this mess. But they could not. The bottom line is that if they try to stop the demolition, the owners might file a lawsuit against the city, which the Mayor wants to avoid at all costs."

"Has the Mayor tried talking to the owners about this matter?" Grandmother Celia asked with some desperation, sensing she was probably going to lose the argument, but hopeful she could still bring some good news to her neighbors.

"Yes, the Mayor has already talked with the owners and tried to convince them not to demolish the buildings. But they were not swayed, and insisted they wanted to build lavish new apartments there. The fact is, the owners are very powerful real estate developers from Cali and if we give them trouble here, other developers will want to avoid Nueva Vida in the future. We don't want a bad reputation. It is all about money. I hope you understand."

"What is the Mayor's proposal then to us?" the old woman asked.

"Well, the Mayor does not have a real proposal for you and your neighbors," the representative responded hesitantly, nervous that Grandmother Celia would react angrily to such a suggestion. "What the Mayor would like to ask of all of you, though, is to let the buildings go. He would like for you, Ms. Duarte, to personally call off the protests, to tell your neighbors to put an end to this stand so that no further trouble will ensue from this. God knows, enough trouble has already been generated! There is absolutely nothing the city can do at this point, so the protests are futile. By convincing your fellow neighbors to walk out, you will be doing Nueva Vida a huge service."

The official's well-crafted arguments had won over Grandmother Celia, as she believed now that Mayor Rivera and his people had done all they could to help the protesters. If they were indeed telling the truth, there was really no way she could continue arguing. The only thing she was upset about was the Mayor not telling her this in person. That did bother her and she was still a little suspicious about the whole thing, but the charming official had convinced her for the most part of the Mayor's integrity in the matter. "It seems to me there is nothing any of us can do about this, unfortunately," she said sadly. "What is your name, by the way?"

"Oh, my name is Geraldo Ayala," the man replied happily, sensing the old woman was giving up the fight. "Pleased to meet you, Ms. Duarte," he said as he leaned over his desk to shake her hand. "I wish we could have met in other, better circumstances."

"You seem to be a nice young man," Grandmother Celia told the official with a trace of affection. "Anyway, I am going to leave now and tell my neighbors to end this struggle. But what if some of them decide to continue protesting, despite my pleas? Will they suffer any consequences?"

"Yes, they may be thrown in jail and face charges of some sort," he answered quickly. "This is exactly what the Mayor wants to avoid! He desperately does not want any more problems resulting from this. He does not want to throw any people in jail over this."

"I will do my best to persuade my neighbors to act accordingly, although my heart is broken." With that she walked out of Mr. Ayala's office. Within a couple days, she was indeed able to convince all her neighbors to end their stand. A week later, the three apartments were demolished, and nine months later, the new condominiums were standing in their place, forever changing the face of the old neighborhood. The residents felt sad, but accepted the changes as the will of fate, or more precisely, for those who were religious, the will of God. They gradually went about their lives, recovering from the blow of losing a cherished part of their lives.

However, some disturbing news regarding the apartment demolitions soon leaked out. A newspaper photograph would show the portly Mayor Rivera hamming it up with Juan Amalia Torres, the real estate developer responsible for knocking down the old apartments, during a lavish ceremony sponsored by the city. The title of the article read: "MAYOR RIVERA WELCOMES DEVELOPER TO NUEVA VIDA". The article went on to reveal that the Mayor actually had courted Torres and high-profile developers for a long time before they finally decided to invest in Nueva Vida. According to the newspaper, the Mayor had thanked Torres during the ceremony for accepting his invitation and "changing the face of the city". It was also disclosed that Torres had worked closely with the Mayor's office in choosing which neighborhoods were to be revitalized, and how they would be changed.

When Grandmother Celia got hold of this news, she was overwhelmed with anger. "I will kill that man!" she yelled. Of course, she now took all the responsibility for allowing the buildings to be demolished in the first place. "How idiotic I was to trust that man!" she complained to her friends. "It is all my fault. How will I live with myself, now?" She really loathed herself for a short while until she decided to take action against the Mayor. It might have been too late to save the apartments, but not her self-respect.

For about a year, she did everything in her power to raise hell wherever the Mayor went, whether it was city hall or a public event. She would raise objections to many of the Mayor's bills in city hall, which soon became her favorite hang-out. She would take the microphone and loudly lambaste every one of his initiatives. While she ranted, the Mayor would just sit there and laugh along with those close around him. Yet, it was not such a laughing matter when Grandmother Celia seriously considered filing a lawsuit against the city for deceiving her over the demolition of the apartments. After all, she was a senator's widow and could afford a good lawyer. Many of the city's occupants would also be on her side.

Mayor Rivera recognized the severity of this threat and went into action himself. Through the carrot and stick, he was able to persuade all the law offices in town not to take on the case. Grandmother Celia was either told by the law offices that they were too busy with other cases or that her case was not going to win. Some decent individuals were more honest, telling her that they did not want to risk their careers by taking on such a controversial case. With no cards left on her deck, Grandmother Celia began losing hope. She would go to city hall a few times more, but many people there mocked her. "There is that crazy old lady again," many of them would say. Her family and friends had long pleaded with her to end her personal fight with the Mayor, and she finally began to listen to them. "I will no longer be an object of ridicule," she told Aunt Teresa one day, and with that, she never returned to city hall. Her feud with the Mayor was over.

*   *   *

So when Grandmother Celia watched her big flag of Colombia hanging from her balcony in honor of Vicente Sanchez's upcoming visit, she was proud of her country for the first time in a very long while. Sanchez was a symbol of hope for her, someone who was honest and was going to change her country for the better. In fact, he reminded her of her long-deceased husband, whose mission in life was to serve his country without getting wrapped up in vanity and wealth. With the likes of Sanchez around, Colombia no longer would be brought down by corrupted, deceitful politicians of the new age. The humbler world of her youth would come back under their wings, supplanting the rotten one already in existence. In a way,

Grandmother Celia likened the youthful presidential candidate to Jesus Christ during Judgment Day, returning to save the good souls while casting away the bad ones. People like her would be saved while those like Mayor Rivera would be banished forever from Nueva Vida and Colombia. At long last, she would be vindicated!

CHAPTER TEN

PARTY ON THE BUS

When the news of Vicente Sanchez's planned visit to Nueva Vida first broke at about eight in the morning on Tuesday, October 22nd, people suddenly stopped what they were doing and flocked to the streets. Many of those who already started working simply left their jobs to celebrate. Seeing the festivities already forming on the streets, our friend Gabriel wondered if he had to work later that evening. Soon after hanging the Colombian flag on his grandmother's balcony, he decided to walk over to the language institute and find out for himself. It took him longer than usual to get there because of the throngs of people already crowding the streets. When he did get to the institute, he saw the short, slender Dr. Granados standing outside the front entrance and viewing the emerging spectacle before him. When he saw the tall, gangly Gabriel approaching, the professor beamed a hearty smile. "Wow! Isn't this amazing!" he told Gabriel. The two then stood side by side in front of the entrance for some time, watching the people gathering in the streets. They engaged in some small talk before Gabriel asked him if he still had to go work that evening. "No, there will be no classes this evening," the professor replied. "In fact, I have called off the rest of the day. I just told my morning class to leave a little while ago."

"I had a feeling you would call off classes," Gabriel said. "It's nice to take a day off once in a while."

"Yes it is. Anyway, it would make no sense to have classes today since most of the students will not even come."

"That's true," Gabriel said. "What do you plan on doing now?"

"First, I am going to close this place up," Dr. Granados responded. "Then, I will go home and open up a bottle of my finest whiskey. I'll have myself a drink and then join the party! Sounds like a good plan, don't you think?"

Gabriel then bid farewell to the jubilant Dr. Granados and began walking back to his grandmother's. With so much to see around him, Gabriel walked very slowly, gathering everything in. People were marching down the streets arm in arm, carrying pictures of Vicente Sanchez along with Colombian flags, and chanting "Viva Colombia!" Our young friend could not help but get swept up by it all, as he chanted along with the people and raised his fist in the air with each chant. He was truly happy to see such public fanfare everywhere. When a *chiva* bus rolled in his direction and the people in it pleaded for him to enter, Gabriel could not hold himself back. He jumped into the slowly moving vehicle to the delight of everyone inside. As soon as he got in, Gabriel was mobbed by some of the passengers, as they embraced and grabbed him. "Welcome, my friend!" shouted a muscular man with a Stalin mustache and modest beer gut. He was terribly drunk and red as a lobster. "Let's celebrate to Colombia's future! Would you like a beer?" Gabriel gladly accepted a bottle of good Colombian Pilsner beer from the man, who retrieved it from a large cooler behind him. This man seemed to be in charge of the carnival ride, as he gave orders to the driver and talked to everyone inside.

Soon after Gabriel entered, all eyes focused on him again, since he did not look like a native. The host took advantage of this moment to butt in and entertain everyone. "My young friend, I am sorry but you don't look like a Colombian," he told Gabriel quite solemnly. Gabriel did not know what to make of the situation, since it suddenly was dead silent. He became very uncomfortable with all the attention he was receiving. He did not know exactly how to

107

respond to the man's query, for it seemed rather awkward, if not condemning. "You are right," he told the man quietly in decent Spanish, but certainly not native. "I am not from this country. I am American."

"You are a gringo?" the man asked with all seriousness, as if upset.

"Yes," replied our young friend, looking at his inquisitor with more alarm and suspicion. Nothing was said for a while as the man just stared into Gabriel's eyes. This long pause only made things more nerve-racking for the young American, as he began to squirm a bit. "You are a gringo?"

"Yes."

"A gringo?" the man asked in a serious tone for the third time.

"Yes."

"A gringo?" the man uttered again, though this time with a laugh as he glanced back at the audience. "Ladies and gentlemen, we have a gringo on the bus!" he declared, laughing hysterically now. "What are we to do?" The others inside the bus then started laughing as well. Gabriel could only look on with a bemused smile.

"Forgive us, young man, we just wanted to have a little fun, that's all," the man explained, which put Gabriel much more at ease. He was somewhat familiar with the town's belittling sense of humor, but had not always been sure where they were going with their jokes. Thus, the youth had learned quickly to stay cool and patient in those situations, and let the jokes play out lest he make a fool out of himself by saying anything inappropriate or even getting emotional. "I thought you were going to kick me out of this bus," he jokingly told the host, eliciting more laughter from the passengers. He then lifted his beer bottle up to take a swig when another man cautioned him not to do so, for there might be police around. "Really?" replied Gabriel. The man then began laughing with the others, making Gabriel really feel like a fool this time. "You got me there!" he said with some embarrassment. The engaging host boldly stepped in again and asked what the American thought about Colombia.

"I love this country!" Gabriel enthusiastically responded.

"That's good! What is it that you like about this country?"

"Ever since I was a young kid, I have loved this country . . . its natural beauty, its spirituality, its warm and friendly people . . ."

"So, you have been here before?" asked the host while the others quietly listened.

"Oh yes, several times," Gabriel replied.

"Really?"

"Yes. I have even lived here for a short while when I was a kid. My mother is from Nueva Vida."

"Your mother is from Nueva Vida?"

"Yes she is."

"Well I'll be damned," the man said with much surprise.

"Yes, much of my mother's side of the family still lives here," Gabriel explained. "I have come here many times before to visit them."

"I noticed your Spanish is pretty good, but I didn't figure that you have ties here."

"Yes I do."

"Well, well, well . . . then you are a part of us. And even if you were not, we would have been all too happy to have you here aboard with us on this bus. That is the kind of people we are! Once a person has stepped onto the soil of this town, they will be welcomed with open arms. And when they leave it, a part of their hearts will remain here! That is the kind of town this is!" The host then lifted his half-empty beer bottle in the air. He looked at Gabriel first, then at the passengers. "I want to make a toast!" he declared.

"No, not another one," someone in the crowd remarked sarcastically.

"I will make as many toasts as I want, for this is my bus!" the host retorted. While he continued looking at the passengers with his drink raised in the air, the man seemed to have forgotten what he was about to say. He wavered a bit on his heels, stumbled, and fell to his side, where Gabriel caught him and propped him back up again. As Gabriel held him up steady by the elbow, the host, with his bloodshot, drunken eyes seemed to have recaptured his senses. "Now, I remember what my toast was going to be for," he said, drawing some laughter from the crowd. "Ladies and gentlemen, I would like to toast our new friend here . . . what is your name, son?"

Gabriel, still holding the host by the elbow, offered his name, and wondered when he was going to get off the hook. He was being a very good sport about it, but now desperately wanted nothing more than for the attention to be diverted away from him. "Gabriel?" the host asked. "That is an interesting name. Well everybody, I would like to give a toast to our new friend Gabriel. Salud!" Everyone who had a drink, whether it was a beer bottle or a flask of rum, raised it in Gabriel's direction and took a swig. The host turned to Gabriel and introduced himself. "Gabriel, my name is Herman. I am very happy to meet you."

"I am very happy to meet you too, Herman," the youth replied, as he happily noticed the attention was no longer on him, for the passengers began talking with each other.

"I did not embarrass you, did I?" Herman asked.

"No, not at all," Gabriel answered.

"I did not mean to put you on the spot."

"No, that was fine."

"This is a great day for this city," Herman said. "This is a great moment for all of us who are from here. We will never forget this day."

"This is certainly wonderful," Gabriel said.

"We deserve it!" stated Herman, who was still being propped up by Gabriel. "We have suffered so much from this war. Now, this man has arrived on the scene to save our country. Hopefully, he can do it. Or, at least, I hope he will be given a chance. But, we will enjoy this moment and celebrate, for this is great for our city and for our country!" After saying this, Herman began talking with someone else. Gabriel took advantage of this opportunity to walk away from the front of the bus and move towards the back where he could blend more easily with the people. He left Herman behind after helping him maneuver towards a nearby pole he could hold onto.

The young American found an empty seat all the way in the back of the cramped bus, which was good since there were not many seats to start with. In fact, the bus was stripped of most seats to accommodate such parties on wheels. He considered it a bizarre but wonderful idea. "You don't see this in America!" he thought. Gabriel then looked down on his seat and wondered if he needed it at all, for most of the passengers were standing anyway. The passengers were either gathered in the middle or standing along the sides where they were chanting slogans and talking with people on the street. He decided to look out from where he was in the back and observe the festivities outside the bus. It was all a daze, as people and vehicles flooded the street. Some people shouted friendly words at Gabriel, asking him how the party in the bus was going.

Gabriel looked with amazement at the people standing on the balconies of apartments lining the streets, waving their Colombian flags. Those without balconies would lean over their windows and wave at the crowds below. It seemed like a moment from the past, Gabriel thought. This type of street celebration was reminiscent of the old ticker-tape parades in New York's Times Square during the 1940's, or more ominously, Hitler's victory parades through Berlin or Vienna. These were images he had studied in history books, but was now experiencing first-hand in Nueva Vida. It was a strange but exhilarating feeling. Yet, Gabriel was not able to really gather it all in, for there was so much going on around him. He was swept away like a piece of confetti flying through the air.

One thing that struck Gabriel was the appearance of unity everywhere, as people walked with their arms interlocked or hand-in-hand, laughing and crying together. He thought it was interesting that for a few hours at least, all the people, rich and poor, law-abiders and criminals, clerics and laymen, old and young, were bound together as one. Spotting any hint of division among the crowds was like trying to find a needle in a haystack. There was no cursing, fighting, suspiciousness, or other sorts of tension to be found. "Could this be the closest thing one gets to a heavenly kingdom?" Gabriel pondered. This spirit of unity would soon drag Gabriel in from his detached spot in the back corner of the bus, as a short woman grabbed him by the hand. "Come over here," she said.

As he was brought to the middle of the bus, where most of the passengers were now gathered, lively cumbia music began playing from a large amp in the front. Many of the couples in the bus then started dancing together, while the rest formed a circle around them. The short woman took Gabriel inside the circle and asked him to dance with her. He shyly accepted, which made the woman very happy. At first, she tried to teach the young foreigner a few steps, but soon realized he did not need any help for he already knew how to dance to cumbia. They danced through the first song without saying a word to each other. Gabriel felt a little awkward dancing inside of a slow-moving bus amid happy crowds of people. He did not envision this happening to him when he woke up only a couple hours before. He thought it was going to be just another average day. Instead of grading papers at a cafe though, he was now dancing with a woman in a strange looking bus. It was not even noon yet. During the second song, Gabriel's dance partner began talking with him. She introduced herself very affectionately, gently pulling him down so he could hear her. "My name is Mayra. What is yours?"

"My name is Gabriel," he spoke into her ear. "It is nice to meet you." The two talked throughout the song, and Gabriel quickly sensed that this attractive, slightly older woman was very interested in him. She held him very close to her, especially when they were speaking with each other. The young American did not know quite how to handle such overt affection from this woman. For the time being, he kept dancing with her for he had nowhere to go, and he enjoyed the attention he was receiving. Being shy, he appreciated not having to carry the conversation, for she initiated most of the talking. "So you are from the United States," Mayra said with a friendly smile. "Do you miss it?"

"No, I actually do not miss it much," Gabriel responded. "I needed to get away from there."

"Why?" she asked.

"I don't know. I guess I needed a change of scene. So here I am."

"So why are you here?"

"I am here working as an English teacher. But I am also visiting my relatives." This ignited a flurry of inquiries from Mayra about his ties with the city, his life in the United States, and his future, among other things. While they were talking about his uncertain future, Gabriel grew uneasy and switched the topic of conversation. He began asking questions about her and discovered that Mayra had a daughter. She also worked at a clothing store. Mayra then asked Gabriel how long he was going to be staying in Nueva Vida. When he said he was going to stay indefinitely, she flashed a big smile. The excited young woman then embraced him and ran her hand through his hair.

Gabriel now knew for sure that Mayra liked him, but was not sure if he wanted to continue being there with her. The woman was indeed attractive, with her long flowing dark hair and golden skin, but, for some reason, she did not exactly strike his fancy. Anyway, he had a hard time deciding what to do. The song had ended and they stopped dancing. Our conscientious friend did not want to suddenly abandon her for fear of appearing rude. He really wanted to leave the bus soon and go back to his grandmother's to eat lunch, for he was hungry.

But Mayra was making it all the more difficult for him to leave, as she asked Gabriel if he wanted a beer. When he could not make up his mind, the woman started to work her charm on him, spinning her webs around him slowly but surely. "Have a beer with me," she pleaded in a most enticing manner which Gabriel could not resist. "You must loosen up and enjoy this wonderful moment. What do you say?" Without even waiting for his response, she walked toward the front to get beer. Our friend could only watch as his fate was at the mercy of this assertive woman. She soon came back with two beers and happily gave one of them to Gabriel. They opened the cans of beer, gave a toast to each other, and chugged down.

They talked and drank some more, as the bus slowly moved along with the parade. Little by little, Mayra was winning over Gabriel. He certainly liked the affection he was receiving from her. He also admired her down-to earth personality, for she was not putting on any airs. She was candid and sincere, and not pretending to be someone she was not. This comforted Gabriel since he could also be himself. After finishing their beers, they danced some more;

the two were even talking about doing something together the following day. After dancing to a couple songs, Gabriel retrieved more beer at the front of the bus and encountered Herman. He was standing there beside the big cooler, grinning from ear to ear with his yellow teeth as he looked at Gabriel.

"So, I see you are enjoying yourself here very well!" he said while nodding in the direction of Mayra. "That woman is my best friend's niece. She's got a reputation, if you know what I mean." Gabriel just stood there smiling, not knowing how to react to such a comment. Before he could even say something in response, the wily Herman told him he was only kidding. "Nah, she's a nice girl." Gabriel then asked him for a couple beers. Herman gladly bent down and grabbed the beers for him, prompting Gabriel to inquire whether it should be paid.

"No, no, no," the proud host replied with almost a growl on his sun-burnt face. "No payments are required. This is on me, all of it! Actually, this is not on me for I stole this from some depot outside of town. I did not mean to steal it, but it was right there for us to take. Nobody was around, and we just took it. Loads and loads of alcohol! So, it is not on me for I didn't buy it with my own money. But, what the hell! Why should I feel ashamed when I, like Robin Hood, give back to the people all that I have stolen?"

"I'll toast to that!" a tipsy Gabriel declared.

"Yes! Cheers to Robin Hood and Colombia!" Herman answered. With that, Gabriel walked back to the rear of the bus where Mayra was waiting. She was conversing with some people and then abruptly stopped when she saw Gabriel. She offered a big smile and grabbed his hand when he gave her one of the beers. "How nice of you," she said tenderly. "I was already starting to miss you." Our young friend was beginning to feel like he was on cloud nine, in the middle of a joyous parade with a nice companion, but there was something missing. He wanted a cigarette and reached for his shirt pocket. His pack was not there. He began to panic, reaching all over his shirt and pants for his pack of cigarettes. "Oh no!" he cried, remembering he had left them at his grandmother's. Mayra looked very concerned as she asked Gabriel what was wrong. When he told her he left his cigarettes back home, the considerate Mayra started asking some people around them if they had any cigarettes to spare. However, Gabriel implored her to stop. "No, we can get off the bus and go to a store. What do you think?"

"Sure, we can do that," Mayra replied.

"Good," Gabriel said. "Now, we have to stop this bus." The two could have easily jumped off the vehicle since it was rolling slowly ahead, but Gabriel wanted to be a gentleman and have it stop for her. They went to the front and asked the driver if he could stop the bus so they could get off. However, the drunken Herman overheard their request to the driver and leapt to his feet. "What do you guys think you are doing?" he demanded to know.

"Oh, we want to get off," Gabriel responded sheepishly.

"Why the hell would you want to leave this boat?" the man barked. "Are you crazy? We are celebrating a wonderful day for our city. This party has just begun!"

"Well, I wanted to buy some cigarettes."

"You want to buy cigarettes? Why didn't you just ask me? Here, have three. That should keep you satisfied for a while." Herman reached for a cigarette pack in his shirt pocket, drenched in motor oil, and took out three, then four. He gave them to Gabriel.

"Thank you very much, Herman," the gratified youth said while Herman helped light his cigarette.

"Now, don't think about leaving this bus again, you hear?"

"Loud and clear!" answered a happy Gabriel.

The two then returned to the back where they retrieved their beers and continued talking to each other. Many of the people kept dancing to the uplifting cumbia rhythms. At this point, Gabriel was content with just looking on, standing there with Mayra, who was now holding his hand. The youth was pretty drunk now, although not that badly for he was still able to make sense when he spoke. But thanks to the vast amount of alcohol coursing through his veins, he was bold enough to kiss his companion on the lips without even pausing. Mayra was a little startled by the kiss, but was not unreceptive. She then pulled away, smiled sweetly and told Gabriel that it was a 'very, very nice kiss'.

After that, they were continually in each other's arms. The party on the bus, as well as on the streets, was lasting well into the afternoon with no signs of abating. By about three o'clock, Gabriel remembered he had not informed his grandmother and aunt of his whereabouts. However, he shrugged it off an instant later, realizing they must have assumed he was somewhere out in the parade. "Don't worry," Mayra reassured him. "They know you are somewhere out here having a good time. Besides, you are grown man. They know you can take care of yourself." He was having fun and did not want the party to end. Neither did Mayra.

Yet, a look of terror suddenly overcame her face. "Oh my god," she said breathlessly. When Gabriel inquired what the problem was, she could only keep looking at one particular spot in the street. Gabriel turned around to look at what it was and saw three police officers on motorcycles motioning for the bus to stop. They were holding out their pistols. Herman saw the police officers and ordered the driver to stop. No one dared leave the vehicle for fear of being shot at by one of the officers. Two of them slowly walked around the bus before winding up at the front, where they called out the driver. The driver looked back at Herman to receive directions. Herman, still drunk, hastily told him to go out. There was complete silence inside as everybody looked at the officers with some apprehension. When the driver finally came down, one of the officers asked him what was taking place in the bus. "We, we are just enjoying the festivities like everyone else, sir," he meekly replied.

The other officer then informed the interrogator that the bus was not registered. Hearing this, Herman stormed out of the bus and confronted them. "This is my bus!" he angrily declared. "What do you mean it is not registered? The sticker is right here." For a while, there was silence as Herman showed them where the sticker was on the other side. The officers nodded approvingly when they saw the sticker, and then returned to the front entrance door of the vehicle. They asked Herman if they could go inside. "Why?" he asked, quite startled. "We have not been doing anything wrong." The lead officer simply told him he was going to conduct a search of the bus. "Go ahead," Herman told him. "You won't find any drugs or guns in there." Crowds of people had already been gathering around this scene, as it was unusual to see the police involved in anything other than simple ground patrols at certain sections of the city.

The lead officer went inside and immediately discovered the cooler containing the beers. He picked up one of the beer cans, looked at it, and then continued the rest of his search inside. When he went to the rear, where Gabriel and Mayra were, he gave them a strange look, especially at Mayra. It seemed like he was about to say something to her, since he paused in front of her for a brief moment. But he said nothing and walked away. "What was that about?" Gabriel asked Mayra. "He's a dirty cop," she whispered back. "He was looking down my dress!" The cop returned to the front of the bus and went down to confront Herman. He held up the can of beer for Herman to see. "This is unacceptable!" he told him.

"What do you mean?" Herman asked.

"There is a huge cooler inside full of beer," the officer said menacingly.

"What is the big deal?"

"To distribute and consume alcohol in public, especially on a bus, is against the law."

"Since when?" Herman inquired. "I didn't know that! This has been going on forever during parades and public celebrations. I understand that on a normal day, this is not to be tolerated. But on a day like today, this has always been accepted by the authorities."

"I don't want to get in a conversation with you about this," the officer replied sternly. "The law is the law, and I am going to have to put you and the driver under arrest."

"You've got to be kidding me!" Herman protested. "You are going to actually enforce the law on a day like today. This is ridiculous!" The three policemen proceeded to place hand-cuffs on the two men. They called a squad car over to the scene. Shortly thereafter, a car with lights flashing away, arrived, eliciting a chorus of boos and whistles from the large crowd. The booing and whistling got louder when the two men were being led to the car. However, the crowd cheered boisterously when Herman, like a fallen hero vowing to return, raised his handcuffed hands in the air just before he was pushed into the squad car. As soon as it left, the crowd continued booing and heckling the three policemen. They quickly got on their motorcycles and scooted off.

As soon as the police left the scene, there was a sudden mad dash towards the bus. Several members of the crowd wanted to get at the booze inside. Gabriel and Mayra were stuck inside the bus amid the chaos, as people pushed their way into the bus. The large vehicle then began to rock back and forth with some drunken revelers outside desiring to tip it over. Gabriel immediately sensed the danger and told Mayra they should jump out. A couple others had already done that, so Gabriel offered to help Mayra down. He lifted her up over the side and she then fell the short distance to the ground. Gabriel then climbed over the siding and cautiously fell to the ground, a tricky maneuver with the bus rocking so vigorously.

Landing in a narrow space amid the crowd, Gabriel then looked around for Mayra. She was nowhere to be found. By then, the crowd around the bus had grown larger and rowdier with much pushing and shoving going on. Mayra apparently got swept away by the crowd and Gabriel continued looking for her. He tried finding her amid the crowd close to the bus, but there was no luck. Then he decided to leave the crowd and ventured gingerly to the adjacent sidewalk. He figured Mayra would show up eventually if he waited there. But ten minutes later, there still was no sign of Mayra. "Oh well, it looks like she's gone," he lamented. He left the crazy scene around the bus behind, as indeed a party continued on it like before, only with a different group of people taking over.

It was mid-afternoon and Gabriel was beginning to get tired. He decided to make his way towards his grandmother's. Having walked two blocks down the street, the young American was amazed by the throngs of people congregating and marching along. It was a happy scene, but Gabriel could only wonder about Mayra. "Is she okay?" he pondered. He was about to go back to the scene of the abandoned bus and look for the girl when he stopped himself, figuring it was futile. "She must have just left on her own accord," he thought, concluding dejectedly that the girl had had her kicks with him and moved on.

Gabriel finally put any thoughts of Mayra behind him as he ventured towards his grandmother's. He was still a few blocks away and the traffic was moving very slowly. The youth took the opportunity to take in the scene some more and enjoy it. A smile reappeared on his face as he saw all the happy people around him chanting and singing. "What a glorious sight this all is!" he thought as he was fast approaching his grandmother's. As he crossed a street going west, Gabriel looked to his left for any motorcycles or bikes knifing through the crowds. As he did this, he saw someone familiar in the distance. As he looked closer, he noticed a girl that looked like Sandra. She was walking down the street with some other young man. They were going the other direction. They were holding hands.

The mere sight of Sandra with another man startled Gabriel. Half-crazed, he ran in the direction of Sandra to make sure it was her. As he got close to the couple, he slowed down and eventually settled right behind them. He kept walking behind them and began inspecting the girl directly in front of him. He was not sure it was Sandra, so he continued along. A few moments later, Gabriel decided to stop, not knowing if this girl was indeed his beloved Sandra or not. He preferred it this way. He stood on the sidewalk of the small side street, where there were fewer people. He watched the couple disappear in the distance. He stood there on the sidewalk, trying to come to terms with what he had just witnessed. "That was not her!" he thought desperately. "It cannot be her!" At that point, a man bumped into him from behind, momentarily snapping Gabriel out of his anxiety-riddled thoughts. He then turned the other direction and slowly walked away from this quiet quarter of town.

As Gabriel got back on the main street leading to his grandmother's, the vibrant spirit of the crowds had no affect on him. Such were his feelings of sadness that everything was blocked out. But then he looked ahead and saw Luisa the volcano. The sun was beginning to set behind her. The clear blue sky was now giving way to a canvas of brilliant yellow, red and violet hues. Against this glorious backdrop, the volcano seemed to take on a life of its own, a sight which could have inspired poets to write, painters to paint, and in the case of saddened individuals like Gabriel, to feel hope. Luisa was so beautiful at that moment! The big pine trees on her distant flanks also stood proud and tall, so far away, yet so visible to the youth's yearning eyes. The sight instantly transported Gabriel from the festive streets of Nueva Vida, away from the heartache of having possibly watched Sandra with another man. The timeless beauty Gabriel was observing from the crowded street had a most calming effect on him.

As he slowly walked in the direction of Luisa, Gabriel felt as if the volcano was speaking to him. He felt she was trying to soothe him although he was unable to make out the words. It did not matter at that point. Gabriel could understand the message. There was a *grander purpose* in his life, and it was only a matter now of discovering what it was. Minor romantic setbacks, such as those involving Sandra and Mayra, paled in comparison with this quest for meaning and purpose. Luisa, like a prophet sent from heaven, confirmed that belief to him, and he was able to make it back to his grandmother's a little more happily.

CHAPTER ELEVEN

THE VISITORS

Mayor Juan Carlos Rivera was slumped in a chair in his office after his early morning meeting with his staff, feeling dizzy and weak, when the phone suddenly rang. He jumped out of his chair to answer the phone and was told by his secretary that a couple members of the government had just arrived and wanted to meet with him. When he was informed upon further inquiry that the two individuals were high ranking government officials, the Mayor told his secretary to let them in.

A few seconds later, the two men entered the Mayor's stuffy office. One was dressed in a neat army suit while the other wore civilian clothes. "Good morning, Mayor Rivera," began the man dressed in civilian clothes. "My name is Leonel Perez, Deputy Interior Minister, and this here is Lieutenant Colonel Ricardo Bolan, liaison for the high command of the armed forces." After shaking the hands of both gentlemen, the Mayor politely told his two guests to sit in one of the two sofas in the room. Both refused and continued standing before the Mayor. "What in heaven's name could this be about?" the old patriarch wondered. The Deputy Interior Minister wasted no time in getting things started.

"Mr. Mayor, we were wondering if you would be interested in having some breakfast with us," Perez began. "We have some very important business to discuss. The meal will be our treat. Please be so kind as to come with us." Mayor Rivera cautiously accepted the invitation to eat breakfast with the two mysterious men. He immediately sensed they were in no mood to be refused. The three soon walked out of city hall and entered a shiny, black SUV a block away. Perez took control of the wheel while Lieutenant Colonel Bolan courteously offered the front seat to the Mayor, who gladly accepted. Once inside the vehicle, the two visitors asked the Mayor what restaurant he would like to go to. "*Estrella Norte* would be fine," he replied. "It's just a mile up this street."

"Mr. Mayor, as I said before, we are here to discuss with you some very, very important business," Perez stated once he had the truck moving steadily on the road. "It involves the upcoming visit of Vicente Sanchez."

"What about it?" the Mayor asked.

"Mr. Mayor, there are some serious plans being devised by the higher-ups concerning Mr. Sanchez."

"Oh yeah?" the Mayor asked. "What may they be?"

At this moment, Lieutenant Colonel Bolan lit a cigarette in the back seat. He rolled down the window and threw out the match. Leonel Perez, in the meantime, was struggling to find the right words with which to answer the Mayor's question, impatiently tapping his chin with his forefinger. There was tension in the air. "Well, Mr. Mayor," he spoke at last, "there is a desire by certain high officials in the government to *remove* Mr. Sanchez, if you know what I mean."

"Yeah?" the startled Mayor uttered after a pause, slowly realizing the Deputy Interior Minister meant assassination.

"Yes," Perez affirmed quietly.

"Well, what does that have to do with me?" asked the Mayor.

"*It* will take place here in Nueva Vida," Perez calmly answered while keeping his eyes focused on the road. Both of his hands were now gripping the steering wheel so tightly that his knuckles appeared like white tortoise shells.

"Oh," the Mayor replied in shock. There was silence for about a minute as Mayor Rivera pensively stared out the window. "Well, I don't know if I like that idea," he commented after the lengthy pause.

"What's the problem?" Perez inquired, momentarily turning his head over to look at the Mayor.

"I don't know if I want that to take place in my city," a concerned Mayor Rivera responded. "I can care less about that son of a bitch Sanchez, as I am sure the both of you know. My opposition to him is widely known throughout the country. But I am worried about what will happen to my city and its reputation. I have spent many, many years building up Nueva Vida from scratch. When I took over this city fourteen years ago, there was nothing here but a few cows roaming about. Now, it is the biggest, wealthiest city in southern Colombia. I have worked very hard to build this city up and I don't want anything to ruin that."

"Look, bad things can happen anywhere," Perez reasoned. "You shouldn't have to worry about the reputation of your city being ruined."

"I don't know," the Mayor said. "I would like this operation to take place somewhere else. I strongly feel that this will bring Nueva Vida nothing but terrible problems. I intend to retire soon, perhaps in two years, and I want things to go smoothly until then. I don't want something like that to take place here. There could be riots everywhere. The media will descend upon this town like a swarm of locusts. Then there will be all the investigations popping up." At this point, the Mayor's two guests were growing very frustrated with his objections to the government's proposed plans to murder Vicente Sanchez in Nueva Vida. At this point, the Deputy Interior Minister rashly decided to play the card intended to soften the Mayor Rivera's stiff resistance. "Mayor Rivera, do you, by any chance, know that you are on Sanchez's list of government officials to be tried for corruption when he takes over?"

"What?" the startled Mayor asked.

"Yes," Perez confirmed. "Sources within the government have recently discovered the existence of a list that Sanchez has drawn up which targets corrupt officials throughout the country. Forty-five officials are on the list and you're one of them."

"This is absurd!" barked the angry Mayor. "What evidence does he have?"

"We don't know," the Deputy Interior Minister calmly replied, sensing full well that he had touched a sensitive chord with Mayor Rivera. "All we know is that this list exists and that Sanchez intends on proceeding with these high-profile corruption trials."

"Can I see this list?" the Mayor asked impatiently. "Is there a copy of it anywhere?"

"No, there are no copies of it," Perez answered, keeping his left hand on the steering wheel and freely gesturing with his right to deliver his points. "We know it exists and that Sanchez is planning on using it to gather defendants for these corruption trials. This should be no surprise since he has long been talking about cleaning house. However, if there is no Sanchez, there are no trials. The sooner this can be resolved, the better it is for you and the country. These corruption trials would be a terrible thing for Colombia right now with all the problems swirling around. It would demoralize the nation! Stability is what we need and that pretty much rests squarely on your shoulders, Mayor Rivera. It all depends on if you follow our plan or not."

"I need some time to think about this," the confused Mayor responded.

"What is there to think about?" Perez asked, now really annoyed. "Look Mr. Mayor, your cooperation is needed. I don't understand why you are having such trouble with this. In your case, this should be a no-brainer."

"You should cooperate," advised Lieutenant Colonel Bolan, speaking for the first time. He stretched out from the back seat and placed his hand on the Mayor's shoulder reassuringly. "This will be best for you, your city, and the country," he added in a deep, firm voice after a drag of his cigarette.

Ultimately fearing the tarnishing of his own reputation more than that of the city, Mayor Rivera then posed nervously, "If I go along with this plan, what do you need from me?"

"Not much," answered Bolan reassuringly. "I believe you will be expected to supply very little police security when he visits here. I actually don't know what the exact plans are. Someone will get in touch with you later in the upcoming days to inform you about the specific details of the plan. Until then, you just hang tight and, of course, you wouldn't say a word about this to anyone."

"Well, I don't know about this," the Mayor said, unconvinced.

Lieutenant Colonel Bolan continued persuasively from the back seat in between drags of his cigarette: "Look, we know this is very difficult for you, Mayor Rivera. This is not an easy situation. This is not easy for anybody. We didn't want to have it end up this way. But this is where we're at and this is what we need to do for the sake of the country's stability. We need to take action, but we need your help."

"Fine, you will have my help," the Mayor stated nervously. He was none too pleased.

"If you have no other concerns to express, then we will . . ."

"There is one concern," the Mayor interjected. "I don't want this in any way to be traceable to me."

"You will not have to worry about that," the Lieutenant Colonel replied. "Nothing will be traceable to you."

With that, Perez changed the topic of conversation to the restaurant, specifically its location. The Mayor told him they were very close to it. Within a minute, they reached the restaurant and parked right in front of it. They went in and got a table. There was hardly any conversation between the three individuals and before they could order, Mayor Rivera had to excuse himself. He told Perez and Bolan that he was not feeling well and needed to go home. He ended up taking a taxi back to city hall.

*   *   *

Throughout the morning, all sorts of emotions went through Mayor Rivera. First, there was fear. As already mentioned, he was worried about the possible consequences resulting from the assassination. Then there was aggravation. "What a pain in the ass this will be!" he thought. This was indeed a terrible mess which the Mayor was embroiled in. He had encountered all sorts of problems during his fourteen years in office, but nothing like this. The assassination of such a high-profile figure like Vicente Sanchez, a popular presidential candidate on the verge of winning, was sure to generate trouble. There was no way the Mayor was going to gain anything positive from this and he knew it. Yes, he would not have to worry about Sanchez's corruption investigation. However, he would have to answer an indefinite number of questions connected with the assassination. Police security would only be the tip of the iceberg! He would also have to conduct his own bogus investigation of the crime scene and launch searches for the assassins while maintaining a straight face. Besides all of that, the city would have to be united after such a tragedy, which would be no small feat. The Mayor wondered if he was going to be able to cope with all that pressure. Ultimately, he sensed that the impending events could very well leave his career tarnished in some way.

Lastly for the Mayor, there was rage. The high levels of anxiety and frustration were now leading to an intense feeling of anger. The anger was specifically directed at Vicente Sanchez, his nemesis. As he finished his second glass of scotch in his office, the anger kept mounting. More than ever, he now firmly believed that the source of all his problems since the time of the small corruption scandal in city hall was Sanchez. The discovery of Sanchez's 'list' only confirmed in the Mayor's increasingly delusional mind that the presidential candidate was behind that particular scandal. In fact, he believed Sanchez masterminded all the recent plots against him, including the political opposition against his airport expansion proposal.

"I was right all along!" he thought. "Things have been going badly for me ever since this ingrate first came around." His paranoia and hatred rose to new heights, to the point where he wanted to kill Sanchez with his own hands. He threw the empty glass in his hand against the wall. The usually even-tempered Mayor had lost control of himself. What made him go further over the deep end were thoughts of his family being harmed along the way. "He will go after my sons too!" he yelled inside his office.

In a mad dash, he called police headquarters and ordered them to clamp down on the celebrations taking place outside. When the reasonable head of the police, Luis Sandoval, who was liked by many people in the city, asked him why there should be a clamping down of the celebrations, the Mayor coldly answered that such spontaneous actions by the populace, without the consent of city officials, were illegal. "Are you aware we are going against the will of the people here?" Sandoval asked. This sensible observation enraged the Mayor further, as he cursed and yelled back at his chief of police, telling him how stupid he was for asking such a 'ridiculous' question and asking him, in turn, if he wanted to keep his job. Sandoval replied that he wanted to keep his job, but then posed questions to his boss regarding how the festivities were to be broken up. To this, the Mayor merely responded that the police should do whatever they could to enforce an end to the parades and restore order. This left the police chief utterly puzzled, but he did his best to enforce the Mayor's strange and vague orders.

At first, the police fully intended on breaking up the celebrations. They told people to leave the streets and go back to work. Many people initially followed orders and left the street while the police were there; but when they left, the people went back out to the streets to resume the celebration. In some instances, the officers, looking at the huge crowds, did not even bother issuing the Mayor's crazy orders. After an hour, the police realized their mission was impossible. They were content with just containing the crowds, making sure no violence or destruction of property occurred. When Sandoval, the police chief, heard of this, he was terribly alarmed and angrily ordered his men to start making some arrests. With the arrest of some people, he could at least demonstrate to the Mayor that there was an attempt to restore order.

*   *   *

Herman and his bus driver were among the unfortunate few arrested that day, to be delivered on a platter to the Mayor. Luckily for Herman and the others, the Mayor had lost interest in the matter by the following day, when things reverted back to normal in the city. They were all eventually released. The Mayor had other important things to worry about, like the assassination of

Vicente Sanchez. He was told late that morning by a high-ranking military officer in Bogotá that the plot had indeed been devised for some time and that everything was set. The killers had already been hand-picked and were to be in Nueva Vida the day before Sanchez's arrival. The military officer told the Mayor, just like Lieutenant Colonel Bolan had the day before, that his only task was to supply as little police security as possible so that the assassins could effectively do their job. He told the Mayor not to worry about anything else and that they would be in touch.

This telephone conversation with the military officer left Mayor Rivera feeling a lot easier about the situation. He regained his composure completely and even apologized to his police chief for lashing out at him the day before. The Mayor was under strict orders not to tell anyone, even his closest advisors, of the assassination. This made him feel like the whole affair was out of his hands; not only would things be easy for him, but he also would not even be vaguely culpable. After all, the government was calling the shots, not him. He was just a hapless pawn in this plot, for in the end, Vicente Sanchez was going to be killed with or without him, in Nueva Vida or some other town. So why should he have to lose any sleep over the matter? He was powerless to stop this even if he wanted to. If anything, the government was doing him a terrific favor since Sanchez was an enemy who needed to be done away with.

And even if he was implicated with the murder, that would not be so terrible. Many great leaders throughout the world, past and present, have had some blood on their hands. Besides, the Mayor felt deeply in his heart that the killing of Sanchez would be a service to the country. Colombia would be saved from total anarchy! Most importantly, the old order of things would be preserved, guaranteeing that he and other government officials to be charged with corruption would not have to sit through shameful trials. "What would that do to the morale of the people?" he thought. "How could that be a good thing? It would make us Colombians lose our dignity at a time when we cannot afford to."

Even if the country was in dire straits for the moment, there were other better solutions for ending the civil war and drug trafficking than allow some 'lunatic' to take over. The Mayor was a champion of the system in place, and though it was in terrible shape, he was convinced it could still solve all the country's problems. Concerning the civil war, he believed more money simply needed to be pumped into the army so it can be equipped and trained well enough to take on the guerrillas. If that was not enough, diplomacy could be used to at least halt the fighting periodically in order to provide valuable respites for the troops. Diplomacy had actually been used by the government to end its wars with smaller guerrilla groups in the past, and still could be used in the future. And as for drug trafficking, the system defeated Pablo Escobar and the Medellin cartel a couple years before. So the system can work, provided that everyone is unselfish, patriotic, and on the same page!

In defending the system, Mayor Rivera felt like a true patriot. Even though most of his countrymen were not in agreement with him, he believed they would come to their senses sooner or later. "They are thinking now with their hearts instead of their heads," he thought. "That will change with time." More than ever, he felt good about himself and his country. Being a devout Catholic, he considered the murder of Sanchez to be an evil act in and of itself, but necessary for the common good of the nation. The Mayor had a strong belief in the omnipotence of God and that humans were not free entities. Like ships tied to an anchor, everyone was bound to God, who determined the events that would shape each of their lives. People might do evil things but in the grand scheme of God's plan, they might be good. There was a purpose for everything. It was God's intentions to have goodness conquer all in the end and have everyone welcomed into the kingdom of heaven. Thus, the root of Sanchez's assassination was goodness, for everyone involved with the plot, no matter how despicable they were, would play an invaluable part in carrying out God's plan. The Mayor could not in any way resist God's plan!

It also helped that Mayor Rivera personally disliked the presidential candidate. This only led to further rationalizations serving to protect him from any lingering feelings of guilt and wrongdoing. "He's the one that got himself into this predicament in the first place," he thought in reference to Sanchez. "He's taking on the government, the whole system, and he knows how dangerous that is. So if the stupid jerk dies, that's his fault." These convictions allowed the Mayor to retain his wits and proceed with his life normally. He had nothing to hide for he was serving his country and God to the best of his ability. With this self-righteous mindset, he could calmly face the storm that was about to rock Nueva Vida. Whatever the outcome, the Mayor would never experience fear or shame again if he could help it. He fully intended to continue serving his term with a measure of self-respect and honor. "Let the chips fall where they may," he told himself. "I will try not to lose my cool."

So complete was Mayor Rivera's transformation that he ordered more festivities to take place on the day before Sanchez's arrival. He planned to make speeches for that particular day and, of course, when the presidential candidate arrived. He made a radio address officially announcing Sanchez's visit, in which he declared how great it was for Nueva Vida, and what was being organized for the historical visit. No longer was the Mayor consumed with hatred, as he now was jovial with everyone. Many in his office noticed the change in his behavior right away and considered it to be strange. Nevertheless, they were delighted to see him in better spirits. "Better to work for a happy boss than an angry one," one of them commented.

CHAPTER TWELVE

NO TURNING BACK

In Vicente Sanchez's camp, things were as rocky as ever. His three remaining advisers pleaded with the stubborn presidential candidate not to go to Nueva Vida. They told him the visit was unnecessary with victory all but wrapped up. Above all, they reasoned that Mayor Rivera was a sworn enemy of his, and visiting the town might lead to some trouble. "That's his turf, Vicente," one of them warned. "God knows what might happen to you over there." Sanchez brushed off all the warnings, stating that Mayor Rivera was powerless to do anything against him. His most trusted aid, Jose Xeno, continued to plead with Sanchez about not visiting Nueva Vida. "I don't know, Vicente," he told him. "I have a bad feeling about this."

"What is there to feel bad about?" Sanchez asked. "Mayor Rivera's hands will be tied. The whole country will be watching."

Xeno was unconvinced: "My God, Vicente, you have a short memory, or maybe you have not read enough of our beloved country's bloody history. Nothing will stop these people from killing you if they really want to. By going to Nueva Vida, you arc just making it easier for your enemies. You're entering their territory! You think Mayor Rivera's hands are tied if you go there? That's very naïve."

"Well, you may be right," Sanchez calmly responded. "Perhaps we are entering the dragon's lair. But I am not worried. There have been no death threats of late. If the death threats had continued,

I would be a bit concerned. But we have managed to survive this long, so I am not about to panic now."

"The fact that there have been no death threats in a week worries me even more," Xeno said. "It does not leave me feeling relaxed at all. I find it very strange and ominous." The two other aids were in total agreement with him. "They may just want to give us a false sense of security," one of them added nervously. All these warnings and talk of death threats deeply disturbed the presidential candidate. He unloosened his tie and plopped down onto the couch. They were in a hotel room in Cali, the last stop before Nueva Vida. He was visibly agitated and gave an angry look, his bulging eyes swimming around, surveying the room for answers. He finally exploded. "Oh, I am tired of all this! I am tired of having to worry about every little move I make. If I go to Cartagena, I will be in danger! If I go to Medellin, I will be in danger! If I go to Nueva Vida, I will be in danger! If I stay home, I will be in danger! To hell with all this talk of danger! I am surprised I have not lost my sanity after having listened to all your warnings over the past couple months."

"Vicente, I am sorry but we are only doing our job," a startled Xeno responded, desperately attempting to soothe his boss' frazzled nerves. "We don't want to make you afraid. No, no, not at all! Your life is not at risk at the moment. For all we know, these death threats may not be genuine. But we are only advising you to proceed with caution in case some of these threats are real. Now we had advised you not to travel over the past couple of weeks, but you have done so anyway and it's been fine so far. At present, we are telling you not to go to Nueva Vida because it is hostile ground for us and we have never been there before. We are not the least familiar with the place and that's got us a little bit worried, that's all. We are only communicating our concern to you and you should not, in response, be flying off the handle."

"I am sorry guys," Sanchez said, much calmer after the blowup. "You are right, Jose. I should not be flying off the handle, as you say. I have hired you three to counsel me and that's what you have been doing. In the end, it's up to me to either take your advice or not. I understand I have not been taking some of your advice in recent days, which may have left you guys feeling a little frustrated. Yet, the three of you have been very loyal to me and I appreciate that very much. Excuse me if I sometimes lose my temper, for these have been very stressful days."

"Oh, Vicente, you don't have to explain it to us," Xeno answered. "We know you are going through a terrible amount of pressure. Please don't excuse yourself for this minor blowup."

"I'm glad you understand. There is a lot hanging in the balance right now with the election right around the corner. The last thing I should do is lose my cool. You are right about that, Jose."

"Yes, you can't lose your cool," Xeno confidently suggested. "We, your advisors, also cannot lose our cool, as we are compelled by necessity to analyze things objectively, without a hint of any biases or personal feelings. In order to win this election, we all have to be on the same page. We all have to think in an objective and reasonable manner. That should be the basis of our relationship while we work towards an election victory."

"I could not have said it any better, Jose," the exhausted presidential candidate added. "Without all of your help, I would be completely lost."

"Without you, boss, there would be no hope for this country," one of the advisors said.

"There will always be hope for this country," Sanchez proclaimed. "Whether that hope is realized or not is solely up to the Colombian people themselves."

"Yes, Vicente, the people are a big factor when social changes come about," the cerebral Xeno remarked. "But the people need individuals to lead them. You, Vicente, have been that leader our people needed so badly and, without you, this movement would never have come about. Let's be honest with ourselves, the movement would be unimaginable without you, for you are its personification, its soul. You have brought it to life."

"Oh, stop flattering me so much, Jose!" the humble Sanchez pleaded. "I'm just a regular person like everybody else."

"Yes, we know you, Vicente. You don't like to receive any credit for all the wonderful things you have done."

"I don't like to set myself apart from everyone else, that's all. My destiny is intertwined with the citizens of this country. I am not more special than anybody else. You mention, Jose, that the people need me. Well, I disagree with that. If anything, I need them more than they need me, for they lead me and tell me what do, not the other way around. I am only their chosen representative who communicates their sense of frustration, nothing more. After all, what am I without the people? Nothing at all!"

"Well said, Vicente," Xeno said. "You are a truly noble and selfless man. That's why the people love you so much and why you are the perfect embodiment of this movement. But we now need to make a decision regarding Nueva Vida. Are you going to go or not?"

"I am going."

"Are you sure?"

"Positive."

"Vicente, this visit is not necessary. The people need you. You should not put yourself in a situation that might jeopardize this campaign . . . this movement . . . this hope of the Colombian people. Please reconsider your decision."

"I understand perfectly where you are coming from, Jose," Sanchez replied in a firm voice. "One must act wisely and make good decisions. You don't want anything to get in the way of my election victory. I know for sure that your intentions are good. However, I must reject your advice once again. I am a man of my word. I told the people of Nueva Vida that I would pay them a visit. I cannot cancel this trip after I have given these people my word. What kind of a message would that send to the people of Nueva Vida and the rest of the country? That just because I have victory at hand, I can no longer keep my promises? That when I become president, I'll sit around and do nothing? That's a terrible message! There is no time to bask in the sunshine. Everything is in constant motion and there is always something to do, and I am not going to be resting on my laurels. The people expect me to be continually working on their behalf. So I am going to Nueva Vida to fulfill my duties and promises. There is no turning back."

"Okay, my friend, we will go to Nueva Vida," Xeno solemnly affirmed. With that, Vicente Sanchez and his staff began making arrangements for the trip to Nueva Vida. Xeno immediately placed phone calls to Mayor Rivera's office, informing him that Sanchez would arrive in town on the 26th of October, which was only three days away. They got their plane tickets ready and patiently waited for that day to arrive.

∗   ∗   ∗

In the meantime, Mayor Juan Carlos Rivera calmly organized the city for Vicente Sanchez's arrival. He even had a brief phone conversation with the presidential hopeful, but cut it short lest he began establishing feelings for the man. He did not want to start feeling guilty so soon. "I don't want to know this man more than I have to, especially now in light of what's going to happen," he thought. The official plans for Sanchez's two day visit were already sketched, which included a motorcade tour and rally on the first day, and a farewell ceremony on the second. The Mayor planned on attending only the motorcade procession through the city, which would mark the candidate's arrival. He was not sure about attending the rally later that evening because he neither wanted to show support for this man he so publicly detested nor deflect attention away from his guest. He was going to play that by ear. His deputy, Victor Ascencio, was scheduled to be at the farewell ceremony in the Mayor's place, for he was planning on having his usual Sunday outing with his family. These plans were communicated to Sanchez's camp so they knew more or less what to prepare for in Nueva Vida.

In anticipation of this historic visit, the town was being cleaned and fixed up, as hundreds of city workers and volunteers removed garbage from the streets, trimmed bushes lining thoroughfares, hung posters of Sanchez and the Mayor onto walls and street lamps, and placed barricades in certain areas. The stadium was also being readied for the rally, as seats, loud speakers, lights, and the stage were quickly set in place. The stadium seated about forty thousand people, which city officials anticipated was going to be filled to capacity for the rally. The only hard part for Mayor Rivera during these preparations was estimating the exact amount of police necessary for the visit and where they were to be stationed for patrols. What made things complicated and tricky for him was the knowledge that there was to be an assassination attempt. Yet, the Mayor did not know where and when the assassination was to take place. He was specifically ordered to provide as little police protection for the presidential candidate as possible, but the lack of further details left him scrambling for a definitive plan of action. The Mayor desperately waited for word on the situation from the government, but as of Thursday night, less than two days before Sanchez's arrival, no new information had arrived.

This lack of communication on the part of the government angered Mayor Rivera. "The future of my city and my career are now in their hands and the bastards don't even bother to tell me what's going on," he thought. "What negligence and lack of consideration! No wonder this country is in total disarray." Later that night, his patience ran out. With no further information from Bogotá, he went into action and drew up a plan for police security in the city. He called his police chief, Luis Sandoval, and told him to place most police officers in major street intersections during the motorcade tour, with only two officers on motorcycles traveling with the candidate, one leading the procession and the other trailing. The vital part of the security plan had to do with the stadium. The mayor guessed the assassination attempt would occur wherever Sanchez was going to make a major speech, which was scheduled to take place during the rally in the stadium. He ordered Sandoval to place no more than thirty officers at the site of the stadium during the rally, most of them outside of it to direct traffic on the street and control potential disturbances around the area. When Sandoval asked about the interior of the stadium, the Mayor remarked that only a couple officers should be positioned there since all probable trouble would occur outside.

"What about Sanchez himself?" the police chief asked. "Shouldn't there be any of my men close to him in case of an assassination attempt?"

"No," the Mayor responded confidently, as he was prepared for this obvious inquiry. "I am not worried as much about Sanchez's personal safety as what might happen outside the stadium. The thing I fear most is some sort of stampede or riot occurring outside the stadium. Sanchez will be fine."

Sandoval was satisfied with this observation, as he approved the Mayor's security plan. This made Mayor Rivera feel good for the moment, as he was doing all he could to take care of the loose ends resulting from the government's negligence. It was late Thursday night and there still was no word from Bogotá. "I can't believe they have not informed me of anything!" he fumed in thought. He was impatiently waiting in his office, sitting in his leather chair. The doors were closed as they had been for the previous couple days. He did not want this terrible secret of the assassination plot to be leaked. The anxiety of waiting for word from his fellow collaborators made him grab a pack of cigarettes in his desk. He only smoked during times of crisis and always had a pack stored somewhere in his office in case such moments arrived.

What bothered the Mayor more than anything was keeping this secret to himself. He yearned to talk to one of his intimate friends and advisors about the plot. Above all else, he wanted to complain to someone about the government's folly and negligence in this matter. The Mayor was a terribly social individual who always sought to confide in someone about problems affecting him. But this was one problem that warranted strict confidentiality. He considered calling Victor Ascencio, but decided against it. "God knows how he will react to such news," he thought. Talking to his wife, brothers, or other family members was totally out of the question. Thus, the aging patriarch of Nueva Vida, the most powerful man in that part of the country, felt utterly powerless. His anger and resentment with the government increased with each passing minute without a phone call. He fumed on: "They tell me not to worry even though the plot hinges on what I do. They expect me to draw up the whole security plan without a clue as to when and where the assassins will strike! They tell me not to worry. What a bunch of assholes!"

After finishing his cigarette, he finally left the office. It was close to midnight.

As he walked out of the building and was entering his car in the parking lot, the Mayor was observed by none other than Victor Ascencio. "Juan Carlos!" he shouted from his car, which came to an abrupt stop in the middle of the street. The Mayor turned around, startled, and squinted to see who it was. Ascencio drove up to the parking lot and approached the Mayor. "What in the world are you doing here so late?" Ascencio asked.

"Oh, I fell asleep. I woke up a little while ago."

"The secretaries didn't wake you up?"

"I don't remember . . . Oh, yes they did! At least one of them did. But I guess I continued sleeping."

"Yes, you look very tired my old friend," observed Ascencio, who was a little drunk.

"What brings you over here?" the annoyed Mayor asked.

"I had just left a party. I'm on my way home right now."

"Well, drive safely. I'll see you tomorrow morning."

"Okay, boss."

Ascencio was backing out of the parking lot, when he suddenly asked the Mayor when they were going to play poker again. "We haven't played in a long while," he said.

"I don't know," the weary Mayor replied. "I guess we should make some time for that soon." As he drove away, Ascencio noted how strangely his boss had been behaving lately. First of all, there was the weird meeting about Sanchez's visit, in which he contemplated retirement. Then, there was the attempted crackdown on the street celebrations shortly thereafter, which was followed by a mass release of all offenders from jail and a warm-hearted attitude toward Sanchez's visit. Now, the Mayor was seen leaving his office at a very late hour, something he hardly ever did. "Something is up," the shrewd Ascencio thought.

CHAPTER THIRTEEN

SNATCHED AWAY

Dr. Ricardo Granados was an affable man who got along well with all his students and employees. His genteel and wise demeanor drew many people to him. He was a worldly figure who taught at some fine schools in Colombia and abroad, but settled down in a small city to run a modest sized school. He had a genuine fondness for teaching English and helping others. Despite his elite educational background, Dr. Granados was not the least bit arrogant, which made him all the more popular around the school and community. Many people who knew the professor had advised him to go into politics, but he never considered it. He always thought of politics as a rotten business and was perfectly content directing the language institute, which he considered to be a dream job. Besides, he always believed politics wasn't for him, for he was too private a person for such a life. The thought of going into politics was always there because other people continued making suggestions, telling him he would make a great congressman or senator. He just never took such advice to heart.

Yet, behind the façade of broad smiles and pleasant gestures was a profound sadness deep in the core of Dr. Granados' being. Not everyone sensed this sadness, but Gabriel was one of those who did. The way the professor stood alone in his office, at the rear exit doorway, or end of the second-floor hallway, looking down at the floor or out the window with drooping shoulders, confirmed

Gabriel's suspicions that the professor was sad about something. He eventually would find out what was long tormenting the decent man when the two went out to a local tavern one day. After a couple drinks of aguardiente, the professor opened up to Gabriel and told him a tragic, horrifying tale. It was about his daughter and only child, Sara, and how he lost her to kidnappers.

"It changed my life forever," Dr. Granados explained to his young friend. "It was obviously the worst moment of my life and I really haven't recovered yet. In fact, I don't think I ever will."

"My God, that is terrible!" Gabriel told him. "I am sorry this happened to you, Dr. Granados. Who kidnapped your daughter?"

"We will never know. She just disappeared one day and we never saw her again." The professor went on to tell the whole story of his daughter's abduction and death. According to him, Sara was kidnapped along with five others in February, 1993. She was traveling with her best friend's family to their farm house, which was about twenty minutes outside of Nueva Vida. The only way to get to the farm house was through some isolated back roads, and somewhere along the way, they were stopped by armed men and forcibly taken away. The vehicle, a 1980 Toyota Land Cruiser, was left abandoned on one of the roads, with one of its doors open. Nothing of any value or substance was left behind. The evidence around the scene clearly pointed to a kidnapping.

The abandoned vehicle was located only a couple minutes from the farm house. The back road snaked around a lush valley deep in the Andes, so it was assumed the kidnappers either went down into the valley or up the mountains. It would have been almost impossible to track them down, especially in an area so remote and treacherous. Gabriel's uncle once told him that if a man was to die somewhere outside of Nueva Vida amid the mountains, jungles, and steep ravines, no one would ever find him. Such was the terrain around the area that few people dared to navigate through it without a knowledgeable guide.

The local police informed the professor and his wife, Angela, that they would investigate the matter further. They asked the couple to contact them as soon as they received a call from any kidnappers.

The news of his daughter's sudden disappearance shocked Dr. Granados and his wife. They desperately waited to hear from either Sara or her abductors. They just wanted to know that their little girl, who had just turned 16 a couple weeks before, was still alive. Their hopes were finally answered when one of her abductors called their residence about four days after her disappearance. The professor was informed that Sara was indeed kidnapped, but was otherwise doing fine. No harm had been done to her and she was located in a safe place. After all the anxiety of waiting for any information pertaining to her daughter's whereabouts, the professor was more than delighted to find out she was still alive. He sounded almost thankful about the news, but Dr. Granados' sense of euphoria would come crashing down once the mysterious man on the other line demanded an extremely heavy ransom of twenty million pesos.

"20 million pesos?" the startled Dr. Granados asked.

"Yes."

"That . . . is too much! There is no way I can come up with that kind of money!"

"Well, that is something for you to figure out," the captor replied icily. "If you don't, your daughter will pay the ultimate price."

"How much time do we have?"

"The sooner you come up with the money, the better. Bye."

The phone dropped from the professor's hand, as he stood there motionless, paralyzed with anxiety and dread. His wife, who was so happy moments before, stood alongside her husband crying. These loving parents now encountered a cruel situation of having to save their daughter's life without the actual means of doing it. They gladly would have given up their own lives for her, but were powerless to do anything at the moment. They did not have the money to free Sara. They did not know where she was being held. Lastly, they had no way of contacting the kidnappers. They were left with only two options: figure out a way of gathering as much money as possible or go to the local authorities and report the call. The couple decided to opt for the latter, as they hurried their way toward police headquarters.

*   *   *

When Dr. Granados and his wife arrived at the nearest police station, there were a few people standing in a line at the front desk. Yet, there was nobody tending to them. About fifteen minutes had lapsed and there still was no sign of a clerk. Finally, an angry Dr. Granados walked up to the desk to see if there was someone in the backroom. "Is anybody there?" he yelled at the top of his lungs. "Hello? We have been waiting here for a long time!" With no reply, he went around the room, pounding on the doors of surrounding offices. They were all locked and there were no responses. He then took his wife and walked around the vicinity of the building, looking for anyone who could help them. They managed to find a staircase inside the lobby area leading up to the second floor.

With no sign of security anywhere, the frantic couple raced up the stairs. Not finding anybody in the second floor, they went up to the third floor. Once again, there were no signs of people. "Does anybody work in this place?" the professor asked bitterly. The floor was shaped like an 'L', and not wanting to leave any stone unturned, they went down the hall to check out the other wing. As they made their turn around the corner, Dr. Granados and his wife saw a man walking in their direction. They flung themselves toward him.

"We need your help!" the professor pleaded, weary and out of breath.

"Yes," the alarmed man replied.

"Our daughter has been kidnapped!"

"You will need to go to the investigations office."

"Where is that?"

"That's on the fifth floor."

The two then ran once again towards the stairs and hastily went up to the fifth floor. Much to their surprise, it was teeming with people. The investigations office was not too far down the hall, and upon entering it, the couple was pleased to find there were no lines as a receptionist sat behind a desk and promptly received them. The young woman gave them a warm smile and asked what they needed. Dr. Granados politely asked her if they could see an investigator.

142

She replied that there were no investigators then available and that they would need to make an appointment. This unfavorable reply, along with the anxiety and frustration of losing his daughter to cold-blooded kidnappers and not finding immediate help in the police station, caused the good professor to blow his top. His thin, usually calm face turned red with uncontrollable rage. His dark eyes bulged out from underneath his thick glasses. "My daughter has been kidnapped!" he shouted. "We've been running around this god-damned building, looking for anyone who can help us! We haven't been able to find anybody who can! What kind of a place is this? Where's the sense of decency and responsibility around here for god's sake?"

"I'm sorry, sir . . ."

"Don't sorry me! I didn't come all the way here to be pitied! I came to talk to someone who can help us bring our daughter back!"

"I'll see what I can do," the receptionist said, as she walked out of the office. A few minutes later, she returned with the news that someone would tend to them shortly. While they sat and waited in the room, Dr. Granados apologized to the young receptionist. She kindly told him not to worry about it. "I just hope and pray your daughter is okay and will return to you both," she told them with genuine concern. At that moment, a large, bear-like man in a dark suit and tie came into the office and asked the couple to follow him. They went out into the hall and walked not too far down to another office.

As soon as they entered, the man closed the door and invited the professor and his wife to sit on the chairs facing his desk. He then introduced himself as Investigator Juan Ignacio Parra, shook both their hands, and calmly sat behind his desk. After Dr. Granados told the investigator what happened to his daughter, he was politely asked to provide general information about her. Investigator Parra patiently wrote the information down on a yellow form. This all took about ten minutes, when suddenly the investigator placed the form aside and began asking the stressed couple more questions regarding the disappearance of Sara.

"Now, you say that a man has called you today and claims he has your daughter, right?"

"Yes."

"Okay, what else did he say?"

"He said that Sara is doing fine and that she is in a safe location," replied the teary-eyed Dr. Granados. "He also said that he wants 20 million pesos for her."

"Did he say anything else?"

"No, that was all. The conversation was very brief. He just told me that and hung up."

"Did he, by any chance, provide a deadline for the money?"

"Oh yes, I forgot. I asked him about that and he said the sooner he receives the money, the better."

"Is there anything else that you remember from the conversation?"

"No, that's all."

There was a brief pause as the investigator finished writing the professor's answers on a notepad. Then, he looked up at the ceiling, searching for other questions to throw Dr. Granados' way. He was nibbling at the end of his pen and continuing to look up at the ceiling when he suddenly refocused his attention on the couple sitting before him. He proceeded to ask the professor and his wife a series of questions regarding the place and time of Sara's abduction. The couple went on to describe what they knew of the kidnapping, that it took place about four days before in a remote area twenty minutes outside of Nueva Vida and that the jeep was left abandoned with few things left inside. The investigator continued writing down this information on his notepad, carefully assessing the situation. After Dr. Granados was finished with his testimony, the investigator left the room momentarily with his notepad and form in hand. He returned about ten minutes later and told them that the case of their missing daughter and her friend's family was already on file. He also explained that a preliminary investigation had been taking place, with nothing substantial uncovered yet.

"So, what is the situation then?" asked the professor's wife, Angela. "What are you able to do about the situation?"

This terse question caught Investigator Parra off-guard a bit. "There really is nothing I can personally do at the moment, other than to gather this information, do some research, and wait for any new developments to take place."

"So, there is nothing you can really do for our daughter?" Angela asked, irritated at the investigator's vague reply.

"Mrs. Granados, I can be of help to your daughter, but you have to be patient. I cannot, with the snap of a finger, bring her back from wherever she is. This is going to take some time and we will need to be very patient."

"Well, what exactly are you going to do to bring Sara back?" asked Dr. Granados, whose eyes were bloodshot from lack of sleep. "What will be your plan of action?"

"What we will do over the next week is continue combing through the abduction scene to see if there are any clues or trails of evidence," Investigator Parra calmly explained. "We need to find out who these people are and where they could have gone. We will certainly talk some more with the locals who live around there to see if there were any potential witnesses. One of them might know something about the kidnapping. But I want to let you both know once again that this, unfortunately, may take some time. I do not have a lot of men at my disposal to comb through the area, let alone to conduct a manhunt. Our office doesn't have a lot of resources from which to use in this case, so I am not in a position here to offer you any promises. All I can tell you is that I will do the best I can to bring back your daughter with the resources allotted to me."

"Who do you think has our daughter, Investigator Parra?" Mrs. Granados asked. "Do you think it's the guerillas?"

"Oh, I can't say right now. It certainly could be the guerillas, but it could also simply be a group of criminal bandits. This is not a domain exclusive to the guerillas, which makes kidnapping cases very frustrating. Sometimes, one will never know who the kidnappers actually are, even after the ransoms are paid and the captives are safely returned. The captives usually have no clue who their abductors are because they are not told their identities. Their descriptions of the men usually are not helpful, because they can fit a wide range of people. Some wear army fatigues, others don't. Even if they wear fatigues, that doesn't mean they are guerillas. Without any real confirmation, their identities can never be known. But I will say that the guerillas, in the case of your daughter, are suspects for sure."

"Do you think these people will kill Sara?" a teary-eyed Mrs. Granados asked.

"I don't know, but these types of kidnappings sometimes end in death if the ransoms are not paid."

"Well, they expect us to pay them 20 million pesos!" Dr. Granados angrily stated. "I don't even come close to having that kind of money!"

"That is their initial demand," the investigator said, attempting to ease the fears of his clients. He moved his big paw of a hand in slow little circles through the air as he talked, which had a calming effect on the professor and his wife. "If they sense more or less what you're worth, they will work their way down from the initial demand, sometimes very far down. What you have to do is be frank with them, and simply tell them you don't have the money. You cannot show any fear. You have to be straightforward with them. I can't stress that enough."

"That sounds easier said than done," Angela said, as she was holding a handkerchief to wipe away the tears constantly streaming down her face. "We will be bargaining with these criminals over the fate of our daughter. This is not like going to some auction to buy merchandise. Our child's life is at stake!"

"I understand that your daughter's life is at stake. I know this won't be easy, but you both have to be cool and firm with these kidnappers! You guys can't give in to fear because they will take advantage of that and use it against you. They will milk every peso from that fear and make it harder for you, so please be cool and firm with them. I have been involved with kidnappings before, and I know some of their tactics. I know what works with them and what doesn't. You have to realize, first of all, that these people don't consider your child to be a human being. They only consider her to be a mere object . . . a means to an end. Whereas with you, this is a struggle over the life of a loved one, with the kidnappers, it is like a business transaction. Their main tactic involves scaring people, and they use that fear to get what they want, which in the end, is ransom money. Yet, one must *always* remember that the kidnappers are never in total control of the negotiations. The captives' families are actually in control because they are the ones who have the money! That's what nobody ever realizes! People always want to believe the kidnappers are in control of these situations and that the families are powerless victims, but that is the wrong way of looking at it. Both of you have something that they want, so you have to dictate terms to them, and place the ball on their court."

"But this is not a game!" Mrs. Granados declared. "My daughter's life is at stake!"

"If you think that way, Mrs. Granados," the investigator replied just as passionately, "and you give way to fear, I guarantee you will lose Sara! I have seen too many families lose their loved ones because they were gripped with fear. What this fear does is make the families act more desperately and carelessly than they should, which endangers their loved ones. When the kidnappers call again, which they will for sure, you will simply tell them the truth, which is that you *don't* have the money. You don't get angry with them, threaten them, or ask too many questions. Let them ask the questions, to which you give simple, honest replies. If they sense you are honest, they will work with you and seek a quick resolution to the situation. Is that understood?"

This advice had very much satisfied Dr. and Mrs. Granados, and they thanked the investigator. They asked him if he was in charge of the case, and he told them that he was. This made the couple very happy because they felt they were now in good hands. The investigator gave the professor and his wife his card and instructed them to call him immediately after they talk with the kidnappers again. "Until then, we will keep in touch and I will let you both know if there are any new developments."

*   *   *

Investigator's Parra's advice seemed simple enough: be honest and straightforward with the kidnappers. His advice would soon be put to the test when the kidnappers, as expected, called again a couple days later. The kidnappers made the same request of twenty million pesos. "I am sorry, but I don't have that kind of money," the professor replied. The man on the other line then threw a curve ball, which surprised Dr. Granados. He reminded the professor that he was the director of a large school. He could acquire the twenty million pesos by asking his students for money. Dr. Granados was a bit stumped by the suggestion, and he thought about it a little. He then flatly told the kidnapper that he would not drag other innocent people into the situation. "I will not do that," he firmly told the kidnapper. The kidnapper asked the professor if he was sure, informing him at the same time that a machete was lying nearby his sleeping daughter. This horrifying image alarmed the professor, as he momentarily lost his composure. But he emerged securely from that feeling of terror once he remembered Investigator Parra's advice about being cool and firm, and he reiterated his initial answer. "No, I will not do that," he said. "I refuse to drag other innocent people into this."

"Are you sure about that?" the mysterious man asked one more time.

"Yes, I am sure."

There was a brief pause thereafter, during which time the kidnapper could be heard conferring with someone else over the phone. The man soon returned to the phone and requested five million pesos. Dr. Granados again responded that he did not have that amount of money. "We will talk later," the man said before abruptly hanging up the phone. The professor, as instructed, called Investigator Parra immediately, and told him what had just happened. The detective was ecstatic, telling Dr. Granados he conducted himself perfectly. "Now, they have dropped their demand from twenty million pesos to five million!" he happily told him. "You see! You were cool under pressure, you did not give way to their demands, and now you have them sweating!"

Parra went on to tell Dr. Granados that the kidnappers would continue lowering their demands as long as he remained firm. The investigator also told the professor that nothing had been uncovered around the abduction scene, but he would continue combing through the area and talking to locals for another week. Dr. Granados and his wife were certainly happy about these turn of events, and were confident their daughter would return to them. They were appreciative of the investigator's help and considered him to be indispensable in their efforts to bring her back.

The Granadoses, for their part, would continue doing the little things to save Sara. They would help search for clues around the abduction site along with the other investigators, which involved grueling hikes up and down the mountainous area. They wondered how their daughter could ever be found in such a rugged area. "Just to search one mountain," the professor remarked wearily, "would take a month. There are literally dozens of mountains in this area!" They also talked to the locals, asking them if they had witnessed the abduction of Sara and her friend's family, or had seen them lately. They carried photographs of her and showed them to the people, to no avail. They posted messages on the lampposts and walls of the village, imploring witnesses of the kidnapping to contact the police. The Granadoses also went to church every morning, praying for things to end well. If there was nothing else to do, the couple waited patiently for the next phone call.

*　　*　　*

The call came soon enough. But nothing could have prepared Dr. and Mrs. Granados for what they were about to be told. They were coldly informed that Sara was dead. "What?" the shocked professor asked.

"She died last night," the mysterious man said matter-of-factly. "She got sick late yesterday afternoon, and died within a few hours." For a minute, the professor did not say anything. The kidnapper told him Sara's death caught everyone by surprise, since it was initially believed the illness was not serious. "When we realized it was serious, it was too late to do anything." There were no apologies or offers of condolences. After a prolonged silence, Dr. Granados finally asked where he could recover the body. He was told the body was left behind. "We had to leave the area lest we got infected with the strange disease," the man explained. "We could not tell you where the body is." With that, the man abruptly hung up.

Dr. Granados refused to believe his beloved daughter was dead. He quickly called Investigator Parra to inform him of the news, and was anxious to know how he would interpret it. He was desperately hoping the kidnapper was just bluffing, that the news of Sara's death was a part of the whole scheme to get more money. However, Parra would quickly shoot down those unfounded hopes. He told Dr. Granados that the kidnappers were probably telling the truth, since there was no need for them to be lying about the girl's death. "It just would not make any sense for them to be lying about something like that," he reasoned.

Parra went on to explain that the phone call was indeed strange. "Rarely do kidnappers go out of their way to inform a family that their loved one had died unless it's to demand a ransom for the body," remarked the puzzled detective. After some thought, Parra concluded that there may have been a purpose to the call. He guessed that the kidnappers, through revealing the news of Sara's death, were attempting to put more heat on the families of the surviving captives to pay up. "It's still bizarre," the investigator admitted. "Maybe they felt bad about the whole thing and wanted to let you know personally. It might have been as simple as that, especially if they didn't demand money from you. This, however, is unusual behavior for kidnappers, very odd indeed."

The professor was forced to realize that his daughter was probably dead, but he did not lose hope entirely for another month. He waited for the kidnappers to call him back to explain there was a mistake or hoax, and that Sara was indeed alive. He dreamed several times about her appearing on the front steps of the house one day, after having escaped from her kidnappers, and leaping into his arms. She would be immediately fed, showered, and consoled in such dreams. After a brief period of recovery, she would be readied for school. She would have had so much to live for.

Alas, there was no phone call. The kidnappers would never be heard from again. Sara was dead, he would finally admit to himself. Five weeks after Sara's reported death, the ransom money for the remaining captives was paid off by a group of relatives, and they were subsequently released. The family of five immediately met up with Dr. and Mrs. Granados, and they confirmed their daughter's death. Everything the kidnappers had said about Sara dying suddenly from a strange disease turned out true. They went on to tell the couple that the girl was hastily buried in a wooded area not too far from Nueva Vida. Unfortunately, they could not remember the exact location of the grave for they were constantly on the move and blindfolded much of the time. This spurred the couple to go looking for their little girl's body, as they gathered a group of friends to help in this incredibly difficult mission. The professor and his wife wanted to give Sara a proper burial, as they dreaded the thought of her buried in an unmarked grave in some remote location. "I don't want my baby to be alone!" Mrs. Granados would cry hysterically. After three unfruitful days of intensive searching through the mountainous area, however, the couple gave up.

Sara's sudden death and missing body would haunt her unfortunate parents. It was a terrible blow, especially for Mrs. Granados, who would never be the same again. Whereas her husband would continue working at the language institute and recover some pieces of his shattered life, Angela Granados would stay inside their house much of the time, mourning the loss of her daughter. She would be bedridden for days. It got so bad that the professor contemplated sending her to the hospital to receive psychiatric treatment. He even threatened to leave her at one time, so frustrated he was with her. But he chose to stay by his wife's side during those tough times, hoping she would slowly emerge from her depression.

"So that's my story," the professor told Gabriel in the bar.

"How's your wife these days?" the somber youth asked.

"She's better," Dr. Granados answered. "She now clings on to the hope that she will be reunited with Sara in heaven. She has rediscovered her faith in God and is starting to go to church again. That has helped her immensely. After almost three years, I feel we are getting better."

CHAPTER FOURTEEN

A DAY WITH PUMA

On the morning of Friday, October 25th, Gabriel was returning from the language institute, where he collected his paycheck. As he walked down the street, he noticed a certain buzz in the air. Even though Fridays were usually busy, there was more activity than usual on this particular morning. The unusual sight of several police officers appearing together in street corners or riding past on their motorcycles was the most obvious indication that something was afoot. Gabriel had never seen so many police officers around and about in Nueva Vida before. The streets were bustling with people passing out leaflets, hanging up posters, and sweeping the sidewalks. Gabriel was not only aware that the elections were a couple weeks away, but that Vicente Sanchez was visiting Nueva Vida the following day. The proud people of this city were getting ready for this historic visit.

The gangly American was passing through a street corner when he saw Puma, in his usual red jumpsuit, walking in his direction and waving at him. The semi-retired civil servant asked Gabriel if he wanted to help him for a short while putting up posters of an old friend who was running for alderman. The youth gladly obliged and they both walked over to Puma's car, which was only a block down the street. They both got in the car, which was an old Renault 4 sedan, and sped off to collect the posters.

The drive was a treat for Gabriel, as he enjoyed watching Puma maneuver the little, old car through the narrow, congested streets. His rough, big hands would pull and push the odd console mounted stick to and fro with some difficulty, causing a loud thud whenever the gears shifted. "You certainly don't have cars like these in the States," the youth thought. In one moment, the old man would angrily honk at the slow-moving traffic ahead of him, cursing loud enough for everyone in the vicinity to hear him; while in the next, he would be shaking hands with some acquaintance walking by, a broad smile replacing a mean growl in an instant. Puma gave the impression he knew the town like the back of his hand, and it thrilled Gabriel to see this man operate in his turf, his environment.

The retired civil servant drove deep into the congested heart of Nueva Vida, just south of downtown. The area was by no means attractive with all the little stores tightly bunched together and litter strewn all over. This was a rough part of town with shady, scheming men staked out in front of their stores and haunts, looking for easy money to walk by. Gabriel made sure his paycheck was securely folded into his wallet, and that it was deep in his pants pocket. He did not want to leave anything to chance in such a neighborhood. Puma finally parked the car right in front of a three storey office building. "Perfect parking!" he declared.

The two made their way inside the building, as they entered a large, empty lobby. Puma walked into a backroom. He noticed Gabriel halted just beyond the entrance and encouraged him to follow him inside the backroom. "Come on," he told him. "There's nothing to worry about." To the youth's surprise, the backroom led to a rather large warehouse topped by a glass ceiling. There were about a dozen people working inside. Two cars were parked off to the side along with three large loading machines. Two huge crates were sitting at the rear of the warehouse, beside an entrance large enough for a semi-truck to go through. "What the hell do they do in this place?" Gabriel immediately wondered. Puma asked the first man he saw if he had the posters. The man, slender and with a cigarette sticking out of his mouth, went behind a desk and retrieved the rolled-up posters. "There should be about fifty in there," the man said.

"Good!" Puma said. "Then I'll be going."

"Wait!" the thin man called out. "The boss wants to see you upstairs."

Puma seemed a little startled. "Am I in trouble?" he asked. Puma then told Gabriel to go with him as they walked toward a spiral staircase in the back of the warehouse. From both sides, one could see the windows and doors of other offices on the two floors above with balcony walkways connecting them. They went up the staircase to the second floor and walked over to a nearby room. The door of the room was slightly open and Puma gave it a quiet, respectful knock. "Come in!" barked someone from inside. The room was rather large and a short, heavy-set man was sitting behind a desk in the back corner. He was wearing a white dress shirt with gold cufflinks and a navy blue tie. His graying hair, perfectly combed to the back, topped off the neat appearance.

He was talking on the phone and motioned his two visitors to sit on the two seats facing him. He soon hung up the phone and began addressing his visitors. He first inquired about Gabriel, since he had never seen him before, and Puma happily introduced the two. The man's name was Alfonso Costa and he was mildly interested in Gabriel's background. "I have always wanted to go to the United States but never had the chance," he said upon introduction. "Maybe I'll go there sometime before I die." Mr. Costa, who seemed somewhat harried, then quickly turned his attention to Puma and requested some favors from him. He handed him an enclosed envelope. "I just need for you to give this to Jaime."

"Okay, boss."

"I also need for you to tell him to meet me here at six, all right?"

"He is at his house, right?" Puma asked.

"Yes, he should be there. If not, try him at his brother's restaurant. If you can't find him anywhere, try him later this afternoon."

With that, Puma and Gabriel left for the home of Jaime Calderon. Gabriel soon found out that Calderon was the man who was running for alderman, and whose posters they were going to hang up throughout town. Puma did not seem too happy about having to run around as a messenger. He was not talkative during the short drive to the house except when he complained of his predicament once they entered his car. "First, they want you to hang up posters and deliver leaflets. Now, they have me working as a delivery boy. What do they have lined up for me next? Shining shoes?" Gabriel could not understand what Puma was doing. The man was supposed to be retired and yet he was performing all these strange services for this mysterious Alfonso character. Gabriel originally thought Puma was just helping some friends during the elections. The youth now learned it was something more than just helping friends as Puma seemed to be entangled in some murky operation. He was about to ask about this but stopped short of doing so, lest Puma got irritated further. "It's not really any of my business," he thought, and left it at that.

Things got stranger when the two arrived at Calderon's house. The man was at his house and he gruffly invited Puma and Gabriel inside. Like Alfonso Costa, he was short, plump, and dapper in appearance. The man knew Puma was there to hand over the envelope and asked for it as soon as they entered. Puma reached into his pocket, took out the envelope, and gave it to him. In front of them, Calderon opened up the envelope and took out what appeared to be a check. He looked at it and immediately became enraged. "How in the world does that imbecile expect me to win the election with this meager amount of money?!" he demanded to know, waving the check in the air as though it was toilet paper. He was yelling from the top of his lungs. The two maids inside the lavish living room scurried away. "Is this how that fat crook treats me after all the favors I have done for him over the years? I knew this was going to happen! I knew he was going to give me nothing!"

"Perhaps, Jaime," Puma quietly chimed in, "he will give you more money in the coming days."

"More money in the coming days, you say? Hah! Puma, the both of us know him damn well. We both know how he operates. He doesn't count his chickens before they hatch. He probably feels that I will lose against my opponent, so he gives me this meager amount. If he felt I had a real chance of winning, then he would have given me more. That's how he treats all the other candidates of the Mayor's party. He only gives money to those who have a chance of winning. But what he doesn't understand is that I have a chance of beating my opponent! The people are not happy with this guy. It just doesn't make any sense. Maybe he knows something that I don't."

"I agree with you, Jaime. The people in this district are not at all happy with Suarez. You really have a shot at winning. In fact, I think you're going to win easily. Costa must not be reading your race correctly. He's probably miscalculating the whole thing."

"No, I think he's calculating it correctly. He knows what he's doing. He's no fool."

"Well, I think he's a fool to think you're going to lose to Suarez."

"Whatever the case may be, he has only given this piddling amount!" Calderon declared angrily. He then held the check up in the air and began tearing it up into tiny pieces, dumping it all over the floor. "I refuse to speculate more on the matter."

"There is also one more message I need to give you," Puma said, stuttering a little. He seemed to be bracing himself for yet another tirade from Calderon.

"What's that?"

"Costa wants to meet with you at six this evening."

"No way in hell will I meet with him!" Calderon roared. "In fact, I have an idea!" The man called for the maids to come into the room and rudely demanded they pick up all the pieces of the check on the floor. "Hurry it up!" he yelled at them as they slowly began collecting the small pieces of the check. After every piece had been picked up and given to him, Calderon placed it all inside the envelope and handed it to Puma. "Here! Give this back to that imbecile and tell him to shove it up his stingy ass! Tell him I don't need him or his money!"

"Are you sure?" the weary Puma asked.

"Yes, I am sure! That money won't make a difference. I might as well just run this campaign on my own!"

With those words, Puma and Gabriel quickly departed for Alfonso Costa's office. "I hate this," the displeased Puma muttered in the car. He said nothing else while on their way to the office. He was too busy honking his horn at the cars in front of him, trying to move traffic along. The irritated, old man pushed and pulled on the gear stick so hard, the youth thought it was going to be yanked off the dashboard. Yet, the strong, little Renault finally made its way to the office building in one piece. There were no legal parking spots available in front of the building, so Puma chose to illegally park his car a few feet off to the side of the entrance, halfway onto the sidewalk. "We'll be here only for a short while, hopefully," he told Gabriel. They went inside the building, walked through the warehouse in the back, climbed up the stairs to the second floor, and marched over to Costa's office where the door was open. Puma, with his characteristic toothpick sticking loosely out of his mouth, walked in and handed Costa the envelope.

"What, you could not find him?" asked Costa, who was puffing away at a cigar while sitting behind his small, simple desk.

"No, I found him," the out of breath Puma replied in between puffs of air, "but he did not accept your check."

"What? What do you mean?"

"He said there was not enough money. He claims he needs much more money to win the election. Quite frankly, he was very upset."

"Very upset?" the angry Costa wondered. "Why, that fat ingrate should be grateful I gave him that amount of money! There's easily more than enough in here for him to win the election. That good-for-nothing bum! I have bailed his ass out of so many jams in the past and this is how he treats me? By throwing my money back into my face? He's a heavy favorite to win his race and if he can't with this amount of money, he truly is an idiot! After all, from what I know, Suarez is despised by his constituents." Gabriel was so humored by this situation, he was about to break out in hysterical laughter before biting hard on his own tongue. He certainly did not want to laugh aloud during that tense moment.

"Well, Jaime thinks he's got a good chance to win," Puma said, "but he actually thinks the race is close, or at least close enough to require more financial support from you."

"No, he is not going to get any more money from me! I am going to give him a call right now and tell him to meet with me at six."

"He said he is not going to meet with you," Puma informed the flustered Costa. "He says he is going to go his own way and run the campaign himself."

"Why, that idiot," the portly Costa muttered, as tiny beads of sweat were rolling down his forehead. He got up from his chair and began pacing the room, taking a couple of deep puffs of his cigar. The room had a strange odor, as the scent from the cigar and Costa's cologne were doing battle within the confined space. As he paced the room, Costa opened up the envelope and noticed his check was torn into pieces. "What's this?" he inquired with much surprise, dumping all the pieces of the check onto his desk. Then, to the utter astonishment of Puma and Gabriel, he began laughing hysterically. This prompted Puma and Gabriel to laugh along with him for quite some time. "Oh, that's funny!" remarked the red-faced Costa, as he was beginning to lose his breath from so much laughter. "That idiot never fails to humor me!"

When the laughter finally died down, Costa sat back down behind his desk and rewrote another check. "He should be satisfied with this," he told Puma, showing him the check, then stuffing it inside the envelope "Tell him not to worry about the meeting at six. I'll talk to him later." He gave Puma the envelope and dismissed him and the dazzled Gabriel. Just when they exited the door, Costa called them back. As they came back, he offered Puma and Gabriel each a cigar. "These are Cubans! I know you Americans love them. I have a ton of them. One of my friends goes there once a year and keeps giving me boxes of these cigars. They're wonderful! Please take these!" Puma and Gabriel gladly accepted the offer.

The two then headed off for Jaime Calderon's house with the check and cigars in hand. At that moment, Gabriel felt like he was partaking in some clichéd scene from a mobster film. It was so very strange and shady, with all the transactions involved. On their way to the house, Puma declared the trip would be the last for the day. "If he doesn't take the check this time," he stated, "I will tell him to drive his fat ass over to Costa and give it back himself. I'm tired of this already! I'm nobody's slave!"

When they arrived at the house, Calderon seemed a little annoyed at first but quickly understood his two visitors were probably bringing him good news. He then cordially invited the two inside and asked Puma why he had returned. Puma told him that Costa had decided to provide more money for his campaign after all, and handed over the envelope. Calderon took the check out of the envelope, observed it, and smiled broadly. "Now, that's more like it!" he declared enthusiastically. "This amount will allow me to win!" The jubilant man invited his guests to a cup of coffee. When Puma refused, Calderon began pleading. "Come on Puma, have a cup of coffee while you are here. We have not had a good talk in such a long time. Stay here and tell me what's going on with you. Tell me who this friend of yours is."

"Well, I am doing fine," Puma replied half-heartedly. "Nothing has really changed in my life. Just keeping my head above the water, you know. This here is my friend from America, Gabriel. We met on the street one day. He's a very nice kid. Anyway, thanks for the invitation, but we must really be going."

"Are you sure?"

"Yes, but thanks anyway."

"We must get together and have a good talk, my friend," Calderon cheerily told Puma, "just like the good old days. Feel free to stop by." As they were walking out of the door, Calderon called Puma over, took out a wad of cash from his pocket, and gave some of it to him. "Take this," he told him. Puma's protests over accepting the money fell on deaf ears, as his old acquaintance emphatically told him to leave with the cash. As they walked out of the house, Gabriel noticed a smile on Puma's face, his first of the day. Once inside the car, he gave the youth some of the kickback money. "That should last you a couple weeks," he said with a wink of the eye. Gabriel counted exactly ten thousand pesos in his hands. He now understood why the old man went through all the trouble to serve these people.

* * *

Puma and Gabriel went to a café right after they left Jaime Calderon's house. "We need to go somewhere to relax and enjoy these Cuban cigars," Puma told his young friend. They went to a small café not too far away from Dr. Granados' language institute. It was right across the street from Nueva Vida's biggest park, the Parque Infantil. Many people were strolling around inside the park while others were napping on the benches. It was almost noon, which marked the beginning of a lengthy siesta break for most residents of Nueva Vida. Even though Vicente Sanchez's historic visit to the city was to take place the following day, most people stopped working and went home. Everything took a back seat to this time-honored break during the middle of the day.

As soon as Puma and Gabriel arrived at the café, they ordered a couple aguardientes and lit up their cigars. This was indeed a moment of triumph for them. They earned a good amount of money in two hours by just delivering messages. The whole ordeal was a real eye-opening experience for Gabriel, which further aroused his curiosity. Who exactly was Alfonso Costa? What did he do for a living? What were people doing at the warehouse? How did Puma know Jaime Calderon? The mesmerized American was dying to ask Puma these questions and felt the time was perfect. When Gabriel fired away with his first question regarding Costa, Puma hesitated a bit. Gabriel was not sure if his friend wanted to answer the question or knew how to go about answering it. The old man looked straight ahead, his keen, tiny black eyes betraying cool reflection. The cigar smoke swirled around the dark, weathered face of Puma, making him appear like some Indian shaman. The sight would have made a poet happy.

"Is he some sort of mobster?" Gabriel asked eagerly.

"No, he's a businessman," Puma finally answered. "He has no ties to the cartels from what I know."

"What business is he in?"

"He's made most of his money in distribution. He's also involved in real estate."

"What does he distribute?"

"All sorts of goods: foods, cosmetics, clothes, toilet paper, you name it. He's got a fleet of about thirty trucks that are sent all over the region. You probably have seen these trucks. You can't miss them. They are all colored bright green. The name of the company is Hatuelongo Ltd."

"Yes, I have seen those green trucks," Gabriel affirmed. "They are all over the place! It must be a lucrative business."

"It certainly is."

"By the way, what does Hatuelongo mean?"

"Hatuelongo was a local Indian prince who died fighting the Conquistadores," Puma replied after taking a puff of his cigar. "He has become a mythical hero in this area."

"That's interesting. I have never heard of this man."

"You haven't heard of him probably because you haven't lived here long enough. He became a hero by saving hundreds of his own people. By fighting the Conquistadores with some of his men and keeping them at bay, he allowed most of his tribe to escape into the jungle. The battle took place a little east of here. He was killed in the battle."

"Is he buried anywhere around here?" the intrigued Gabriel asked.

"His body never has been found," Puma responded.

"That's sad. At least Costa has kept Hatuelongo's name and legacy alive through his company."

"That has angered some people because they consider such use of Hatuelongo's name, for the sake of profit, to be disgraceful."

"As for Costa, how did he get involved in politics and what is his role?"

"Costa is an old friend of Mayor Rivera. He is one of Rivera's moneymen. He helps oil his machine, as they say."

"So, he gives money to Rivera and his party," Gabriel inquired after puffing on his cigar.

"Yes, I would say that is correct," Puma answered. "Of course, Costa does not do this for nothing. Rivera helps Costa's businesses in return. He has allowed, for instance, Costa to monopolize the entire distribution market in the city. Nobody is allowed to compete with him. That has allowed Costa to become very rich. They both really scratch each other's backs."

"So, what we saw today was an instance of Costa offering his help to Mayor Rivera."

"Yes, because Calderon is a member of the Conservative Party. A victory for Calderon will be a victory for the Mayor."

"In the United States," Gabriel went on to explain, "we have a term for people like Costa: political boss. These men are not politicians themselves, but they are wealthy and donate a lot of their money and time to a particular party, ensuring its survival. Within that party, they are very powerful and influential."

"I would say that fits the description of Costa pretty damn well," Puma remarked with a wry smile.

"How did you know Costa?" the youth asked Puma with some reservation. He sensed these questions were annoying the old man to some extent. After all, Puma just wanted to relax for a while and have a light conversation over some booze and cigars. The last thing he wanted to do was talk about his own complicated life. But Gabriel could not help himself, so fascinated he had become of these shady figures running Nueva Vida. Puma took another sip of aguardiente and looked at his long Cuban cigar for a brief moment. The brown leaves of the cigar seemed to have a calming effect on him. He realized there was nothing wrong with giving his young friend some background information about himself. "I actually knew Costa through Calderon," Puma finally replied. "I eventually became his chauffeur."

"You were his chauffeur?" Gabriel asked.

"Yes, I was his chauffeur for about seven, eight years," the old man responded somewhat embarrassed. "Then I retired about three years ago, and have since worked for him once in a while, doing odd jobs. It never hurts to earn more money, especially when one's retirement package is as meager as mine. Costa, though, is a strange cat. I have worked for him for a good number of years, but I really can't say I know him well. I think that's odd because chauffeurs usually get to know the men they work for very well, since they are with them a lot of the time. But he has always kept some distance between himself and his employees. He probably feels things will be easier for him if he doesn't know the people who work for him too personally. I can't fault him for that."

"I noticed he did not pay you for what you did today," Gabriel said.

"Oh, he will later. The good thing about him is he pays well. That is why I have not been able to retire completely. I can't complain about my life right now. I have been fortunate."

"Do you like the guy?"

"I can't say I really like the guy, but I also can't say I hate him either. The man is a smooth operator. He is wealthy and powerful. He has his way of doing things, which may not make some people happy. You can't always make everybody happy, you know."

"How did you know Calderon?"

"I have known him for a long time. We worked together at City Hall in the sanitation department. We were both clerks. We worked together there for twenty years until he moved up the ladder and worked for the Mayor. That was about ten years ago. Once he moved up to be one of the Mayor's assistants, he became very big-headed. He became a big shot. He never talked to me again really. It was as if he had never known me. Whenever we passed each other in the street or in City Hall, he would just wave and say hello, nothing else. Sometimes, he would say nothing at all!"

"I noticed you weren't too happy to be in his house," Gabriel noted.

"No, I wasn't too happy to be there," Puma agreed. "I don't care for people who aren't genuine. This guy was a pretty good friend of mine for a long time and then suddenly refused to even acknowledge my presence. However, I am pleased he did give me some of that money today. I guess that was a nice gesture. Perhaps, he feels a little guilty about how he has treated me in recent years and wants to make amends."

"Yes, he did invite you to go over there whenever you wanted."

"Well, if he wants to salvage the friendship, he can call me up. I certainly won't be going over there, knocking on his door unannounced."

"What kind of work did Calderon do for the Mayor?"

"He has been his accountant. His big job was handling the city budget. Calderon was always a great mathematician. He did very well."

"How did he get the job?"

"Ten years ago, the city budget kind of spiraled out of control. Someone was needed to help make sense of the situation. The men running the city's finances at the time were complete idiots. They were the Mayor's cronies, many of whom had no qualifications whatsoever in administering the city's economy. These people could not even do simple first grade math. It was ridiculous! Calderon had a bachelor's degree in accounting and had done a good job managing the budget of the sanitation department. Our boss put in a good word for him to the Mayor and, from what I've heard, was hired on the spot a couple minutes into the interview. To Calderon's credit, the city has experienced no fiscal problems since."

"So now he wants to run for alderman," Gabriel commented while Puma was ordering another round of aguardiente shots. The strong, licorice-flavored liqueur was putting the old man in a rather relaxed mood. He seemed now very comfortable talking about his old friend and the backroom politics he was so familiar with. He was letting everything go—all the secrets, frustrations, and fears that loomed large over much of his life. "Yes, he now wants to run for alderman," Puma told the youth. "He wants a change of scenery, I guess."

"Do you think Rivera asked him to run for alderman?" Gabriel asked.

"I think it was a mutual thing. Rivera absolutely adores Calderon. He thinks very highly of him and with good reason. He saved his butt ten years ago. Rivera probably believes Calderon will strengthen his political base in the south side of the city if he becomes alderman of the seventh sector, which is quite large. Rivera feels his support in the south has slipped a little, so he needs a trusted guy there to whip things back into shape. Meanwhile, Calderon, from what I've heard, would love to succeed Rivera as mayor. The alderman's seat would make the ideal stepping stone. He knows he needs to get his feet wet in politics if he wants to be mayor in the future. So, running for alderman makes perfect sense for Calderon and the Mayor as well."

"Do you think Calderon will be the mayor one day?"

"It's possible. But there are a couple things going against him. First of all, Calderon is old. He is around my age. He must be at least sixty. He doesn't have much time left. He needs for Rivera to retire soon, but nobody knows when that will happen. He may be there for another ten years for all we know! Time, therefore, is working against Calderon. Nueva Vida is also getting younger by the day, as most people who have moved over here recently tend to be young. These people will not want to vote for an older guy to be mayor. They will want someone younger. Another problem for Calderon is the competition he will face if he ever decides to run for mayor. The list of potential candidates as it stands now is incredibly long. And many of these candidates would have more experience, influence, and money than Calderon. Even if he wins the alderman's seat, I would still consider him a long shot to be the next mayor of this town at this point."

"Have you ever met Mayor Rivera personally?" the inquisitive Gabriel asked as he continued sipping his second glass of aguardiente.

"Yes, I have met him on several occasions in City Hall. But we don't know each other personally. I hear he is a real jerk. Someone told me once that he doesn't even know the names of his own secretaries! Can you believe that? In this way, he is kind of like Costa. They are very stand-offish, stuffy, arrogant individuals. No wonder they are friends! If Rivera had to run for mayor on personality alone, he never would have won. His personality is shit! Many people here don't like him. But they keep voting for him because he is effective and has done some good things for the city. More than anything, he has the support of some very powerful people. That has helped him for sure. In fact, that is how he became mayor in the first place. He worked in City Hall for many, many years, and befriended several powerful individuals during that time. When Rivera ran for mayor, they literally bankrolled his whole campaign. He won in a landslide. Ever since, he has been invincible. Anybody who runs against Rivera doesn't stand a chance. People who want to challenge the Mayor on legislation won't be heard, whether they are city alderman or common citizens; and any business that seeks to break up the monopolies of Rivera's friends will not stand any chance of surviving long. The Mayor and his friends have complete control of the city."

"Where does Costa stand among these men?"

"Oh, he's stands heavy among them all right," Puma answered. The aguardiente in his bloodstream was not only loosening his tongue, but working on his emotions. Anger was rapidly building up inside of him. "In fact, Costa is ranked pretty high up there because of his involvement with politics. His closeness to the Mayor makes him all the more powerful. He does have one rival, however. His name is Ricardo Perez. He owns most of the farms around here. He's got a huge dairy enterprise. Perez is also close friends with Rivera, and very involved with politics. Like Costa, Perez personally donates a lot of money to the Conservative Party, bankrolls campaigns of local politicians, and even has a hand with important decisions made by the Rivera regime. As far as the aldermen and the daily handling of affairs are concerned, Perez controls the north side of town and Costa the south side. These two guys despise each other, but the Mayor has played off that rivalry brilliantly to his advantage. It's called divide and conquer. The Mayor is always above the fray, never harmed by what goes on."

"The Mayor is a smart man," Gabriel said.

"Yes, he is," Puma agreed. "But, he is a dirty scoundrel. So are Costa, Perez, Calderon and the rest of them! They're all really terrible! They just care about power, nothing else. Their vanity knows no bounds! They have done some horrible things. I have witnessed them myself . . . some really horrible things."

"Like what, murder?"

"No, not murder," the old man responded as he took another puff of his cigar, which was already halfway done. "I have not personally witnessed something like that, although it would not surprise me if they did have a hand in some killings. They have wronged a lot of people in other ways. They have clobbered folk who simply got in their way. They have kicked them while they were down, taking away their businesses, jobs, and homes. They have destroyed many lives and families for the sake of acquiring more power and money. What makes it worse is their smugness about the whole thing. You would think they were Roman emperors the way they behave so inhumanely! They think they have the right to do whatever they want. They don't care who gets hurt. It's this arrogance that is appalling! I tell you, Gabriel, I would respect a cold-blooded killer more than any of these hypocritical bloodsuckers. That's the damn truth!"

The two sat there in silence for a while. Puma suddenly looked at his cigar and developed a pained expression on his face. "Oh, I am almost finished with this," he observed sadly. "Let's enjoy these fine Cubans while they last. I don't want to talk about those thieves anymore." They would remain at the café for another half-hour, spending most of it talking about the upcoming visit by Vicente Sanchez. Then it was back outside, where things were still a little quiet with the siesta not finishing for another hour. Gabriel went back home to rest. Considering what he went through during the day, the youth had a hard time believing it was only one in the afternoon.

CHAPTER FIFTEEN

THE DEADLY ANDEAN WINDS

On the early morning of October 26, Vicente Sanchez and his team were ready to board a small turboprop in Cali. They had to walk a long distance from the airport to the plane waiting on the tarmac. It was already hot and humid in Cali. Many of the passengers were sweating profusely after the long walk. One of them joked about trading in his short-sleeved shirt for a thick sweater upon arrival in cold Nueva Vida. "That's the only place in Colombia where they actually drink alcohol to warm themselves up," the man said. Sanchez and his small team of advisers and attendants, as was by custom, were the last passengers to board any plane to avoid getting hounded by people.

Sanchez reluctantly agreed to this only for the sake of making things easier for his staff. They had a lot to do in the plane, and could not be bothered by people clamoring to chat with the presidential candidate throughout the entire duration of the flight. So they had arranged this special treatment with every airline that served them through the campaign. The plan usually worked very well, for most passengers would be completely unaware of the candidate's presence in the aircraft. Once in the plane, the team would seat themselves up front in first class. The curtain would be closed at all times. These were one of the few pained moments Sanchez would experience during the campaign. "Here I am, running as a candidate for the common people and sitting in first class!" he would complain. "How terribly hypocritical that is of me!"

Despite his reservations about such exclusive treatment, Vicente Sanchez soldiered on that morning like every other during the campaign, and boarded the turboprop. Once they got seated, the team went over some last minute details concerning their trip to Nueva Vida. They discussed, among other things, what places they should visit during the trip, which people to see, what message the candidate should deliver during his speeches, and even which clothes to wear. They also discussed Mayor Rivera.

"I really don't know what that man has planned for us," said one of the advisors. "He is a staunch backer of the government. I don't trust him."

"It should be no different than all the other towns we've visited," said another advisor. "All the mayors of these towns have been staunch supporters of the government and nothing has happened to us yet, right?"

"I don't know," replied the first advisor. "Something about this man concerns me. I hope my fears are unfounded." Sanchez stayed quiet during much of this, letting his advisers do all the work. He figured he needed to conserve more energy than them, since he was going to be doing all the walking and talking during the visit. Besides, he was in no mood to discuss the trustworthiness of Mayor Rivera, knowing it was too late to wonder about it now. "We are on this plane ready to leave and they are *still* talking about Mayor Rivera!" he thought. To avoid any further damage to his psyche, Sanchez would simply ignore the gloomy talk of his aids and prepare himself mentally for the trip. This he did by simply looking out the window of the plane to regain his composure or gloss over his planned speech in Nueva Vida.

Shortly after Sanchez and his people boarded, the plane's propellers began spinning around as the engines roared to life, eventually moving the aircraft toward the runway. With hardly a hint of wind around, the takeoff conditions were ideal. After a short burst down the runway, the small plane gracefully lifted off, heading for Nueva Vida. The flight was to last about an hour and fifteen minutes. Once the plane reached cruising altitude about twenty minutes later, Sanchez and his assistants were enjoying coffee and pastries. As his men continued talking strategy, Sanchez silently prayed for his safe return home. He dreaded staying apart from his family for any length of time, long realizing it was a terrible price to pay for becoming president. He often felt guilty for leaving his family behind during such trips and engagements, resorting to prayer for emotional healing. He would miss his wife and daughter so much at times that he would cry like a little boy in the privacy of his hotel room.

During these vulnerable moments, other concerns would relentlessly bombard his mind. The pressures of becoming the next President of Colombia, with all the work and personal sacrifice it entailed, loomed large and heavy over him. He yearned for the simpler life he left behind, when he did not have to worry about so many things. On top of that, the threat of his assassination was omnipresent wherever he went, which forced him to update his will a few times during the campaign. These grim realities caused Sanchez to even faintly contemplate quitting the race and, even once, committing suicide. "Why not get it over with now?" he would think. However, these dark moods would pass instantly with a simple prayer for his family or upon hearing the jubilant cheers from a crowd. Only then, would he regain focus and march ahead with his mission, realizing that it was not just about him. Thoughts of his embattled country, bleeding from years of drug violence and war, would reignite the fires within him. The survival of his country was at sake and he was determined to save it, even at the cost of his own life. These enlightened, patriotic thoughts would always win over the darker ones in the end. This brought him peace of mind.

*   *   *

While Sanchez continued to pray silently during the flight, the plane began to rock up and down. Unbeknownst to him and the others, the plane was entering a very turbulent part of the trip. It was heading right over the Andes Mountains. Since the turboprop could only reach an altitude of about twenty thousand feet, it could not cruise above the crosswinds that swept through the mountains on occasion. The route from Cali to Nueva Vida was in fact so dangerous, only the best pilots in Colombia were assigned to it. Most of these pilots usually had some background serving in the Colombian Air Force and were already familiar with the hazards of flying through the mountainous area. They were trained on how to maneuver around the swirling wind patterns and, most crucially, how to handle extremely turbulent situations. Such situations often required not only a lot of experience, but plenty of piloting skill.

But all the experience and skill in the world could not guarantee safe passage through this infamous route. Many planes flown by seasoned pilots would not make it over the years. Most would be found crashed along the side of some remote mountain or buried in the dense jungle foliage of a ravine. Of the several planes lost to the Cali-Nueva Vida route, there were no survivors. They were victims of the same savage winds that caused Inca warriors fleeing from their enemies, in desperate search of a hideaway in the interior jungle basin, to die frozen in their tracks; wreaked havoc on ambitious Spanish Conquistadores looking for gold, often forcing those fortunate to have survived to take other safer routes; and brought a sudden end to various mining and oil-finding expeditions during the early Twentieth Century, which left the lives of at least a hundred men unaccounted for.

So when the flight got bumpy, the pilot of the turboprop was none the least surprised. He did all he could to make the flight as smooth as possible by often changing altitude, speed, and direction. However, the sudden bumpiness caused a slight stir among the passengers. Most of them immediately sat upright and refastened their seatbelts. Vicente Sanchez's camp voiced their concern about the turbulence. One of the advisors asked the flight attendant what was going on, to which she responded they were simply encountering some bumpiness characteristic of the route. "Is this going to last for a long time?" the advisor asked.

"It may," the flight attendant responded calmly. "Just make sure to keep your seat belts on."

After the initial waves of heavy turbulence, the flight settled down to a slightly bumpy affair. It was smooth enough for Sanchez's team to conduct their business once again. Sanchez continued remaining quiet for the most part as he looked out the window. About fifteen minutes later, the flight became very shaky again. This time, the pilot, sounding harried, informed all passengers to put their seatbelts on and place their seats in the upright position. This nervous announcement alarmed everyone. The flight attendants quickly scurried to their seats in front of the cabin.

After encountering the turbulence, the pilot decided to descend the plane about five thousand feet. The descent was very abrupt and steep which elicited terrified shouts from those within the cabin. Once the plane made its descent, it continued to rock heavily. The lower altitude had not improved the situation, so the pilot decided to increase speed for the purpose of knifing through the perilous crosswinds. This only made things worse as the plane bobbed more heavily than ever. The pilot then made one last desperate decision. He attempted to maneuver around the pocket of turbulence by changing directions and descending another three thousand feet. As he made the plane turn right and descend, the situation improved significantly as there was far less turbulence.

But after a minute, the pilot suddenly realized he was lost. All his attempts at changing altitude, speed, and direction to avoid the heavy winds only served to make things more difficult for him. In a rash attempt to rediscover his location, the pilot checked all his navigational equipment and computers. What made things worse was that the aircraft was now hurtling through a dense layer of clouds, adding to the pilot's sense of confusion. Within seconds, the man was able to rediscover his location, prompting him to redirect his course and turn left. However, a mountain stood in his way which forced the pilot to make an abrupt climb. The turbofan engines began to scream loudly as the plane began climbing higher and higher. But the mountain was too close and the pilot realized there would not be enough room to maneuver out of the situation. His eyes widened as the earth was closing in from his cockpit window.

CHAPTER SIXTEEN

WHEN THE MUSIC'S OVER

The city of Nueva Vida was ready for Vicente Sanchez's visit on the morning of Saturday, October 26th. The streets were cleaned, pro-Sanchez banners were aloft on every city block, flowers were planted along the highways, and the stadium where he was to make a speech that evening was adequately touched up for the occasion. The people of this town were anxiously awaiting the arrival of the next President of Colombia, which was scheduled for around ten o'clock. Some were sweeping the sidewalks in front of their homes or businesses, while others gathered confetti for the occasion when the presidential candidate's motorcade would pass through. Most people were simply standing around, conversing with friends and neighbors or anxiously listening to their portable radios for the latest information.

The portly Mayor Rivera arrived at the airport at about seven-thirty. The flight was due to arrive at eight-thirty. Rivera was feeling pretty good that morning because he finally received a call from an anonymous official in Bogotá, in which he was informed of the latest information regarding Sanchez's assassination. It was to take place in the stadium sometime after the speech. This pleased the Mayor because he had correctly anticipated where the assassination would take place, and planned accordingly. With little police presence within the stadium, Rivera was sure the plot would succeed.

By 8:15, the Mayor and his retinue of men stood on the tarmac of the airport, waiting for Vicente Sanchez to arrive. The tall and elegant Victor Ascencio, the mayor's right hand man, and Gerardo Ayala, his high-powered attorney, were among the men. A long motorcade of assorted cars and SUV's were positioned nearby to transport Rivera and Sanchez to town right away. It was sunny but very gusty, as everyone struggled to keep their hair in place. Even the Mayor's famed silver hair, always fixed and neat, was flying all over the place. "This wind is driving me mad!" he complained after several failed attempts to keep his hair down. At 8:30, most people, who had been cheerfully mingling until then, turned silent as they nervously waited for Sanchez's plane to touch down at any moment. When the much anticipated plane had not arrived by 8:55, the Mayor, growing increasingly impatient, ordered Ascencio to go to the airline ticket counter to check the progress of the flight. Ascencio soon returned and told Rivera there was no news of the flight, other than it might be running late due to the windy conditions.

At 9:15, with no sign of the plane yet, Rivera finally lost his nerve and bolted for the control tower. "I am going inside to find out what the hell is going on!" he declared furiously. When some of his aids began to follow him, the Mayor told them to remain on the tarmac. He insisted on going by himself. He walked, in his portly, wobbly manner, to the airport building. Once inside, he asked a security guard to take him to the control tower. The guard ended up escorting Rivera to a locked doorway in the back of the airport, which led to a staircase. The Mayor was told the staircase ascended to the top of the control tower about four stories up, where the air traffic controllers were. Rivera was, at first, displeased about having to walk up all those stairs. The guard, noting this, offered to retrieve one of the traffic controllers from the tower. The Mayor agreed and the young man ran up the stairs.

While he waited at the bottom, some thoughts entered Rivera's mind. At first, he thought of ways of preventing himself from giving the air traffic controllers a severe tongue lashing. He was so upset about the utter lack of knowledge regarding the whereabouts of Sanchez's flight. He wanted to yell at somebody, but also did not want to lose his cool. The Mayor, considering what was planned for that evening, desperately wanted everything to go smoothly. Any delay or postponement of the flight could create serious trouble. God forbid if the flight came very late and the presidential candidate, tired from the long ordeal, wanted to postpone or cancel the speech scheduled for that evening! He was very fearful of this possibility and dreaded the news of any flight delay.

However, another thought popped up. This particular thought excited the Mayor—the plane may have *crashed*. He knew well the infamous history of the Cali-Nueva Vida route with all the crashes that took place over the years. He suddenly realized that Sanchez dying from a plane crash would be a wonderful blessing for him. With the assassination attempt aborted, he would not have to worry about the subsequent media frenzy and, worst of all, the public speculation of his involvement in such a crime. This possible scenario, which seemed too good to be true, made Rivera all the more anxious to talk to the air traffic controller. He now was hoping the plane had crashed. The excitement and tension was too much to handle, forcing the Mayor to light up a cigarette.

At that moment, the guard had brought down one of the air traffic controllers, who looked quite nervous. The Mayor had a reputation for firing men who were harbingers of bad news. He immediately asked the man what had become of the flight. The man, diminutive and bald headed, could not reply at first. He only gave a frightened look. The Mayor then placed his hand on the man's arm and tried to encourage him to speak. "C'mon! You don't have to worry with me. I just need to know what happened to that flight."

"I'm sorry, Mayor Rivera, but I just don't know how you will take this," the man replied.

"What is it?"

"We have lost contact with the flight!"

"What do you mean you have lost contact with the flight?"

"Well, we have not been able to communicate with the plane anymore and it also has disappeared from our radar."

"How long ago did you lose contact with the plane?" calmly inquired the Mayor.

"We lost contact with it a little more than an hour ago. We have been trying to reestablish contact several times, but each attempt has failed. We have talked to the controllers in Cali in an effort to determine if the plane may have returned there or rerouted somewhere else. They have told us that they have lost contact with the plane as well."

"Oh my God, what does this mean?" the Mayor asked. "Does it mean the plane may have crashed?"

"Yes," the man responded timidly.

"Do you know for sure?"

"No, we don't. But this is a terrible sign. In any case, we have alerted the federal authorities to conduct searches of the area where it may have gone down."

"Good! Could you give me your telephone number so I can be kept informed of what's going on?" The air traffic controller took a page out of his little note pad and wrote the number on it. After handing away the number, he was warmly embraced. "Thanks for everything you have been trying to do," Mayor Rivera kindly told him. "You should be commended for your efforts." Of course, these uncharacteristically nice gestures from the Mayor stemmed from his exultant spirits at that moment. He was beside himself with joy. The air traffic controller then raced back up to the control tower with a big sigh of relief.

The men on the tarmac outside were nervously pacing to and fro, waiting for either Sanchez's plane to land or their boss to return from the control tower. When they saw their boss returning, they knew right away from his rather deflated posture that something bad had happened. The Mayor slowly walked toward them, with his head down, and upon reaching them, told all of them what had happened. They were all stunned at the news. With a government search of the plane already in progress at that moment, the men decided it was best for the Mayor to return to Nueva Vida to make some sort of an official announcement to the people. A few of the others would remain at the airport to keep tabs on the situation.

On the way to Nueva Vida, Rivera received a call on his cell phone from the same official who had spoken with him the night before. He told the Mayor what he had already known, that Vicente Sanchez's plane was missing and a search was being administered. The official sounded happy and relieved as he told the Mayor that Sanchez was probably dead. "If he is indeed dead, we're off the hook," he said. He also informed him that the news of Sanchez's missing plane was being released throughout the country, so citizens of Nueva Vida probably already knew about it. "Just make sure you console them at this time," the official said, "and tell them that everything is being done to find that plane and rescue those who might have survived."

As it turned out, Mayor Rivera and the rest of Colombia would not have to wait long to discover what had become of Vicente Sanchez. Search teams, which included the Colombian Air Force, discovered the smoldering wreckage of the plane that carried Sanchez and thirty-two others at around one in the afternoon, only four hours after it was officially declared missing. Rescue crews, dropped by helicopters flying low over the mountains to avoid the treacherous crosswinds, soon investigated the crash site meticulously and found no traces of any survivors. There was absolutely nothing left of the plane but some burning, smoking heaps of metal, leaving no doubt the impact of the crash was severe enough to have killed everyone on board. Rescue efforts ended by four in the afternoon and the first photographs of the crash site, both from air and land, were released to the media. By five o'clock, the government released a message officially pronouncing Sanchez's death from the crash. It also stated that the President would address the nation on television at seven in the evening.

*   *   *

Mayor Rivera was extremely happy through much of the day. With each passing minute, the likelihood of Vicente Sanchez's plane having crashed somewhere grew steadily through the morning. There were no reports of the plane returning to Cali or landing somewhere else. He had his spokesman issue a brief statement over the radio at about two in the afternoon. It informed the citizens of Nueva Vida that he and his staff were working very hard with the government to help search for Vicente Sanchez's plane. The Mayor waited anxiously like everyone else to find out what ultimately happened to the popular presidential candidate. He called the airport's control tower several times to check up on the situation. With no change in the news by three o'clock, he sensed his wishes might come true.

When images of the charred plane were aired on television at five o'clock, which were shortly followed by the government's official confirmation of Sanchez's death, the old politician leaped into the air like a happy little boy. "This is the best thing that could have happened to me!" he thought. "Now, I don't have to worry about the assassination and covering it up! I don't have to worry about being implicated with it! There will be no media circus! I am free as a bird!" He could hardly believe his good fortune. He poured himself a glass of his finest Scotch and reveled in the moment. Mayor Rivera was so overcome with happiness that he almost forgot his responsibilities to the public. A phone call from Victor Ascencio, who asked what was going to be done for the city in light of such terrible news, shook him out of his euphoric stupor. He decided to address the townspeople personally over the radio after the President's televised statement in the evening. "I will declare that tomorrow be a day of mourning for Sanchez," the Mayor told Ascencio.

"That will be a good idea," Ascencio agreed.

"I did not like the son of a bitch, but protocol dictates that I act properly and help the people of Nueva Vida get past this trauma."

"You'll pull it off like always, boss."

*   *   *

But the sympathetic words of the President and Mayor would do little to soothe the sense of shock and sorrow now felt by the people of Nueva Vida. Since Sanchez's death was confirmed, these feelings gradually intensified. At first, many people gathered on the street to console each other. They had just lost their hero and were having trouble coming to terms with it, some weeping hysterically while others just stood around quietly. Some even refused to believe Sanchez was dead. Their thoughts ranged from him having miraculously survived the crash and looking for rescuers somewhere in the mountains, to him being kidnapped by the guerillas. The sound of weeping and depressed chatter had replaced the festive music which blared throughout town in the days leading up to Sanchez's anticipated visit. The music which had come to symbolize hope to everyone was nowhere to be heard now, as an ominous silence hung over much of the city.

After the Mayor's brief radio address, however, in which he declared 'it was a sad time for Nueva Vida', the quiet grieving and sense of shock was increasingly being replaced by an angry rumbling in the streets. Mobs of people began forming in many parts of the city, where individuals would harangue the crowds and suggest the government's complicity in the deadly plane crash. Fueled by alcohol, they became more vocal and restless. By midnight, the rapidly growing mobs began to march through the city. The situation quickly turned disastrous. The roving throngs of drunken firebrands wreaked havoc wherever they went, overturning vehicles as large as buses, igniting large garbage dumps on fire, and breaking into stores. Some unfortunate women who got in the way were even raped by criminals joining the fray with the sole purpose of breaking the law to their hearts' content.

At about one o'clock in the morning, the dazed city authorities finally deemed the situation serious enough to take swift action. Policemen, who were allowed to take the night off in order to mourn the passing of Vicente Sanchez, were now urgently ordered to report back to duty. Additional policemen and security personnel who were off duty at the time were also called into action.

By the time most of the officers entered the streets, much of the city had undergone significant damage. Huge fires continued blazing in several areas. On top of that, the mobs turned on the police. They hurled stones and Molotov cocktails at them, challenging them to shoot their firearms. Even with their entire force on hand, the police were badly outnumbered. They were also ill-prepared for such a fight since many of them were not equipped with tear gas and riot gear. Nueva Vida had been a peaceful town for such a long time, that local officials never considered buying such equipment in large quantities. Outnumbered, ill-prepared, and under a hail of stones and even bullets in some places, the police would soon be in full retreat. The victorious mobs responded by looting, pillaging, and raping even more. Nueva Vida was quickly falling into chaos.

CHAPTER SEVENTEEN

A NIGHT TO FORGET

The night of October 26th was particularly horrifying for Gabriel, his Aunt Teresa, and Grandmother Celia. The three of them were hardly able to get much sleep. Through their second floor windows in the living room, they viewed with shock the madness unfolding below. Like an avalanche of destruction, drunken men rampaged through the street with Molotov cocktails, stones, rifles, and handguns. The sound of broken windows, gunfire, and raging fires tore through the walls of Grandmother Celia's apartment like a buzz saw. Gabriel tried covering his ears with his hands to no avail. What may have been worse were the hateful, vengeful voices of the men wreaking havoc outside. With scorn, the men would contemplate, loud enough for all in the neighborhood to hear, which homes to break into and which ones to leave alone. Most times, however, the sadistic men would end up doing nothing but break a couple of windows before moving on to terrorize the next unfortunate street block.

Besieged inside their apartment, Gabriel, Aunt Teresa, and Grandmother Celia could do nothing but pray for the riots to end. But their prayers would continue to go unanswered. One wave of marauding rioters would shortly be followed by another, leaving hardly any time for those in the neighborhood to rest. Unable to sleep, Gabriel frequently ventured to the window to view what was going on outside. When the riots began, he observed one terrible scene involving an old man attempting to stop the madness. The man slowly walked toward the mob and was seen trying to speak to them. Some words were exchanged, with the man trying to plead with the rioters to stop what they were doing. Many in the mob were laughing at the man, making fun of him. Finally, one of them, carrying a crude torch, stepped toward the old man and kicked him in the stomach. The brave gentleman was left to lay on the street, barely moving at all.

Gabriel immediately wanted to go out and tend to this poor victim of senseless violence, but was stopped by his aunt and grandmother. "Don't you dare go out there!" Aunt Teresa told him. "They'll do the same thing to you!"

"But the man could be dying out there," an angry Gabriel replied. "We just can't leave him alone like that! He was trying to help!"

"Do you want to put yourself in danger?" Aunt Teresa asked.

"I don't care!" Gabriel responded. "Let them do what they want with me. I got to help that man!"

"Well, what if you do go out there to help that man? And what if the mob gets to you and perhaps kills you? Then your aunt and grandmother will be left all alone in this apartment, defenseless against these hordes of madmen. In that case, then the poor man out there on the street, yourself, your grandmother, and I could all end up dead. Is that what you want?" These words of Aunt Teresa finally convinced Gabriel not to go outside, but he was nonetheless frustrated about not being able to help the old man. He peered out of one of the windows right away to see how the man was faring. He was pleased to discover that some neighbors came to his aid and were helping him get up and move out of the street. He was taken inside one of the apartments and seemed to be recovering fine, as he was able to walk and talk with those who were helping him.

However, it was only a matter of time before the next wave of rioters arrived in the neighborhood, which triggered a thought in Gabriel's mind. More than anything, he desired a gun. "That would keep these scoundrels at bay!" he thought. He asked his frightened aunt and grandmother if they had a gun anywhere in the apartment.

"Of course not, Gabriel!" was Aunt Teresa's stern reply. "We don't keep guns in our home. You know that!"

"Well, I didn't know for sure!" Gabriel fired back. "Besides, it would be a very good idea to have one, especially in moments like these! How are we supposed to defend ourselves?"

"God will come to our defense!" Aunt Teresa declared almost hysterically. "If we pray hard enough, he will help us survive through the night!"

"Well, that's good, but I would still feel a little safer if we had a gun in our possession right now."

Gabriel and his aunt were about to continue squabbling when Grandmother Celia told the two to stop. "Gabriel, we do have a gun!" she declared from her bed. "It's in the garage, inside a long cardboard box with the word 'lamp' scribbled on it. You can't miss it. Go now and retrieve it." Gabriel enthusiastically went downstairs to the garage, while his aunt remained sitting on the living room sofa with a dumbfounded look on her face, unable to speak. There being a gun in the house was certainly news to her. "Why, I never bothered to even look in that box," she told her mother, astonished she never was informed about the weapon.

"Your father placed it there a long time ago and I never kept my eyes off of it," Grandmother Celia explained.

With looters bearing down on her home, Aunt Teresa was not about to complain further about it. The apartment could now be adequately defended and that brought some relief to her. When Gabriel returned with the long, heavy box, which had to be carried with both arms, he immediately opened it. He anxiously grabbed inside and pulled out a powerful, 1930's vintage German rifle. The youth marveled at it while his aunt cringed, as she visibly shook in the presence of this fearsome weapon. "Look how big this thing is!" he observed excitedly. There were also about thirty bullets inside the box, more than enough to defend the apartment. Gabriel checked inside the weapon and noticed it was already loaded. "Good, everything is ready" he remarked. "Any man would be stupid to enter here with this thing facing him. I guess our prayers have been answered."

Unfortunately, Gabriel spoke too soon. They were not out of the woods yet. For the next hour, they were to witness more acts of savagery from the mobs. A man was shot and killed down the block, the shoe store directly across the street got broken into and looted, and an apartment not too far away began burning up uncontrollably. The most terrifying moment of the night occurred at about three in the morning, when some rioters entered the neighborhood and began contemplating what to do.

"What place should we hit now?" asked one.

"Well, well, well, look at this place here!" loudly said another, referring to Grandmother Celia's apartment. "It seems to be untouched! Ha! Ha! Ha! It seems to me that it has some money inside. Let's find out! Let's break in!" Gabriel quickly ran to the top of the staircase with his rifle and waited for the men to enter. His aunt and grandmother were trembling with fear.

"Wait! Wait!" ordered one of the men. "This place is familiar to me! I believe this is where Celia Duarte lives!"

"Who the hell is she?"

"She was this old woman who always fought Rivera in City Hall. She was the wife of Senator Duarte."

"That probably means she's got money! Let's go in!"

"You idiot, she fought the Mayor and lost! She was noble! She's got my respect! Let's leave her alone and move on!"

With that, the men who were just outside the door of the apartment, ready to break in, now moved away and walked down the street. Gabriel just stood at the top of the stairs, trembling with heavy rifle in hand and sweating profusely. He did not move from that position for quite some time. His aunt finally had to grab him by the arm and forcibly move him away. Gabriel placed the gun down on a table in the hallway and began to cry. "What's going on?" he asked his aunt. "Why are these people doing this?" Aunt Teresa took him to the kitchen towards the rear of the apartment, which was safe from the violence taking place in the street, and offered her rattled nephew a glass of water. He drank half of it but could not continue. He began crying again, mumbling about being back home in the United States. He once again asked his aunt why

185

such terrible things were happening. "Things are just getting out of control," she responded while stoking her nephew's hair.

"But shouldn't they be attacking the government?" he wondered. "Why are they taking it out on innocent people?"

"Because many of them are drunk, Gabriel," she replied, "and they don't know what they are doing. There are also some criminals out there who don't care about anything or anybody, and are just taking advantage of the situation. These kinds of things happen sometimes in our country. We just have to wait this out until daybreak, and hope things will turn out all right." She then encouraged him to finish the glass of water, which he did, and led him by the arm back to the living room. She managed successfully to calm Gabriel down, rubbing his shoulders, and telling him things were going to be okay. With his nerves almost fully soothed, the youth went out to the hallway to retrieve the rifle. He waited patiently by the window, with both his hands tightly clutching this weapon 'sent from God', for the next round of trouble to hit the neighborhood

*   *   *

Meanwhile, Mayor Rivera was busy trying to quell the uprising from his lavish residence thirty minutes outside of Nueva Vida, yelling at his underlings over the phone and issuing orders that were not being strictly followed. How things had changed—only a few hours before, the Mayor was drinking champagne with his brother and some other close associates who despised the fallen presidential candidate. They warmly talked about how the old order would remain in place with the unexpected death of Vicente Sanchez. Above all, they celebrated the fact that Sanchez, the 'immoral, ungrateful troublemaker', was dead. "Thank God I didn't have to go through the humiliation of playing host to that jerk, taking him around this town like I was his servant!" the Mayor told his guests. "I am glad he did not set foot on my city!" They drank several glasses of champagne, so elated they were.

The men celebrated well into the night, not knowing what was actually happening in Nueva Vida. Finally, a phone call came a little past midnight. It was Victor Ascencio, who informed the drunken Mayor about the serious disturbances occurring about the city. When the Mayor announced he would return there at once, Ascencio pleaded with him not to. "No, it's too dangerous," he said. "There are hundreds, maybe thousands of thugs roving the streets destroying everything in sight right now. Fires are burning everywhere! Please stay at your residence! You'll be safe over there."

"What shall I do?" the stunned Mayor asked.

"Stay where you are," Ascencio replied. "You can issue orders from your residence in the meantime. I've already contacted police headquarters and told them to get the entire force out there as soon as possible."

Mayor Rivera thanked his most trusted advisor, hung up the phone, and stood there motionless for a while. He was breathing heavily and his face turned deathly pale. He informed the others in the living room of his residence what was happening in Nueva Vida, and they could not believe it. They began pressing him with questions but he could not speak, so shocked was he. For a few minutes, the Mayor did nothing but walk a few paces back and forth. The others dared not ask him anymore questions. There was a terrible silence in the room. Finally, the Mayor's brother told him to snap out of it and do something. "You don't want to lose control of the city," he warned. This advice brought the Mayor out of his trance. He decided then and there to leave for city hall immediately. "I must be there to take care of the situation!" he declared much to his brother's enthusiastic approval. "I don't want to remain here, cowering like some timid dog." The Mayor stormed off to his car accompanied by his valet. During the ride to city hall, he made a flurry of phone calls, first to Ascencio to find out more information about the riots, as well as telling him he was on his way to city hall; then his police chief, Luis Sandoval, to issue direct orders; police headquarters to see if units were being mobilized; and lastly, to the fire department to make sure all major fires were under control.

This rash of phone calls, even though they brought more bad news, made Mayor Rivera feel better. By issuing orders and making inquiries, he felt like he was back in control. "These riots stop right now!" he would tell everyone over the phone. However, the quiet seclusion of city hall, far removed from the destruction and violence racking other parts of his city, would bring a false sense of security to the Mayor. He would continue issuing unreasonable orders that were mostly ignored. When the bad news continued to pile up through the night, he would get more angry and desperate. He lashed out at Sandoval, his police chief, when he found out many police units were backing away from the mobs. "How can we restore order in the city when our god-damned police are shaking in their boots, shying away from their duty to protect the citizens of this city?" he scornfully asked Sandoval. "They should be ashamed of themselves! You are responsible for lighting a fire under their pathetic asses! Do something about it for Christ's sake!" When Sandoval began pleading his case, the Mayor refused to listen and hung up the phone.

Rivera also lashed out at the fire department chief for not putting out enough fires. What he failed to realize was that the city, with only twelve antiquated fire trucks at its disposal, could in no way put out twenty raging infernos, some engulfing four-storey buildings whole. On top of that, firemen had to deal with the crazed mobs as well, who often blocked the paths of the fire trucks intentionally and even, in some cases, attacked the firemen themselves. The Mayor simply refused to believe the upheaval was uncontrollable. He only could blame his underlings for not doing enough to turn things around. His rage, like the city itself, was getting out of control. He could not stand the fact that things could go so wrong after the wonderful news of Vicente Sanchez's death. He cursed at god for teasing him by having him endure such a dramatic turn of events. "Just a few hours ago, I thought I was saved from Vicente Sanchez," he told one of his guests. "Now, I have to worry about being saved from my own people!"

As the riots continued to spiral out of control, the Mayor was faced with an important decision: whether or not to call the federal authorities in the capital to send in troops. He desperately hoped the upheaval would be contained by the city's police and fire department within a short period of time. He did not want to have to make the call to Bogotá. If federal troops were sent in to save the city, his political legacy would be overshadowed by the riots. At the very best, if the riots were crushed rather quickly, say within a day, there would still be a noticeable smudge on his record. However, if the Mayor did not call in federal troops while his city burned to the ground, he would be all the more damned for it. It was a no-win situation. With things not getting any better by three in the morning, and under the persistent prodding of his brother and Ascencio, Mayor Rivera finally made the call to Bogotá.

CHAPTER EIGHTEEN

THE RIOTERS

By three in the morning, approximately when Mayor Rivera was making his call to send in federal troops, things began calming down in Nueva Vida. For mysterious reasons, the rioters, the very men who took complete control of the city and terrorized it, stopped what they were doing and scattered away. Perhaps their desire for revenge and loot had been satisfied. Maybe they were growing tired at so late an hour, and with no more booze to be had, the need for sleep had overcome them. Others, witnessing the horrible destruction they inflicted on the city as they sobered up, may have run home to avoid being incriminated.

Whatever the reasons, the rioters suddenly disappeared from the streets. The police, who were nowhere to be found during much of the night, suddenly emerged from their hiding spots. They reentered the streets with something to prove, as their collective pride had been badly bruised. They went rounding up as many suspects as they could find. They managed to collect a few drunks roaming about, most of who probably were not actively involved with the riots anyway, and sent them, bloodied and bruised after being mercilessly whacked with Billy clubs, to headquarters. Peace had finally been restored.

*   *   *

As for the actual rioters, no one could explain what their motives for destruction were on the night of October, 26th. The death of Vicente Sanchez obviously had something to do with it. It triggered the maelstrom that followed later that evening. However, exactly what caused hundreds of men to act with such reckless, medieval savagery? Some people would say it was the alcohol, but that is certainly disputable. The booze might have contributed to the men's aggressive behavior only to a degree. Many of the same rioters probably get drunk every weekend, but they usually have not gone out burning homes, looting stores, and raping women in the process. The wholesale destruction of a city is not what most people yearn for when they have had too much to drink. Could people get angry and possibly commit acts of violence while under the influence? Certainly for some, that is possible. Could it lead them to randomly kill innocent people out of the blue? If they are sane and not compelled to do so, probably not. Thus, alcohol could not have been the sole reason for what happened that fateful evening.

Still, some others would say it was an acute sense of frustration. That certainly could have been a principle cause. Many citizens of Nueva Vida wanted to see the popular presidential candidate, but were denied that privilege. Not only were they robbed of the chance of seeing him in person in their own hometown, which would have made them swell with pride, but they forever lost their hero. The man who they felt was going to change the fortunes of their country and lead it in a new direction, was now dead. Suddenly, the hope for a better life, one not plagued with rampant poverty, crime, and violence, was extinguished. The frustration felt by the people, which had been building steadily over several years of civil war and ineffective government, finally erupted in a most violent manner right after Sanchez's death.

This is indeed a good argument. Any riot would to some degree result from frustration and anger. The urban riots in America during the late Sixties were a result of racial discrimination and the deaths of such leaders like Dr. Martin Luther King and Malcolm X, among other things. During the French Revolution, the poor masses protested their unfair treatment by the nobility. Regarding King

191

Louis XVI as the chief symbol of their repression, they had his head chopped off. Nonetheless, could mounting anger and frustration alone be the cause of horrendous crimes committed during the upheavals in Nueva Vida, 1960's America, or revolutionary France? Maybe, but there could be something else involved.

Others might say it was class struggle. It was widely believed in Nueva Vida that many of the rioters were from the poorer classes, and they were exacting their revenge on the wealthy elite. In fact, many of the homes and stores that were pillaged and burned were located in affluent neighborhoods. Several rioters were heard slandering the rich through the night, claiming they were targeting the 'bloodsuckers' and 'parasites' who abused the poor. It cannot be denied there was an undertone of class consciousness and conflict in this particular revolt. However, affluent citizens were not the only victims of mob savagery that night. Poorer communities were equally ravaged by random acts of crime and violence as well. If the rioters were so concerned about the poor, why did they target them as well? Somehow, the class struggle argument does not hold up here.

So what reasons are we left with to explain the behavior of the rioters? Alcohol, frustration, and class struggle have been at least partially ruled out. There is one possible explanation left: *freedom*. Now, freedom is a profoundly vague term, although it is mostly perceived as something positive. When people, for instance, are freed from a terrible situation, like a house fire or a cruel dictatorship, the meaning of the word is most definitely positive. The state of living in freedom, whether it is spending money lavishly or going away on a fishing trip, also has good connotations. In all respects, freedom represents not being shackled down physically or emotionally. It symbolizes the power to overcome or avoid any obstacles that may cause some sort of distress. However, for human beings living on earth, this is impossible. They will always be shackled in some way, first and foremost by their own flesh. Nobody can avoid illness and death.

Nevertheless, people can still experience freedom, but only in fleeting, short-lived moments. In the strictest sense, it is the act of *fleeing*. More specifically, it is the act of fleeing from one restrictive moment or place. When someone goes out on a shopping spree, the freedom he or she may experience is actually flight from some sort of mental or physical bondage, whether it is a tense home environment, responsibility to the family, a bad day at work, depression, and so on. Similarly, when a few men go on a fishing trip for the weekend, they are intentionally leaving society behind. They would like to think they are escaping from reality, the very things in life which they believe are holding them down.

Their freedom, however, is only confined to the act of escaping. Once they have reached their intended destinations, the shopping mall or lake, their freedom ends. When the person arrives at the mall, for instance, he or she has to then worry about what to buy, how much it costs, whether to buy something or not, going back home after the purchase is made, and think about what to do for the rest of the day. In other words, that person, once at the shopping mall, returns to the reality of being bogged down by niggling concerns. The men on the fishing trip, once they arrive at the lake, also are greeted by the necessities of booking a room at the lodge, getting acquainted there, readying all the equipment, renting a boat if they don't own one, making sure the boat has enough gasoline, hoping the weather and fish will cooperate, and so forth.

Such freedom or escaping is usually welcomed by every person at certain times of the day or week. It provides a momentary release from the pressures of life, a way of coping with the endless difficulties of one's daily existence. This is widely considered healthy and good. Yet, the very freedom which so many people seek can unleash their worst impulses. In unique situations, it can lead people to lash out and inflict harm onto others. When a person seeks to hurt someone else, it is the very manifestation of freedom in the form of escaping feelings of anger or helplessness. The act of hurting someone else, whether through a punch or verbal insult, represents the actual moment of freedom. The freedom of unleashing this attack also generates an overwhelming feeling of power. Once that punch or insult has been thrown, the perpetrator's freedom ends as the consequences of the deed loom immediately thereafter.

In some cases, such destructive impulses can be justified, as when people are defending themselves. Yet, other instances are not. When a master whips his slave for no other reason than to free himself from feelings of boredom, frustration, or an inferiority complex, the act is unjustified. This senseless cruelty is an unfortunate product of freedom, which can largely explain what happened to the rioters in Nueva Vida on the night of October 26th. The terrible acts committed by these men can at first be traceable to an urge to free themselves from feelings of sadness over Sanchez's death, anger at the government, frustration with the civil war, and weariness from the rigors of their burdensome lives. This proved to be a potent combination of emotions, which led them to a path of senseless destruction.

The freedom of fighting back against the injustices of their predicament would spawn an intense feeling of power among the rioters. They turned the situation around and now were masters of their own fate, something they never experienced before. These men were so accustomed to being pushed around by life that they thoroughly enjoyed this new sense of power. Some conscientious men used the occasion to lash back at the government by overturning buses and burning federal buildings. There was purpose in their actions, as they sought to make a political statement.

Other rioters were not as mindful, they being of a more criminal and unscrupulous disposition. These were the men who truly did not know how to handle their newfound freedom and power. They were the ones who ended up terrorizing Nueva Vida throughout the night, indiscriminately lighting homes on fire, raping women, looting stores, and murdering innocent civilians. Like the master mindlessly abusing a slave, these particularly sadistic rioters committed such crimes for no justifiable reasons. These ranged from simply ridding themselves of boredom and frustration to, in the case of rapists, making sexual fantasies come true. These unruly criminals would eventually take over the uprising, forcing many of the conscientious rioters to leave prematurely. "Those idiots just want to burn homes and hurt people," remarked one decent man. With fewer decent men around, things would really spiral out of control.

The crazed rioters would continue to enjoy their freedom, transgressing the law wherever they went. However, after a couple hours inflicting mayhem on the city, some sensible men, perhaps sobering up and feeling a bit tired, began questioning what was happening. They soon realized there was no point in carrying on with their cruel activities, informing the others that it would be best to flee the scene. "If any of us are caught," one man said, "they'll hang us in the square!" This created panic among them, as they all suddenly disappeared from the streets. They ran to their homes as fast as they could. With that, their freedom ended. No longer would their dark, destructive impulses terrorize the citizens of Nueva Vida. They would rejoin their ranks, going home to their beds, trying to sleep and forget about what had happened. Many were unable to sleep, so scared they were of being snitched by others. From marauding lions to quivering sheep, bold lawbreakers to fearful abiders of the law, the remarkable transformation among the rioters was now complete.

CHAPTER NINETEEN

AFTERMATH

By the early morning of October 27th, most of the fires that raged through the night in Nueva Vida were either put out or dying away in the cool mountain air. The destruction leveled upon the city was severe in some areas, but it was not to the extent warranting major rebuilding projects. The city was a mess and several weeks if not months were required to clean up and reconstruct certain areas, but it clearly was going to survive. Considering the amount of huge fires that engulfed the town, many citizens were expecting far worse damage. They were pleasantly surprised the following morning to discover most of the businesses and stores were not only left untouched from the riots, but some were even open as well.

While most people were happy to have survived through the night, Mayor Rivera was seething with rage. He viewed the smoldering condition of his city on a brief car trip during the early morning, and immediately called for revenge. "Look at what those animals did to my city!" he told his chauffeur. "I want their heads on a platter!" Not only would the riots probably ruin his legacy, but he had to now clean up the terrible mess left behind. He also had to make sure the hospitals were fully staffed to care for a growing number of injured people. As it turned out, a remarkably small number of civilians were killed during the riots. The authorities would later report the number of deaths to be at twelve with about three missing.

Nevertheless, the very first thing the Mayor did after touring the city was summon his police chief. After giving him a good tongue lashing, he ordered Luis Sandoval to lead an investigation to round up as many rioters as possible. "I don't care if you have to resort to the cruelest torture methods," he told Sandoval. "I want you to get as much information as you can! I want all the ringleaders locked up!" The big, burly Sandoval was all too happy to walk out of the Mayor's office with his job still in hand. After having been embarrassed the previous evening and hoping to get even with the rioters, he gladly took on the investigation. It was one of the few times the cranky Mayor and lucid police chief were on the exact same page.

Mayor Rivera then turned his attention to the federal government. He did not want the federal troops to enter the city. Having called for them a few hours before out of desperation, he suddenly had a change of heart now that things seemed to have calmed down. The Mayor feared the presence of troops in the city would demonstrate weakness on his part. He wanted to appear strong before the people of Nueva Vida during such a crisis. He was also concerned about his power diminishing once the army arrived. "Don't kid yourself, the generals will start calling the shots around here when they come," he told Victor Ascencio.

Ascencio agreed with his boss about the problems the army's presence in the city would pose, and suggested they give Bogotá a call. "The President is a sensible, understanding man," Ascencio told the Mayor. "If you strongly state your case, he will listen and perhaps grant us our wish." They were in the process of making the call when, lo and behold, the Mayor's secretary stepped into the office and informed him that the President was on the line. The Mayor quickly picked up the phone. The President eagerly asked about the situation in Nueva Vida. The Mayor gave a brief description of what had occurred the prior evening and finished by saying that they had regained control of the city. The President was pleased by that bit of news and Mayor Rivera figured it would then be a good time to inform him of his problem. He then pleaded with the President not to send in the troops. "You can even station them right outside of town," he added. "I just can't have them set foot inside. It would kill me politically. I need to let my people know that I am still in charge. I hope you understand. Would you do that for me, Mr. President?"

"I am sorry Juan Carlos, but I can't do that for you," the President firmly replied, much to the Mayor's disappointment. "Those riots in your town have become big news throughout the country. Have you seen the television this morning? The news programs are showing footage of what happened last night, with all the fires and looting."

"What?" the stunned Mayor cried in disbelief. "It's on television?"

"Yes, it's on television!" the President responded scornfully. "Not only is it on television here in Colombia, but everywhere in the world too. Foreign networks have shown footage of the riots. They are also mentioning how your police were apparently overwhelmed and could not stop what was happening."

"Oh my God," Rivera uttered quietly.

"Yes, your town is receiving worldwide attention," the President continued. "Because of all this attention, there is no way I can allow the situation over there to get worse. The troops have to go in. I have to send a message to the Colombian people. I can't allow what happened in Nueva Vida to occur in other cities. The last thing I want is an epidemic of rioting spreading throughout the country while I'm leaving office. We already have our hands full with the guerrillas."

"Mr. President, I understand your situation," the Mayor said, attempting to reason one last time with the head of the country. "I am in a similar situation myself right now. Since we are kind of in the same boat, let's try to work something out. I can tell you right now it is peaceful here! People are actually going back to work! I have just ordered an investigation on the riots and dump trucks are already out there cleaning things up. The entire police force will be patrolling the streets tonight. Please, Mr. President, give me one more chance to assert myself here!"

"No, I am sorry Mayor Rivera, I can't do that. You know damn well that if the people there decide to riot again, which is a good possibility, your police force won't stand a chance of stopping them.

The people know that too! I heard that none of your police were equipped with riot gear. If that's true, you should be ashamed of yourself! This is the end of the Twentieth Century and you haven't equipped your police units with the most basic riot gear? That's absurd! No, I am sending the troops in! You spoke of political suicide a moment ago. Well, I would certainly be committing political suicide if I don't send the troops in!"

The deflated Mayor relented, knowing well that the President was rightfully not going to change his position, and wearily asked when the army was to arrive. The President informed him that the troops were to arrive in Nueva Vida sometime in the afternoon, definitely before the evening. "From my understanding, they are only a couple hours away and proceeding toward the city as we speak," he said. "General Manuel Torres will report to you as soon as he gets there. I hope things go smoothly between the two of you." With that, the conversation ended, leaving Mayor Rivera demoralized. "The army is coming," he told Ascencio. "It only keeps getting worse, doesn't it?"

*　　*　　*

Meanwhile, Gabriel along with his aunt and grandmother were waking up that morning, grateful they survived though the torturous night. The dazed youth woke up on the sofa beside the window with the long rifle lying right next to him. He apparently fell asleep while on watch, gun in hand. His two loving relatives were already awake, quietly moving about, preparing breakfast and checking for any damage to their old apartment. When she saw Gabriel walking toward the bathroom along the hallway, Aunt Teresa ran to him and gave a big hug. "We survived the night, my dear," she told him with tears in her eyes. "The Lord is with us and will continue to be."

"I hope so, Aunt Teresa," Gabriel answered, still tired from a lack of sleep. "I hope we don't have to endure another night like that."

"Well, I just heard some interesting news from the radio," Aunt Teresa said.

"What it is?"

"The army will be coming here today, some ten thousand troops they say. We won't have to worry about anymore riots for the time being. Things will definitely quiet down around here."

This was certainly welcome news for Gabriel. He was still in shock from the previous evening. The youth, having grown up in a quiet suburb of Detroit, where the closest thing to danger and excitement were the shenanigans committed by teenagers during Halloween, had a hard time coping with things. Dodging shaving cream and tossed eggs certainly doesn't compare with preparing to shoot crazed men carrying Molotov cocktails and guns! Having witnessed such random, cruel acts of violence, Gabriel's perceptions of life and humanity were shaken to the core. The ivory tower he had been living in for so long had come crashing down.

Gabriel came to South America for the very purpose of descending from that tower, to break free from the boring, isolated life he had led. That crucial, symbolic moment had now come but he was surprised to be feeling the way he was. He expected during such a point in his life, at last wading through the swamp of humanity, to be feeling some exhilaration and fulfillment. Instead, there was a dread he never felt before, an eerie sense of fear, loneliness, and vulnerability all at once. The youth understood that he could have easily died the night before. God knows what would have happened if those rioters intent on entering Grandmother Celia's apartment had their way and broke down the doors! That thought haunted him through the morning. "Life is really a numbers game," he thought in existentialist fashion regarding his pure luck of surviving the riots. The randomness of it all left him feeling quite insignificant, as though he were a mere pawn in the whole scheme of things.

Gabriel would snap out of this listless state when Dr. Granados called him later in the morning. First, the professor would inform the youth that the language institute would be closed the following day, Monday, because of the riots and Sanchez's passing. He then asked Gabriel if he wanted to go to a demonstration to be held that afternoon. The youth asked what the demonstration was about. "It will be, I guess, a demonstration against many things: the death of Sanchez, the Civil War, corruption, and even the riots. My God, what those people did last night was terrible! Anyway, the demonstration will take place downtown in the plaza. I have a feeling a lot of people will show up. Would you like to come?"

"Sure, I would like to go," Gabriel timidly answered, not sure what he was getting himself into. "Who is organizing this demonstration?"

"From what I know, a bunch of university students and professors are organizing it," Dr. Granados replied. "I heard this on the radio. It's seems to be a very spontaneous thing and I don't know how well it's going to be run. But sometimes, the more spontaneous the event, the more interesting it can be."

"How long do you think it will last?" the youth asked.

"God knows how long it might last. I guess it depends on how many people will show up. If a lot of people show, which I expect it will happen, then it might last fairly long."

"I'm just asking these questions because I'm concerned about what happened last night. I'm worried about another round of riots occurring again."

"You shouldn't worry now," Dr. Granados said. "I believe the worst is over. There won't be any of that type of senseless violence here. Things got out of control because the criminals took over. Now that they have had their fill of loot, they won't show their faces again, especially now that the federal troops will be arriving shortly. Anyway, Gabriel, I thought you came here looking for some excitement. You've been telling me about this global revolution taking root here in Colombia. Well, you got a taste of some rioting last night. I figure that may have gotten you a little excited."

"As I have told you several times before," Gabriel retorted with a chuckle, "I would prefer to witness such things from a safe distance. Did you know I was wielding a rifle most of last night?"

"Ah, my young Gabriel," the professor replied, laughing at the story, "you have just learned that nothing can be witnessed from a safe distance here in Colombia. I also was clutching a rifle through most of the night as did many others I am sure! You might be a little ruffled now, but you will soon get used to how things are here. You should actually be feeling grateful you survived to live another day. Some others were not that fortunate."

Despite agreeing to go to the demonstration with Dr. Granados, Gabriel still felt rattled by what he experienced the previous couple days. He was terribly sad about Vicente Sanchez's death and horrified by the riots. After eating his breakfast quickly, he felt the need to take a walk and sort some things out in his head.

CHAPTER TWENTY

A MORNING STROLL

It was about ten o'clock in the morning when Gabriel departed from his grandmother's apartment. He figured a nice, long walk through town would do him some good. A couple blocks into his walk, Gabriel already noticed some of the destruction from the riots: a burned out building here, a looted store there, a wrecked car somewhere in between. Shattered glass was a common sight on the sidewalks and streets, as were bullet casings, beer cans, rum bottles, gasoline, jerry cans, rubble, graffiti, strewn garbage, and, most disturbing of all, blood. Looking at the smattering of blood stains on the sidewalk not too far from his grandmother's apartment, Gabriel pondered if someone had died at that spot. Of course, there was no way he could have known and the uncertainty of it only served to further trouble his mind. Yet, Gabriel was an optimist at heart, and he kept recalling what Aunt Teresa and Dr. Granados had told him earlier that morning about being fortunate enough to have survived the ordeal. These positive thoughts enabled him to continue his walk through town.

What also helped Gabriel was that most of the city had remained intact. His fears of total annihilation were unwarranted. Having seen so many fires dot the landscape the previous evening from his grandmother's second storey window, the youth could not believe how little damage was actually done. "It's a miracle!" he thought. Despite the terrible mess, all the familiar sites and sounds were there. The enormous Church of St. Peter was still standing, with its huge pilasters and bronze dome glistening in the morning sun. The splendid plaza in downtown was intact as well, though the streets were a tad littered. Looping around and heading back north toward the direction of his grandmother's apartment, Gabriel encountered his favorite panaderia on 19th Street. Not only was it still in one piece, but it was open too! With his feet a little tired from all the walking, he decided to enter and take a momentary brake.

Like usual, Gabriel ordered a coffee with a piece of sweet pastry. He then sat in a table which already had a newspaper on it and began reading away. The customary half-hour spent in the panaderia, usually every afternoon right after the siesta break, was always Gabriel's favorite time of day, when he could truly get away from everything, relax, and catch up on some news. Being there in the morning was a bit strange for our young friend, however, since there was no sunshine yet on that side of the street. The panaderia was completely shaded and a bit cold, which took Gabriel some time to get used to. He was accustomed to having that wonderful afternoon sunshine splashing on his face whenever he was there, which was comforting in the cool mountain air. He now had to curl up to warm himself in the shade, frequently rubbing his hands and legs together. Few places in Nueva Vida had any sort of heating aside from the occasional fireplace, forcing people to wear thick sweaters indoors most of the time. Only between noon and three o'clock in the afternoon, when the sun was directly above the city, could people afford to be without a sweater.

As he picked up the paper, Gabriel noticed it had not covered the riots. The upheaval took place too late in the night for it to be even mentioned. He read it anyway, particularly the latest news on Vicente Sanchez's death. He was surprised to learn how dangerous the Cali-Nueva Vida air route was. "I have taken that same flight several times before," the youth thought. "I'm never taking it again!" He was also puzzled over how quickly the crash site was found, within a couple hours after the plane's disappearance. Considering how difficult such a search and rescue mission must have been, with all the mountains and ravines covering the area, Gabriel pondered if the government already knew where the plane was. Indeed, many people in the street were saying the government was involved with the plane's demise. These conspiracy advocates suspected either a time bomb, all too popular a weapon in Colombia, or sabotage.

Once he finished reading the paper, Gabriel lit a cigarette and took in the scene around him. Everything seemed to be slowly going back to normal. The street was now teaming with cars and people, which further reassured our young friend. The early morning shock was gradually replaced by a need among the citizens of Nueva Vida to proceed with life, to check up on loved ones, friends, businesses, and somewhere in between, go to church, since it was Sunday. No calamitous event could keep these proud people from retaining some control over their own lives, from doing what was necessary to survive. As he watched the big black birds hovering effortlessly in the distance, close to the majestic Luisa, Gabriel realized nature also had that same quality. Like humanity, nature would always have the *will* to endure and survive. He gained strength from what he saw around him, whether it was a homeless man panhandling outside of a store or a sunlit cloud floating past. Humanity and nature mirrored each other in their efforts at self-preservation, and this, Gabriel thought, is what made both truly admirable.

With those encouraging thoughts, a rejuvenated Gabriel left the bakery and reentered the streets. The youth was making his way toward his Cousin Rosa's house, walking past Parque Infantil, where he played basketball during the weekends, when he bumped into the jaunty Puma. He was wearing his familiar red jumpsuit and, like always, appeared to be in a rush. "It's amazing how we always meet like this!" Puma joked. "Three hundred thousand people live in this town, yet we always bump into each other everywhere. Are you sure you are not a member of the C.I.A.?" The old man told Gabriel he was going to check up on some family members. "Yeah, I am doing the same thing," Gabriel replied.

"Who are you going to see?"

"My cousin, Rosa, and her family," the youth answered.

"I hope they are all right," Puma said. "I can't believe what those criminals did last night. They have no dignity, no decency. They should all be executed for what they did!" The old man began to shake visibly with fear when he discussed what happened to him during the riots. "I hid like everyone else," Puma described, "hoping nothing would happen to me. I live in a tiny apartment on the first floor. Aside from the front door, there are no other exits and the two windows have protective bars over them. If one of those thugs had decided to break in, I would not have been able to escape. Hell, I also worried about those Molotov cocktails. If there was a fire right outside my front door, I would have been in big trouble! It really was a nightmare! Thankfully, nothing happened to me, but I really was shitting in my pants for a long while." Before they went their separate ways, Gabriel asked Puma if he was going to the demonstration later that afternoon. "For what?" the cynical old man asked. "What will that solve? It also could not have come at a worse time with the army arriving here later today. They'll make sure to squash any sign of a revolt in this city. The demonstrators will be risking their lives!"

*   *   *

When Gabriel arrived at Rosa's home, her jovial husband, Eduardo, was the only one there. He had just arrived from seeing his parents and warmly greeted Gabriel at the door. Gabriel was glad to find out nothing bad had happened to Eduardo and his family. He really cared about them for they were down-to-earth, decent folk. As Gabriel entered the home, Eduardo described how he and his neighbors went out to the street with their rifles and guns the night before. "We dared the rioters to enter our neighborhood," he proudly recounted. "There were about twelve of us standing together with our guns cocked right at them. They did not even give it a thought. They turned away and never came back! We've learned over the years that the police here can never be relied upon. The people have to defend themselves." Eduardo then invited Gabriel to eat lunch there with his family, since noon was fast approaching. He was the type of man who never took 'no' for an answer, finally convincing Gabriel, after some gentle prodding, to accept the invitation.

Soon thereafter, Rosa slowly entered the small house with her ten year old daughter, Juana. They both were distraught, weeping uncontrollably. Eduardo, who was then sitting in the sofa with Gabriel, leapt to his feet and asked them why they were crying. Rosa, so traumatized that she was not even aware of her cousin's presence in the living room, could not answer immediately. She continued to sob hysterically along with Juana, who clutched onto her mother tightly. Eduardo continued looking at the two as they wept, waiting anxiously for either one of them to speak. Finally, Rosa began to tell what happened, although very slowly for tears were still streaming down her face. She eventually informed her husband that one of her good friends had not survived the riots. The woman had been murdered in her own home.

Her name was Eileen and Gabriel had met her a few weeks before at Rosa's. They were playing cards on a Saturday night. Eileen stayed for a brief time, so Gabriel did not get to talk to her that much. What he did remember was that she was a widow who was living alone. He also remembered her being quite attractive, but somewhat shy and reserved. "They slit her throat and left her on the floor of her bedroom!" Rosa described in terror. "When Eileen's family did not hear from her, they went over to her home and discovered her body lying there. She had bruises . . ." Rosa could not continue with the story, as she walked with her daughter to one of the bedrooms in the back.

Eduardo was left standing in front of Gabriel with a serious, shocked expression on his face. He stood there paralyzed for quite some time. Gabriel, feeling uncomfortable, stood beside him, looking down at the floor with his hands on his hips. After what seemed to be an eternity, Eduardo finally moved about the room and told Gabriel he was going to go comfort his wife and daughter. "This might not be a good time for lunch," he said. "Maybe you should go and come back a little later."

"No problem," the youth replied quietly before slipping out.

CHAPTER TWENTY-ONE

THE DEMONSTRATION

Gabriel was saddened by the tragic death of Rosa's friend. He was grateful nobody close to him was hurt or killed. Returning to his grandmother's apartment, the youth ate a hearty lunch of vegetable soup along with a plate of flavorful baked chicken and boiled potatoes. When Gabriel informed his grandmother and aunt about Rosa's friend, they were genuinely saddened. "How terrible!" remarked Grandmother Celia, shaking her head in disgust. "Let's hope she is in God's hands now. It's never good when things get out of control like they did last night." She expressed shock over the riots, claiming Nueva Vida was never known for such huge outbursts of disorder and violence. "This town has always been peaceful," she claimed, "but I guess everything is now changing." She went on to blame the city's rapid growth and, of course, her mortal enemy, Mayor Rivera, for the recent catastrophe. "Nueva Vida is getting too big," she explained. "Criminals from all over the country are moving here to make easy money. They are ruining this city thanks to that pig of a mayor we have. It's so sad!"

When Gabriel then mentioned he was going to the demonstration, they both communicated their disapproval. "The army will be here shortly, Gabriel," Aunt Teresa said. "It might be dangerous for you to go."

"Why should it be dangerous?" Gabriel asked. "It's only going to be a demonstration. Isn't this a democracy?"

"Gabriel, you should know by now how things are here," Aunt Teresa responded. "You have been to this country several times before and you should be familiar with how the Colombian military operates."

"Yes, but people are just going to gather and voice their dissent. It's not like they are going to take over the city. It's supposed to be a peaceful protest organized by some college students. You are not telling me, Aunt Teresa, that the military will start shooting at the crowd unprovoked?"

"Yes, Gabriel, I am telling you precisely that!" Aunt Teresa stated emphatically. "Don't be naïve! Just the sight of people gathering at the plaza might provoke the soldiers to shoot, especially after what happened last night."

"Well, I think that's terrible for the government to allow that," the youth angrily said. "I mean, there is a horrible civil war, a popular presidential candidate is killed under strange circumstances, and to top it off, a bloody upheaval erupts here. The people of this city are entitled to voice their concerns and frustrations."

"The government, at this time, does not care about the people's feelings here," Aunt Teresa remarked, hoping to dissuade her nephew. "They are only concerned about restoring order and won't care if a few innocent people are killed in the process. Please Gabriel, don't go! It won't be safe. You must understand that!"

However, Gabriel insisted on going to the demonstration. He told them it was something he needed to do. He was not going to be stopped, despite the pleas of his aunt and grandmother. "I don't want to be cooped up here, hiding behind these walls like a mouse while something important is happening out there," he explained. "I want to experience life! That is why I came here to Colombia in the first place. I want to start learning about the truth of things first hand for a change, rather than through some newspaper or book. That is what I have done all my life and I am tired of that! I would rather be dead than to continue living like that!"

Gabriel's grandmother and aunt, being older and more cautious, ultimately did not understand his reasons for going to the demonstration, but they finally relented knowing he was not going to change his mind. They allowed him to go only under the condition that he kept a safe distance from the crowd. "You don't want to be stuck in the middle if something bad happens," Aunt Teresa warned. She also told him to leave the scene immediately if the troops arrived. Gabriel promised to follow those suggestions and keep himself safe.

*   *   *

Dr. Granados and a couple friends arrived at Grandmother Celia's apartment at around three to pick up Gabriel. When they were all about to leave, Aunt Teresa reminded her nephew to stay out of trouble and asked the good professor to look after him, which drew much embarrassment from Gabriel. "I am an adult," he told her. However, Dr. Granados told her he would make sure her nephew would be out of harm's way. "She's your aunt and she loves you, Gabriel," he told him in her presence. Aunt Teresa thanked him and they left after she made the sign of the cross on them.

On their way to the demonstration, Gabriel was introduced to Dr. Granados' two friends, Javier and Maria. They were married to each other and appeared to be in their thirties. They used to be students of Dr. Granados but had stayed in close touch with him for several years. The couple first met in one of his classes. Maria had a large flag of Colombia draped around her shoulders while Javier carried an umbrella in case it rained. Indeed, dark clouds were now forming overhead, covering the sun completely. A cold, howling wind began blowing from the west. What Gabriel immediately noticed was the large number of people seemingly headed toward the plaza. Many of them were carrying flags of Colombia and singing old folk songs. "It looks like many people will be there," Dr. Granados commented.

Indeed, when they finally arrived at the plaza, it was packed! Once in the square, it was hard to move around without bumping into someone. Dr. Granados' friend, Javier, suggested they get onto a balcony of one of the public buildings surrounding the plaza. The professor agreed and the group ventured toward a particular office building which Javier claimed a friend worked in. After a lengthy journey across the square, through the burgeoning crowd, they finally reached the building and entered it. They went up four flights of steps, walked through a long hallway, and arrived at the office of Javier's friend. His friend, Rolando, was there and happily greeted Javier. He allowed them all to get onto the balcony to witness the demonstration. "This is going to be interesting!" he commented excitedly.

When he got on the balcony, Gabriel was awed by what he saw. A sea of humanity lay beneath him, waiting for the protest to officially begin. People were jockeying to get closer to the center of the square, where a large wooden platform, holding four large amplifiers and a couple of microphone stands, had been erected. A couple of the organizers were already standing there, apparently waiting for someone to signal the beginning of the event. Loudspeakers were still being set up around the square to further accommodate the unexpectedly large crowd. They probably were not anticipating such a huge turnout of people. Like Gabriel, Dr. Granados and the others were also shocked by what they saw. "I have never seen anything like this here in Nueva Vida," the astonished professor remarked. "There must be at least fifty thousand people down there!" The balconies and rooftops of buildings surrounding the plaza were also beginning to be filled with people, making the already dazzling scene all the more breathtaking.

Despite the recent memory of Vicente Sanchez's death and the subsequent riots, there was a certain buzz in the air. The Colombian flag was everywhere, waved by people on the ground below and hanging from balconies and rooftops above. The flag's three colors, yellow, blue, and red, bombarded one's visual faculties from all corners, to the point of disorientation. The omnipresence of these national colors struck an unmistakably positive chord among the throngs of people in the square, encouraging them to sing, chant, and lock arms with one another in a scene of patriotic unity. Gabriel had never witnessed such a show of solidarity before in person. "What a magnificent spectacle!" he thought.

Javier's friend, Rolando, suddenly entered the balcony with a bottle of rum and called everyone's attention. "My friends!" he declared. "Today will be an important day in the history of Nueva Vida and Colombia! I have a good feeling about what's going to happen down in that plaza. Let's drink to a new era in Colombia!" Rolando then raised the bottle in the air, took a swig, and passed it around. The exceptionally strong local rum, made in a distillery only a few miles outside of Nueva Vida, hit Gabriel right on the spot. He immediately felt more relaxed and began to contemplate further on what he was witnessing. "This is a symbol," he told Dr. Granados, "of man's crusade to save humanity from the jaws of modernity and oppression!" The professor could only laugh at this bold, silly comment, telling the youth not to get overzealous. "This is only a symbol of Colombia's desire to save itself from its own problems," he retorted.

At that moment, a group of young people assembled on the platform in the heart of the square. They stood along the back of the platform, on each side of a large Colombian flag standing from the middle. A young woman then stepped up onto the platform, walked to the microphone, and began testing it. Within a couple minutes, the loudspeakers were working well enough for the demonstration to commence. The quality was not very good, but everyone within the large plaza could still make out what was being said. The courageous woman made a brief introduction, informing the crowd what the purpose of the demonstration was and who the organizers were. She explained that the event was to serve both as a demonstration against Vicente Sanchez's death and a rally for continuing his struggle. After rattling off the names of professors and students involved with putting the event together, the girl then presented the head organizer, a Dr. Carlos Ghetti, philosophy professor from Occidental University.

The crowd cheered loudly for this man as he made his way to the microphone. They were desperately hoping he would provide some inspiration during this moment of crisis. They were not to be disappointed. The tall, balding philosophy professor delivered a fiery speech, as he begun by insinuating that the government may have had a hand in Sanchez's death. "The timing of his terrible death, so shortly before the election, conjures up many questions, which, I am afraid, will never be answered. What a shame!" His rhetoric was much the same as that of the dead presidential candidate, as he attacked the government, armed forces, right-wing paramilitaries, and guerillas for their corruption and bloodthirstiness. "They have ruined Colombia!" Dr. Ghetti boldly stated. "As Vicente Sanchez said, we the people must save it ourselves! We cannot allow those butchers to keep hacking away at our country until we are left with nothing but splattered blood everywhere!"

The university professor went on describing how great a man Sanchez was and how he must never be forgotten. "He was the only man who really spoke bluntly on behalf of the people," he passionately explained. "He was the only man who sought the truth and attempted to solve the problems afflicting our country. He was not afraid to stand up to those who were keeping our nation tied down, as he was dedicated to fighting the good fight and giving all of us hope. Vicente Sanchez, we the people will *never* forget you! Even though you departed this world physically, your spirit, your dreams, your hopes, and your ideals will continue living on in our hearts!" Dr. Ghetti then made the suggestion, to the delight of everyone in the plaza, that a new political party should be formed in Sanchez's honor. "The fundamental ideals and values of this party should be the exact same as Vicente Sanchez's. What better way for his spirit and vision to live on than in the form of a new political party? Therefore, today, right here in Nueva Vida, I have decided to form such a party!" This drew thundering applause from the jubilant crowd.

Before ending his speech, Dr. Ghetti touched briefly upon the riots of the previous night, imploring people not to resort to violence. He expressed intense shame for the rioters' deplorable actions. "Why should we be committing such brutal acts among ourselves? This is absolutely senseless! We are just chopping our own heads off! Such divisive conduct goes against Sanchez's calls for unity among the Colombian people. We cannot have this anymore!" When he finally ended his hour-long speech, Dr. Ghetti received a lengthy, enthusiastic ovation. The hopes of the people of Nueva Vida showed no signs of dimming away just yet.

✳   ✳   ✳

As the huge demonstration continued in the town's central plaza, Mayor Rivera was impatiently awaiting the arrival of General Manuel Torres and his troops. He was uneasy about meeting the general, having just learned from Ascencio, his aid, that he was notorious for corruption. "He supposedly has made a fortune from arms trafficking," he told him. "Of course, most of the arms have 'miraculously' ended up in the hands of the guerrillas." Even for the Mayor, who was not averse to certain forms of corruption throughout his long career, such criminal behavior was appalling, especially since it was treasonous. Selling arms to the guerrillas along with drug trafficking were considered by the conservative, patriotic Mayor to be truly indefensible offenses. "So you are telling me I have to work with this crook," he asked Ascencio, "a man who should be hanged for his crimes?"

On top of that, Mayor Rivera now had to deal with the protest. Upon hearing reports about it, he ordered police to go there in small numbers to enforce some order and protect property. Considering the overwhelming number of people at the plaza, that was really all the police could do anyway. "Let the army take care of that problem," the Mayor told Ascencio. "I am not doing anything." At around four-thirty in the afternoon, the army finally arrived in Nueva Vida. The roughly ten thousand troops were to be stationed, as previously arranged, at an old army barracks just outside of town. While his troops were settling in, the gruff General Torres decided to follow a strict presidential order in paying Mayor Rivera a visit to city hall. He was not all too happy about it. "Why should I go there to visit him as though he were some king on a throne?" he bitterly asked one of his lieutenants. "If anything, he should have greeted me at the barracks. After all, he's the one who lost control of the city and I am now here to save it!" The Colombian President made the order not only to ensure some semblance of protocol while much power was being transferred over to the general, but to also throw a bone at the luckless mayor. "I guess I'll have to go and tell him in person that I'm the new sheriff in town," he added with a chuckle, scoffing at the senselessness of the order.

While on his way to city hall in his jeep, General Torres soon found out about the demonstration. He drove there to see for himself and was shocked upon discovering how massive it was. He was particularly displeased about the lack of police presence in the area. Without hesitating, he called for all his elite troops, via radio dispatch, to arrive at the scene immediately. He also ordered the rest of his forces to enter the city at once and begin their patrols. When one of his aids inquired if he was going to consult first with the civilian authorities, the arrogant general lashed out at him. "If I wasn't so close to your father," he barked, "I would have you shot right now for asking such a ridiculous question!"

While their senior commander was waiting at the scene of the demonstration, all ten thousand soldiers abruptly stopped what they were doing in the barracks and quickly boarded the trucks and jeeps prepared to take them into the city. This had been an unpleasant day for these young men, as they spent much of it on the twisting mountain roads leading to Nueva Vida. Some of the large diesel trucks had trouble making the steep climbs up the mountains from the jungle ravines where the army base was located. A couple of the trucks even died at times and needed to be pushed along by dozens of soldiers. After countless starts and stops, remedied temporarily by some towing and pushing, throughout the long, grueling journey to Nueva Vida, these troops were irritated and tired. Sensing this, General Torres had allowed the men to relax at their new barracks for a couple hours before their inevitable entrance into the city. This brief respite had now been denied to them and they left the barracks with much fuss and resignation. Some soldiers, unhappy to have left their base in the countryside, proclaimed they were going to wreak havoc on the city.

CHAPTER TWENTY-TWO

THE PIGEONS TAKE FLIGHT

Gabriel was very much enjoying the demonstration. The patriotic speech of Dr. Carlos Ghetti had electrified the huge crowd. There was an incredible feeling of camaraderie in the air, as people chanted and sang amid a colorful backdrop of waving flags and falling confetti. Sadness and fear were replaced by a newfound sense of hope for the future. One particular slogan was being chanted in unison throughout the plaza: "WE WANT CHANGE!" The demonstration showed no signs of winding down once night had fallen. One by one, university students made stirring speeches against the government and the civil war, further exciting the crowd.

Things were falling right into place for Gabriel and his vision of global change. Despite Dr. Granados' contrary opinions, the youth remained adamant about Colombia serving as a beacon for the rest of the world. What he was witnessing in the plaza only confirmed his beliefs. "It is a mystery why this had not occurred sooner here in Colombia and why it is not taking root faster in other parts of the world," he told the professor. But he believed it was only a matter of time before the developments in Colombia would catch on with the rest of the world. Gabriel was certainly excited about these prospects and looked upon the protest unfolding before him with a beaming sense of pride. The death of Sanchez had indeed threatened to squash his hopes for global revolution, but they were completely restored by the demonstration. He could now breathe easier and take pleasure at his vision being played out before his very eyes. The more rum he consumed, the more convinced he was of his own genius.

However, before he and the others on the balcony could finish another toast to Colombia, with the bottle of rum almost finished, federal troops were spotted entering the fringes of the plaza. Everyone in the balcony took immediate notice and were at first nervous. However, the drunken Rolando, who worked at the office, began yelling obscenities at them. He was then joined by Javier, his wife, and even Gabriel. Only Dr. Granados remained quiet. The professor appeared to grow angry at the sight of them. "Bloody assholes," he murmured. Most people in the plaza were not aware of the troops' presence for quite some time, but word soon got around. They turned around to view the army surrounding them and began hurling insults in their direction. The crowd quickly settled on one simple chant, which they delivered in unison, further drawing the ire of the soldiers and their head commander, General Manuel Torres: "GET OUT! GET OUT! . . ."

At this point, the students on the podium had long stopped with their speeches as all the attention was diverted to the troops. Dr. Ghetti stood on the platform looking composed, letting the masses unleash their frustration against their oppressors. Nothing changed for what seemed like an eternity to Gabriel, as the crowds continued with their chants of 'GET OUT!' Finally, one of General Torres's aids, through his own portable loudspeaker, ordered the crowd to disperse at once. Dr. Ghetti immediately went to the podium and vehemently defied the order. "What we are doing here is legal!" he proclaimed boldly into the microphone. "We do not live in a police state! You cannot order us to disperse!" The crowd enthusiastically supported his incredibly courageous stand against the troops. They then continued with their chanting. "This is going to turn bloody," Dr. Granados remarked almost in a whisper. Gabriel suddenly heard a whole bunch of pigeons taking to the air all at once from above the building. At that moment, gun shots could be heard in the distant corner of the square.

Complete pandemonium ensued as people attempted to flee the scene. Their screams were drowned out by the steady gunfire, which lasted for a good thirty seconds. Through the darkness, for night had already fallen, Gabriel could see the sparks of machine-gun fire from across the square. He judged there must have been at least ten soldiers firing away at the crowd. He was suddenly pulled away from the balcony and brought inside by the others, where they gathered to avoid being hit by any stray bullets. Rolando, Javier, and his wife wanted to leave the building immediately, but Dr. Granados wisely implored them not to. "You would be crazy to go out there right now!" he told them. He insisted they wait inside until everything had calmed down. "They won't be so trigger happy later," he added.

In the meantime, Gabriel managed to peek through one of the small windows, enabling him to continue watching the terrible events taking place outside. The shooting had stopped since much of the large crowd had dispersed. The few protesters that remained were still scrambling to exit the plaza, horrified they might get shot in the back. The armed troops could be seen moving into the square to clean things up. It only took a couple minutes for them to accomplish their mission, but Gabriel made out what appeared to be about twenty to thirty bodies lying on the ground. Much to his disgust, the troops did not tend to them for a long while. Many were simply left to die in their own pools of blood. Not until the entire area was cleared of people did the soldiers at last check on the dead and wounded.

A couple of ambulances arrived within twenty minutes to transport those who were still alive to nearby hospitals. A little while after the ambulances departed from the scene, a couple of pick-up trucks drove in to haul away the dead. As though they were large sacks of potatoes, the bodies were unceremoniously heaped onto the flatbeds. With help from the light of lampposts throughout the square, Gabriel counted eighteen bodies. Dr. Granados and the others could only shake their heads in disbelief. "What a horrible massacre!" the professor angrily declared. "This shall not be forgotten!" Much to everyone's chagrin, it was decided that no one should leave Rolando's office that night. They were all to wait well into following morning, when it would be a lot safer.

*   *   *

Mayor Rivera was enraged when he found out about the massacre in the plaza. "I can't believe this!" he cried, pacing nervously back and forth in his office. "The goddamned army has come here and ruined everything! I knew this was going to happen! Worst of all, I have not even met with General Torres yet!" His aides were also pacing the room, deeply troubled by the situation. They were unable to figure out a solution to the Mayor's mounting problems. The Mayor eventually plopped down onto the sofa and laid his head back in resignation. He stared vacantly at the ceiling for a few minutes, hardly blinking his eyes. He was much disheveled. His hair, which normally was combed back neatly, was a tangled mess while his dress shirt was unbuttoned all the way down to his belly. The sleeves, usually held together at the end by a pair of cufflinks, were now uncharacteristically rolled up. The sweat gathering around the sides of his face and neck was now drying up, for he no longer was pacing around. Agitation was replaced with the pale look of defeat.

It seemed nothing could cheer him up. Whatever his aides said had no affect on him. "It's all over," he finally said, with his head still lying back against the sofa. "This is truly the end for me. I thought there might have been a glimmer of hope after the riots, but this massacre will ruin everything for sure. There is no way I can get out of this with my reputation, my legacy intact." The others had nothing to say immediately, for they were in silent agreement with their boss regarding his unfortunate predicament. They could only listen to their boss' rambling monologue about his unsalvageable situation. "Its funny how one or two events can wipe out an entire lifetime of work. I have struggled hard for forty years to build my career, and it will be shot down by the events of the past twenty-four hours! Can you imagine that? One day wiping out forty years? How cruel is that!"

As Mayor Rivera continued moaning from the sofa, two individuals stormed into the office. They were his two biggest political boosters, Alfonso Costa and Ricardo Perez. They wanted to know what was happening to their beloved city. They wanted to specifically know why the massacre occurred. When the Mayor told them that he had nothing to do with it, for the federal troops were not under his control, they were outraged. "Do you know what those troops have done, Juan Carlos?" Costa asked the Mayor. "By killing those innocent people, the town will go against us. Our party will be in big trouble! We will lose control of the town! We can't allow this to happen!"

"What do you suppose we do?" Mayor Rivera asked as he got up from the sofa.

"Get the troops out!"

"I cannot do that. They're here under presidential orders."

"Presidential orders, you say?" Costa asked.

"Yes."

"Then, there you have it! We don't have to worry about anything. The responsibility for this massacre will fall squarely on the shoulders of the President."

"But I made the request to bring them here," the Mayor added. "I would have to shoulder some of the blame as well."

"There must be something we can do!" said the tall, dignified-looking rancher, Ricardo Perez. He and Costa were longtime rivals, but the troubling circumstances brought them together for one of the truly rare times. They certainly did not want to see their power and influence diminished in the wake of the riots and massacre. Their presence in the office reinvigorated the Mayor, since Costa and Perez were not fawning aides or unsympathetic superiors. They were his equals, associates he had known and worked with for many years. The two were responsible for helping the Mayor build and maintain the impressive political machine which had run Nueva Vida for so long. The presence of his two powerful allies brought a sense of urgency, if not pride, to the Mayor, as he no longer contemplated giving up just yet.

"I can tell you this for sure," Mayor Rivera quipped, "the President will not take responsibility for this."

"Well, nobody will want to take responsibility for this," said the plump, dapper Costa. "The question is who will take the fall? We certainly cannot take the fall."

Perez chipped in: "If you get blamed for this, even partially, then we are finished. There must be something we can do."

"What course of action shall we pursue, my friends?" the Mayor asked eagerly.

"I think the only real option we have left is to go after the general," Costa explained. "Like you said, Juan Carlos, there is no way the President will take responsibility for the massacre. So we have no other choice than to pin everything on General Torres, which should be rather easy for us since he ordered the shootings himself. If there is any way you can call the President and try to get him on our side . . ."

"There is no way that's going to happen," the Mayor asserted bitterly. "That's just wishful thinking on your part, Alfonso. You should know better than that! The President, or at least the government, will not take sides against General Torres right now. I would bet my life on that. We're really in no position to do anything right now. All we can do is hunker down and wait. I am sure the massacre will not sit well with the President, and he will seek to wash his hands of it. General Torres will probably do the same. They will probably talk to each other soon and figure something out. They likely will claim it was an accident or something and leave it at that. At this point, it would be best for me to keep quiet and let those two to sort out the mess. After all, the general is already behaving as though he runs this town and the President entrusts Torres with maintaining the city's defense. Let them deal with the problem."

"What if they end up dumping the blame on you anyhow?" Perez asked.

"I don't think it will come down to that. They will probably claim it's an accident. In that way, all respective parties will be absolved of guilt and responsibility. That will be the easiest and safest way out."

Convinced the Mayor had things under control, Costa and Perez left the office feeling a little better about the situation. Victor Ascencio, who stood quietly throughout the entire conversation, was not so convinced. He sensed the situation would continue growing worse, even if the President and General Torres worked things out. "I fear the situation is worse than they would like to believe" he thought. He obviously did not want to convey these feelings to the Mayor, so he remained quiet. All he could do was hope his boss was right.

*   *   *

During the massacre, General Manuel Torres did not panic. After all, he had ordered it. He coolly witnessed the shootings from atop his jeep as though he were reviewing his troops during a parade. This was by no means the first and only massacre he had personally witnessed through his long career. On several occasions in the countryside, he had ordered and overseen the mass executions of innocent villagers suspected of aiding the guerillas. Dozens of men and even children would, on his sudden whim, be forcibly taken out of their homes, lined up against a wall, and summarily shot. Their desperate pleas of innocence would be of no help. Even the protests from mothers, wives, and daughters of the accused would be waved aside.

There usually was never any hard evidence linking the accused victims with guerilla activities. In many instances, the executions would be ordered by General Torres solely for appearances, to demonstrate to his superiors his tenacity in the bloody campaign against the insurgents; and also to assert his authority in the countryside. Despite such illegal killings, the military hardly ever was hit with serious criminal charges. The few charges brought forth in the courts would either be reduced significantly, amounting to slaps on the wrist for convicted offenders, or disappear altogether. This probably resulted from the government's desire to not have the courts interfere with the military's efforts to root out the guerillas. With such little success, judges and prosecutors gradually pursued fewer cases against the armed forces; and with the judicial system rendered weak and ineffective, there was no need for court-martials within the military. Thus, the unsavory conduct of General Torres and men like him were allowed to continue and, at times, even encouraged.

Yet, General Torres' bloodthirstiness would not go entirely unnoticed by the government and military hierarchy. The general was considered too ambitious and reckless by many of his superiors, increasingly drawing their attention and concern. Too many mass executions and murders were being committed under his watch. Wholesale acts of theft and rape were also not uncommon. His troops were as feared in the countryside as the guerillas and right-wing paramilitary groups. On top of all that, there were the persistent suspicions of General Torres orchestrating a vast arms and drug trafficking network in and around his base of operations, encompassing a large area in southern Colombia. Indeed, the general had become very rich. A couple of luxurious, newly constructed homes, one close to his command post and the other nestled along a remote lake, were a testament to his abundant wealth.

Despite the increasing concerns among military and government leaders, General Torres was left alone. He was deemed indispensable in the war against the guerillas. Although there had long been widespread speculation of him selling arms to the guerillas, he was one of the few frontline generals actually holding them off along his part of the front. With the war going so badly for the government, Torres' steadfast defense of his area was indeed one of the few bright spots in the entire campaign. After a string of several embarrassing defeats, the guerillas mostly steered clear of his territory, which enabled commerce to continue flowing freely through much of southern Colombia. This was very appreciated by the government.

General Torres was also left alone because he was very popular with his troops. Several victories against the guerillas along with a healthy dose of kickback money from the lucrative arms and drug trade kept them happy and motivated. Torres may have been terrible to most people but he was good to his troops. Their happiness was all that mattered to him for he saw them as an extension of his own power. He realized that without his troops, he was nothing; he would be unable to run his criminal empire and seize control of so much land. With approximately 25,000 men under his command, Torres' superiors chose not to remove him for fear of a mutiny. That was the last thing they needed during such a critical time in Colombia's history.

This laxness, however, on the part of the government regarding their handling of General Torres would lead to some serious consequences. With the government looking the other way, the general was emboldened to commit more atrocities and crimes. With nothing standing in his way, he eventually considered himself the final arbiter of law in these remote areas. He bullied local and provincial leaders into submission, making sure any administrative links to Bogotá in the region were severed for good. If any brave soul questioned the legality of his methods, the general would always cleverly reply that such 'abuses of power' were perfectly justified in a time of war, and even necessary to wipe out enemy insurgents. "I am mandated by the Colombian government to combat the guerillas in this area," he once told a local judge attempting to curb the general's bloody activities. "It has instructed me to use whatever means necessary to win this war. I am only following orders."

So self-assured he had become of his own authority over the region that General Torres likened himself to a colonial-era viceroy, where he ruled on behalf of a distant government. He frequently derided the Colombian government for its ineffectiveness and weakness. "If I wasn't here," he once confided to his aides, "the government would have lost control of this area a long time ago." Like ambitious conquistadores and governors of colonial past, General Torres was often resentful of his superiors and even dreamed of completely taking over his 'assigned' territory. "Why shouldn't this land belong to me?" he posed to a friend. "This region is cleared of guerillas, thanks to me! I am actually administering this area, not them!" He once played with the idea of running for politics, becoming a governor. But a life in politics did not suit him, as he squirmed at the thought of acquiring and maintaining power through the ballot-box.

With the passage of time, he would become arrogant and defiant to the point of no longer caring how the government felt about his legal transgressions. It seemed to his superiors that he directly baited and challenged them on several occasions, whether by massacring innocent civilians or selling arms to the guerillas. This behavior would certainly irk them, but it was never enough to force their hand by relieving him for instance, or even issuing a minor reprimand. So General Torres would aim to stretch the very limits of the government's patience, engaging it in a nasty psychological game, to see how far he could go without getting his hand slapped. And when Bogotá did nothing to curb his activities, the general would push farther ahead with his unscrupulous agenda. So brazen he had become that he kicked out all the right-wing paramilitaries from his command front. "We don't need them here!" he would declare proudly. "We are better than them at doing their job!" When it came to massacring and pillaging the countryside, his troops indeed were arguably more efficient than the paramilitaries.

It goes without saying General Torres had his share of friends and admirers within the military hierarchy as well. They most definitely did not represent a majority, but there were enough of them to usually tip the balance in his favor. During important meetings, these allies of the general would always make sure to say good things about him. Whenever his various crimes were brought up, they provided seemingly logical justifications and rationalizations: arms were sold to provide more food and material rewards for his troops; the looting of villages was a natural occurrence of war since the 'dawn of time'; and massacres, lastly, were a necessary evil in the desperate struggle for land and power.

The support of these men certainly helped to keep General Torres in command of his army. One such supporter was General Francisco Alba, the deputy chief of the Colombian armed forces. He was perhaps the second most influential man in the military, and made sure his friend, General Torres, was not moved away from his command post. Alba's close relations with Torres fueled rumors of him being directly involved with the latter's arms and drugs operations. Another widely held belief within the ranks of the military was that Torres' allies at the top were receiving substantial bribes from him. Whether through drug money or mutual respect, the general undoubtedly had powerful connections and made good use of them at every opportunity. This made him all the more unstoppable within the military and the remote mountains and jungles of southern Colombia.

Thus, when General Torres ordered the shootings in the plaza of Nueva Vida, he was at the height of his powers. He was going to treat Nueva Vida no differently than any other village that had defied him. He exacted his punishment on the protesters in the plaza the same way he had with so many other suspected enemies in the countryside: with a hail of bullets. His cool demeanor during the shootings indicated nothing unusual going on. There was no expression of shock, horror, sadness, or regret on his hardened face. He had seen it all before and had every intention of killing innocent civilians. When the plaza was mostly cleared of demonstrators, the general calmly gave the order for his troops to stop shooting.

Then, with a simple hand gesture, he gave the signal for his men to storm the plaza, with some in quick pursuit of Dr. Ghetti and the other leaders of the demonstration. With both hands on his hips, General Torres walked a little inside the now deserted plaza, surveying the scene. Once he determined the area was fully secured, he casually walked back to his jeep. From the passenger seat of the vehicle, he gave instructions to his subordinates regarding what to do with the dead and injured victims, as well as the leaders of the demonstration. "Whatever you do," he told them, "don't kill the ringleaders! Bring them to me alive. They can still be of some use to us." He then triumphantly motioned his driver to depart and the jeep was on its way, leaving the bloody carnage behind. It was just another day for the general.

CHAPTER TWENTY-THREE

THE INVINCIBLE GENERAL

Shortly after General Torres arrived at his headquarters just outside of Nueva Vida, he received a phone call from the President of Colombia. When the President asked how things were going, he calmly told him what had just happened. The President was stunned to say the least. This was exactly what he had feared, a massacre in a big town. "How many do you think were killed?" the President asked timidly, hoping the figures were small.

"I don't know exactly at the moment," the general replied. "My guess would be at least about twenty to thirty people."

"Twenty to thirty people . . . that is too much!"

"You are overreacting, Mr. President."

"Overreacting?" the astonished president retorted. "Let me tell you something, General Torres. What you have just done was incredibly stupid! You can get away with massacring people from little villages and hamlets in the countryside, but not civilians from a large town like Nueva Vida! Now you have put me in a terrible bind! This will make headline news all over the country. The media will go over there in droves! The last thing I wanted was for something like this to happen. How are you going to handle the situation if people over there decide to rise up against you? The population there is about 300,000. That's an awful lot of people you have to contend with."

"Mr. President, we are ready to handle any crisis. My troops are well motivated and have overcome many challenges in the past. You are simply overreacting. We have everything under control. There is nothing to worry about."

"You tell me there is nothing to worry about?" the angry head of Colombia asked. "Okay, obviously you are living in some fairy tale. You clearly don't understand what the hell is going on! If you can't comprehend the political and social implications of this massacre, then you are unfit to continue serving as commander of those forces. As of this moment, I am relieving you of your command! This perhaps was long overdue." He then abruptly hung up the phone.

*   *   *

After hanging up the phone with General Torres, the President began the process of officially removing him from power. He called his liaison to the army high command and informed him to get the ball rolling. "Tell them I want Torres replaced immediately!" the President instructed over the phone. After barking out this order, he began working on all the necessary paperwork. The President had reached his breaking point with the general, as there had long been serious problems between them in the past. He felt it necessary as acting president to dispose of the disrespectful, reckless Torres. "For the sake of our country," the President told an aid, "and the democratic principles that we Colombians hold so dear, I must get rid of General Torres!" So angry was the President with Torres that he considered charging the general with several criminal offenses, including conspiracy to commit mass murder. But the President refrained from that course of action, instead being satisfied with just firing Torres. "That should be enough," he thought.

However, the President was soon to receive a phone call from none other than the head of the Army, General Juan Guillen. When Guillen got wind of the President's rash decision to fire Torres, he was stunned. "This is madness!" he told one of his underlings. "How can he do something so stupid? I cannot allow this to happen!"

He went ahead and called the President. The President went on to explain his reasons for dismissing Torres from his command of the southern front. "I will no longer permit General Torres to commit any more crimes!" he told Guillen. "This massacre is the final nail in his coffin! How could he have done that in a big town like Nueva Vida? That was incredibly stupid! It's one thing to act like Genghis Khan in the countryside, but in a big town? That's crazy! Now we are going to have a hell of a time trying to control Nueva Vida, which has a population of 300,000. If the town decides to revolt, how on Earth are we going to stop them, especially when we are in the middle of a civil war? We also have to worry about riots in other cities in the wake of this terrible massacre. Torres has put me in a quandary of monumental proportions. For so long, he has skirted the law down there, acting as if he is king. I am tired of his reckless and lawless antics! I have no choice but to fire him!"

"Before you do that, Mr. President," the startled General Guillen interjected, "can you listen to me for a moment?"

"Go ahead."

"You are absolutely correct, Mr. President, in pointing out the difficulties of controlling a big town. Yes, that may require a huge effort on our part. But I have total confidence in Torres and his troops. He has about ten thousand men at his disposal down there and they have plenty of ammunition. If need be, another ten thousand men stationed not too far away are at his beck and call. I believe he can control the town until things ease up. Torres' men are well seasoned and motivated. They have endured a lot of hardships in the past and always came through. I am sure they'll measure up in Nueva Vida."

"That's good you have such confidence in Torres and his men," the President said sarcastically. "But tell me, why did he shoot at those people?"

"I was going to get to that," General Guillen responded. "Quite frankly, Mr. President, the situation was not looking so good. From my reports, there were probably about fifty thousand people crammed in the heart of the city, where this demonstration was taking place. The ringleaders of this protest were talking about overthrowing the government and starting a revolution. The crowd was really worked up. Torres and his staff were very concerned there was going to be some serious trouble with all those people there. Considering what happened the night before, he felt he had no other choice but to break up this demonstration. First, he had his troops surround the plaza. Then, he ordered the people to leave at once. But they wouldn't listen and kept heckling his troops. The crowd would not budge and shots were fired. It was a very tense situation."

"General Guillen, I still don't believe the shootings were necessary," the President sternly reasoned. "Torres could have simply positioned his forces throughout the town to serve in a security capacity, patrolling the streets, safeguarding property, and so forth. That would have been the best course of action. But now he has opened up a Pandora's Box of troubles with this massacre. There was absolutely no need for his troops to step into that situation with their guns blazing! I am sorry, but I am going to go ahead and remove him from his command immediately."

"So, you think that will solve everything?" General Guillen asked with contempt. "You think that by sacking him, this terrible problem in Nueva Vida will just go away, vanish into thin air? Well, let me tell you Mr. President, that would be wishful thinking on your part! It's not so simple."

"I believe that removing Torres will improve the situation!" the President said. "His recklessness has made things infinitely worse."

"How so?" General Guillen asked. "The demonstration has been broken up and order has been restored. I guarantee there won't be any trouble brewing there tonight."

"What about tomorrow night and the night after that? Torres was not considering the future and the people's resentment building up over that time. It was a horrible miscalculation on his part!"

"I disagree wholeheartedly, Mr. President. General Torres had the future in mind when he broke up that demonstration. If he had not stepped in and did something about it, the situation would have spiraled out of control. The demonstration would have turned into an outright rebellion in a matter of hours. We would then have to worry about similar rebellions spreading to other parts of the country. He just saved you a lot of trouble by taking swift, decisive action, but now you are reprimanding him for it."

"Well, it is still my belief this massacre could really make the situation worse and will actually increase the chances now for a full-fledged rebellion to take place in the coming days."

"There was already a full-fledged rebellion taking place, Mr. President!" the general explained. "There were fifty thousand people assembled in the heart of the city and they were calling for revolution. The crowd showed contempt for his troops and even dared them to shoot. If that is not an uprising, I don't know what is!"

"I still believe he could have exercised more caution," the President replied. "We live in a democracy and there are, as you know General Guillen, limits to what the military can do. There is a certain code of ethics that all members of the armed forces must abide by. To my knowledge, it does not include troops open firing on innocent civilians."

"Mr. President, I am going to be blunt with you," the general firmly said. "If Torres is relieved of his command, you now will have two rebellions to worry about: one from the civilians and the other from Torres' troops. His men will not take orders from anybody else! They love that man to death and if he is removed, there will be an outright mutiny in your hands! Look, we frankly don't have anybody else that could replace him down there. Despite some of his shortcomings, Torres is the only man right now who can effectively take control of the situation in Nueva Vida. He knows the area well and has maintained order along the southern front. Of all our commanders, I have to say he has been the best in taking on the guerrillas. They avoid him at all costs! Aside from the recent upheaval in Nueva Vida, have you heard of much trouble brewing in that region in the past six to seven years? Thus, if you decide to remove Torres from his command down there, you will be making a huge mistake! We will lose control of southern Colombia!" For the first time during the long conversation, the President was silent.

*   *   *

For some reason, General Torres was not too concerned when the President fired him over the phone. He had a feeling his sacking would ultimately not be carried out. He understood the President had to confer with the military bosses regarding his removal, and that it probably would not be permitted. It would be too much trouble, a 'logistic, strategic impossibility' he described to his aides. As it turned out, the general was right. After much heated debate with General Guillen, the President finally relented and allowed General Torres to remain in Nueva Vida under the sole condition that an *accident by way of a premature discharge from a soldier's firearm* be listed as the official cause of the shootings. "No way in hell do I want it known that General Torres actually ordered the massacre!" the President told General Guillen.

Thus, the President, with much embarrassment and regret, had to hire back Torres a mere two hours after firing him. The phone conversation was short, with the general being warned not to do anything foolish. "Under these extraordinary circumstances, I am allowing you to stay," the President bitterly explained to the general. "But if there is another massacre, you will not only be removed from your command, but you will face criminal charges in a federal court." The general laughed off such tough talk, realizing the lame duck head of Colombia would not be able to back it up. This would prove to be a disturbing turn of events. What nobody wanted to readily admit at the time was that the fate of Nueva Vida and even the entire country was now entirely in the hands of General Torres.

CHAPTER TWENTY-FOUR

HOLED UP

With a bloody massacre on his hands and no word yet from General Torres or the President, Mayor Rivera became increasingly distressed. It was nine o'clock in the evening and he was at his office in city hall with his staff, further contemplating the nightmarish situation. It turned out he was having a hell of a time following his own strategy of waiting around quietly. He simply could not do it, especially with his city falling apart. Throughout his long political career, the Mayor was known for not letting problems fester too long. His aggressive style got him results, and he now started to question whether the waiting strategy was the right one. "This is still my town!" he told Victor Ascencio and the others. "Despite the military occupation, I am still the acting mayor. I feel an obligation to do something. There must be something I can do!" He suddenly got up from the couch and began pacing the room. The resigned, weary look on his face was replaced by that of determination and grit, as he sought a way out of the mess he was in. His large ego would not allow for him to remain ignored and uninvolved any longer.

After a few minutes of frenzied pacing, the Mayor stopped dead in his tracks and looked up at the others, who were all seated. "I know exactly what I'll do," he declared. "I am going to call the general himself!" He ordered Ascencio to find the telephone number of the army barracks where General Torres was stationed. Within five minutes, Ascencio returned with the number. "Are you sure you want to call General Torres right now," he asked the Mayor, still clutching the number. "Maybe he should be contacted tomorrow instead, when things have settled down."

"No, I need to call him now!" Mayor Rivera replied boldly, quickly snatching the number from his chief aid. "If I don't assert myself now, I will really be left out of the loop."

"What are you going to say to him?" Ascencio asked.

"Nothing out of the ordinary," the Mayor responded. "I will introduce myself and then inquire about certain matters, such as how he intends to take control of the city. Of course, I will offer my help. Perhaps, it will be a meaningless conversation, but at least I will make my presence known to him. I figure it will be worse if I don't call him. What kind of a message will that send to the general? He'll think I'm afraid of him. I can't let him think that way of me! I need to assert myself and give him a call for the sake of my reputation."

The Mayor picked up the phone and then put it right back down. He needed a cigarette and took one from his desk. He lit it and then looked at the others, who were still seated. This had easily turned out to be one of the most difficult days in his life, but his decision to call General Torres made him feel reassured. He knew he was doing the right thing. "Maybe something good will come out of this," he told the others before picking up the phone again. He then calmly dialed the number and waited for what seemed like an eternity until someone finally answered on the other line. The Mayor, with much pride, introduced himself and asked to speak with Torres. He was told to hold on. The Mayor was again forced to wait for quite some time, and he began to shake his head in frustration at the drastic turn of events over the past couple days. "I was walking tall just a few days ago," he told the others. "Now look at me! I have to *wait* to speak with some goddamned general who has taken over my city. What does that tell you about fate and destiny?" He continued waiting for several more minutes, prompting him to consider hanging up when someone finally spoke on the other line. It was General Torres.

"Hello!" the general barked.

"Yes, General Torres, this is Mayor Rivera. Hello!"

"Yes . . ."

"General, I just wanted to contact you," the Mayor began somewhat nervously. "I was led to believe that we would meet upon your arrival."

"Well, I got tied up with things," the general explained arrogantly.

"I understand," the Mayor said. "By the way, is everything fine over at the barracks? I understand it has been used sparingly over the years."

"It's fine."

"Good, I am glad to hear that," said the Mayor, who was a bit annoyed with the general's curtness.

"You know, I am kind of busy right now," the general said. "Is there anything else you want to ask me?"

"No, that will be all," the Mayor responded meekly.

"Perhaps we will meet later," the general blandly stated. "Have a good evening."

This extraordinarily brief conversation only served to make the Mayor feel more distressed about the situation. He was particularly astonished by the general's lack of consideration. "I have met several generals throughout my life and none can compare to this Torres character!" the Mayor ranted. "What a callous jerk! I spoke to him in a cordial and respectful manner, but he chooses to say nothing and abruptly end the conversation! He gave me no information whatsoever! He did not even direct a question at me! You would think he would have provided some bits of information out of respect for me, the Mayor of this city . . . out of simple protocol, but nothing! Nobody has been that rude to me since I have been mayor! Well, it's safe to say that General Torres and I have no working relationship to speak of."

The Mayor complained bitterly about what could be done under the hazy circumstances. He was specifically troubled by the massacre. Victor Ascencio suggested he keep doing his job, considering the general provided no information. "I have to assume," Ascencio added, "that he will handle security while you take care of everything else. How else can we interpret the situation? As for the massacre, let the general worry about that." This, however, did little to ease Mayor Rivera's concerns. He left the office for the evening with his head bowed and shoulders drooped, the very picture of defeat. Never before in his political career had he felt so isolated and powerless.

*   *   *

In the meantime, Gabriel, Dr. Granados, and his friends were still holed up in the building along the downtown plaza where the demonstration and massacre took place earlier. At first, it was agreed they would stay in Rolando's offices overnight to avoid arrest or harassment from the troops patrolling the streets. However, as the night progressed, there was a growing need among everybody to get out and go home. They were encouraged by Dr. Granados' wife, who insisted in driving them all home. "As long as we are in a car, there should be no problem," she explained. She added that several cars and taxis were still driving around, despite the presence of troops everywhere. By ten o'clock, it was unanimously agreed, without much fuss, that Ms. Granados would pick everyone up and take them home. "Even if we get stopped," Dr. Granados said, "they can't prove anything. This is a big town and people have things to do. They can't just stop living because the army has arrived." Gabriel dared not call his aunt to inform her he was coming lest she vehemently objected to such an idea. "She would become hysterical," he thought.

Ms. Granados arrived at the building at around ten-thirty. The group was actually picked up at the rear entrance of the building, since the plaza was closed off. Everyone hurriedly got into the medium-sized Mazda and the car sped off without a hitch. Through the pale blue light of lampposts, Gabriel was able to see soldiers patrolling the streets, at least two per block. There were usually around ten of them in each big intersection, doing nothing but standing guard. They were just making their presence known at the moment, not yet enforcing any sort of curfew. There were indeed a good number of cars and taxis running about at that late hour, perhaps because people were too afraid to be walking in the street. The only people who were seen walking outside were the drunks, as they were mostly left alone by the army. Aside from some vehicles darting through town, things were very quiet. Making things appear quieter in Gabriel's eyes was the little amount of light turned on inside homes and apartments. People obviously did not want to draw the attention of soldiers, who might be privy to knocking on doors and badgering people for all sorts of reasons.

Gabriel would be the first person to be dropped off. Ms. Granados waited while the youth knocked the door, making sure someone answered. She did not have to wait long as a harried Aunt Teresa opened the door. Delighted to see that her beloved nephew had returned in one piece, she gave him a big hug and kissed his forehead. She and Gabriel then waved good-bye to the others in the car as it sped off. Noticing a couple soldiers rounding the corner about a block away and walking in their direction, Aunt Teresa grabbed her nephew by the arm and dragged him inside. She then quickly closed the door behind her and locked it. As they climbed up the stairs, her hands were visibly shaking. The events of the whole evening had evidently traumatized her. "We need to go upstairs right away!" she whispered.

"What's wrong, Aunt Teresa?" Gabriel asked.

"Those soldiers are terrible!" she said, as they got to the safety of the second floor.

"What happened?"

"They took Humberto!"

"Who is Humberto?" the puzzled youth asked.

"He is the grandson of Don Francisco, our neighbor," answered Aunt Teresa, sounding terrified. "They took him away!"

"Why did they take him away?"

"I don't know! Nobody knows! According to Don Francisco, they knocked on the door and asked for Humberto. There was a big argument between the soldiers and Don Francisco. As they continued fighting, the soldiers then barged into the apartment and dragged the poor boy away. He looks younger than you! He must be only seventeen or eighteen. They shoved him into a truck and drove away with no explanations, nothing! Don Francisco was left in the street, screaming and yelling at them. A couple of neighbors went out and tried to calm him down but he just kept yelling in the middle of the street, demanding an explanation from other soldiers who happened to be walking by. The neighbors then grabbed him and took him inside his apartment before things got any worse. It was terrible!"

"Could you hear what was being said?" Gabriel asked.

"Yes, I could hear them," Aunt Teresa answered. "The soldiers demanded for the boy to come outside. Don Francisco kept insisting he didn't know where Humberto was. It went back and forth like that for a couple minutes. They threatened to shoot him if he didn't retrieve his grandson, but he wouldn't budge. He just kept arguing with them. The soldiers finally stormed into his apartment. When the whole thing was finished, I then became so concerned about you, holed up somewhere. I was afraid they were going to take you away as well. I couldn't bear the thought!"

"Don't worry Aunt Teresa," Gabriel said, "I am here now and everything is all right." They gave each other a big hug. Aunt Teresa started to cry. Gabriel sensed she was crying out of concern rather than happiness. "Why are you crying like that?" he asked his aunt.

"Well, my dear Gabriel, you say thing things are all right," she replied, backing herself away from her nephew quite suddenly and seizing him by the arms. "They may be fine now, with you having returned safely, but the situation here in Nueva Vida is not so good. I would die if something bad were to happen to you. I love you so much. And then there's your mother. How could I even tell her? She would be absolutely devastated if something bad happened to you! Because the situation is so bad here at the present time, perhaps it would be best for you to go back home. It's too risky for you to stay here. I know your parents will be very concerned about you once they find out what's been going on here. It would be in everybody's best interests for you to return to America at once. I know I will be able to sleep better with you being removed from this dangerous place. You can always come back when things settle down."

"I will not go, Aunt Teresa," said Gabriel.

"You must go, Gabriel!"

"No, I will not!" the obstinate youth answered back with a firm voice. "I can't go back!"

"What do you mean you can't go back?" Aunt Teresa asked, growing more hysterical by the second. "You *can* go back. You have the money to buy a plane ticket. There will be no problem for you to leave here. Don't be foolish."

"You don't understand," Gabriel said. "You don't understand what I am saying! I *refuse* to leave here. I don't want to leave. That's my choice. Do you understand now?"

"No, I don't understand," Aunt Teresa asked in confusion. "Why don't you want to leave? How can you not want to leave this dangerous place? They are going to take you away, my dear Gabriel. Don't you see? They will take you away. You boldly stick out. You look like a foreigner. You will attract their attention and they will want to ask you questions. They then will take you away and god knows what will be done to you!"

"Aunt Teresa, you are not making any sense!" said the fiery youth. "Stop talking like that!"

"Why do you want to stay here?"

"I want to stay because I don't want to leave you and Grandmother Celia here alone at this critical time!"

"But we have our family and friends here who can help us," reasoned Aunt Teresa.

"I refuse to leave the both of you alone in this apartment!" Gabriel angrily declared. "I am staying here and that's the end of it! I will remain here until things subside." The youth made his point with such strong conviction that his aunt finally backed down from her demands that he leave at once. With nothing else to say, the two walked into the living room where Grandmother Celia was lying quietly in her bed. Gabriel walked over to her and gave her a big hug. She was elated to see him. He and Aunt Teresa sat there in the room beside Grandmother Celia. They did not say anything to each other. The lights were all off. Through the white moonlight peeking though the window, Gabriel was able to make out the old German rifle on the floor off to the corner. "That will be useless now," he thought, realizing the army would be a much more formidable foe than the crazed rioters from the night before. They all soon fell asleep in the living room, with Gabriel's grandmother and aunt sleeping in their respective beds while the youth dozed off in the chaise by the window. Unlike the night before, they were able to sleep soundly.

CHAPTER TWENTY-FIVE

DR. GRANADOS TAKES A STAND

The following morning was in many respects no different from any other in Nueva Vida. It was Monday and people were determined to go back to work and proceed with their lives, despite everything that had happened over the weekend. Like usual, Gabriel was awakened by the familiar horse-drawn milk carriage moving slowly through the street. The horse's resolute galloping and the large cow bell, rung by the milkman to signal his arrival in the neighborhood, would force Gabriel's eyes to open. However, the youth would remain in bed half-asleep, unwilling yet to get up and begin the day. He would lay there for about a half-hour, listening to all that was going on around him. There were the cars and trucks motoring through the street below; the people walking and talking outside; his grandmother watching some television with her cup of freshly-brewed coffee; and his aunt busy taking a shower, fixing herself up, tending to her mother, and taking care of other things in the apartment. "She is just like my mother," Gabriel once thought in reference to Aunt Teresa, "always staying busy with things."

Not until the maid rang the doorbell at nine o'clock would our friend finally get up from bed. That is precisely what happened on that particular Monday. Once he heard the doorbell ring, Gabriel ran to the bathroom to freshen up. Then he walked over, still in his cotton pajamas, to the kitchen to get some coffee and pastry, which was assembled neatly on a plate on the counter off to the side. He sat in a small table in the middle of the kitchen and began eating his breakfast. It was not much of a meal, but it was enough to give him a kick-start to the day. Besides, lunch was only a couple hours away. There was no need to eat a big breakfast.

After finishing with his pastry, Gabriel walked over to the hallway window just outside the kitchen with his cup of coffee. It was here where the youth occasionally would look at the lush garden tucked away behind the apartment. Since Grandmother Celia was then too old and weak, the garden was no longer tended to. It had grown a bit wild, with tall grass dominating much of it. One could hardly see the trails anymore because of the dense vegetation. Yet, the garden still was a magical place for Gabriel. Its charm and mystery retained a grip on his soul after all these years, despite having lost much of its beauty. The child in him with that natural predisposition to curiosity and wonderment had not left him. Stories of giant bats, poisonous frogs, mean cats, hairy spiders, and ghosts living within the garden's confines no longer dazed and fazed our friend, for he was now a grown-up. Nevertheless, whenever he looked at the garden or walked inside of it, a tingling sensation would jolt through his body. He enjoyed it very much. It was confirmation that his perception of the world was not completely jaded yet. "Thank God for that!" he would often say to himself in such moments, desperately holding onto his childhood memories.

Once he finished his coffee and had been sufficiently warmed by the sunshine poking through the window, Gabriel returned to the kitchen and left his cup in the sink. He then hopped into the shower and dressed up. By ten o'clock he was ready to grade some papers, but decided to call Dr. Granados first to find out if classes were also going to be cancelled the following day. The youth was informed by the professor that classes were not to be cancelled the following day, Tuesday. "I'm sorry there, Gabriel," the professor replied light-heartedly, "but you are going to have to work tomorrow." Dr. Granados then went on to tell the youth that he was going to attend a secret meeting later that evening at Occidental University. According to the professor, the meeting was to address the sudden disappearance of Dr. Ghetti and several of his students.

"There has been no word on their whereabouts?" Gabriel asked.

"None at all," answered Dr. Granados. "It is believed they were captured by the army. All what is known for sure is that Dr. Ghetti's wife and the families of the other missing students have reported them missing."

"That's interesting," Gabriel said. "A young man living in this neighborhood was rounded up by the army last night. I wonder if he was one of the students."

"Maybe he was," the professor commented wearily. "It's hard to say at this point why that boy may have been taken away. There could be a number of reasons. Maybe he did nothing at all and they rounded him up for no other reason than suspicion. That's how they operate. God knows how many people they actually took away last night!"

"What can be done about this?" the agitated youth asked.

"That is precisely what the organizers of this secret meeting are going to try to figure out tonight," the professor replied. "Of course, the police and local authorities won't do anything about the disappearances. The organizers probably realize that and figure they have to handle this problem on their own. It's an unfortunate situation. In a way, I can understand what they are going through."

"How did you know about this meeting, by the way?"

"An old student of mine, who is now attending Occidental University, told me about it," responded the professor. "She says the meeting will take place in the auditorium tonight at around six. That's the only information I have."

"Well, I would like to go," Gabriel said enthusiastically.

"I don't know if your aunt will like that," the conscientious professor remarked. "I can tell she really cares about you. She would be worried to death if you went. I don't think she should be put through anymore agony."

"I love my aunt very much," the youth explained. "However, I am not a child. I want to attend this meeting. I also don't want her to agonize any further over my safety and wellbeing. The best thing to do is not to tell her I'm going to this meeting. I'll tell her I will be eating dinner with my colleagues from work. That should do the trick."

"That will be good," the professor agreed. "I just hope things go all right. It would be bad for your aunt to go through any needless suffering. Anyway, why don't you come over to my house at around five-thirty? From there, we can go together to the university."

"Okay," affirmed the youth.

∗　　∗　　∗

Until he departed for Dr. Granados' house, Gabriel spent the day no differently than any other. He corrected some students' papers in the morning at his grandmother's cozy apartment, had lunch at noon, took a siesta nap right afterwards, and then at around two o'clock, took a walk to his favorite bakery at 19th Street to read the newspaper and have a cup of coffee. What was *unusual* about that day was all the commotion stemming from the massacre of the prior evening. Of course, it was front page news not only in the local papers, but the national ones as well. Everywhere in Nueva Vida, people were talking about it. They passionately discussed every known detail of the massacre, from when it began to how it unfolded. What incensed many people were the rumors about the dead being unceremoniously piled onto the back of pick-up trucks. "I saw it for myself," Gabriel sadly reflected. The youth overheard a man at the bakery describing the army as 'a bunch of cold-hearted, fascist pigs'. "They have no consideration for human life," the man's companion added.

All eighteen victims were finally identified by late morning, whose names were pronounced over the radio. By the early afternoon, a small but vociferous group of people gathered in front of city hall, within ear shot of Mayor Rivera himself, demanding to know why the massacre took place. When a representative of the Mayor finally went out to address the crowd, they overwhelmed him with a flood of questions. When the representative responded merely by saying he had no answers at the moment, the crowd got angry. "The Mayor is running this city!" one shouted. "He should know what's going on!" Under frenzied attack, the representative nervously saluted the crowd, spun around and went back inside.

Another unusual aspect of that day was of course the army's presence in every quarter of town. They certainly did not ease the mounting tensions among the populace. Aside from some isolated instances of pushing and poking individuals who got in their way, the soldiers did not cause any trouble through much of the day. They were strictly patrolling the streets. Yet, their quiet presence was all the more unnerving perhaps because people sensed they might be transformed by nightfall, when they could get away with more aggression under the cover of darkness. Rumors quickly spread about the sinister reputation of this infamous army and the man who led it, General Manuel Torres. Stories of the army's conduct in the countryside, with their penchant for bloodshed and rape, made the rounds all across Nueva Vida. These grisly tales only served to heighten the peoples' distrust and fear of the troops patrolling their neighborhoods. Accounts of General Torres' notorious corruption schemes also made the rounds, arousing a sense of repugnance from most civilians. While most people preferred to stay away from the troops, there were some who dared to confront them, telling them to get out of Nueva Vida among other things. Having walked the streets during the afternoon, Gabriel judged the situation in this once peaceful, pastoral town to be unhealthy. "It is damn tense around here," he thought.

Once he returned to his grandmother's apartment, Gabriel rested for a while before having some tea with his aunt. The youth described what he saw on his walk through town, telling Aunt Teresa that the general atmosphere was one of 'bleakness and uneasiness'. Aunt Teresa was not surprised about her nephew's depiction of the situation, but remained hopeful the army would soon leave with peace being restored. "I know there are a lot of injustices in this country," she explained, "and the people have a right to feel upset about Vicente Sanchez's death. But what people need to realize is that things were not so bad before, at least here in Nueva Vida that is. Yes, there is a lot of poverty here, but there was peace! The civil war never has touched us. When there is peace, there is hope for everybody. People can go about their lives normally. When there is war and conflict, that sense of hope is crushed. Nobody wins with war. Only agony and death prevail! I hope that the people here can understand that and not make any trouble with the army." Gabriel respectfully listened to his aunt's words, choosing not to say anything. It certainly was food for thought. "Perhaps she is right," he pondered, for he was already learning fast how ugly 'war and conflict' can be.

After finishing his tea, Gabriel got ready to leave for Dr. Granados' house. As planned, he told his aunt he would be off to have dinner with some colleagues from work. When she expressed her concerns about him being out at night with all the troops roaming about, the youth told her not to worry. "I promise not to do anything stupid," he said. "Besides, I will be traveling around in a car. Please don't worry." He kissed her forehead and left before his aunt could object further. The youth was out the door by about five o'clock. He walked all the way to Dr. Granados' house, which took him about twenty minutes. When he got there, the professor was ready to leave. He took his car out of the garage and opened the door to let Gabriel in. "Hop in, young revolutionary!" he quipped, "We have some important business to tend to." The young American was slightly nervous.

*　　*　　*

When Gabriel and Dr. Granados entered the auditorium of Occidental University, they were a bit surprised by what they saw. Only about three hundred people were in attendance in the five thousand seat facility. Unlike the night before at the demonstration, there was not much fanfare and excitement. There were no Colombian flags and confetti to be seen, nor singing and chanting to be heard. It was a very somber atmosphere as most people were impatiently waiting for the meeting to begin, hunched in their seats with concerned expressions on their faces. A majority of them were either relatives or friends of the twelve individuals reportedly missing since the end of the demonstration. Some were quietly fidgeting about, while others were visibly crying. "It seems we have just entered a funeral," Gabriel remarked to Dr. Granados. A large, rectangular table stood atop the stage toward the front of the auditorium. Three small microphones, a big jug of water and six small glasses were laid out neatly on it, indicating the meeting would be orchestrated from there.

Gabriel and Dr. Granados would not have to wait long for the meeting to start, for shortly after they took their seats, six individuals emerged from the back of the stage and were making their way to the table. They took their places at the table and, with dour faces, viewed the audience before them. The first to talk was the dark, dapper chancellor of the university, Dr. Rene Delgado, who was seated off to the side of the panel. His appearance, with a smug grin, slightly long hair, and a turtleneck sweater underneath a checkerboard blazer, exuded an air of academic stuffiness. He introduced himself and the five others on the panel who volunteered to run the meeting. Then he went on to explain its purpose. "Last night, an esteemed member of our staff and eleven students went missing," Dr. Delgado slowly stated into one of the microphones in a calm, deep voice. "We are all gathered here to discuss what can be done to procure the safe return of these individuals. I would like to first point out that the university did not in any way encourage the demonstration to take place last night. In fact, the university actually had no knowledge of the demonstration until after it was broken up by that senseless massacre, for it was organized all within a few hours yesterday, outside of campus. The school, as most of you probably know, is closed on Sundays. Although the university did not in any way support the idea of holding last night's demonstration, it will nevertheless strive to undo the damage and find a way to have Dr. Ghetti and his students returned safely. I can say already that the university has contacted the local and federal police authorities about this matter, as well as the Mayor's office. They have all informed us that they are proceeding with their own investigations and will soon contact the army regarding the whereabouts of the missing individuals. We intend to conduct our own investigation as well. We want this to be resolved as soon as possible."

"Has the university made direct contact with the army?" asked one irritated member of the audience.

"We have attempted to contact the army general here," Dr. Delgado replied. "I believe his name is General Torres. Our attempts to contact this general have so far been unsuccessful."

"Why go through the police authorities and the Mayor's office when we know the army has these people," asked the same man. "I don't think they are going to be of any help. The university and all concerned parties should just seek direct contact with the army."

"Like I said, we have been seeking direct contact with the army," the university chancellor answered after a nervous sip of water, "but every attempt has been unsuccessful. I also disagree with your idea that we should only work through the army. We could be stonewalled the entire time. On the contrary, we should seek the help of *other* agencies and institutions, whether government or private, for they perhaps could exert some influence upon the army to at least disclose some information about the missing individuals. We need as much help as possible in this endeavor. The more outside pressure exerted upon the army, the better our results will be."

Contented with this answer, the chancellor left the other members of the panel to run the meeting and answer questions. Unfortunately, things never took off. There were too many unanswered questions and hostile accusations thrown around during the meeting to yield any positive results. Things degenerated into a frenzied argument between those who supported the demonstration and those who opposed it. Even members of the panel were fiercely bickering with each other. The whole affair turned into a fiasco. The one man who could have prevented all this, the university chancellor, was dumbstruck by the chaos and frequently walked out of the auditorium, cell phone in hand, apparently tending to other business. "He wants to get the hell out of here," Dr. Granados commented cynically. After forty-five minutes of such rabble, some people began to walk out of the auditorium. One man, while he was making his early departure, declared: "We are supposed to be saving the lives of our missing loved ones, and instead, you are all fighting about the merits of this demonstration which occurred yesterday.

You all make me sick! With this attitude, we will never get them back!"

Appalled by all the nonsense, Dr. Granados got up from his seat and marched to one of the standing microphones in the aisles. He impatiently waited behind a woman who was comparing the plight of the missing ringleaders of the demonstration to the government kidnappings of liberal politicians during the 1940's. "Excuse me!" interjected one of the members of the panel who was also frustrated by the lack of progress being made. Her name was Elsa. "But how is this historical comparison going to help us retrieve my son and the others who have disappeared? We cannot waste any more time with this kind of talk! We need to address the problem at hand!" This drew everyone's applause. Elsa, who now seemed to be taking command of the wayward proceedings, motioned Dr. Granados to move up to the microphone, for it was his turn to speak.

The professor calmly introduced himself. He then claimed to have a solution to the disappearances, but first went on to tell the story of his kidnapped daughter. "I understand what all of you are going through," asserted the professor, whose dignified voice suddenly grabbed everyone's attention, "the fear . . . the pain . . . the agony of not knowing where your loved ones are, or whether they are alive. I did everything possible to save my daughter's life. I hired a detective. I wrote letters to the mayor, senator, and governor. Yet, despite all my efforts, I was unable to save her life. I firmly believe that I was unable to save her because I was pretty much alone and the kidnappers were unknown. However, your situation is very much different from mine. In this mission to get back your loved ones, you are definitely not alone. The number of people who have gathered together here in this auditorium is a testament to that fact. Secondly, we all know who the abductors are: they are *the army*. Right away, you all have a huge advantage over those families who typically lose loved ones to kidnappers in this country every day."

"Now, how is this advantageous you might ask? Since you are all in the same boat, you can actually use the numbers game to your advantage by banding together against the army. Go out there and make your selves heard! Don't wait for things to happen. Take it to the army! By taking such action, you all improve your chances of winning back your loved ones. I am most certain of that."

"Thank you very much for offering your insights, Dr. Granados," said Elsa, who was quite pleased with the professor's thoughtfulness. "I think you made some very good points and I appreciate you sharing that story of your daughter. I am so sorry that happened to you. You mention that we should band together, make ourselves heard, and take it to the army. How do you suggest we go about doing that exactly?"

"It's quite simple," the professor replied. "You just walk out there with some big signs so that everyone knows what you are demonstrating about. Make sure the signs address the army. That is very important! That will focus everyone's attention solely on the army, which is what we want. The demonstration can perhaps be held in front of city hall, thus placing the Mayor in an embarrassing spot as well. By taking this sort of action, you all will be able to exert far more pressure on the army than going through such conventional channels like the police or local politicians."

"That's interesting," Elsa said, "but wouldn't organizing such a demonstration be dangerous for us? We will be making the same mistakes as our children?"

"I don't see it that way," Dr. Granados answered. "Anything is possible, but I don't see the army attempting to crack the whip in this case. You all will be demanding the safe return of your loved ones. The demonstration on Sunday called for government reform. That was a whole different situation altogether. The army did not blink an eye in shooting and arresting potential anarchists, rioters, and revolutionaries. However, they won't touch mothers and fathers pleading for the lives of their children. They know all of Nueva Vida would pounce on them if they did."

"So you suggest we do nothing more than get together with some signs and march over to city hall?" Elsa asked.

"That's all that will be necessary," the professor responded firmly. "This will be nothing but an old fashioned demonstration, but one that can actually work to your benefit because the whole town will be behind you. I really believe this is something all the respective families must do because it is right! You all must be seen and heard, or else the army will feel free to do whatever it wants. What they have done is terrible. It is illegal! They cannot simply apprehend people for no reason at all. I was at the demonstration and there were no illegal activities taking place. There was absolutely no justification for the army to have indiscriminately massacred so many people and arrest dozens of others. These are heinous crimes which the army should be severely punished for. You have a right to at least demand where your loved ones are, and that right should be exercised now! We live in a democracy for Christ's sake! If you don't protest and exercise your rights as free citizens of one of the oldest democracies on earth, you will be caving in to the forces of repression and tyranny. For the sake of your loved ones and Colombia, you must not allow that to happen!"

When Dr. Granados finished, he received a standing ovation from everyone in the auditorium. They all were thoroughly impressed with his candor and passion. Deep down in their hearts, everyone knew he was right and that something drastic needed to be done. Everyone, that is, except the university chancellor, Dr. Delgado. He nervously watched what was unraveling before him. This cold and pedantic man certainly did not want the meeting to become a springboard to more demonstrations and social upheavals in the future, especially under his watch! He wanted the families to resort to conventional methods of retrieving their loved ones, to allow the police and other civil institutions to do the work. Deeply afraid of the army, he did not want the university to be further tied to any potentially subversive activities. He was now determined to put a stop to Dr. Granados.

"Excuse me, everybody!" Dr. Delgado called out from his place at the edge of the table. "Excuse me, but I don't believe this meeting is going in the right direction. I can tell you right now that the university is certainly not going to support a demonstration. We don't want further unrest. Let's not forget that your loved ones resorted to having a demonstration, and look what happened to them! They are now apprehended and lord knows what will happen to them. You must not commit the same mistake. We must discuss other solutions to this problem or else I will have to ask all of you to leave the auditorium."

Everyone, including Elsa and the other members of the panel, looked in the direction of Dr. Granados to see how he would respond to this challenge from the university chancellor. He was now their leader. "That is fine, Dr. Delgado," the dignified professor answered with restraint. "We don't want to cause you and the university any further trouble. For those, however, who are interested in marching to city hall in the very near future, please follow me. I run a school not too far from here. There are several large rooms there where we can meet." The professor then walked out. Within a couple minutes, the entire auditorium was empty. Only two individuals were left standing inside: Gabriel and Dr. Delgado. Both were too stunned to move.

CHAPTER TWENTY-SIX

A CALL FOR PATIENCE

Once the family and friends of those missing since the demonstration exited the auditorium, they immediately gathered outside around the thin, diminutive Dr. Granados. He went on to tell them they should meet at his language institute the following morning, rather than that night, to further plan their march to city hall. "I was just thinking that if we go there right now," he explained, "the army will be very suspicious. Tomorrow morning will be a whole lot safer with all the hustle-bustle around town to draw off their attention. Nine o'clock should be perfect." Everyone was receptive to this idea. After they were given directions to his school, the professor dismissed them all.

Gabriel witnessed all of this in disbelief. He knew the professor to have some pretty strong political beliefs, but not so bold as to lead a demonstration into the heart of Nueva Vida, in front of city hall! The youth always considered him to be a bit cynical and reserved to take on such an awesome responsibility. Yet, here was Dr. Granados giving a couple hundred of these unfortunate people a voice to be reckoned with, offering them some real hope. In a sense, he was now carrying the torch previously carried by Vicente Sanchez and the missing Dr. Ghetti. In Gabriel's mind, the unassuming professor was not only going to help retrieve the individuals who were illegally abducted by the army, but come to Colombia's rescue in these desperate times. The professor implied it himself inside the auditorium.

When they were finally left alone, Gabriel congratulated his new hero. "I can't believe you did that!" he told him. "You are going to lead these people. You are actually going to continue this struggle begun by Sanchez! This is amazing!"

"As always, Gabriel, you are getting a little ahead of yourself," the shrewd professor retorted. "But perhaps you are not missing the mark by much. My sole intention is to help these poor people get their loved ones back. But in doing so, this simple mission may become a symbol for something else entirely, something bigger . . . something that might strike a chord with many people. If that is what ends up happening, then so be it. However, my ambition here is not to succeed Sanchez or Ghetti. I just want to help these people, for I know what they are going through." Gabriel was not buying any of this. The rationalizations offered by the professor were only serving to blind him of the obvious truth. If a demonstration was going to take place, it would indeed be widely considered a *continuation* of the struggle begun by Sanchez, especially after his death and the abduction of Dr. Ghetti. With a large army, the local and federal authorities, and the rest of Colombia on watch, another demonstration in Nueva Vida would be all the more significant. Every step taken by Dr. Granados and his demonstration would certainly be witnessed and dissected by everyone in the country, especially since members of Colombia's press corps were making their way to the once quaint, sleepy town in droves. Such a march, pleading the safe return of illegally abducted citizens, was going to test not only the army's patience, but its sense of humanity. How the army would respond to such a dignified, passionate march might possibly have very serious consequences for the rest of the country. The fate of Colombia as a nation with long-standing democratic traditions would then be hanging in the balance.

Gabriel understood this and realized how enormous the professor's undertaking actually was. "Dr. Granados must also understand this, but he is not willing to admit it," the youth thought. He became very excited just thinking about all the possibilities. He was dazed by the thought of becoming a major player in the professor's planned march. For once in his short, boring life, the young American could directly partake in something worthwhile. He immediately offered his services to the professor, which was accepted only under the condition that Aunt Teresa not be informed of it. "We don't want her to suffer through more anxiety," the professor remarked as he had earlier in the day. The two did not talk much during the drive back to town. Dr. Granados dropped off Gabriel in front of his Grandmother Celia's apartment. "Stop by the institute at around nine tomorrow morning," he informed the youth.

"I certainly will," Gabriel responded.

*   *   *

That evening, the night of Monday, October 28th, would end up being very calm, which surely delighted the majority of Nueva Vida's citizens. After a calamitous week, which included the festive nights in anticipation of Vicente Sanchez's arrival, the riots following his death, and the massacre of the prior evening, the townspeople were desperate for some peace and quiet. Never before had Nueva Vida encountered so much turmoil in one week. The troops patrolling the city did nothing to further aggravate the situation. To nearly everyone's surprise, the soldiers, since that morning, professionally went about their business, not straying far from their assigned duties of providing security. When they did stray from their respective duties, it was only to play a quick game of cards at the street corner or take a prolonged cigarette break. In every part of town, acts of harassment against innocent civilians were very rarely observed. At times, the demeanor of these troops was even deferential, with a nod of the head in greeting here and a helping hand to an old woman crossing a street there. So impressed were some civilians by their behavior that they heralded them as saviors of Nueva Vida. Many people, however, did not jump to such sweeping conclusions, preferring to give the situation some time. "They are like wild animals," Aunt Teresa told Gabriel when he returned from the university that night. "They may be calm most of the time, but you never know when they will strike and cause harm."

When Gabriel went to bed later that night, he overheard some of the soldiers walking around and talking outside. He went to the window overlooking the street below and saw three of them standing not too far. They were having a light-hearted conversation just across from the building. The youth could not make out exactly what they were discussing, but their frequent laughter indicated nothing more than a good ole' round of jokes and stories. Yet, they were not loud, obnoxious, and drunk, as the sound of their low, muffled voices was actually soothing to Gabriel's ears. He went back to sleep to the sound of that unthreatening conversation taking place just outside. "Those wild animals are definitely calm for the moment," he thought before his eyes shut.

*   *   *

The following morning, Gabriel got out of bed as soon as he heard the milk man's cowbell at around 8:15. He wanted to get to the language institute at nine o'clock sharp. He jumped into the shower, got dressed and ate a quick breakfast. When confronted by his aunt about the abrupt departure from his daily routine of waking up later in the morning, Gabriel did not stray too far from the truth. The youth explained he needed to help Dr. Granados do some odd jobs around the school that morning. Aunt Teresa did not press the matter further as she retired into the kitchen. Within a couple minutes, he was out the door and on his way to the language institute. For the first time in days, things really seemed to be getting back to normal. The streets were teeming with automobiles, while businesses were open and running. Despite the presence of troops, the strain of the previous days now showed less on most people's faces. Yet, Gabriel understood that all was not entirely well with the massacre and disappearances still looming large over the city. There was a sense that the slightest agitation in the street could bring the entire city back down on its knees once again, triggering another round of violence. "Things will really heat up around here with this demonstration," the youth thought in reference to Dr. Granados' plans. "People won't be able to ignore it."

When Gabriel arrived at the institute a little after nine, he was informed by the secretary that the meeting was being held in a room all the way at the rear of the building. "That's the room with no windows," he thought. He anxiously walked down the long, dark hall, passing by several rooms and quickly approaching the one at the end. Gabriel saw the door was open and lights were on, but noticed it was rather quiet. He wondered if he might be the first person in attendance. Once he entered the room, however, there were about fifty people already there, busy getting their large signs ready. He saw Dr. Granados walking around and helping the people, providing them with markers, glue, tape, and long wooden sticks with which to attach the poster boards. He also was giving them suggestions on what slogans and statements to use for the demonstration. Some of the signs read: "WHERE ARE OUR LOVED ONES?"; "WHY ARE THEY MISSING?"; "THEY DID NOTHING WRONG! BRING THEM BACK TO US!"; and "THE ARMY PROTECTS CIVILIANS, NOT KIDNAPS THEM." Other signs were more personal, with some containing nothing more than large blown-up photographs of the missing individuals.

Work on the signs continued for another hour as more people continued arriving into the school. Those who were already finished would help the people who just arrived begin working on their signs. Everybody seemed to be enjoying this activity, as they were doing something creative while mingling with others experiencing the same anguished feelings and thoughts as them. It seemed to be a wonderful stress-reliever for them, despite the fact they would soon embark on a potentially dangerous mission. Yet, these unfortunate people were not the least thinking about their own personal safety, but that of their missing loved ones. They showed no fear whatsoever for what they were about to do, such was their feeling of righteousness. Dr. Granados had done a good job of convincing them that they were doing the proper thing.

Gabriel, at first, just stood in the corner and observed the people working on their signs, but he then decided to follow what Dr. Granados was doing and offer help to others. "It makes no sense to be standing around doing nothing," he thought. Like the professor, he roved about and provided people with markers, posters, glue, and other supplies. He even helped design a couple of poster boards. The young American eventually decided to make his own sign, adopting the slogan "JUSTICE MUST PREVAIL OVER TYRANNY!" which was written in big block letters.

This drew the attention of Dr. Granados, who questioned whether it was too political for their purposes. "We want the army to return the missing people," he told Gabriel. "This type of slogan might be a little too hostile for our purposes." However, someone else read Gabriel's slogan and found no fault with it. "The kid's right," the man said. "That's a great message. We're against the tyranny of the army!" The professor, after a brief moment of thought, acquiesced and allowed the slogan to remain as it was. "Oh, what the hell!" he exclaimed. "Maybe it will help us."

Once most of the signs were completed, Dr. Granados decided to address the people in the large room. There were a little more than a hundred people in attendance by then. He told them that they were finished with their work for the day, and to meet at the institute around one o'clock the following day. This then ignited much discussion about the timing of the protest. Many people wanted to go ahead with it at that very moment. "Let's not wait any longer!" declared one man. "Let's do it right now!" Elsa, the fiery, matronly woman who led the advisory panel the previous evening at Occidental University, and who still garnered much respect among several people, also was in favor of protesting that day. "The sooner we act, the better are our chances of saving their lives," she reasoned, her dark eyes exuding a sense of authority and passion paralleled in the room only by the professor's. "What's the use in waiting when, at this point, every second is crucial to them. We can't afford to waste time and we certainly can't let them wait in agony anymore!" Most of the people were in full agreement with this as they clamored to march the streets right away.

Dr. Granados felt himself backed into a corner, but did not give in to such calls for immediate action. "I understand your point, Elsa," the professor calmly replied. "Time is definitely of the essence here. But I feel the best time to protest would be tomorrow. Firstly, the army is probably just trying to get information from those they have abducted, determining if they are real threats to society and are somehow linked to the riots of Saturday night. That process will take some time. Secondly, I don't think the murder of any of these individuals is an option for the army right now, especially with the whole country watching. Instead, they are probably figuring out if any of the detainees should receive jail time, from which they would then be simply handed over to the federal authorities. I really feel there will be no more slayings. There was more than enough blood spilled during the massacre.

"Lastly, let's give the army one more day to contemplate the matter further. Who knows, they may decide to release everyone today. I just think it is in our best interest to wait one more day to see what develops, to see if the army budges a bit from the existing pressures applied by the media, local authorities, and populace. If they do not budge by tomorrow, however, then we will have every right to demonstrate. Three days would have been enough time to wait. Let us just remain cool for one more day."

The people, including Elsa, quietly agreed with the professor's plan to protest the following day and slowly filed out of the building when they were dismissed. "You won't have to be patient for too long!" Dr. Granados declared to his sullen followers, attempting to raise their spirits. They were chomping at the bit to take immediate action but realized begrudgingly that the professor's prudent course of action was perhaps best.

"They don't look too happy," the exhausted professor told Gabriel when everyone had left. His thin arms were folded behind his head while his eyes gazed up searchingly at the ceiling. "Boy, I did not expect things to turn out so difficult."

"They all want to protest now," the dazed youth replied, "but I think you did the right thing. We should buy a little more time."

"I don't know if I made the right decision by waiting another day," the professor remarked. "We won't really know for sure until tomorrow, I guess. Anyway, Gabriel, we are trying to help these people and I suppose that's all that really matters."

CHAPTER TWENTY-SEVEN

ORDER IS RESTORED

While Dr. Granados and Gabriel were making preparations for a civil march into downtown Nueva Vida, General Manuel Torres was already planning an exit strategy. He yearned to leave Nueva Vida. "This is no place for us," the general repeatedly told his aids. "We need to get back to the countryside as soon as possible." He was growing wary of his predicament, concerned about all the things that could go wrong with his troops in a large urban setting, especially one with a hostile populace. The calculating general sensed that the longer his troops remained in the city, the greater the likelihood they would encounter serious problems down the road. Thus, he proposed to his staff that they leave Nueva Vida soon, the precise date of departure being on Tuesday, November 5th, which would only leave about another week of occupation. "What's the point of lingering around here?" he asked his chief of staff, the dwarfish Colonel Frederico Lopez-Leconte. "To remain here any longer would be risky and stupid."

Despite believing that the brutal crackdown on Sunday night was appropriate, it left General Torres feeling increasingly precarious about the circumstances. He was growing paranoid about other rebellions, especially those in response to the massacre, taking place in the coming days. Gone for sure was the bravado that marked his arrival upon Nueva Vida. He leaned back on his leather chair at headquarters on the evening of Tuesday, October 29th, attempting to further analyze matters. His graying hair was neatly combed back, revealing a round face that resembled a toad's, with all sorts of warts and pockmarks covering his reddish skin. What prevented his face from being ugly, however, were his radiant hazel eyes, which reflected an air of authority and boldness. He lit a cigar in order to think more clearly and stop the fidgeting of his hands, which was particularly irksome because it revealed to himself and others his sense of fear. General Torres took a couple puffs from his cigar and brooded further. At the moment, he was pondering what to do with the demonstrators that were forcibly apprehended a couple nights before. Within a couple of minutes, the general suddenly came up with a solution. "We will interrogate those people one more day," he told Colonel Lopez-Leconte, "for the sake of appearances. Regardless of whether they give us information or not, they all are to be released tomorrow night. That is my final decision."

"So, even if they give information, they are still to be released?" asked the baffled colonel, who stood in front of his seated boss.

"Yes, that is correct."

"General, that does not make too much sense," the colonel remarked.

"Look, I don't care about the situation here," the general explained. "I just want to get out. If we report that one of our prisoners has important information concerning what happened here over the weekend, we may be forced to stay longer. We will have to conduct more manhunts and interrogations, while exposing ourselves to the danger of an insurrection against us. Now, does that seem like fun to you, my noble colonel? Why should we be breaking our backs like that for the government when they themselves have been so inept and careless? I don't want to make the mistake of staying here any longer than we should. Let's keep those people detained one more day, release them tomorrow night, and prepare for our departure next Tuesday."

"If someone does happen to give vital information over the next twenty-four hours, should we still at least alert the government and have the person handed over to them?" the colonel asked.

"No, no, no!" answered an irritated General Torres, shaking his head vehemently. "That will just make things more complicated! What you need to know, my dear colonel, is that I am not interested in making the government happy right now. I am actually keener on making the townspeople here happy so that there won't be any further problems before we leave on Tuesday. By no means should we detain even one person after tomorrow night! Those are my instructions. I also don't want them to be tortured or harassed in any way until their release. You will personally deliver those instructions once you leave this office."

"Have you informed the government about our departure next Tuesday?" Colonel Lopez-Leconte sheepishly asked.

"No, not yet," quietly replied General Torres. "I don't plan on telling them until the weekend so they won't have much time to think about it. Regardless of what their reaction is, I still plan on having my troops leave this city on Tuesday."

"Don't you think that would be a little unwise?" asked the colonel. "They may court-martial us for not following their orders."

"Colonel, you should know better than that!" the general said, grinning broadly. "How many times have we not followed the government's orders in the past? I can't even count with my hands it's been so many times! And do you recall us ever getting in trouble once? Besides, I believe many in the government will agree with our decision to leave as early as possible. Once I explain my decision to them and describe all the things that can go wrong with an extended occupation of this city, we will receive enough support to leave on Tuesday. I'm sure of it."

"What if they just so happen to not support your decision to leave on Tuesday, General Torres?" asked the cautious colonel. "What will we do then? It's true that we have not gotten in trouble for disobeying government orders in the past, but this is a whole different situation altogether. We are being asked to occupy a major city, which the government takes very seriously for it involves national security in a major way. If we fail to comply with this order, I am afraid they *will* come after us. Yes, we have killed peasants in the countryside and gotten ourselves involved with some illegal operations, but the government always knew we did those things for the sake of our own survival. It never involved them directly anyway, so they would always let us off the hook. But now, we are talking about the government's survival here and the occupation of Nueva Vida directly involves their authority and credibility. We will have no choice but to enforce their directives."

"Oh Colonel Lopez, don't be so naïve!" the general scolded him once again. "If we do not oblige their orders this time around, what the hell are they going to do? You say they will come after us. How are they going to do that? With what forces will they pursue us? Have you forgotten we are mired in a civil war in which all available forces are currently being pressed into service throughout the country? If they throw just one division against us, their own security and survival will be terribly undermined. They will shoot themselves in the foot! They cannot afford to go against us. What you fail to realize, my dear colonel, is that we have all the leverage right now. There is absolutely nothing the government can do to stop us. Don't forget that we are doing them a favor by coming here to Nueva Vida and cleaning up their mess in the first place. Look, we won't have to worry about all this because I will have the government convinced that leaving Tuesday will be the right thing."

"What will you tell them?" the colonel asked.

"I will tell them that keeping our forces here for too long will be a terrible mistake. We will risk losing not only the countryside, but Nueva Vida as well. I will suggest keeping a small force, perhaps a thousand troops, here outside of Nueva Vida for an indefinite period of time. But the brunt of my army should be in the countryside battling the guerillas, safeguarding the roads, farms, and ranches of this region. We have been very successful doing that for the past few years. It would be in Colombia's best interest for us to be out there rather than to be holed up here. I received reports this morning that the guerillas have already made incursions into the Putumayo and northern Narino. The longer we stay here, the deeper they will penetrate into the heart of this area. We simply cannot allow that to happen. I will explain all this to the government. I am almost sure they will agree to have our troops leave here by Tuesday, especially if the guerillas continue moving deeper into the area."

"What if there is another major rebellion in this city?" the colonel asked.

"As I said, there will be a thousand of my troops stationed here indefinitely to take care of such emergencies," the general answered confidently. "If it gets really bad, the army can come here for a short period of time. But, it should not be kept here indefinitely! The countryside is far more important than any individual city. What is a town without the farms, ranches, factories, electric power lines, and roads located in the countryside? It is nothing! It could not survive without the countryside. Too many people overestimate the value of a city. Too many generals and politicians throughout history have made the mistake of placing too much importance on cities. Look what happened to Hitler in Stalingrad! He lost the entire 6th Army, 250,000 troops, in his irrational quest to capture that town. Look what happened to Napoleon in Moscow! Even when a city has been captured, the advantages and benefits can be illusory. Take, for instance, the siege of Constantinople. It took an eternity for the Turks to finally conquer that city, but they expended all their resources in the process, to the point of being paralyzed for several years thereafter. If they had ignored Constantinople altogether, the Turks would have been much better off. What *we* need to do here is learn from history and focus on the countryside, for as long as we control it, we will also control Nueva Vida. I have always believed that cities, in a strategic sense, are irrelevant."

"General Torres, you have convinced me," Colonel Lopez-Leconte affirmed. "I am sure that your strategy of focusing more on the countryside will convince the government as well. You have never been wrong before."

"In the worst case scenario," the general added, puffing on his cigar, "if the government does not agree with me, which is a very slight possibility, we will still leave on Tuesday. If they want to unleash some forces our way, let them! That would be awfully foolish and stupid on their part. I know that will not happen."

*   *   *

So sensitive had General Torres become in regards to treating the civilian population of Nueva Vida with decency in the wake of the massacre that he issued a specific mandate to his troops on the morning of Monday, October 28th. It stated that all citizens were not to be provoked in any way. There were to be no acts of sexual harassment, rape, robbery, intimidation, home invasion, physical abuse or murder committed by any of his troops. They were to stick solely to their patrol duties. Acts of 'kindness and generosity' were even encouraged by the mandate, as it further stipulated that the occupation of Nueva Vida *must* be 'smooth if it is to be brief in duration'. Most soldiers wanted to return to the countryside anyhow, so they cooperated fully with their commander's mandate. This explains why the soldiers had comported themselves so well.

However, there was one individual, a certain hot-headed private, who did not comply with the order. The private was accused of sexually harassing a young woman. Apparently, he raised the woman's skirt with his rifle as she walked past him in a busy intersection in broad daylight. The soldier, according to several eyewitnesses, then proceeded to follow the girl down the street a few blocks, rudely pestering her with questions about her availability later in the evening. Luckily for the young woman, three of the private's comrades had been closely following them and dragged the indignant private away.

This incident was reported to General Torres. At first, he had the private suspended indefinitely without pay. This particular private already had a reputation for harassing women, so the decision was easy. "I will not allow this type of reckless behavior from any of my troops, especially now!" the general told his aids. "I don't want any further complications." Considering he had ordered a bloody massacre a couple days before, the general's handling of the private came across as grossly hypocritical to his subordinates. Sensing their disappointment with him, the politically savvy general arranged to have the private's bus ride home paid for in full. He also decided to limit the suspension to four months, which appeased his aids enough for they did not want any of the troops to be punished too severely for what they considered mild offenses. In their minds, the private's harassment of the girl certainly fit the mild category, for he had not laid a hand on her. Normally, such acts of harassment and even rape committed by soldiers in the countryside were ignored by General Torres and his staff, but the delicate situation in Nueva Vida required a drastic change in outlook and policy. The private needed to be made an example if the general was to retain any discipline over his troops. The news of the suspension quickly spread among the rank and file of Torres' army, which compelled them to follow the mandate to the letter.

Thus, three days into their occupation of Nueva Vida, things were indeed becoming more peaceful and quiet, thanks in large part to the mandate. Not since Monday afternoon had there been any signs of protests, for people not only were desperate for a prolonged respite, but, unbeknownst to the general, were even growing fond of the firm security provided by the army. The bloody massacre of Sunday night was rapidly becoming a distant memory. As of Wednesday morning, October 30th, there was every indication that General Torres' hopes for an easy and brief occupation would be realized, particularly with the release of detainees scheduled for that very evening.

CHAPTER TWENTY-EIGHT

A VISIT TO CHURCH

On the morning of Wednesday, October 30th, Gabriel woke up feeling extremely excited and nervous. This was going to be a big day for him, for the protest was scheduled to take place that very afternoon. He jumped into the shower after waking up. He hoped the warm water would calm him a little, but it did nothing to abate the youth's increasing anxieties. The subsequent routine of getting dressed and eating breakfast did not help matters, as Gabriel's initial feelings of excitement and nervousness were giving way to a profound sense of dread. Watching her nephew go about his business that morning in an unusually harried and quiet manner prompted Aunt Teresa to ask him what was wrong. Not expecting such a question to be thrown his way, Gabriel had to think about it at first. "Oh, I am just a little concerned about how my students will perform on the test tonight," he finally answered, which did not convince his aunt the least bit.

"Are you sure there isn't something else that's bothering you?" she asked.

"No, not at all," replied the youth, not daring to tell her the truth.

Aunt Teresa left it at that, as Gabriel was allowed to finish his breakfast in peace. He soon left the apartment to take a morning stroll around the neighborhood. As soon as he was out the door, he lit a cigarette but it only left him feeling pretty light-headed, so he dumped it right away. The anguished youth continued meandering about for quite some time, desperately attempting to rid himself of the mounting feelings of dread. Nothing seemed to help, not even the sight of Luisa, which was breathtaking that morning for the skies were clear. The entire volcano, including its slightly snow-capped summit, could be seen, drawing the attention of everyone in Nueva Vida except Gabriel's. It was as if Luisa, momentarily lifting up her perpetual veil of clouds, was attempting to pass along a message to the troubled young man. It might have been a word of encouragement or perhaps a warning. Who knows what it might have been, but the youth was not looking her way and continued wandering the streets.

Just when things could not get any worse, and the dread became unbearable to the point where Gabriel was on the brink of suffering a nervous breakdown, a large church suddenly appeared. The American stumbled upon it not knowing what to do. The large doors were open. At that moment, Gabriel felt he was either going to enter the church or collapse right there on the spot. Wanting to regain his wits, he chose to enter the church. Once inside, the youth was quickly overcome with a profound feeling of tranquility. The tall stain-glass windows, vaulted ceiling, lit candles, and silence, broken occasionally by gentle, echoed sounds of a friar's footsteps, the closing of a distant door, the scampering of a mouse, transported Gabriel to a radically different world, one which seemed to lack a sense of time, direction, and obligation. He felt a whiff of the eternal, as though he was somehow in heaven.

He stood at the back of the church, right behind the last pew. He was a bit mesmerized at first by his impressive surroundings, but began to gather his thoughts soon thereafter. Gabriel's thoughts would not immediately be on the impending march to city hall, but on his childhood. Our friend had not been inside of a church for such a long time, not since he was perhaps twelve or thirteen years old. "I forgot how incredibly beautiful these churches can be!" he thought in wonderment. "Has it been that long?" Gabriel reflected deeply on his youth, when the world was a much cozier place. "I would spend a whole lot of time just dreaming away," he thought blissfully. When he was a child, Gabriel dreamed of being a scientist. He especially loved outer space, airplanes, and animals, and was not sure which one of the three he would choose for a career. However, he was pretty certain as a kid that he was going to be some sort of scientist. Those dreams would sadly come crashing down when he took a chemistry class during his freshmen year in high school. He *hated* the class. He nearly failed it, as it was sadly realized that science was not for him. That dreadful chemistry class, in Gabriel's view, symbolized the end of his childhood.

Until then, life was a very simple and pleasant affair. However, going to church on Sunday mornings as a child was not so simple and pleasant for Gabriel. First, he needed to get ready, which meant jumping in the shower and dressing up at a rather early time. He would always have to be attired in one of his dapper suits, which included, much to the boy's irritation, a tie. Before leaving, Gabriel's mother would observe him one last time. Never satisfied, she would take out a comb and fix his hair nice and neat to her liking. They would then be off to church, which was only a five minute drive from the house. Once inside the church, there was the ceremony to look forward to. It seemed to always last too long, perhaps because the monotonous cycle of sitting, standing, and kneeling made the whole experience feel like an endless chore for the young Gabriel. The homily and Bible readings never made any sense to him, so he usually ended up dreaming he was somewhere else.

The most exciting part of the ceremony was by far receiving the Eucharist because it involved getting out of those uncomfortable pews and doing a little walking. The wafers were quite tasty as well. The Eucharist also signaled the fast approaching end to the ceremony. Yet, when it was over, it really wasn't. Outside of the church, Gabriel's mother would meet up with some friends from the congregation. The conversations would last for a good duration, which would certainly test the boy's patience further. He would begin tugging away at his mother's sleeves. Then, as though by some miracle, the last conversation would end and Gabriel's mother would begin walking towards the car. "Hallelujah!" little Gabriel would always shout out.

Yet, as he stood at the back of this church in Nueva Vida, our friend could not conjure up any negative memories of those Sunday masses. Church certainly represented a form of restriction for Gabriel back then, but he drew a strange comfort from it now. As a child, he yearned for freedom and consequently detested anything that obstructed it, such as going to church or cleaning his room. Oddly enough, Gabriel was presently running away from freedom! He was weighed down by his *free* decision to participate in the impending march to city hall. More than ever, he understood how repressive freedom can be with all the unforeseen burdens and pressures involved. There was the obligation of helping Dr. Granados and the other participants of the march, along with the pressures of not letting them and, most importantly, himself down. The American began to wonder if he had not felt more liberty as a child sitting in those church pews, daydreaming of being a scientist or playing baseball in the park. The comforts of such a carefree existence created a feeling of security, if not unbridled liberty. The restraints of church, school, and parental rules were a constant source of irritation for the young Gabriel, but this somehow made life more manageable and predictable.

A cozy sense of security is exactly what Gabriel was now longing for. He had run inside of the church out of desperation, seeking some solace in a very crucial moment in his life. The youth realized he could easily come away from the march either dead or imprisoned, and he was despairing over this possible fate. The noble choice of helping the people of Nueva Vida, made of his own free will, was by no means glamorous. Shaking with fear inside some church was proof that he was not basking in any glory! He was having persistent doubts and the church seemed to be giving him a warm embrace, as if to shield him away from Dr. Granados' march. "The Ivory Tower is so different from reality," he bitterly thought. Gabriel was being lured by the all too easy option of giving up on the demonstration. He would no longer have to worry about encountering immediate danger later that afternoon. Our anguished friend imagined how relieved he would feel if he just gave Dr. Granados a call and told him he was sick and could not make it. "I would not have to go and I would be saving face at the same time!" he thought euphorically.

However, Gabriel would not be fooling himself with such a lie. "I could not live with myself," he realized. He could not turn his back on Dr. Granados and the others. He was determined to not miss out on the demonstration. The youth then left the church. He knew there was no turning back.

CHAPTER TWENTY-NINE

THE MAYOR'S UPBRINGING

Late in the afternoon of Tuesday, October 29th, Mayor Juan Carlos Rivera was left alone in his office. It was another frustrating day for him, as he had not yet heard from General Torres or the government. "I hate being stuck in limbo!" he told Victor Ascencio. "If they only had the decency to tell me what's going on, at least I would be feeling better about things. I wonder if I should even come to the office tomorrow. What's the point? They might as well put a monkey in here, for it would hardly make any difference." Ascencio and the other aids tried in vain to make their boss feel better by convincing him to keep working through the crisis, for it would end shortly. "The army won't be here for long," Ascencio insisted. "Once they leave, you will have your city back." But the Mayor knew that would not be the case, for he now believed that Nueva Vida would never be *his* again. The military occupation would forever be a stain on his legacy, serving to remind him and everyone else of his incompetence and weakness.

Yearning to escape from this humiliating situation, the Mayor poured himself a glass of scotch. Comfortably sprawled on the sofa, he began remembering certain early episodes of his life. He was an only child who led an incredibly lonely existence. The Mayor's father was, in fact, a member of the Colombian House of Representatives, working solely on behalf of Narino province. Before his stint in congress, the man was a high-powered attorney representing several wealthy ranchers in the area. Shortly after his first wife died unexpectedly from cancer, leaving behind six children, he caused a big stir in Nueva Vida by supposedly marrying one of his maids. He was fifty-eight and she was seventeen. This unlikeliest of couples would end up being the parents of Mayor Rivera, as he was born well within a year into their scandalous marriage.

However, little Juan Carlos was only a couple months shy of his second birthday when his father died. His death apparently came as no surprise to anyone since he had long been ill. He reportedly told a friend that he married the attractive, young maid so he could derive some pleasure from what little time he had left on earth. What was perhaps surprising instead is that Juan Carlos and his young mother did not receive a peso from the deceased man's will, leaving the two literally out on the street overnight. This was indeed a bitter slap in the face for the young maid. She strongly suspected that the other members of the family, who had despised her, somehow doctored the will solely to their benefit within hours after the patriarch's death.

Without any proof to support her suspicions, the luckless widow had no choice but to pick up the pieces and move on with her life. This she did by taking up residence with her parents and finding a job in another household. Things were definitely looking up for this little family when tragedy would strike again. Little Juan Carlos' mother was suddenly killed under mysterious circumstances. The official cause of death was that she was trampled to death by a horse belonging to the family she worked for. However, there were strong rumors that she was actually raped and murdered brutally by a friend of the family. No autopsy or criminal investigation was ever performed, as Juan Carlos' grieving grandmother accepted the official explanation from the family, as well as a generous hand-out of money that came with it.

Thus, the Mayor had lost both parents by the time he was five years old, too young to even remember them. Fortunately for him, his grandmother, now widowed, would come to the rescue and raise him. Her name was Imelda, and she would devote the rest of her life to the little boy. Working as a maid herself, she desperately wanted a better life for her grandson. "Poverty will only bury you," she would tell little Juan Carlos. "You will need to dig your way out of poverty if you are ever to see the light above." Through the help of the gracious family she worked for, Imelda was able to send her grandson to esteemed Catholic schools until he was thirteen. She realized that a solid education was the key to her grandson's success in the future, and drove him to do well in school. The boy turned out to be an excellent student, usually outperforming most of his peers who came from more privileged families.

Despite all the academic success, little Juan Carlos was struggling terribly with other aspects of his life. He became very withdrawn because he was unable to fit in anywhere. The privileged kids looked down on him because he came from a poor family, while the children from his humble neighborhood were scornful of his refined manners and schooling. "You're not one of us" was a phrase he became accustomed to hearing throughout his youth, which forced him to retreat further into a corner. On top of that, the boy had a difficult time coming to grips with what happened to his mother, which led him to harbor intense feelings of resentment towards his father. The boy would forever blame him for his mother's death, since she probably would not have had to work another day as a maid and succumb to that dreadful accident if his will had included her. Being left off his father's will also killed him in a way since it made him feel like a bastard, a 'piece of shit flushed out of his existence' as he liked to put it. These painful thoughts coupled with his loneliness were often too hard for the boy to bear, as he would occasionally lapse into lengthy periods of depression.

Little Juan Carlos would often cope with his pain and loneliness by reading in his tiny bedroom. He particularly enjoyed adventure tales involving pirates and sea treasures. As he grew older, he took a liking to war history and science fiction, which would certainly help him forget the drab realities of his own life. Whenever he tired of reading, the boy would go outside with a soccer ball. Not too far away from the house was a yard behind a small, vacant shop, where he would kick the ball against a wall, endlessly practicing his shot by aiming at certain spots. In between shots, little Juan Carlos would sometimes attempt to improve his dribbling skills by maneuvering the ball around bushes and trees in the yard. After a couple years of this, he was convinced of his ability to play the sport well, but there was no one for him to play with.

Whenever these two options were exhausted, the boy would sometimes visit his cousins' house. He would resort to this only out of desperation. His cousins, consisting of two boys and three girls more or less his age, were always a lot of fun and played all sorts of games, but Juan Carlos never wanted to bother them too much. He was deathly afraid they would eventually reject him like everyone else had if he spent too much time with them, so visits were kept to a minimum. "They will find some reason to dislike me," he always thought. Suspecting the worst from people, he chose to avoid them as much as possible. The sad truth was that there were a good number of individuals, including his cousins, who did genuinely like him and would have enjoyed his company. Instead, they were always left wondering why he was so aloof and distant. The youth figured there was no sense in building bridges if they were going to be burned anyway.

Whenever little Juan Carlos was not occupied with reading books, practicing his soccer skills, or spending some time with his cousins, he would be overcome with sadness. However, Imelda would not put up with these bouts of depression for too long, encouraging her grandson to break out of this vicious cycle of self-pity and look at the brighter side of things. She would remind him that he was a special boy with a wonderful future. She would also tell little Juan Carlos not to give up hope for the sake of his mother, who was 'watching over him from heaven'. "What your father did was terrible," she would tell him, "but you cannot punish yourself and your mother by getting so angry and depressed over it." Imelda served as the boy's coach and cheerleader, constantly pushing him forward and making sure he did not falter along the way. When he needed some good advice, a pat in the back, or a kick in the rear end, she was always there to deliver it personally. Through her guidance, the boy was able to caste away any demons threatening to derail him from his goals of graduating from high school with honors and attending college. "If it had not been for her," he would often tell his friends, "I would not have made it."

The day he graduated from high school was indeed special for both of them, as they celebrated the occasion with family and friends. Imelda tearfully spoke in front of everyone about how her 'darling' grandson had made her and his mother proud. Not to be outdone, Juan Carlos talked about how Imelda was the anchor in his life, the one person who always believed in him and provided all the 'encouragement and love in the world'. His graduation from high school was the culmination of a long, turbulent journey for them both, as they overcame many difficult obstacles. "Now we look forward to Juan Carlos becoming the first member of our family to graduate from college," Imelda cheerfully announced to everyone while they toasted to her grandson's future. A year later, however, Juan Carlos was hit with the disheartening news that his loving grandmother had terminal breast cancer. She would end up dying only a few months later, but inspired everyone with her courage and tranquility in the face of death. "Do good things for others," were Imelda's last words to her grandson from her deathbed at home.

Juan Carlos would be deeply saddened by her death, as it would take a long while for him to recover from such a devastating loss. He took to the bottle for solace and dropped out of college for a semester. He could not fathom living without the only person who had stood by his side much throughout his entire life. So large was the void in his life and irreplaceable the sense of loss that it was as if he had died himself. Late one night, a drunken Juan Carlos was thrown into jail for disturbing the peace. He had stumbled through the streets of Nueva Vida and cursed aloud at God and his father, waking up the residents of each neighborhood he had passed by. When finally encountered by the police, he began lashing out at them as well and resisted arrest. The two police officers were not able to place handcuffs on the belligerent young man until he was knocked out cold by a punch to the face.

Lying bloodied on the floor of his jail cell, just as he was about to pass out again, Juan Carlos had seen a disturbing vision. It was his grandmother, Imelda, standing out in the corridor. She looked sad and did not say anything. He jumped to his feet and was about to tell her he was sorry, but the vision of Imelda then disappeared. "What the hell have I done," he muttered to himself, realizing he was letting down both his grandmother and mother in a big way. The young man vowed at that very moment to clean up his act and move on with his life. When he was released from jail the following morning, the very first thing he did was go to the university and reenroll. He would quickly regain focus on his studies, receiving his degree in economics less than three years later while making the dean's list as well. With absolutely nothing to lose, an emboldened Juan Carlos also began opening himself up to people. No longer haunted by lingering feelings of self-doubt and worthlessness, the youth began socializing like never before, building lasting friendships and partnerships that would serve him well into the future. The rest is history.

The Mayor proudly reminisced that critical moment in his life, when he turned things around in that dingy jail cell. He was still lying on the couch with a glass of scotch in his hand. There was a smile on his face. The smile, however, quickly vanished as he thought of his grandmother. "I hope you are still proud of me, grandmother," he wondered aloud as a tear streamed down his ruddy cheek, a forlorn prisoner of circumstance.

CHAPTER THIRTY

THE SECOND DEMONSTRATION BEGINS

Gabriel had arrived at Dr. Granados' language institute a couple minutes past one o'clock in the afternoon on Wednesday, October 30th, right after finishing lunch at his grandmother's. Most of the people were already there, ready to protest. They had gathered their signs and were waiting for one final briefing from their unassuming leader before embarking on their trip to city hall. The serious, businesslike Dr. Granados would soon appear before them, as he got up on one of the tables in the lobby. "There has been no word yet from the army regarding the missing individuals and their whereabouts," he announced. "Therefore, we will go to city hall right now to voice our concerns. We will not march over there because the army may attempt to block us. Instead, we will go there separately using cars, buses, or any other means of transportation. Once at city hall, we will act with class and dignity. We will not go out of our way to provoke the army with insults or threats. We are simply exercising our rights to dissent in a peaceful manner."

The professor's voice then turned more solemn. "Now, before we go, I would like to raise one very important issue. All of us will be facing a certain level of danger. The army will most likely confront us. If they feel threatened, they might use their weapons on us. That is the reality. I have said before that the army probably won't touch us. Having thought about the matter further, I would now like to take that back. The chances of us getting thrown into jail or being shot at are, I would say, pretty high. Thus, I want everyone to think twice about this. If you don't feel up to the task, there is absolutely no shame in walking away right now. We will all be putting our lives at risk, and I just want everyone here to know exactly what they are getting into before we proceed with this demonstration. I don't want to mislead anybody. So please contemplate right now whether you would like to really go or not, for this certainly will not be a walk in the park."

Dr. Granados' words of warning, however, did not trigger any sort of exodus. Instead, all the one hundred or so individuals standing before the professor were determined to protest more than ever, despite the danger they were going to face. With their missing loved ones most probably in the custody of the army, they felt there were no other viable options left for them. They had to take drastic action. Faced with no questions or responses, the professor gave his last instruction, reminding the protesters not to flaunt their signs on their way to city hall. "We want to make a surprise visit," he added before finally telling the people to head over there at once. They all immediately went out to their cars or to the bus stops on the streets. Those who were taking the bus or walking were not allowed to bring their signs personally unless they had brought large enough bags with them. The leftover signs were to be transported by cars, where they would be concealed.

In a matter of minutes, the language institute was empty. With everyone gone, Dr. Granados and Gabriel then took about ten remaining signs and stuffed them into the professor's car before heading over to city hall. Not one word was exchanged between the two during the trip. The professor appeared both determined and apprehensive, as he kept nervously tapping the steering wheel with his ring. Gabriel, on the other hand, was more relaxed. The trip to church earlier that morning helped remove some of his anxiety. He just looked out the window as the car sped on its way to city hall, appearing unusually tranquil in light of the circumstances. Mostly positive thoughts were now running through his mind, as he became very excited about the prospects of the demonstration. Above all, he was feeling proud about making himself useful for a good cause. "I am finally doing something that will make a difference in people's lives," he thought.

*   *   *

Due to a lack of traffic during the siesta break, Gabriel and Dr. Granados were able to reach San Sebastian Square in front of city hall rather quickly. Within a half-hour, all the protesters had assembled at the smallish square, gathered their signs, and begun demonstrating in front of the Mayor's office. There were no elaborate loudspeakers to rally more people around them. They had only their signs. However, their spirited chanting and singing would soon draw everyone's attention in the area, including the soldiers stationed there. Immediately upon seeing the budding demonstration, the commanding officer on the scene contacted General Torres. The general told him not to lose his cool. "Let them protest for the time being," he calmly informed the officer. "If it continues to grow over the next fifteen minutes, ring me up again."

However, the protest continued to grow. Once other civilians in the vicinity got wind of what the demonstration was about, they entered the square immediately. As Dr. Granados fully expected, the protest instantly received the people's support. They sympathized with the demonstrators' wishes of having their loved ones returned to them. Suddenly remembering what had happened only a few nights before, people became incensed that the army would stoop so low as to unlawfully apprehend and detain innocent civilians. "This type of behavior is what we would expect from the guerillas or criminal bandits, but certainly not the army!" cried one man who joined the protest. Soon enough, the square became filled with people making all sorts of demands on the army, from returning the missing detainees to leaving Nueva Vida at once. Much to Dr. Granados' satisfaction, the demonstration did not get out of control as most people comported themselves well. There were no angry, drunken calls for violence. People perhaps did not want to disrespect the families who were leading the demonstration. Following their lead, they all just looked in the direction of city hall and made their demands in a peaceful, organized manner.

Meanwhile, inside his office, Mayor Rivera looked at what was developing outside his window with much concern. "Not again," he whispered through his lips. Nevertheless, the Mayor did not sit idly on the sidelines this time around. He felt somewhat rejuvenated after having reflected on his childhood the night before and was determined to handle this emerging crisis the *right way*. He immediately ordered police units to the scene. When Victor Ascencio wondered whether this might offend General Torres, the Mayor erupted with anger. "Do you see any troops out there doing anything?" he asked Ascencio. "Am I supposed to sit here and do nothing while hundreds of people are gathering outside my office? That would be criminal on my part! Besides, how could General Torres be offended by my ordering the police over here when he has not bothered to tell me anything since his arrival? I have no idea what's going on around here. He has not cared to fill me in on anything, so it's his fault that there is this lack of organization. As you have said, I can only worry about doing my job, certainly not his or anybody else's."

After having ordered police over to the square, the Mayor then asked one of his aids to bring the leader of the protest to his office. "I need to speak with this person at once!" he declared. "We must figure something out." The young aid ran out looking for this individual, and after several minutes of pushing his way through the crowd and conducting inquiries, was eventually led to Dr. Granados. Upon being informed that the Mayor wanted to talk to him, the professor, suspicious of the strange request, declined. "If he supports our cause," he told the aid, "tell him to do something about it. Tell him to help release some of those detainees. But I am not going to leave from this spot right now." When the aid returned to the office with the professor's answer, Mayor Rivera was disappointed but not surprised. His subordinates in the room, however, were thoroughly embarrassed for him. The townspeople did not even want to consult with him!

Yet, the Mayor did not lose hope, as he continued plotting ways to resolve the matter. He stared out the window, deep in thought, while his aids looked on haplessly. The telephone suddenly rang, breaking the stifling silence in the room. It was the police chief, Captain Sandoval. He angrily informed the Mayor that the entry of police units into the square was being blocked by soldiers. "They are being told to go away," the police chief added. "The army, I guess, will take care of the situation." Utterly frustrated, the Mayor hung up the phone without saying anything. He now realized there was nothing else he could do. He proceeded to tell the others what had happened to his police, calling it another slap in his face. He went on to lambaste the army's arrogance and secrecy, bitterly complaining for some time about their handling of the occupation. "How do they intend to run this city if they don't even *communicate* with the civil authorities?" he asked. He sat down on the sofa and began loosening his tie, looking dejected as ever.

Sensing things would only deteriorate further, with the crowd outside growing considerably larger by the second, Victor Ascencio suggested that the Mayor leave at once. "It makes no sense for you to remain here," he told his boss. "You should just go home, or better yet, go far away to your farm. We can say that you're sick and need to recuperate in seclusion."

"No, I won't do that," the Mayor responded after a brief moment of contemplation.

"Why not?" asked the insistent Ascencio. "Why do you want to subject yourself to further humiliation or even danger by staying here? Those hooligans out there may storm this place any moment. The army is sure to arrive soon and god only knows what they will do."

"How will leaving here be any less humiliating or dangerous for me?" asked the Mayor. "I believe there is nothing more humiliating than to flee from trouble. That has never been my style!"

"I just don't think," Ascencio went on passionately, "it will make you look good if the people out there know you are in here and powerless to do anything about this dilemma we are in. It will make you appear terribly weak. Remember Juan Carlos, you have a reputation to protect! This crisis will subside soon enough and the troops will be out of here eventually. It is only a matter of time before you will regain control of this city. Therefore, until then, it is important that you keep yourself out of harm's way with your reputation intact. Staying here will be suicide in every sense of the word."

"Look, Victor, I will not leave," the Mayor proudly answered. "I know you mean well and you may be right about the whole thing. But as of now, I belong here. I may surely lose all my credibility as a result, but I will not lose my sense of dignity. I would rather be accused of incompetence than of cowardice. I agree that it indeed might be dangerous to remain here, so it would be best for all you gentlemen to leave here immediately. But, I will be staying."

The others protested this decision, but the Mayor remained adamant about staying. When they then refused to leave, the Mayor ordered them to go at once, explaining that it would be best for everyone to be separated. "A couple of the secretaries will remain here with me," he said from the sofa, while he rolled up his sleeves. "You guys can tell me what's going on in other parts of the city. You can also try to contact the general, if you want. You can make yourselves more useful outside of this place." The Mayor was only saying this to make his aides feel better, for he really did not care what they would eventually be doing after they departed. He escorted them out of the room and told them not to report to city hall until things settled down. Ascencio and the others finally left the room, quickly heading for the rear exit to make a clean getaway. They all wondered whether their boss had gone mad, for they could not understand why he was acting so irrationally. "He seems to want to make some sort of a stand," Ascencio said to his concerned colleagues, "but why now? The timing is not right. And what sort of a stand is he making?"

*   *   *

In the meantime, the commanding army officer at the scene nervously observed the square filling up with people. He waited

Mauricio F. Ochoa

fifteen minutes, as instructed, before calling General Torres again. He informed the general that the crowd had swelled to about a thousand people and recommended that troops be sent in. The general was displeased with the news. He asked his officer how the people were behaving and what they were protesting about. "Right now, there are no signs of violence," the officer answered. "They are just chanting slogans. The protest seems to be about the individuals we have detained. Their relatives are demanding their safe return." The general went ahead and sent a couple thousand reinforcements into the area with the strict order that nothing be done until his arrival. "These people could not wait another day to do this," the general thought in reference to the bad timing of the protest.

While putting on his chest-protector, he discussed the situation further with his long-time deputy, Colonel Frederico Lopez-Leconte. "I can't believe this demonstration is taking place only a few hours before we were going to release those damned detainees!" he ranted. For one of the rare occasions, General Torres lost his cool. He kicked a small wooden chair in his office, which crashed against the wall. "Now, my plans are ruined!" he raged.

"What do you mean your plans are ruined?" Colonel Lopez-Leconte timidly inquired.

"We may not be able to leave by Tuesday, you fool!" the general barked.

"Well, we can release the detainees right now and avoid the mess of having to break up this demonstration," the colonel explained. "That's the only other option we have at the moment, and we might still be able to leave by Tuesday."

"That is an option we can ill-afford to take," the general said after some thought. "If we release the detainees now, that would open up a big can of worms. The people would demand more and the government would be on our backs for caving under pressure. We cannot show any weakness right now! We have to go in and end this right away!"

"I think you should reconsider this, General Torres," the colonel firmly said. "We crushed a demonstration a few days ago, only to be out there yet again crushing another one at the moment. When will this cycle of violence end? Perhaps a more diplomatic, tactful approach might best resolve this problem."

"There is nothing to reconsider at this point," the general affirmed. "My decision has already been made. We are going to do what any other army would in this situation, and that would be to crush this demonstration now. That's the only option we have. Let's get going!"

Having fully regained his composure, General Torres gathered his pistol that was on his desk and left the room, followed by Colonel Lopez-Leconte. They headed for the two command jeeps parked just outside, already with the drivers seated and ready to go. As soon as he was seated in the vehicle, the general summoned another couple thousand troops to the scene of the demonstration. He then gave an order, which went to all field commanders assigned to the protest: "I want this demonstration crushed immediately! Order your troops to start shooting in the air when they enter the place. If that does not work, then they are to shoot at the crowd. You do not have to wait for my arrival to commence."

CHAPTER THIRTY-ONE

NO TIME FOR REFLECTION

At the head of the demonstration, directly in front of city hall, was where Gabriel stood right beside Dr. Granados. The youth marveled at how quickly things had changed. "A few days ago, Dr. Granados and I were viewing another protest atop some third floor balcony," he thought in amazement. "Now, we are directing this one!" He seized the moment by helping to lead the chants and cheers. He was also busy conveying Dr. Granados' instructions to others and making sure they were being followed. From time to time, he would confer with the professor about the direction of the protest, discussing whether they should embark on a march through town at some point later in the afternoon, if it should continue into the evening and so forth. Never before had Gabriel felt so important in his life.

Such assertiveness was uncharacteristic of the reserved Gabriel. Brooding or dreaming away, whether in the lonely confines of his room or off on a deserted park bench, had always been one of his favorite activities. It was a form of therapy. Over coffee or cigarettes, Gabriel would reflect, sometimes painstakingly for hours, on the steps he had taken through the course of his life. He would ponder whether those steps were correct or misguided, and if anything valuable was learned along the way. Much of the time was spent justifying prior actions and decisions rather than admitting any mistakes. Our friend needed to stroke his own ego with such rationalizations, for the last thing he wanted was to be afflicted with more doubts and regrets.

As much as he obsessed over the past, he always had his eye on the future and becoming somebody important. The lad just loved to reflect endlessly on this and other matters dear to his heart. "You spend so much time thinking that you never get anything done," his mother once complained to him. If only his demanding mother had the chance to witness her son there in Nueva Vida, standing proudly in front of city hall that afternoon! She certainly would not be able to accuse him of inactivity. So wrapped up was Gabriel with the demonstration that he could not even reflect on some of the more bitter and sad experiences in his life that had long held him back.

* * *

Gabriel could not even think for one fleeting instance during the protest about his beloved grandfather, who would often take him out fishing as a child. During those trips, the old man would delight the little boy with stories about the huge groupers he caught off the shores of Chile. "They were so big, it would take ten of us to carry them off the boat," he would recount. He would always laugh at the tiny freshwater fish they caught in southeastern Michigan. "These fish are not even large enough to serve as adequate bait for the groupers we caught off Chile!" he boasted once. Gabriel was only eleven when his grandfather suddenly fell over on the boat one hot summer afternoon, clutching his chest. He painfully gasped for air a couple times before collapsing and losing consciousness. Little Gabriel navigated the row boat alone onto the river bank and desperately looked for help. It was no use. Paramedics arrived thirty minutes later and immediately pronounced him dead. Losing his grandfather that day was the first tragedy in his life.

The youth also could not reflect on other disturbing moments of his childhood, such as suffering at the hands of his grammar school classmates, who often referred to him as 'space cadet'. One obnoxious kid by the name of Nick Orville would often get behind him in line and attempt to trip his feet. "Hah, hah, space cadet's got pigeon feet!" he would say. This would go on for months until the gangly Gabriel turned around one day and took a swing. Nick barely ducked out of the way and managed to push Gabriel, off-balanced after taking the wild swing, to the ground before they got separated. Gabriel received a big tongue-lashing from the school principal along with a couple detentions for this display of aggressive behavior, but he was never bothered by Nick or the others again.

Despite finally taking a bold stand against his chief tormentor, the reticent youth would continue to struggle relating with his peers. They considered him too odd. They had a difficult time figuring him out and were ultimately put off by his quiet demeanor. The poor child was one of the few kids in the class who never got invited to any sort of party or gathering. Gabriel often wondered if it was not better to be ridiculed, for at least he would receive some attention from the others. He figured that any attention, whether good or bad, was better than none at all.

Things would continue to get worse for Gabriel in high school. The boy could never adjust to its incredibly large size and diverse student population. This was worlds apart from the smallish schools he had attended until then, where everybody knew each other's names. The distressed youth felt like a mere number rather than a person, which had a numbing effect on him. "Those were the four most boring, depressing years of my life," he would often tell people later. Feeling stifled in the large school, Gabriel simply crawled away from view. He avoided social contact with others and spent most of his free time at the library doing homework or reading books.

He was able to survive these difficult years by dreaming away, living vicariously through the characters he read about in books. This provided a healthy release for him at the time, for he could have easily sunk into despair and drugs otherwise. Gabriel, the awkward adolescent, would imagine himself being in Napoleon's army at the onset of the campaign at Austerlitz, voyaging with Captain Ahab in search of the terrifying white whale, or sitting at a New York City night club with Holden Caulfield. Gabriel certainly preferred retreating into his own little fantasy world than face reality. To face reality and live normally was too stressful an option. Joining a club, meeting girls, and getting a job all required too much socializing! The shy youth figured he would fail at these endeavors anyway, so there was no sense in even trying. If anything, his dignity and sanity would be preserved as he would be kept out of harm's way.

It was by his third year in high school, after a lifetime of feeling rejected by his peers, that Gabriel began feeling contemptuous of people in general. This is when he willingly chose to turn away from society and become an outcast. Being frowned upon by his peers, he frowned back at them. No longer was it necessary for him to be like everybody else. Instead, Gabriel aimed at being different from his peers and, in time, became proud of his status as one of the truly misunderstood characters in the school. He began reading Nietzsche, Marx, Sartre, and Machiavelli, books he figured none of his peers would venture to read. As the divide between he and his peers widened, Gabriel would derive from such readings an explanation for his position outside of society, or what he deemed 'the herd'. Such readings would confirm in his mind the shortcomings of society. In Gabriel's mind, choosing not to follow the herd was a virtue, a sensible attempt at preserving one's freedom and individuality.

But Gabriel, thanks to his mother in particular, was never quite the doomsayer. Despite his outcast status in high school, he had remained an optimist and sought answers for all the problems of mankind. His mother always instilled a belief in him that he could make a difference in the world one day and do something good. Therefore, Gabriel was determined not to remain in the sidelines for long. Instead, he would eventually seek to change society and was convinced that revolution was the answer. What that revolution would be, he was unsure of. But he would continue reading and finding answers, and soon enough Gabriel would discover his heroes, men like Che Guevara, Vladimir Lenin, Thomas Jefferson, Martin Luther King, and Mohandas Gandhi. He began writing journals containing his ideas about how to change the world for the better. Many of his thoughts were indeed aimless and random, but there was an increasingly coherent message within, that the world of the early 1990's was full of injustice and unfairness, and that it needed to be 'righted' somehow.

Gabriel would identify himself with the underprivileged lot of the world, those who were cast away from society. He was convinced these people needed to rise up against the forces oppressing them. He, of course, likened himself as one of these people, perhaps one of their leaders in the future. Reading and writing was indeed what kept Gabriel Ferrero grounded and sane through those years of loneliness as an adolescent, how he wiled away the time. It gave him hope and a sense of purpose in his life. But the misunderstood youth was still human and longed for some meaningful interaction with others. All the reading and writing he was doing was no longer enough. The loneliness was certainly taking its toll on Gabriel by his senior year in high school. "This is no way to live," he thought at the time.

Thus, upon leaving for college, Gabriel was desperate to make some changes with his life. It was time for him to reach out and grab a piece of the world. After all, the tall and dark Gabriel had developed into a decent looking young man. Once he arrived on campus, he began growing out his hair, which attracted more attention from girls. People wanted to meet this interesting looking person and invited him to parties. "Gosh, why wasn't it this easy in high school?" he often wondered. Pleased with all this newfound attention and acceptance, he gladly welcomed the opportunity to make friends and hang out. For the first time in his life, he felt vaguely *popular*. Gabriel partied like a fiend during his first year in college, not knowing exactly what to do with all the freedom of university life. One thing he certainly did not do was focus on his studies, as his grades suffered through much of his first year. But this was of no concern for him at the time, considering all the boredom and loneliness he had endured throughout his life. Academics were certainly not a priority.

Gabriel continued his easygoing ways well into his sophomore year when he met a girl named Anna. Our friend immediately fell for her sparkling blue eyes and soft manners. They began courting each other and Gabriel liked her more with each date. The youth could not stop thinking about this girl as he was convinced he had fallen in love with her. "I have never felt this way about a girl before," he admitted to friends. Unfortunately, three weeks into their courtship, Anna dumped Gabriel for another man. The only consolation for Gabriel was the knowledge that this other man was much older than him and in his fourth year of medical school. "There is no shame in losing out to a much older man," his friends told him.

Nevertheless, these comforting words could not shake Gabriel out of despair. He simply could not believe Anna left him and was convinced that she would run back to him in time. When he had not heard from her in two weeks, however, our friend realized she was gone for good. This first encounter with heartbreak truly devastated the once carefree and clueless Gabriel, who would become an emotional wreck for a few months. It was another taste of cold reality which literally sent the youth reeling back to the Ivory Tower once again, as he desperately climbed up to the safety of its lofty heights. "I don't want to deal with that type of pain ever again," he thought.

This experience with Anna was a watershed moment for Gabriel, as it was a reconfirmation of his outcast status in society. It was a bitter reminder of his prior life, of his fractured relationship with society. The girl came to represent society itself, rejecting him and kicking him to the curb. He thought he could win her over and, in doing so, become an accepted member of society at long last. But this was not to be and Gabriel, rather than taking such a blow in stride, became angry and resentful. He just gave up. With his confidence shattered, Gabriel reverted back to his old ways. He partied less often and began writing in his journals again. He began living in the cafes, taking up smoking and reading more than ever before. Having reverted back to his reclusive ways, our friend was at least able to improve considerably in school, eventually graduating with a Bachelor's degree in political science. Yet, he was as confused as ever and did not know exactly what he wanted out of life. His loving parents, who patiently stood behind him through all the highs and lows, were growing increasingly concerned about his apparent lack of direction.

By traveling to Colombia shortly after his college graduation, Gabriel sought to find some direction by perhaps getting a job. This is what he explained to others about the purpose of his trip. But he also went there for another reason: he was unconsciously attempting to undo the damage inflicted by the heartbreak from a couple years before and other setbacks in his life. Without knowing it himself, he was right there at that demonstration *because* of Anna, Nick Orville, his grandfather, and many others such as Sandra who had come to represent the disappointment and sadness of his own existence. In fact, they *drove* him there to that spot in front of city hall! In the midst of that tightly packed square in Nueva Vida, Gabriel finally felt himself letting go. All the demons were being exorcised. Any rankling thoughts of the past were now the furthest things from his mind, as they were drowned out by a sea of chants demanding the Colombian Army to let go of its prisoners.

CHAPTER THIRTY-TWO

TAKING AIM

When General Torres ordered the demonstration crushed, his field commanders knew exactly what to do. Not only was the crowd to be dispersed, but the organizers were to be rounded up. Last but not least, the leader was to be killed on the spot, if possible. The general adopted this brutal philosophy from several years of fighting insurrections in the countryside. "By killing the leader," he stated once to his cronies, "you have one less troublemaker to worry about. You also send a message to any other fool who wants to follow in that person's footsteps, that he won't be walking for long." It's a doctrine that served the general and his staff very well through the years, as their not so subtle employment of fear and intimidation had enabled them to maintain control over the rugged and vast countryside of southern Colombia.

The leader of the prior demonstration, Dr. Ghetti, managed to survive because General Torres did not want his head on a platter. He wanted information from him instead. However, the general was extremely concerned now with the situation and was determined to put an end to the turbulence in Nueva Vida once and for all. His credibility with his own troops and the government was at stake. On his way to San Sebastian Square, the general made one last call to his commanders. "There has been a change in plans!" he urgently announced. "Not one shot is to be fired until I authorize it! Tell your men to take their positions around the crowd and hang tight. I will be joining you there shortly. Again, not one shot is to be fired until you hear further word from me!" Unbeknownst to the field commanders, General Torres dispatched his four best snipers from the rifle division onto the scene. Troops were not to do anything until the snipers, working from the heights of surrounding buildings, located the leader of the protest and had a clear shot. This slight change in plan reflected the general's desire for a clean and swift operation this time around, with far less bloodshed and political repercussions.

To demonstrate his sense of confidence to his driver and staff sergeant sitting in the rear of the jeep, General Torres engaged in benign conversation with them after issuing his last orders. This was typical behavior from the general just before a significant undertaking. Such light conversation was his way of coping with stress, having the effect of not only relaxing him but others around him. In reality, these dialogues only masked the underlying tension the general was really feeling, the sudden gregariousness being nothing more than a nervous habit. Yet, this habit served the general very well with his troops since it gave him the reputation of being cool under fire. General Torres' conversation with his aids about the finer qualities of Colombian rum would soon be interrupted by a call from one of his snipers. He confirmed that the leader of the demonstration was now in his sights.

"Are you sure that's him?" the general asked.

"Yes, I am sure it's him," the sniper responded confidently. "He fits the description of people we talked to. He is in his sixties, thin, and wears thick glasses. His name is Dr. Granados. He is standing right in front of city hall and people seem to be hovering around him. This must be the man."

"Good! Don't lose sight of him," the general told him. "Have the others sighted him as well?"

"Yes, Dominguez and Rollo have also sighted him from their locations," the sniper replied. "Correa is still looking for a spot."

'With three, that's enough," the general stated. "We can go ahead and take this man out. Now, from your vantage point, is it a clear shot?"

"Yes it is. It is a fairly easy shot."

"Good! Then you and your comrades are authorized to take action. But remember to wait for the troops to move in first. Once they begin moving in, shoot."

"Yes sir!"

"Thank you, Sergeant Lima. If you succeed with your mission, you will be duly rewarded. I will now order my commanders to move in their troops. Good luck."

General Torres did just that a few seconds later. He called on his commanders to begin the assault. After that, he put down the receiver and continued conversing with the driver and staff sergeant accompanying him in the jeep. As they were quickly approaching the square, the general began talking about the rare yellow tulips found in his hometown. As a connoisseur of flowers, he was disappointed in not having been able to spot any beautiful tulips, roses, or lilies in and around Nueva Vida.

CHAPTER THIRTY-THREE

THE SHOTS

The demonstration had already showed signs of tapering off by the time the army had arrived. Many people were actually leaving the scene to return to work or avoid the trouble of being pinned in by the army. After what happened a few nights before, most civilians were not willing to risk their lives for the sake of a few missing people. If it had been night, more individuals, emboldened by booze and the cover of darkness, might have joined in support of the protesters. The bright, early afternoon sunshine certainly did not help the cause of Dr. Granados and his followers. Thus, the crowd had shrunk by half by the time the troops entered San Sebastian Square a half an hour later. A couple hundred more fled the area immediately upon spotting the soldiers, leaving only two to three hundred people there.

Observing this rather small gathering of people, the cautious head commander on the scene waved off the assault until he conferred one last time with General Torres. What he was witnessing definitely contradicted earlier reports that the square was crammed with angry protesters. Since the circumstances apparently changed, the head commander wanted to make sure General Torres still approved of the assault. He called the general and explained the situation to him. "The square is not even a quarter full," he told him.

"What?"

"There are only a couple hundred people here right now," the commander described further. "A lot of them fled when we arrived."

"Are more of them still fleeing?" asked the general, who was also puzzled with all the conflicting reports.

"No," answered the commander. "Those who have remained seem committed to staying."

"How are they responding to the presence of our troops?"

"They have taken notice, but they are staying put for now," the commander said. "They continue to chant and carry on with their activities despite our presence, although some of them appear a little scared. Should we still carry out your orders?"

There was a pause that lasted for about half a minute. The commander, who was anxiously waiting for a reply, could hear the general conferring with Colonel Lopez-Leconte on the other line. There seemed to be a heated exchange going on through the muffled reception. General Torres finally spoke into the receiver. "Yes, carry out the orders," he affirmed, sounding somewhat irritated. "You may begin moving in the troops."

*   *   *

Gabriel was one of many protesters who grew concerned over the sudden entrance of troops into the square. Nonetheless, much like the others, he toughed it out and remained where he was. Not giving in to fear proved to be incredibly difficult, for there was a side of him that desperately wanted to flee the area. The soldiers were armed to the teeth and looked very menacing. The American immediately sensed danger. Yet, he was able to retain his composure. "I cannot be a coward now and run!" he thought. Dr. Granados told everyone to remain calm. "We will stay right here and hold our ground!" he declared in a calm voice. "If that means we'll be thrown in jail, then so be it. God will take care of us."

In a matter of seconds, the troops had completely surrounded the protesters and were marching forward when they were suddenly ordered to stop. Gabriel could hear several women crying out of fear.

"Are they going to shoot at us?" one asked hysterically. Others were tearfully imploring the troops not to harm them. "We are mothers who want to know where our children are," said another. "That's all we want to know! You must try to understand!" The troops did not seem at all fazed by what the women were telling them. They stood about twenty yards away, objectively sizing up the group of people courageously standing before them. With their machine guns cocked and ready, they anxiously awaited the next order.

Gabriel continued to nervously watch the troops for what seemed like an eternity. The soldiers remained in their positions for several minutes, without as much as a word being spoken among them during that time. It was deathly silent. Suddenly, a whistle blew emphatically from a distance. The troops began moving in. Shots were fired in the air. Gabriel could hear several soldiers ordering the protesters to move out. He could also hear the terrified screaming of protesters around him. Others defiantly resisted the soldiers as they approached, calling them 'pigs' and 'butchers'. Major scuffling ensued around the periphery as some resisted arrest. Gabriel and Dr. Granados were still deep inside the crowd, which was a good distance from where all the scuffling was taking place. The professor, out of concern for the safety of his followers, ordered the protesters not to resist arrest. "Let them take us away!" he declared.

Right after he uttered those words, Gabriel heard a rifle shot echo through the square followed by a crashing thud right behind him. Blood splattered all over the back of his head and on the faces of those standing before him. The dazed youth turned around and saw Dr. Granados lying lifelessly on the floor in a pool of blood, the back of his head partially blown off. By that time, two other rifle shots had discharged from a distance, one not hitting anybody and the other barely grazing Gabriel's arm. The youth and others in the crowd instinctively fell to the ground once it was determined they were under rifle fire. While he was lying there, Gabriel immediately felt severe pain in the triceps muscle of his right arm and clutched at it with his left hand. He noticed some blood on his hand and proceeded to look at his wound. He was relieved to discover that the wound was only superficial, for there was nothing more than a piercing of the skin. But it was painful and he continued grasping at it, making sure the bleeding stopped by applying pressure with his hand.

The rifle shots had momentarily startled the troops as well, for they also crouched down to the ground. They were not so sure if they were being targeted by some fanatical demonstrators around the vicinity of the square. However, the soldiers were soon told by their own commanders that they were not the intended targets. They were ordered to proceed with the task of clearing the area of demonstrators. In an effort to ensure the success of his operation, General Torres apparently had decided to wait to the last minute to inform his commanders of the snipers and their mission. With the flurry of rifle shots seemingly finished, the troops got back on their feet and continued dragging away protesters from the scene. Two large army transport trucks had just arrived to haul the prisoners to an undisclosed destination.

At this point, most of the protesters were either lying or crouching on the ground, allowing themselves to be individually taken away by troops without putting up any fight. They were following Dr. Granados' last order. However, many of them did not know that the professor was in fact dead. Those who did know, like Gabriel, were in such shock that they were unable to do anything but quietly stare at his body. Finally, Elsa, who had directly challenged Dr. Granados the day before, began screaming hysterically at the sight of her fallen leader. "Oh my God!" she despaired. "They have killed him! They have killed our leader! They have killed Dr. Granados!" The matronly woman ran to the body, turned it over to check if he might still be alive, and began wailing away upon discovering he wasn't, occasionally burying her head into the dead man's chest. "How can they do this to this man?" she wondered aloud. "He was such a good man!" Elsa then viewed Dr. Granados' face, which was rapidly losing all flushness and vitality, and began patting his hair back. His eyes were still open. She promptly took off his thick glasses, placed them on his stomach, and lovingly shut his eyes, triggering another intense bout of sobbing from her.

Most of the attention around the square was now directed at Elsa and the dead Dr. Granados. Rather than assume leadership over the protesters, she simply crumpled beside the professor. She could not go on. The others began weeping along with her. They could not understand why such a decent man had to pay the ultimate price, especially when he was not asking the army for much. Despite all the anger they might have been feeling toward the army at that moment, there was no fight left in them. The chanting and singing had stopped. There were not even words of accusation leveled at the soldiers, besides those from the broken Elsa. In calm and orderly fashion, troops moved out the grieving demonstrators who remained huddled around the pieta-like scene of Elsa cradling the dead professor. If anything, they were now peacefully resigned to being reunited with their loved ones in jail.

All this proved too much for Gabriel to handle. Angry at the army, sad about what happened to Dr. Granados, and scared for his own personal safety, the youth was simply overwhelmed by the whole terrifying experience. By the time he was placed inside one of the transport trucks, Gabriel had lost all sense of himself or reality. He was in a state of shock and unable to communicate with others around him. He just stared vacantly into space as the truck rolled away.

CHAPTER THIRTY-FOUR

LOST AND FOUND

In the subsequent days, there were many interesting developments in Nueva Vida. The army's crackdown on Dr. Granados' demonstration finally ended all the turbulence which had riddled the town for five long days. No protests or riots were to resurface again. The professor's quixotic stand against the army proved to be the last gasp of a rebellious spirit which hovered over Nueva Vida since the untimely death of presidential candidate Vicente Sanchez. With peace restored, General Torres was able to proceed with preparations for a major withdrawal of his troops from the city planned for the following Tuesday, November 5th. On the night of Saturday, November 2nd, the calculating general released all of his prisoners from the two demonstrations, thereby cutting all ties with Nueva Vida and paving the way for a smooth exit.

The only prisoner not to be released that day was Dr. Ghetti, leader of the first demonstration which ended violently in the hands of Torres' troops. The philosophy professor was handed over to federal authorities for further questioning over his role in that uprising. The investigation would not last long. After a couple days of intense questioning in a remote farmhouse not too far from Nueva Vida, the government chose not to press charges against Dr. Ghetti and thereby released him. In return for such leniency, the professor agreed to leave Nueva Vida immediately and never return under any condition. Considering he had no family there, this was

301

not such an unreasonable demand by the government. He was also warned not to indulge in any 'treasonable' activities in the future. "If you do not comply with any of our wishes," the lead investigator threatened Dr. Ghetti, "things will end up bad for you, really bad." Broken and defeated, the professor reluctantly boarded a plane headed for the capital the very next day. He did not even have time to say goodbye to anybody, only leaving frantic instructions for his secretary to handle all unattended business, which included first and foremost his resignation from the university and the termination of his apartment lease.

As for General Torres, everything went according to plan. The government not only accepted his request to withdraw the brunt of his forces from Nueva Vida, but even went so far as to congratulate him. "Your handling of the situation in Nueva Vida was superb," the defense minister told him in person. "Your actions there have elevated the tattered image of the armed forces to new heights in the eyes of the Colombian people and the rest of the world." In the crack of dawn on Tuesday, November 5th, the general began rolling out his forces, surely ending the bloodiest chapter in the history of Nueva Vida. The general was truly relieved to be leaving, vowing he would never return. "If they do call me up here again," he told his deputy, Colonel Lopez-Leconte, "I'll just send a few of my forces with one of my commanders. That's all that will be required anyhow. There's no way I'll ever set foot here again!" A thousand troops were left to monitor the situation there for another six months.

Upon returning to his base in the jungle, General Torres' first order of business was not to plan renewed campaigns against the guerrillas, but to check up on his vast criminal enterprises. Once all the money was counted and it was determined that the smuggling operations had not missed a beat while he was away for more than a week, the elated general offered most of his troops a three day break. This despite great incursions made by the guerrillas throughout the region in recent days! However, the crafty general was not concerned. "The guerrillas will be stretched too thin if they continue to go any further," he explained to the worried Colonel Lopez-Leconte.

"They will be in a parlous state. In three days time, they will be ripe for defeat."

General Torres and his staff celebrated their successful mission in Nueva Vida later that evening amid plenty of cigars, rum, and young women from the area. The general called the mission a triumph over 'evil insurgent forces'. Of course, there was no mention of the nineteen civilian casualties coupled with countless violations of human rights and civil liberties required to gain such a triumph. One such violation included barring scores of newspaper journalists and television reporters from entering the town. A road block was set up on the main roads leading to the city from the north and south. Anyone who was entering was subjected to questioning by soldiers. Those who were discovered or suspected to be working for the media were simply not allowed to pass through and told to go home. With the media essentially out of the picture, the general was free to act with extreme ruthlessness. The government essentially did nothing in response to the pleas and protests made by the embittered journalists and reporters who were camped outside of town. "And they call this a democracy!" one columnist sarcastically remarked.

*   *   *

Without the media around, the outside world was unable to witness the heroics of Dr. Granados. The news of his death and General Torres' brutal handling of his demonstration was not even covered by local papers, so tight was the army's grip over Nueva Vida. Dr. Granados' body was taken by the army to headquarters soon after the other protesters were hauled away. Once his true identity was discovered, the army called the professor's wife, Angela, to inform her they had his body. They told her he was killed in a firefight with troops during an insurrection earlier in the day. Angela dropped the phone, unable to listen any further. She began wailing in disbelief. A friend who happened to be at the house picked up the phone and was able to get directions to the army barracks. Angela was driven by her friend to the barracks in order to confirm the identity of the body. Upon recognizing her dead husband lying unceremoniously on a stretcher in a barren, damp room, she fainted and dropped to the floor. It was too much to bear. She was now alone in the world, without her husband and daughter who were both lost tragically.

Soon after recovering from her fainting spell, Angela quickly regained her composure and set up arrangements to transport her husband's body to a cemetery. "I need to take him away from this terrible place," she told her friend. The funeral would take place two days later. It was attended by a small group of family members and close friends. To everyone's surprise, Angela remained composed and strong throughout the proceedings. Her touching farewell speech drew tears from everyone gathered there. "My husband was the rock in my life, a solid, dependable man who was always there for me," she stated. "I will now attempt to serve as a solid rock for him and my daughter, to live in their memory for the rest of my days here on earth so I can be reunited with them later in God's paradise. This I will do with all the energy that is left in me."

This quiet funeral, however, would not close the book on Dr. Granados. Tales of his bold self-sacrifice began to spread throughout Nueva Vida. Those individuals who personally witnessed the events which unfolded in San Sebastian Square on October 30, 1996 were immediately compelled to unleash word of the professor's heroic death. His courageous stand against the army made such a great impression on these witnesses that they went on to cultivate his legend. "May the brave and noble actions of that divine man on this day never be forgotten!" one of them feverishly declared when he saw the professor's limp body slowly being carried away from the square. Everyone in Nueva Vida would soon be talking about Dr. Granados. Significant details of his simple yet tragic life would be unearthed and known to all, particularly the loss of his daughter to kidnappers. The professor's decision to defend the rights of the protesters unlawfully abducted by the army was all the more moving for everyone, since it obviously was done in memory of his daughter. It all proved too irresistible. Within a few weeks of his death, he had become a local hero.

*   *   *

Lastly, there is the case of Gabriel. Upon witnessing the death of Dr. Granados and being spirited away by the army, the young American suffered from what appeared to be a severe nervous breakdown. He was unable to communicate with anybody and just stared off into space, oblivious to everything around him. Elsa tried to snap the youth out of his stupor by trying to engage him to talk, even grabbing him by the arms and giving him a good shake a couple times, to no avail. Soldiers also attempted to get his attention by yelling threats to him, which also did nothing.

The army eventually realized there was something genuinely wrong with their young captive. The army doctor came in to check his condition the following day, and was unable to diagnose anything specific. "He's not reacting to any stimuli," the doctor noted. "This concerns me. It could be post traumatic stress disorder, but it's too early to tell. I suggest he be taken to a hospital for further tests and treatment." The suggestion was not taken up by the army immediately, and poor Gabriel was forced to stay at the makeshift detainment facility outside the barracks, which consisted of two cramped, decrepit houses. When the doctor came the following day to check up on the young American, he noticed no improvement. What really drew his concern was Gabriel's frail condition, since he had not eaten anything for days. The doctor was obliged this time to make a stronger case for the youth's transfer to a hospital, and called over a sergeant who was nearby. When the sergeant refused to have Gabriel transferred to a hospital, the irate doctor blew up. "Look, this boy needs to be sent to a hospital!" he demanded.

"I am sorry my dear doctor, but we cannot let any of these people go," the sergeant calmly replied. "Those are standing orders."

"What the hell is the use of keeping this boy here when obviously he is in no condition to be interrogated?" the relentless doctor asked sarcastically. "Just take a good look at him! How on God's earth will he be of any help to you?" The two continued to heatedly discuss Gabriel's situation when General Torres suddenly stormed into the house. "What's with all the commotion in here?" he barked.

"General, I fear this lad here could be suffering from a severe nervous breakdown," the doctor firmly explained. "I request that he be taken to a hospital immediately. His condition has gotten worse and he is not eating." The general quickly glanced at Gabriel and then hastily accepted the doctor's request. "Go! Go! Take him away!" The youth was driven to the nearest hospital by a staff officer accompanied by the triumphant doctor. Once Gabriel was officially registered by the hospital, he was released from army custody. "Take good care of this boy," the good doctor told the hospital staff as he left.

Shortly after he was admitted into a room, Gabriel's condition improved dramatically. The airy, bright environment of the hospital was a monumental contrast from the dreary confines of where he was detained by the army. Gabriel started to become aware of his surroundings and taking more of an interest in things. There was a beautiful view of the volcano, Luisa, from his room, which inspired him further to recover his senses. He spoke for the first time in days when he was asked to provide the telephone number of a close relative. "23-851-7476," he replied faintly to a nurse. "That is the number of my aunt, Teresa." Sensing help was on the way, he broke a smile. Within an hour, a relieved Aunt Teresa arrived. "Thank god!" she declared with happy tears in her eyes. "Thank god I found you!" She went beside his bed and began kissing him all over his face and head. She held his hand and did not let go for a long time. "Why do you continue doing this to us?" she asked. "No one knew where you were or what happened to you. We thought you were dead. You can't keep scaring us like this anymore, you understand?"

By late afternoon, Gabriel was almost fully recovered, which was amazing considering he was in such hopeless shape earlier in the day. The presence of his aunt certainly helped, along with a renewed desire to *live*. A nice big meal and visits from other members of his family were icing on the cake. Gabriel would proceed to tell his aunt and the hospital staff what happened to him. "Bullets started to fly and I felt somebody get hit behind me," he recounted. "I turned around and saw Dr. Granados lying on the floor, all bloodied on the ground, his head in pieces. Then I got hit on my right arm, just nicked. The troops came in shortly thereafter and hauled us away, and that's all I can remember." The doctor assigned to Gabriel went on to explain that his condition, due to the trauma incurred from that day, was not abnormal. "Many people initially go through some shock in the event of a serious traumatic experience," the doctor said. "The problem becomes serious, however, if the individual cannot overcome such shock and stress within, let's say, a couple of weeks." The doctor suggested Gabriel stay overnight at the hospital for observation, and if his condition continued to improve, he would be released the following day.

When Gabriel's condition continued to improve through the next day, the doctor, to Aunt Teresa's relief, gave the youth his walking papers. "If the symptoms come back in a major way, you will have to make an appointment to see me again," the doctor instructed. The young American was in good spirits after leaving the hospital, despite still feeling a bit numb and shaken. With his job lost at the institute, there was no reason for him stay in Colombia any longer. "My time is done here," he admitted to his aunt. Satisfied with all he had experienced and learned in Nueva Vida, Gabriel was now ready to return to the United States. Arrangements were being made to buy airline tickets for the return trip the following week. He was really looking forward to going back home.

CHAPTER THIRTY-FIVE

NOT OUT OF THE WOODS

When General Torres released all his prisoners on the night of Saturday, November 2ⁿᵈ, the government, suspicious of the army, wanted to conduct their own investigation. It actually began with the questioning of Dr. Ghetti, but there weren't enough answers. The government especially wanted to know more about the second demonstration led by Dr. Granados. To tie up all the loose ends, another investigator was sent down to Nueva Vida. He was Dr. Luis Galeano, a very ambitious, famous attorney from Bogotá. With an insatiable craving for publicity, Dr. Galeano was renowned for taking on high-profile cases against corrupt politicians and members of the drug cartels. He was rather young, in his late thirties, tall and dapper, who relished his popularity. The man was always seen wearing the finest Italian suits, so conscious was he of his appearance in front of the cameras. Many members of the government were put off by his vanity, but realized his extraordinary gift for cracking difficult cases and finding bad guys. "He can always be relied upon to do the dirty work for us," a senator once said of him. Thus, when the investigation in Nueva Vida required mopping up, Dr. Galeano loomed as the best candidate for such an assignment, immediately prompting the government to call upon his services once again.

When the high-powered attorney arrived in Nueva Vida on Monday, November 4ᵗʰ, a day before the army was to depart, he went directly to see General Torres at the barracks. The meeting, which only lasted ten minutes, proved to be a productive one for Dr. Galeano as he was handed by the general a list of all those who were previously detained. He was also given a backpack of one of the detainees, which was apparently left behind by accident. That was all the information and evidence the general was willing to provide his intrusive guest, but it was certainly enough to get things started.

When Dr. Galeano returned to his hotel room, the very first thing he did was to go through the backpack. There was a workbook for an English class and a notebook inside. He proceeded to check the notebook and noticed the name 'Gabriel Ferrero' scribbled on the inside cover. He then began reading through it, which seemed to be some sort of diary composed in English. This diary, written in Nietzschean prose, consisted of Gabriel's thoughts on various topics ranging from politics to music. A lot of it was done when the youth was still in college. Since he was fluent in English, Dr. Galeano understood everything that was written in the notebook. He was astounded by some of the passages, especially those emphasizing global revolution and a new world order. One passage stood out in the investigator's mind: "The next major revolution to take place in the world will probably occur in a Third World country such as Colombia or Indonesia, serving as a springboard for other similar movements to take place and spread throughout the world."

This alarmed and angered Dr. Galeano. "This man wants to *use* Colombia to spread revolution throughout the world," he told his humble partner in the investigation, Officer Jose Gaudio, a law enforcement agent who was also working directly on behalf of the government. "That is why he is here now! How dare he consider using our country like that! How dare he think of our country as nothing more than a pawn in some misguided scheme to wreak havoc upon the world!" Having discovered through other passages that this author was also American, the unscrupulous investigator came to the sudden realization that he need not look any further. He had found *his man*. "This arrogant American is going down!" he proclaimed after tossing the notebook on the table. Gabriel was to become the sole focus of the fledgling investigation.

For Dr. Galeano, this was perfect. The case was now certain to become high-profile. It involved a foreigner from a powerful country attempting to topple the Colombian government. "This will draw everyone's attention!" the attorney gleefully told Officer Gaudio, who disliked his colleague's sensationalist rhetoric and narcissism from the outset. As the lead investigator and prosecutor, Dr. Galeano was certain he would become a symbol for national pride and unity, heading the crusade against foreign saboteurs and terrorists. There was a lot for him to gain from such a case, particularly as it concerned his political aspirations, and he knew it. He already figured what charges would be leveled against the suspect if enough evidence was gathered: 'crimes against the state' and 'terrorism'. With a conviction, these carried a possible life sentence.

What Dr. Galeano needed to do now was find this man and question him. He went back to the army barracks alone to inquire further about Gabriel Ferrero and his whereabouts, and was told he was transferred to the nearby Simon Bolivar Hospital a couple days before. The investigator then sped toward the hospital, desperate not to lose track of his quarry. Gabriel, of course, was not there as he had already been released by that time, but the hospital did provide Aunt Teresa's address. Having found what he was looking for, an elated Dr. Galeano went to a restaurant across the street to have some lunch and take a much needed break. "I plan to pay this man a visit later today after we have done some more investigative work," he told Officer Gaudio before quickly feasting on a dish of garlic trout.

*   *   *

At three in the afternoon, someone knocked on the door of Grandmother Celia's apartment. Aunt Teresa went down to answer the door, and was startled to discover who it was. She instantly recognized the man as Dr. Luis Galeano, the famous, handsome attorney, and was momentarily excited about his presence before her. However, she quickly realized that he probably was not going to be a harbinger of good news. She correctly guessed that he was there to question Gabriel. In an effort to calm her sudden fears, Dr. Galeano, who was accompanied by his partner, Officer Gaudio, gently informed Aunt Teresa that he would like to speak briefly with Gabriel about the latest demonstration that took place in Nueva Vida. "This is just a simple investigation into what happened that day," the duplicitous investigator told her. "Nobody has been charged with anything."

Aunt Teresa then welcomed the men inside and told them to sit in the anteroom beside the entrance while she fetched Gabriel. Gaudio opted to remain outside, perhaps not to further alarm Gabriel when he got downstairs. A couple minutes later, a nervous Gabriel walked into the anteroom and shook hands with Dr. Galeano. The investigator tried to put on a cordial front to ease the youth's concerns, but it did not work. Our friend somehow sensed the slick attorney was up to something shady. Gabriel's suspicions, of course, were well justified for not only had Dr. Galeano made him the focus of the investigation, but also discovered a short while before that the youth was indeed a former employee of the deceased Dr. Granados, thus linking him directly to the supposed leader of the last demonstration. This was a big piece of evidence not only linking Gabriel with the demonstration, but with its organization; thus, as far as the case was concerned, tying him possibly with a conspiracy to overthrow the government of Colombia.

Dr. Galeano began by asking Gabriel general questions about the demonstration, such as the time it began, what its purpose was, and its size. The investigator then went on to the army's crackdown of the demonstration, asking how many troops were present, how many shots were fired, what prompted the soldiers to fire, and so forth. These background questions were used to soften up the youth by leading him to believe he was clearly *not* the focus of the investigation. That is precisely when, it was hoped, the suspect might become careless and incriminate himself. Gabriel gave succinct answers to these questions, but when asked about Dr. Granados, he became, to his interrogator's utter delight, very loose-tongued.

"I understand that you worked for Dr. Granados," Dr. Galeano commented.

"Yes I did," Gabriel answered without hesitation. "I enjoyed working for him. He was a great man and I am still in shock that he is dead. I am very saddened by this." By that time, the short, muscular Gaudio had entered the room through the open front door. Touched by Aunt Teresa's candor and graciousness, he suddenly wanted to make sure her nephew was not railroaded by the ruthless lead investigator. The officer wanted to provide a calming presence for Gabriel, whom he considered to be the unfortunate victim in this increasingly sordid affair. "I will not let this boy be sacrificed for the sake of Galeano's career ambitions!" he thought while taking a seat on the sofa beside Dr. Galeano, opposite Gabriel. He offered the youth a genuinely friendly smile and humbly introduced himself.

"That must indeed be sad for you, and we are sorry you are going through such emotional turmoil," Dr. Galeano continued. "What made him so great in your eyes?"

"Dr. Granados was a very good man," Gabriel answered. "He was very honest and fair. He helped a lot of people and was always there when you needed him." Despite mistrusting his interrogator, the American was unaware the noose was actually being fastened around his neck. He was not exactly sure where the investigation was headed, and certainly had no inkling that the focus was indeed on him. For the time being, he felt there was absolutely nothing wrong with telling the truth about the deceased professor and his relationship with him. Believing the investigators were only there to close the books on the demonstration, Gabriel even felt compelled to tell as much as he knew about what went on in order to clear the professor's name for posterity.

"How did he help people?" the attorney asked.

"In many ways," responded Gabriel. "Nothing specific comes to mind. He was good at giving advice, I suppose. Students and teachers who worked for him all looked up to him. He was just a very decent man who gave a lot of his time and energy for others."

"Sounds like he really was a good man," Dr. Galeano agreed, his large dark squid eyes not straying from Gabriel the least bit. "Now, for the sake of the investigation, we need to ask you why the good Dr. Granados felt the need to organize this demonstration, that is, if you know what the reasons were."

"Yes, I know what the reasons were," Gabriel replied cooperatively. "Dr. Granados was horrified at what happened during the first demonstration, the one led by Ghetti. He was saddened not only by the deaths of those eighteen or nineteen people, but also by the fact that dozens more were apprehended by the army. He felt that the army's actions were illegal. He wanted the army to let go of those people, especially because they had not broken any laws. He organized the demonstration for the purpose of freeing those who were unlawfully detained."

"That seems like a noble cause," the attorney commented deviously, hoping to convince Gabriel that he was on his side. "The army had no right to act the way that they did. It's a real shame that it turned into such a tragedy. Did Dr. Granados consider other ways of freeing those people other than through a demonstration, or was he left with no other choice?"

"Yes, other ways of freeing those people were actually attempted," the youth answered. "The local police was contacted, but they were of no use. The army was also contacted several times by various family members of the missing detainees, but they gave no information whatsoever. It was not until all these measures were exhausted that Dr. Granados finally considered organizing a demonstration. Thus, we were, as you say, left with no other choice."

Gabriel would go on to describe in detail how the demonstration was organized, from the time Dr. Granados first rounded up his followers at Occidental University to the day it actually materialized. Not only did he provide incriminating information directly tying him to the demonstration's formation and organization, but he also offered up one last valuable piece of evidence for his interrogator. "I hoped that this protest would spark some real change in Colombia," our friend concluded gallantly. "I wanted people throughout the country to open up their eyes to the injustices not only occurring here in Nueva Vida, but all around them." Dr. Galeano was content to end the interrogation at that point, fully satisfied to have extracted so much evidence from the suspect himself. He thanked the youth for his cooperation and got up to leave. "You will not be leaving Nueva Vida in the next couple days?" the brash attorney inquired hesitantly. "I am asking this lest we need to ask you more questions in the future."

"No," the youth responded. "Not at least for another week."

"Good," Dr. Galeano remarked. "Then we will be in touch the next couple days if something pops up." Gabriel, incognizant of the terrible damage he had done to himself, warmly bid the two guests farewell. "I am glad I was of help," he told them. Dr. Galeano, pleased that the investigation was going so well, left the residence beaming from ear to ear. He secretly tape recorded the whole conversation, knowing full well that the case against Gabriel was perhaps a slam dunk now. His partner, Officer Gaudio, walked a good distance behind him, absolutely disgusted by what was developing. "This poor boy's goose is cooked already," he thought.

CHAPTER THIRTY-SIX

THE ARREST

Officer Jose Gaudio, however, had not given up on saving Gabriel's life. When they returned to their hotel, Gaudio confronted Dr. Galeano about his handling of the investigation. "I think it is wrong to just go after this kid," he told his colleague. "What about the others that were involved?"

"We will go after them as well in time," Dr. Galeano replied a bit defensively, stunned that his partner would question him in such a bold manner. "But we have now in our hands an individual who has planned and attempted to topple our government! He is a saboteur, an infidel of the worst kind! We have to focus all of our attention on getting this individual behind bars so that no other foreigner will dare contemplate following in his footsteps. There has to be a respect for the sovereign rights of our country!"

"C'mon, this kid could not hurt a fly!" the incensed officer responded. "He just got wrapped up in the whole situation."

"Oh really?" the attorney asked with sarcasm. "How can you be so sure of this man's innocence? As for him getting wrapped up in the situation, as you suggest, as though he was some harmless bystander in all this, have you even bothered reading his notebook? In page after page, he writes, in such an inflammatory manner, about global revolution, toppling governments, and so on. He came here with the sole intention of causing some serious trouble and if you can't understand that, then you must be blind, deaf, and dumb!"

"I believe he is innocent," Officer Gaudio argued. "You can't tie anything to this boy. It's not like he had some grand scheme from the beginning to overthrow the government. He was working here as a teacher and *his boss* happened to lead and organize a demonstration. He probably only wanted to help out his boss, nothing more. As for what he told us earlier about wanting to spark some change in this country, what's the big deal? Many people in this country also desire change. Whatever he has said or written down in the past doesn't make the kid guilty of anything."

"Look Officer Gaudio, we are here to investigate what happened in this town the past couple weeks," Dr. Galeano stated arrogantly. "This is an investigation deemed extremely important by the government for it concerns national security. Nothing should get in the way of our nation's safety and wellbeing, including your naïve notions that this kid is innocent. If there is any suspicion that the young man planned and organized this riot, we must pursue all the leads and continue investigating him until it has been established without a shadow of a doubt that he is not guilty. Being a detective, you should know that we must follow these strict procedures in determining whether a case should be opened or not."

"Don't resort to this legalistic jargon in justifying why you are going after this boy!" the officer retorted angrily, walking up to Dr. Galeano and getting right in his face. "Just tell the truth! You are going after him only to further your career ambitions. You know this will become a high-profile case and you will receive a lot of attention from it! It doesn't matter if this kid is innocent or not! You don't give a damn about justice!"

"It has become clear to me," the stunned attorney softly began saying while taking a step back, "that we cannot work together. I, therefore, relieve you of your duties here as of this moment."

"You do not have that authority!" Officer Gaudio stated amid sarcastic laughter. "Only the government has the authority to relieve me for they are my employer, not you."

"Then I will ask for your dismissal," the embarrassed attorney countered.

*   *   *

As it turned out, Dr. Galeano would get his wish. Later that evening, the government accepted his request to have Officer Gaudio dumped from the investigation, sending a much more obsequious person in his place. Officials in the capital were delighted with the progress being made by the ambitious attorney, and were overwhelmingly supportive of his efforts to pursue a case against Gabriel. Along with a new investigative partner, Dr. Galeano's superiors offered to provide ten security agents and a private jet the following morning. The suspect was to be apprehended and brought to Bogotá for further questioning. The attorney informed his superiors that he would be returning with the suspect within forty-eight hours, for his work was almost finished. He only needed to take care of some final details.

After having learned of his sacking, Officer Gaudio also found out from Dr. Galeano that Gabriel was to be arrested probably the following day. "I am sure the suspect's defense team will be pleased to have you work for them," the pompous attorney told Gaudio in parting. The officer, however, would not leave Nueva Vida immediately. Angry and humiliated by his firing, he felt compelled to do something to save Gabriel. With time running out, Officer Gaudio decided to dash over to Grandmother Celia's residence to tell Gabriel himself of Dr. Galeano's sinister plans for him. Quickly boarding a taxi, the officer arrived at the residence within ten minutes. It was a little past eight o'clock in the evening. The officer ran up to the door and urgently knocked on it. Aunt Teresa soon opened up the door and was startled at the sight of the nervous man standing before her.

"I need to tell you something very important which involves your nephew," Gaudio told her. He was noticeably shivering in the cold Andean evening air. "Will you please let me inside for a moment?"

"Sure," she responded quietly while stepping aside slowly to allow the man inside. Judging from the look of Officer Gaudio's pale face and perturbed eyes, she immediately sensed trouble.

"Your nephew Gabriel needs to leave this town immediately!" the frantic officer told Aunt Teresa once the door was closed behind him. "In fact, he needs to leave the country now!"

"What?" shrieked Aunt Teresa, loud enough to draw Gabriel's attention above on the second floor. He began walking down the stairs. "What are you talking about?" Aunt Teresa asked hysterically. "What do you mean Gabriel has to leave the country immediately?"

Officer Gaudio then noticed the youth walking slowly down the stairs. He immediately began addressing him. "Gabriel, you remember me from this afternoon?" he asked.

"Yes, of course," the concerned youth replied.

"Well, I have just been dismissed from the investigation because of a disagreement I had with my partner," he began. "I am telling you right now that Dr. Galeano wants to pin everything on you! He has been building up a case against you! The charges are very serious. He believes you attempted to topple the government and has gathered enough evidence to have you tried in court. You may be arrested as early as tomorrow or maybe even tonight! You must gather your belongings and leave right away!"

"But this is ridiculous!" cried Aunt Teresa. "Gabriel is completely innocent! He has done nothing wrong!"

"Of course he is innocent!" the officer agreed. "The charges are ridiculous and I let Dr. Galeano know of this! That's why I was fired from the case! The government apparently is satisfied with the crazy findings of the case and is supporting Dr. Galeano's efforts to bring Gabriel to justice. You must believe me! Gabriel has to get out of here! He must leave immediately!" Aunt Teresa stood at the bottom of the stairwell in shock. Gabriel continued looking at Officer Gaudio in disbelief. He finally asked the officer how he could leave the country in such short notice. The good officer implored him to somehow get to the Ecuadorian border perhaps as early as that evening before the charges were to be officially brought forward. "They will probably arrest you tomorrow," he added, "so if you get to the border by morning, you might still have a chance of getting past the customs officials without any trouble. But you are running out of time!"

"Can you stay and help me?" asked the utterly dazed Gabriel.

"As much as I hate to say this," the saddened officer confessed, "I cannot remain here any longer. I am placing myself at great risk by giving you this information. You are on your own from this moment forward. I recommend you take a taxi down to the border for it would only take about thirty-five minutes. A bus would take about two hours at least. I must leave now. Good luck!"

With that, Officer Gaudio exited from the apartment and disappeared into the night. Gabriel and Aunt Teresa quietly stood at the bottom of the stairwell behind the entrance for the longest time, painfully gathering in all what the officer had told them. Hundreds of confused thoughts crossed their minds, which explained their inaction and silence upon hearing the frightening news of Dr. Galeano's devious plans.

"What do we do?" Gabriel asked, finally breaking the silence.

"We pack your things!" Aunt Teresa answered. "That's what we do!"

*   *   *

Meanwhile, Dr. Galeano began feeling uneasy as he paced inside his hotel room. Not wanting to leave anything to chance, he suddenly decided to have Gabriel apprehended that very evening. "I don't want that boy disappearing on me," he thought. However, with the security agents and private jet not arriving until at least the following morning, he faced a real dilemma. How was he going to make an arrest? Looking out the hotel window and noticing some soldiers patrolling the street below, Dr. Galeano came upon an idea. He decided to go down there and ask the soldiers to help him make the arrest. "The army can detain him until my men arrive tomorrow," he reasoned.

After the swift five-floor elevator descent, he ran through the lobby and out the entrance doors to meet with the soldiers, who were not too far down the street. With an almost theatric sense of importance and urgency in his voice, Dr. Galeano introduced himself to the troops and asked them if they could do him the favor of helping apprehend Gabriel. Despite knowing who he was from television, magazines, and newspapers, as well as being a powerful representative of the federal government, the soldiers were hesitant to help the brash attorney. The soldiers told him, much to his chagrin, that they would need to seek the permission of their superiors first. Dr. Galeano did everything to coax the soldiers to come along with him to no avail. They resolutely stood their ground. "We cannot leave our duties here without the permission of our commanding officer," one of them reiterated firmly.

"Fine," Dr. Galeano finally accepted. "Then we will seek the permission of your commanding officer. I would like to speak with him myself." Through an antiquated portable radio, one of the soldiers contacted the commanding officer and informed him of the attorney's request to use them for making an arrest. The impatient attorney would soon personally address the army sergeant, letting him know how urgent he needed the soldiers at that crucial moment. "We need to arrest this terrorist now!" he went on passionately. "The government has made this imperative!" Dr. Galeano was then made to wait on the line while the sergeant sought General Torres' permission to temporarily hand over the soldiers. Within five minutes, the sergeant was back on line and informed Dr. Galeano that the permission was denied.

"The permission is denied?" Dr. Galeano inquired angrily. "How can that be? The government will not be pleased with this. Both you and General Torres can be charged with treason since this is the arrest of a terrorist we are talking about! You should reconsider your decision."

"I am just following orders here," the sergeant retorted. "Maybe the local police could help you detain this man."

"I am just requesting the assistance of three of your men in detaining this man," the attorney pleaded. "I am not asking much here."

"I am sorry," the sergeant replied. "We cannot help you."

Turned down by the army, the increasingly desperate Dr. Galeano had no choice but to follow the sergeant's advice and seek help from the Nueva Vida police department. He stormed back to the hotel lobby and demanded the concierge to call police over. Two officers arrived shortly thereafter and were received by the attorney. Unlike the military soldiers, these officers would quickly bend to Dr. Galeano's will. They were hooked in so rapidly by his convincing manner and fame that he did not have to resort to threats. They were more than willing to go along with his wishes. The three of them sped off in a squad car in no time, hastily making their way toward Grandmother Celia's apartment.

*   *   *

While Dr. Galeano was rushing toward Grandmother Celia's apartment, Gabriel and Aunt Teresa were scrambling to pack everything up. They had just begun filling up the second and last suitcase when there was a knock on the door. At so late an hour, Aunt Teresa sensed it was trouble. "That's Galeano!" she whispered with dread in her voice. "Oh my god, Gabriel, you must flee now! Go through the backyard!"

"No, this is madness," a resigned Gabriel remarked. "Aunt Teresa, I am not going to flee. If they want to arrest me, they can go right on ahead. I have not done anything wrong and they can try me in a court of law. But I am not going to run the risk of getting killed out there like some criminal on the loose. I have nothing to hide." Against the backdrop of his aunt's loud sobs, Gabriel calmly walked down the stairs to answer the door. As expected, it was the dapper Dr. Galeano accompanied by the two police officers. "You are here to arrest me," the youth nonchalantly told them upon opening the door. "Arrest me then."

Gabriel was quietly handcuffed and placed inside the squad car parked in front of the entrance. Aunt Teresa witnessed this with a mix of anger and horror from the doorway, as her nephew, once positioned securely in the back seat, soon looked back at her in despair. He shook his head in disbelief. The disappointed look on Gabriel's face suddenly triggered a rage in Aunt Teresa. She desperately flung herself onto the squad car, crying out for her nephew and declaring his innocence. "You can't be taking him away like this!" she yelled out from the top of her lungs, rousing the attention of her neighbors. "He has done nothing wrong! You can't take him away! Gabriel, I love you!" The car sped off, leaving Aunt Teresa lying on her knees in the middle of the street. She continued weeping there until a couple of concerned neighbors escorted her back into her apartment. "He'll be back," one of them told her. Once they had reached upstairs, Grandmother Celia was standing in the hallway awaiting them. For one of the rare times at that late hour, she was out of her bed. Like the majority of her neighbors, she had been roused by the commotion surrounding Gabriel's arrest.

"What has happened?" she asked her tearful daughter.

"Mother, they have taken Gabriel away again," she replied sadly. "Gabriel has been arrested for participating in the last demonstration, this time by the civil authorities. This is so crazy! I can't believe how terribly insane this has become!"

"Well, there is no need for tears then!" Grandmother Celia declared with divine fervor, mustering all her strength to keep herself standing on her tired, weak legs. "It's not the end of the world! He will come back to us, for he is innocent. We must remain brave for him. God will find a way to vindicate him!" This valiant pep talk by her mother had instantly helped Aunt Teresa regain some composure. Unable to go back to sleep, Grandmother Celia asked her daughter to make some tea for them and their two guests. They would end up talking about the arrest until a little past midnight.

CHAPTER THIRTY-SEVEN

AN UNEXPECTED HERO

Under the strict orders of Dr. Galeano, the squad car containing Gabriel was driven to the nearest police station. The attorney wanted to make sure the youth was securely locked up while he waited for the arrival of the security agents and government jet from the capital. Once at the station, Gabriel was rapidly booked and placed in a jail cell. Dr. Galeano callously went on to explain to police officers and staff at the station the importance of maintaining vigilance over the new inmate. "This man is to be tried in a federal court for acts of terrorism," he told them. "He is not to move from that jail cell until some federal agents and I arrive to take him away. That should happen within the next couple days. Until then, he is to remain there under lock and key." Content to see Gabriel securely detained and confident the local authorities would not undermine his orders, Dr. Galeano left the police station.

Gabriel, meanwhile, began weeping in his cell. "It's over," he cried. "I will never be free again!" The grim reality of his situation was beginning to set in. He envisioned spending the rest of his life behind bars. He brooded over the possibility of never being able to spend quality time with his family and friends again. Despite all the turmoil of the week, including his two arrests, the death of Dr. Granados, his nervous breakdown, and now facing serious criminal charges, Gabriel had not completely sunk into depression yet. If anything, there was a sense of resignation after the initial feelings of frustration and sadness. "Oh, the hell with it!" he thought an hour into his confinement. "There is nothing else I can do now but wait." There was even a tinge of hope. Knowing full well he was innocent, and with the help of some good people, the young American felt there was still a chance the situation was redeemable. He eventually fell asleep with this positive thought in mind.

*   *   *

The following afternoon, Mayor Juan Carlos Rivera heard about Gabriel's incarceration for the first time. This news had virtually brought him back to life. For a week since the army's repression of Dr. Granados' demonstration on Oct. 30th, the Mayor had gone into full retreat. Stunned by the events of that afternoon, having personally witnessed from his office the merciless assassination of Dr. Granados by a remote sniper and the mass arrest of all his followers, the Mayor was left totally dispirited. What disheartened him most was his utter powerlessness to stop the army. All he could do was stand there and watch the horrific moments unfold before his eyes. Later that evening, he drove alone to his vacation home outside Nueva Vida and stayed there for a couple days. He explained to his family and closest associates that he needed to be by himself for a while. "General Torres has managed to make me feel no more important than a grain of sand on a beach," he confessed to Victor Ascencio over the telephone. He even went on to tell Ascencio that he was considering retirement in light of what happened in recent weeks. "Perhaps I should leave now before things get even worse," he added cynically.

Mayor Rivera, though, could not take that step. Too much pride was still coursing through his veins as he was not going to let two weeks of misfortune prematurely end his fourteen year reign over Nueva Vida. He desperately wanted to reverse his fortunes and hoped that the short time away from office would do some help. If anything, he thought that his short exile would at least rally his closest allies around him. Much to his disappointment, however, he would return to city hall from his hiatus without the fanfare he had expected, despite having informed his colleagues about it a couple days in advance. The building was almost empty on that Tuesday morning, the very morning General Torres had pulled out his troops, with only a few bureaucratic functionaries and secretaries mulling around. Not even Ascencio was there to greet him, confirming his own suspicions of his rapidly waning popularity and influence. Not until well after his arrival did his closest colleagues bother to greet him via telephone.

Angered by such a lukewarm reception, Mayor Rivera called for an emergency meeting at high noon in his office. He urgently wanted to show everyone that he was still *the boss*. There were also several critical orders of business to discuss, including Nueva Vida's reconstruction, modernizing the security apparatus, and administering damage control upon the Conservative Party's sagging image within the city. The Mayor wanted to address all these problems immediately not only for the sake of saving his own political skin, but of guaranteeing the city's survival and wellbeing in the immediate future. Thus, there was a lot at stake when members of the Mayor's inner circle finally gathered in his office.

The meeting, however, would turn out to be unproductive. Intense disagreements arose between the participants, hindering the Mayor's desperate attempts at asserting his authority and helping the city. The main point of contention was the direction of the Conservative Party and whether it should initiate drastic reforms. Mayor Rivera, always having been a steadfast traditionalist, was now wavering a bit after all that had happened. His confidence in the old way of doing things was severely affected and he was now considering other options on how best to manage the city. With the confused Mayor divided over what to do next, his aids felt compelled to jump in and add their two cents. This led to a free-for-all, with the two-faced Ascencio accusing the pro-reformers of weakness. "How can you guys ask the Mayor to initiate changes?" he asked furiously. "That would go against everything the Mayor has done over the years and what this party represents! We can't be viewed by the people now as caving under pressure like a bunch of cowering dogs with our tails between our legs. We need to stand firm more than ever!"

"Weren't you for reform a couple weeks ago?" another aid asked Ascencio. "Where exactly do you stand, Victor? You keep changing your positions!"

The news of General Torres' massive troop withdrawal earlier that morning did momentarily bring the Mayor some delight during the discussions, but the frenzied arguments and accusations would soon prove too overwhelming. After an hour of such nasty rabble, the meeting had to be called off. "I've never experienced a meeting like that, ever!" the Mayor thought, thoroughly disgusted by the lack of progress made. Meetings, impromptu or not, had usually been a cooperative and orderly affair with the Mayor speaking most of the time while the others respectfully listened. One could always count on important decisions being made during such gatherings. The fact that not even one lousy agreement could be reached during this latest gathering was quite telling. It was indeed a bad sign for the Mayor.

Mayor Rivera would spend the next couple hours in his office, feeling utterly hopeless about things. He could not even eat lunch after the meeting, so low were his spirits. So when he received a phone call at four o'clock in the afternoon from his police chief, Luis Sandoval, and was briefed about a strange case involving an American youth who had been held in jail on Dr. Galeano's orders since the previous night, he literally leapt to his feet with excitement. With a renewed sense of purpose, he immediately knew what had to be done. "I'm not going to let that snake take away that innocent boy!" he told Sandoval with zeal. The Mayor knew the protesters led by Dr. Granados did nothing wrong, for they broke no laws. He also understood what Dr. Galeano's real intentions were. "He is going to turn that boy into a scapegoat for all the crap that's happened here!" he explained to Sandoval. "All the while, he will surely use this to prop himself up for a run for the presidency in the future. This has nothing to do with justice and security in Nueva Vida or Colombia. Instead, it has everything to do with this man's ego!" At last, there was something worthy the Mayor could sink his teeth into. This time, there would be no army standing in the way.

*   *   *

Upon hanging up the phone, Mayor Rivera stormed out of his office and drove over to the police station where Gabriel was being detained. He felt ecstatic about leaving the stuffy confines of his office and embarking on this mission to save Gabriel's life. Despite knowing full well the political danger he was getting himself into, the Mayor did not hesitate. He did not care what the consequences would be. What he would later remember most from this particular night was how *free* he felt, especially when he stormed out of his office. It proved to be a watershed moment in his life. Perhaps the act of doing something *good* for a change was liberating in itself, overriding any pragmatic considerations that may have popped up in his mind. The Mayor might have also identified himself with Gabriel, who was now entangled in the government's vast web of conspiracy and deception. In freeing the unfortunate youth, he was basically freeing himself, at least momentarily, from a life which had grown too complicated and confining over the years.

All these emotions had worked up the Mayor to such an extent that, by the time of his arrival at the police station, he literally lost all practical sense. He barged in and demanded to see Gabriel. The guards led him directly to the cell containing the youth, whereupon the wild-looking Mayor, with blazing eyes, unkempt hair, and ruffled shirt, immediately ordered his release. The guards complied and opened up the cell door, revealing a startled Gabriel, who had jumped up to his feet at attention. "Hello young man!" the Mayor said in greeting. "My name is Juan Carlos Rivera. I am the Mayor of Nueva Vida. I know all about your situation. You are unfairly being made a scapegoat for all that's happened here in recent weeks. I am going to make sure that does not happen. Please come with me." Amid the shocked looks of all those at the police station, Gabriel walked out of his cell and followed the Mayor down the corridor toward the exit doors. "He must be on some strange drugs," remarked one spectator about the Mayor's odd behavior.

Just as they approached the doors, however, Victor Ascencio and Luis Sandoval had entered through them. The two men blocked the paths of Mayor Rivera and Gabriel. "Juan Carlos, what on heaven's name are you doing?" Ascencio asked in bewilderment.

"What do you think it looks like I'm doing?" the Mayor retorted sarcastically.

"Have you lost your mind?" Ascencio asked furiously, holding the Mayor by the arm in an attempt to bar him from leaving with Gabriel. "Do you know how much trouble you will get for this?"

"Let go of me!" the Mayor barked, violently shaking his arm free of Acsencio's tight grip. "Nobody is going to stop me from doing what I feel needs to be done!"

"Juan Carlos, I am not going to allow you to do this," Ascencio replied in a more hushed, calmer tone. "You have worked too hard all these years in establishing what you have now. You just can't throw it all away."

"Well, I'll ask you, what is there left for me to throw away?" asked the Mayor. "There is *nothing* left! As a mayor, I am finished! You know it! I know it! Everybody knows it! I suppose the only thing that can be salvaged from all this is my dignity, and that begins by saving this young man's life."

"Juan Carlos, please think this over," Ascencio pleaded in vain. "Maybe we can discuss this problem over some coffee right now. I don't want you making any rash decisions."

"Maybe my decision to save this boy's life is a problem for you, but it certainly isn't for me," the Mayor replied. "If you like, you can join me for some champagne when he crosses the border." With that, the Mayor and Gabriel pushed their way through the outstretched arms of Ascencio and Sandoval and exited the building. From there, Mayor Rivera drove Gabriel first to Grandmother Celia's apartment to pick up his belongings.

Aunt Teresa was astonished to learn that the Mayor, of all people, was helping her beloved Gabriel flee the country. "I cannot believe you are doing this for my nephew," she told him. "God is smiling on you for this." The Mayor went on to tell her that he was going to have Gabriel driven to the Ecuadorian border that very evening. "We'll dump him off somewhere along the border, close to the highway," he explained. "He'll just walk across to the other side and get on a bus. I'll give him some extra money." They quickly gathered Gabriel's things and departed. There was not even enough time for the youth to give his sleeping grandmother a goodbye kiss. "I am confident he'll make it," the Mayor assured as they were leaving. Aunt Teresa walked down the stairs with the Mayor and Gabriel, giving her nephew one last hug when they reached the doorway. "I will tell your mother and father that you will be in Ecuador," she tearfully told her nephew. "I love you so much. God be with you!"

Once inside the car, Mayor Rivera then contacted his longtime friend, Alfonso Costa, and asked him if he could arrange to have Gabriel safely transported to the border. Costa agreed and told the Mayor to drop off the youth at 160 Lucindo St. "There's a man who lives there that can take care of that," Costa said. The Mayor then drove to the residence at 160 Lucindo St., which was not too far. He did not say much to Gabriel on the way there, other than a few words of advice. "Make sure that in case of an emergency, you contact the American embassy in Quito," he told him. "If, by any chance, God forbid, the Ecuadorians consider extraditing you back here to Colombia, seek asylum there immediately!"

Once they arrived at 160 Lucindo St., the Mayor walked up to the front door of the humble single-story residence, adorned with beautiful rose bushes underneath the windows. Gabriel, remaining in the car, was too preoccupied to focus his attention on what the Mayor was doing, so absorbed he was of his predicament. A cousin of his lived in Quito, the capital, and he figured he would go stay with him. "I have nowhere else to go," he thought. Very soon, a car containing the Mayor pulled up on the street. He got out and motioned Gabriel over with a soft gesture of his hand. Gabriel got out of the car and walked over to the Mayor. "Okay, son, you are going on this car to the Ecuadorian border," he instructed excitedly. "The man inside will take care of you." The Mayor then took out a large wad of cash and stuffed it into Gabriel's jacket pocket. "Here's some money for you. Don't lose it. Good luck."

"I don't know what to tell you Mayor Rivera," the baffled youth told his savior while he embraced him. "Thank you so much for what you have done for me." As the car began moving ahead, Mayor Rivera gave the youth a subtle farewell wave before turning back to his car. There was a slight trace of satisfaction on his plump, weary face. For once in what seemed like an eternity, he had achieved victory. It did not come from enacting a new law or winning an election. There were absolutely no political ramifications involved. Nonetheless, the aging patriarch of Nueva Vida still felt happy all the same.

*   *   *

When Gabriel was seated in the car, he looked over to the driver. He was stunned to find out who it was. It was none other than his friend, Puma! He was doing his bosses another favor in driving Gabriel to the border. This favor, unlike many of the others, did not smack of corruption. As always, Puma was dressed in his trademark red jumpsuit and had a toothpick sticking out of his mouth. Both were extremely surprised to encounter each other, and Gabriel would begin telling his incredible story to him. When the youth was done, Puma could only shake his head. "See what politics can do to you," he told Gabriel. "It will only end up making you run away with the tail between the legs. You tried to do something honest and good and now you are running for your life!" Puma was also left feeling a little nervous. "They're sending me on a pretty dangerous mission here," added the semi-retired civil servant. "You may just be Colombia's most wanted fugitive right now. I better get you to the border quick!"

When they arrived at the border town of Ipiales about an hour later, Puma got off the Pan American Highway and drove toward the outskirts of town. He took a dirt road to a remote location along the border where there were no patrol officials in sight. Being about ten in the evening, it was pitch dark all around for the lights of Ipiales were now hidden behind a large hill. Puma stopped the car and turned off the engine. "You are going to go walk that way," Puma told Gabriel, pointing south to the Ecuadorian side. "There aren't that many hills you have to worry about over there, which is a good thing. About a half mile from here, you're going to make a sharp right. Then you keep walking until you reach the town of Tulcan, which you can't miss because it's pretty big. It's not that far at all.

It won't take you long to get there, maybe forty-five minutes to an hour. I think you'll make it no problem." The two individuals then shook hands and embraced each other before Gabriel embarked on his short journey across the border to freedom.

Noticing, however, that Gabriel was lugging his large suitcase, Puma called him back. "There's no need for you to be carrying that," he told the youth. "You'll break your back lifting that thing across this terrain. That will also attract thieves. Mayor Rivera gave you a large bundle of money. That's all you will need, plus your passport." Gabriel subsequently dropped his suitcase, opened it up, and searched for his passport. He soon found it and placed it inside his jacket pocket. He thanked Puma for this sensible piece of advice, waved goodbye, and proceeded walking ahead into the vast darkness.

Once he heard Puma's car rumble away, the youth, now completely alone, was momentarily frightened. The darkness made it incredibly difficult for him to make any headway, so he chose to sit down on the ground for a while to regain his composure. While sitting there, Gabriel looked up at the sky and noticed how large and shiny the stars were. He was dazzled by them. Seized by such beauty, our friend felt it was an encouraging sign from God that things would work out fine for him. With time, he also was able to make out more of the surrounding landscape, his eyes eventually adjusting to the darkness through the help of the stars. Feeling more confident, our weary friend finally got up on his feet and mustered enough courage to continue trekking his way across the border into Ecuador. About a half mile into his journey, Gabriel, remembering Puma's directions, made a sharp right. After going over a couple small hills, he was able to make out some residential lights in the distance. "That must be Tulcan!" the youth thought happily. With all hope restored, he walked ahead with more briskness and determination. The end of his long ordeal had come into sight at last.

CHAPTER THIRTY-EIGHT

AFTERWORD

After Gabriel made his escape from jail, Dr. Luis Galeano was left fuming. He immediately wanted to know how it happened. Under Victor Ascencio's orders, Luis Sandoval, the police chief, told the investigator that a gang of men armed with assault guns went into the police station earlier in the evening and demanded Gabriel's release. "There were about twelve of these men, heavily armed, and there were only about six of my men here on duty," Sandoval said. The police chief went on to say that the identities of the men were unknown. "They all wore masks," he added.

Frustrated over Gabriel's bizarre escape, Dr. Galeano then requested the government to organize a manhunt for the young American. The government, however, was unwilling to offer any more help. The investigator was simply told there were not enough resources for such an ambitious operation. "With our war against the guerillas and drug traffickers, we are in no position to be conducting a nationwide manhunt at this time," a government official explained. Thus, with the big fish, Gabriel, having swum away, Dr. Galeano was forced to end his investigations prematurely, leaving Nueva Vida empty-handed.

Having survived Dr. Galeano's subsequent twenty-hour investigation with the help of Ascencio and Sandoval, Mayor Rivera was able to serve out the rest of his term in office. When it ended a year later, however, he chose not to run for re-election, consequently ending his long reign over Nueva Vida. Dejected and exhausted, he told friends that fifteen years was enough. The Mayor's dwindling support among voters and members in his own party surely played a role in his decision to step down. Had the circumstances been more favorable, he perhaps would have run again. However, things were just not the same anymore. The magic was forever gone and change was necessary for all parties concerned.

Despite ending his political career on a down note, it did not leave the Mayor all that embittered. He no longer was so concerned about his legacy, unloading what had long been a hefty burden from his shoulders. "Who cares about what historians and pundits think," he would tell a friend upon departing the mayor's office. "I did what I could and if people are going to remember me in a bad light, then so be it. I am not going to worry about it." He equated one's survival in politics with pure luck. "If Vicente Sanchez had not died, I would still be mayor today," he told his wife years later. "My luck finally ran out when he died and all those terrible demonstrations and riots erupted in the city. There was nothing I could have done then to prevent all that from happening, no matter how intelligent and skilled a politician I was." The arbitrary, cruel world of politics would only irritate the Mayor in the end of his lengthy tenure, especially when things were no longer going his way. His encounter with Gabriel is what finally made him turn away from politics forever. It made him realize there were other more important things in life.

From then on, Juan Carlos Rivera began spending more time with his family, especially with his seven grandchildren. This renewed interest in family certainly helped him cope with his retirement from political life, which had absorbed him for so long. He regretted not having spent more time with his family over the years, but was grateful that he was able to enjoy their company in the twilight of his life. When he was not spending time with his family, he would take strolls around the neighborhood during the mornings, read the newspaper over a cup of coffee at the local bread shop in the afternoons, and attend church services in the evenings. This tranquil lifestyle proved to be a welcome change for the Mayor, despite other people's concerns that the idleness would drive him crazy. The simple life of a retiree gave him something that a long political career never did: peace of mind.

That's not to say that things were entirely rosy for the Mayor. Being human, he would succumb periodically to dark thoughts. He could not help feeling bitter at times about how his career ended. He was also disappointed about having been largely forgotten by the people he had long served. "I worked faithfully on their behalf for all those years," he once told his wife, "and yet they choose not to remember me in any way. It's as if I didn't exist at all." The Mayor was particularly disgusted with his old colleagues and friends for no longer keeping in touch with him. Not even Victor Ascencio, who would eventually become an alderman and assume leadership of the Conservative Party, bothered to speak much with him anymore. All in all, however, the old patriarch remained upbeat to the end, not desiring to harbor any ill feelings while he was preparing to 'meet his maker'. He died without much fanfare about seven years after leaving office, and his legacy, as he expected, would forever be linked to the social upheaval in the wake of Vicente Sanchez's death. However, the Mayor would not have traded the sense of inner calm he felt at the end of his life for anything. It was something, unlike political power, that could not be snatched away from him.

∗   ∗   ∗

As for Gabriel, he would return home to the United States safe and sound. His experiences in Nueva Vida, Colombia would forever change him. Gone were his wild beliefs about global revolution. Gone also was his faith in the human race. Having returned from his quixotic trip a much more humble person, the youth, by choice, led a rather normal, quiet life thereafter. He went into real estate and developed a respectable business. He eventually married and started a family, his wife bearing him two daughters. Between managing his business and raising a family, there was not much time for him to dabble in anything else.

Gabriel rarely reflected at length on his last trip to Colombia, since it brought back some bad memories. By choosing to block out those memories, our friend believed he would be able to move on with his life. Yet, terrible nightmares would haunt him, especially those involving the bloody assassination of Dr. Granados. It had been very difficult for him to come to terms with the professor's death. It was hard for him to accept that the man may have died in vain, his heroic struggle to defend the rights of his fellow countrymen ending in a hail of bullets. "Fate can be so cruel," Gabriel once remarked to a friend regarding the professor's death. "He died for nothing."

Gabriel also could not rid himself completely of that itch to break out from the straight-and-narrow life he had led since his return to the United States. His adventurous spirit had not died after all the years spent leading a normal existence. His unwillingness to confront the demons from his trip to Colombia so many years before only served to increase his sense of frustration and restlessness. To rid himself of all these anxieties, Gabriel dove further into his work which only made things worse. Selling homes proved not to be the cure he was looking for, neither were activities and hobbies such as playing tennis or tinkering with his 1970 Dodge Charger. These occupations of body and mind proved only to be temporary fixes, not warding off the painful memories for long. Life certainly had become a drag.

Then, one day in his fifty-sixth year of life, something happened. Gabriel was at a local barbershop getting his hair trimmed when a strangely reminiscent image flashed onto the television screen before his eyes. It was a Spanish-speaking channel, for the barber was from Mexico. The stunned Gabriel could not believe what he saw. He had to rub his eyes to make sure. The screen showed footage of a demonstration taking place in Colombia, which included a man holding up a huge poster bearing the image of none other than the bespectacled Dr. Granados. "Oh my God!" Gabriel shouted, pointing at the screen. "That's him! I knew that man!" The long deceased professor had resurfaced as a mythical hero in Colombia. His legend had grown slowly but surely throughout the country. He now had become a prominent symbol for the new popular movements taking shape, his self-sacrifice serving as inspiration for the downtrodden masses.

Once the news segment on Colombia ended, Gabriel, like an excited little boy, engaged in conversation with the barber, proudly telling him he had fought alongside Dr. Granados. "He literally died in my arms!" he recalled. "That happened about thirty-five years ago! It seems like it happened yesterday!" He went on talking to the barber about Dr. Granados and his Colombian adventure for nearly an hour, letting go of any misgivings he may have had since that time. This news about the professor was indeed cathartic for our long suffering friend. He was happy to know Dr. Granados had not died in vain, that his struggle and ultimate sacrifice were not forgotten. This also made Gabriel feel proud about his own participation in the demonstration that took place in San Sebastian Square all those years ago, for it was now serving as a beacon for change in Colombia. It proved to be a worthwhile endeavor after all!

Gabriel would from that moment finally embrace the distant memory of his trip to Nueva Vida. He would view it as the period in his life when he became *a man*. He began talking openly about this remarkable trip to his family, friends, and anybody who was interested in listening. He was no longer afraid of recalling his several close brushes with death that had given him nightmares for so long. Everyone who knew Gabriel noted the extreme, sudden change in him, and was pleased that he was finally coming out of his shell, although they were unsure of what to make of it at first. Was he on some strange medication? Was he having an affair? They were just so accustomed to him being reserved and serious all the time. There was now more of a permanent bounce to his step and glow on his face, thanks to this newfound acceptance of his past.

Gabriel would begin dreaming of going back to Nueva Vida some day with his family. In time, he learned that the town had actually shrunk in size by half due to diminished business in the area. There were several reasons for this. The endless civil war certainly had a negative effect, as Nueva Vida, perhaps because of its remote location, eventually became a favorite target for guerilla operations, particularly the occasional blockade. Coupled with the ineffective leadership of subsequent mayors since the reign of Juan Carlos Rivera, this led to a large exodus of businesses from the town. Luisa the volcano also had become active a few times during that period, which further scared off people.

Thus, in a matter of thirty-five years, Nueva Vida had come to resemble what it used to be: an isolated agricultural outpost. Its decline, however, would not be blamed so much on the guerillas, political corruption, or Luisa's activity. Instead, the blame would fall squarely on Mayor Rivera's shoulders, for, according to many popular historical accounts, he did not take appropriate action against the demonstrators and rioters who brought the city to its knees on those fateful days in October, 1996. People marked that turbulent moment as the turning point in Nueva Vida's fortunes, when its downward spiral began. The Mayor would forever be labeled most unfairly as the 'builder and destroyer' of Nueva Vida.

The boom days may have been long gone, but not all was lost. Much of the city's ancient charms and customs had returned. Grandmother Celia would have loved it! She would have certainly minded the abandoned buildings and stores scattered everywhere, which gave parts of Nueva Vida the appearance of a ghost town. But at least there was peace. Cows were able to roam through the streets unhindered by cars or trucks, so desolate it had become! Without traffic noise, people were able to hear the church bells once again. With fewer criminals prowling the streets, men felt free to perform serenades at night. Gabriel wanted to return to Nueva Vida to visit the graves of Grandmother Celia and Aunt Teresa. He also wanted to pay homage to Luisa the volcano, for she was still there in all her glory. He was convinced that she had *protected* him during his last perilous trip to the city, making sure he survived intact. He firmly believed this. The respected businessman and father of two was now yearning to view the sun setting behind the volcano's flanks one more time.